CW00665442

THE LIST OF THINGS.

THE CHECKLIST ROMANCE SERIES
BOOK 1

EMMA MILLER

Edited by
SABRINA GRIMALIDI

Illustrated by
KASSANDRA CAMPONI

à mes cerises. This is for you.

A NOTE FOR MY READERS.

A trigger warning for the content within this book. There is sexual assault presented in this book in one of the chapters and discussion about it follows. There is also sexual and explicit content throughout the book.
This book is based around football but some of the contents within might not align with accurate football rules or college football regulations. Inconsistencies within the content may occur.
And lastly, every song within this book was completely intentional and deeply thought out before being included. To increase the emotion, and feeling while reading the book I suggest listening to the songs placed within the story during, or after you read the chapter. Music has always been a giant step in my writing. It's inspiring and helps the intricate details come to life in a more vivid picture. Thank you for choosing my book, and listening to my words.

PLAYLIST

Bad Reputation by Shawn Mendes
Lonely Bitch by Bea Miller
Crazier by Taylor Swift
Starving by Hailee Steinfeld
Perfect by One Direction
Wannabe by The Spice Girls
Tattoos Together by Lauv
gentle by Lexi Jayde
Cliché by Cece Coakley
New Year's Day by Taylor Swift
All the Time in the World by Stephen Day
I Don't Know You At All by Lizzy Mcalpine
anything by Dodie
What I Like About You by The Romantics
Ahead of Myself by James TW
magic by John K
Control Freak by Madisenxoxo
Certain Things by James Arthur
Satellite by Harry Styles

CHAPTER ONE

CONTROL FREAK BY MADISENXOXO

THE STUDENT CENTER IS DEAD QUIET AS I FLIP through my notes. It's late, no one else is in the room, let alone the building besides me and him. The doors will be locked after me and my student leave. I look across the table at Bellamy Archer and instantly feel weird calling him a student because he's the same age as me, but that's what he is considering how badly he needs the tutoring.

"You're staring at it like you've never seen math in your entire life. What's the confused face for?" I pull my notes back, double-checking that the instructions are in English, and not in a foreign language.

Nope, still in English like I wrote them.

"Because your handwriting kind of sucks, Hart," Bellamy uses my last name.

Typical football player.

"I'm not on the football team, and I'm not actually your teacher so, once again stop calling me Hart," I raise my eyebrows at him across the table.

He taps his pencil on the table, and smirks. I roll my eyes.

"Okay fine. Kamryn, your handwriting is very messy," He corrects himself, and I nod with a fake smile on my lips.

"Better. If you can't read my handwriting, I'll read you the equation and watch you while you do it," I stand up, and he raises his eyebrows.

"Watch me while I do it? Didn't know you were into voyeurism Har... I mean Kamryn," His golden retriever smile is unyielding.

I sigh deeply and walk over to him.

"Your jokes are a hazard to my health, and also infuriating. Write the equation so I can leave," I cross my arms as I speak out the math problem to him.

I watch him copy my words and slowly work through the problem. I stand behind Bellamy, peering over his broad shoulders to see what he writes. He misses a step, and I clear my throat.

"Did I miss something?" He looks up at me, expecting me to help like he always does.

I lean over and take the pencil from his hands, slightly bending over the table. I tap on the paper, and circle it with my red pen, hoping he'll look back and remind himself to do this step every time.

"You missed this step. You can't forget it," I remind him, and he nods, his eyes trailing from the paper to my face.

"What would I do without you Kamryn?" His voice is so sweet it's dripping with honey, and I know it's most likely sarcasm.

"You'd be absolutely fine, probably benched on the team for having shitty grades, but they'd survive without you, isn't that right... Archer?" I use his last name just like he uses mine.

"If I sit on the bench will you wrap up all my

appendages when you're on the sidelines? I happen to need extreme care," He senselessly flirts, and I ignore him.

As a sports medicine student, it would be a dream to be on the football field with the top college team in the nation, but I haven't been asked to do that just yet, and Bellamy knows that.

"Finish the equation before I finish you," I snap.

"Don't threaten me with a good time," His smirk is unmistakable.

I circle back around the edge of the table and sit back down, leaning in my chair. I go over my notes, waiting for Bellamy to finish. He slides his notebook over to me, and besides the small slip-up that he fixed, the answer is correct, and the equation is perfect.

"You are such a bright pupil, A-plus for you, are we done now? Our hour was up ten minutes ago," I look at my phone which is currently being blown up by my best friend who is already on my couch with about ten rom coms lined up for our movie night.

"I just can't help but want to spend my entire night with you Kamryn," He closes his notebook, and there's no sarcasm in his tone, or the look on his face.

He smiles, and I look away from him, packing my things up.

"You did good today, if I didn't know any better I'd say you'd make a perfect score on our final next week," I smile at him. He shrugs.

"I'll do alright. I'll just sit behind you, and sneak answers from your paper."

My jaw drops, "Bellamy! I pegged you as many things, but not a cheater!" I know he's joking, but still.

"Pegged?" He wiggles his eyebrows, and I swat at him with my notebook.

He stands next to me, towering over me as the two of us walk from the student center together. He opens the door for me, and I walk under his arm, scurrying outside into the warm night air. It's dark outside, the only light coming from the street lamps that cast a yellowish glow around campus.

"I'll see you in a few days. Keep studying okay? Text me with questions if you need me," I start to walk toward my apartment complex, and Bellamy grabs my backpack, pulling me backward.

"You don't think I'm going to let you walk home in the dark all alone do you?" He tilts his head.

We're normally finished before the sun sets but today he had practice which meant we needed to push tutoring. We always seem to work around his football schedule. It's what's expected of me considering how sport-oriented Seattle Pike University is.

"Are you offering me a ride, or are you planning on kidnapping me?" I turn, and he lets go of my backpack.

"Just get in my car, and tell me where to go," He shakes his head and lets out the lightest chuckle.

I walk to his car, seeing the reddish tint of the Jeep. It's far too dark to notice much else about it. He gets in, and I do just as he asks, telling him directions over the soft hum of music that comes from the radio, it's classic rock I don't fully recognize. Bellamy pulls up to the front of my complex, and I grab my things and hop from the tall Jeep.

"Thank you. I'll see you," I wave to him, and he nods.

"See you later Hart!" He calls after me.

"It's Kamryn!" I yell back and escape into my apartment building.

When I finally make it up to my floor, and through my front door, there's a pillow being hurled at my head.

"Hey! Throw pillows aren't meant to be thrown Sienna,

get it together," I throw the pillow back at her and drop my backpack in the middle of the living room.

"You took too long," Sienna grumbles, and I sigh.

"It's Bellamy's fault, not mine, and either way, you had a pre-summer game thingy or whatever it was. Your curls are still wet so you can't lie and tell me you didn't either," I raise my eyebrows at her.

"The drills I called for the team ended hours ago. I just went to the gym, but you're still late!" She pulls the blanket over her body, curling it on her body tighter.

Sienna is captain of the girl's lacrosse team and probably the most active person I know. She and I have been friends since my freshman year, but we didn't get as close as we are now until this year.

I start stripping in the middle of my apartment, leaving my clothes laying on the floor as I walk to the giant gray chair that is my designated laundry chair. By designated laundry chair I mean the chair that is piled with weeks of laundry so bad that it's pouring over the sides and onto the floor.

I'll do it soon. Swear.

"You have a key to my apartment for a reason because I'm never here on time to let you in," I laugh while digging through the heap of clothes.

I change into something comfy, and out of my outfit from the day. I look over to my curly-haired best friend and she's in a lacrosse t-shirt, and shorts. Perfect movie night attire. I get a running start, and Sienna shields herself as I take a giant leap onto the long gray couch. There's a floor-length lamp to the left of the couch that's casting a glow over the room. I look at the TV with my body pressed into the cushions. Sienna has *Love, Simon* queued up and ready to play, and I'm so glad because I absolutely love this movie.

"What took you so long? Were you making out with the hot football player in the student center? Naughty tutor sleeps with her student?" Sienna wiggles her eyebrows.

"First of all, life isn't a porno, and second of all you already know you'd be the first person I would tell if I slept with Bellamy or any other hot football player. I always tell you who I sleep with," I settle into the couch, Sienna and I on opposite sides with our feet meeting in the middle.

I cuddle myself into my light pink throw pillow, and Sienna turns on the movie.

"All I'm saying is that Bellamy is a catch, no pun int-"

"Sienna, I want to work with football players, not fuck them."

We both pause, and I recount the few football players I've already slept with. Sienna jokingly starts counting on her fingers, and we both burst into laughter.

"Shh. Watch the movie, no more sex talk," I turn my attention in front of me and fall in love with this film all over again.

I SIT UP, getting giddy, and emotionally ready for my favorite scene of the entire film. The reveal of who Blue is, and the infamous Ferris wheel kiss. My heart melts every single time. I watch with eager eyes. Sienna sits up too and reaches for my hand as we watch the cuteness overload ensue. God, I love love. Well, I love love when it's in media form.

"God I need something sweet, cute, and perfect," Sienna gushes, and I shake my head.

"This stuff just doesn't ever happen, not in real life," I shake my head.

"Okay miss pessimistic Debbie Downer. Who shit in your love soup?" She nudges me, and I shrug.

"Nobody. You can't tell me this stuff has ever happened to me," I look to her for an answer, and she groans, throwing the pillow at me once again.

I dodge it and watch it bounce on the grayish wood floors below us.

"No, it hasn't but that doesn't mean it won't one day. Romance is not dead. Chivalry is... kind of not dead," She argues.

"Romance is fictional only," I push myself off of the couch, and grab my backpack from the floor. I drag it over to us and pick out a piece of paper from my notebook, ripping it out, and drawing a checklist. "I'm going to do my research, and make a list of the things in these movies that I've never in my life done, and I bet over the next week you won't be able to check one off either. I'm not a pessimist. I'm a realist!" I argue, and write down *Ferris wheel kiss* at the top of the list.

"Fine, but just because I haven't done them doesn't mean I won't one day. It doesn't mean you won't either, you heartless bitch," She keeps watching the movie, and I shake my head.

I'm a hopeless romantic in some ways, but not in the expected way. I love the romance, but hate how falsely it's presented. Where is the heartbreak, and the hurt, and all the crying, and cheating, and breaking up? It's hard to change my mind about stuff like this because it's true, I've never experienced any of it, and it's hard to imagine that I ever will.

CHAPTER TWO

HOT FOR TEACHER BY VAN HALEN

Sienna might have been correct about my time management. Being late is the worst thing in the world. I mean that with everything inside of me; I hate it but as Sienna said, I always manage to end up late.

Today, it wasn't my fault. Really, it wasn't. I was going to be on time to class but then I got stopped by the manager of my apartment building who happens to be my boss, and he had a million and one things to say. I'm regretting working the front desk at the place I live because I have to see that persistent man every morning, inevitably making me tardy.

I've been up every single night for the past few days watching all of my favorite romantic comedies, and TV shows to complete this master list for Si. Because of that, I might have woken up a little bit later than planned today. It wouldn't be that big of a deal under normal circumstances but this isn't a normal circumstance.

Most every class I take at Seattle Pike University is stadium style which means there are at least a hundred students. I wouldn't be missed if I decided not to show up at all. This course, in particular, is one of the only ones I have that's small, made up of only about thirty students. So if I'm not there, I'll be marked absent. I will be there, just five minutes later than I should be, with sweat dripping down my back. *No big deal.*

I walk through the quad surrounded by trees, the math hall in perfect view in front of me. To my left is the street, lined with beautiful blooming magnolias, and cars of students. The other side of the street is lined with the same pretty grove along the sidewalk in front of one of the science buildings. Summer is here already. This is my last hour of lecturing before finals next week which means I must show up. I want to know everything that will be on this test, and Professor Gallen always tells us every detail.

I like school. I like it because it's the calm before the storm of the weekend. Yes, it's stressful. Tests, books, and notes, but it's nothing I can't handle. I've always been keen on going to class all throughout high school and college.

"Hey Kamryn," One of the lacrosse players waves at me, I wave back, flashing a smile.

"Hey, Kam!" Another voice says.

I turn, and see Sienna coming right out of the doors I'm about to walk through.

"Hey, Si," I wave to her as she bounces down the stairs.

"Do you need me to help you study tonight for your human anatomy class?" Sienna asks, and I shake my head in response.

"Nope, I've actually got it covered for once!" That's the only class for my major that keeps me up at night.

Sports medicine wasn't my dream when I was younger, but ever since middle school, I've never wanted anything more than to be on a field. Preferably a football field.

It didn't matter what school I went to for sports med,

but I chose this one because of my academic and in-state scholarships, and the fact that Seattle Pike University has some of the best sports teams in the country. Our football team, lacrosse teams, volleyball, and soccer. I knew I would get the most hands-on experience here considering we have a budget for every sports team. Hell, we even have a Quidditch team. It was also perfect because no one from my small high school decided to come here and it felt like a fresh start.

"Are you headed in for Professor Gallen?" Sienna asks, and I nod. "Good luck. This final is going to be hell."

I sigh deeply at her words. "I'm late, and in trouble now. Great," I joke.

"Are you going to come to Leah's party with me tomorrow?" She passes me, turning around and walking backward as she awaits my answer.

"I don't see why not... I'm late so I've got to run, but I'll text you, we can ride together," I smile at her and she walks off.

I charge the doors and walk to the end of the hall where our class is. It shouldn't be such a big deal that I wasn't here exactly at 10 A.M... other students aren't on time more often than not but I already feel a small bit of embarrassment creeping up in my throat at the thought of everyone looking at me when I enter the room. I peer through the window in the door, and Professor Gallen is already at the front. I take a deep breath and open the door, knowing I just have to rip the bandaid off. Normally I'm partial to attention, but now... not so much. Just as I suspected, eyes turn from the professor to me. I give a close-lipped smile, slipping through desks to the empty one in the middle of the class.

"Thank you for showing up Ms. Hart," Professor Gallen speaks.

"Wouldn't miss it for the world," I say under my breath.

I look up to see the only empty desk and, of course, the one behind it. I already see the smirk. His classic dimple is already formed on his cheek. Pearly white teeth, and a million-dollar smile. His gaze is already set on me.

Bellamy's got a full head of sloppy brown hair that I know he does nothing with to make it look as good as it does which is annoying in and of itself. Just like the pretty bright blue color of his eyes. Bellamy Archer, quarterback, heart-throb, charmer, and complete annoyance. I haven't seen him once since I tutored him a few days back, but he seems happier than ever to see me.

"I was starting to think I'd be missing that beautiful face of yours today."

Bellamy has hardly ever been able to control the fact that he's a grade-A flirt. I've been tutoring him since this semester started, and he hasn't ceased his irrational flirting. I don't mind it, but part of me thinks he's a bit delusional because he's never going to win this game.

"I don't have time for you today Bellamy," I whisper.

I feel a soft tug on my hair. I turn slightly. One of my lengthy black strands is curled around his long finger. I stare blankly at his annoyingly handsome face.

"Make time?" He gives an innocent smile, his cute dimple carving into his cheek.

Okay, I have a slight weakness for dimples. *So what?* I move my head forward, the strand of hair falling from his finger. I like Bellamy's attention, but it's distracting right now so I ignore him instead of replying.

Bellamy is probably one of the most sought-after guys on

campus... and it's a large campus. He's like royalty here, him and his best friends and roommates Griffin and Lawson. Quarterback, running back, and wide receiver, like three peas in a pod. Though all of our teams are incredible, our football team really is the best that there is. National championships. Some of the highest-ranked players in the nation. The highest NFL draft rate too. If you play football, you come here. Everyone knows our team, and if you go to this school, you know Bellamy Archer, Lawson Bennet, and Griffin Jones. Especially since Bellamy is a shoo-in for the Heisman next year.

I watch Professor Gallen, trying not to get motion sick from his excessive hand movements today. He's a great instructor, he just makes my head spin sometimes. I follow along, writing what's important, and making a star in my notes by everything he says will be on the final. I'm ready as it is, but there's no harm in going over the materials a few more times this weekend.

Class is over before I know it, and we're even let out a little early which is great. I make my way toward the double doors leading to the quad.

"Hart! Hey, Hart!" Bellamy's calls, with an obnoxious use of my last name.

I know that there's no use in trying to outrun a football player. I stop and turn around. He jogs to me, coming to a slow stop right in front of me. I stare up at the tall man in front of me.,

"Yes?"

He wears loose-fitting jeans that are cuffed at the ankles and a pair of Vans. He has on a white t-shirt that's bigger on him but still shows off how muscular his chest and arms are. Part of his tattoo is peeking from the left sleeve of his shirt, it's the only sign of ink he's got on his body. He has on a backpack as well, with only one strap resting on his shoulder. My eyes roll over his body until they meet his eyes.

"Tutoring, I need you before the final," He makes his demand, and I raise my eyebrows at him.

He looks at me, hesitates, and flashes a full smile, his perfect teeth revealed to me.

"Alright, fine. Tonight," I offer, but he sucks in a sharp breath between his teeth.

"I can't tonight I have-"

"Practice?" I already know what he's going to say.

This is a common occurrence with him. This man might as well take a sleeping bag and rest his head on the football turf instead of his bed. The boys have all been off for the past three months from practicing from what I know, so I wonder why there's practice tonight.

"How did you know?" He jokingly nudges my shoulder, and I glare at him.

I'm not easily annoyed by much, but Bellamy's consistent joking is something that might get on my nerves more than I'd like to admit. He's never serious, I don't know if he's capable of being serious unless it's from a relationship standpoint.

"I'm glad you find this amusing, but tonight is all I've got. The final is on Monday," I remind him.

"What about tomorrow?" He asks.

"Party that I refuse to miss because I'm tutoring your sorry ass."

His jaw drops. "How rude," He jokes.

He's got to be at least 6'1, possibly taller, which is significant compared to my 5'4. He's a skyscraper in men's clothing. A skyscraper with a heart-melting smile that he's flashing at me right now.

"Why do you have practice? The season is over, can't you-"

"It's not actual practice. You know summer sessions are happening in a few weeks and I have to go do the drills that coach called. Come on Hart, give me something, anything," He practically begs, and I tighten my hold on myself, keeping my arms crossed over my chest.

He's persistent and charming, which are two very dangerous qualities to have.

"Can you stop calling me by my last name like I'm a football player? And I can't help you, Bellamy, I'm sorry. We tutored the other day, you said you were fine," I shrug.

"Saturday?"

I shake my head at his suggestion, "I'm working, and then I have plans."

"Fine, Sunday?" He gives another option.

"The student center isn't even open on Sunday."

We've never studied anywhere other than the student center. Bellamy gets distracted far too easily, even in a place designed for studying. I'm not trying to make excuses. I don't mind tutoring him, but I'm not going out of my way to make it possible.

"So come to my apartment then," Bellamy stops talking when he hears me laughing at the silly proposal.

"Do you really think we could get any studying done with Griffin and Lawson?" I mention his roommates who are both loud and rowdy just like Bellamy, and every other player on their team.

"Good point... I can come to you then," He offers. I stare at him blankly. "Please... Pretty please with me on top? I'll do anything, Kamryn. Please."

If he actually needs help, I'd be a complete dick to say

no. I've been tutoring him all semester to prepare for this test. I would hate for it to be for nothing.

"I mean I do know where you live. Technically I can just show up, and beg you on your doorstep. I have great puppy dog eyes, and I'm phenomenal at begging," He tilts his head, his full lips pressed into a suggestive grin.

He wiggles his eyebrows at me, only making me roll my eyes. That doesn't change the fact that I'm smirking too.

"Fine, you can come to my apartment. I swear to god, you better not be late," I say.

He smiles a big toothy grin now. We've worked around his football schedule all semester so I don't see why I can't do it one last time. Normally he tries to do anything but study but he seems to have improved in class considering the coach doesn't have a problem with his grades since earlier this semester, so I guess something must be working. He's going to be in my home though which is different... Very different. No funny business is allowed, not at all.

CHAPTER THREE

ANOTHER MAN'S JEANS BY ASHE

I WAKE UP TO MY PHONE BUZZING RIGHT NEXT TO MY ear. I sit up instantly. My eyes can barely focus on anything as I come out of my haze. I slap the bed, my hand haphazardly searching through my large white comforter until it finds my cold phone. I see the time first, and then the call coming in from Sienna. I answer, and tuck the phone between my ear and my shoulder, using my hands to pull my hair up and out of my face.

"Hello?" I take the phone in my hand now.

My clothes are sprawled every which way across my bedroom. I'm not gross. Most of these clothes are clean, I just hate putting them away after I try on outfits that don't make the cut. Hence my laundry chair, and the fact that you can't see my bedroom floor anymore due to clothes. I sift through the clothes, and I can't find anything I want to wear.

"I'm almost at your place."

I fully forgot that I had set up a ride to the party with her yesterday.

"ETA?" My eyes frantically search the room for the

outfit pieces I'm imagining in my mind.

"About six minutes. Are you good?" She asks.

I laugh a breathy laugh into the phone, "Wonderful, I just woke up."

She's the one laughing now, "Why did you take a nap?"

I find the jeans I was looking for, and tuck my phone once more, the device resting between my cheek and my shoulder.

"I didn't mean to. I sat down in my bed, and next thing I know I woke up to a phone call. Don't worry, I'll be ready with a minute to spare."

I'm always late. I think it's inevitable at this point.

"Sure you will," She laughs, and the line goes dead.

I slide the jeans I grabbed from the floor over my waist, the jeans feeling a lot looser than normal. I move to the clothing rack in my room and grab one of the only things actually hung up. I tear off my baggy shirt and pull the tight black long sleeve shirt on my body to replace it. The material hugs my body perfectly while the jeans hang loosely. I put matching black and white sneakers on my feet quickly.

I run into my bathroom almost falling as I make it through the door. I let my hair fall back down. My black hair hangs right down to my belly button, loose second day curls making it look effortless. I spray it down with one of the million things scattered on my counter, and then I brush it out, trying to untangle the rat's nest that's settled on the back of my head while I slept. My skin is tan, and most of my makeup from earlier today is still sitting fine. I take the stick of eyeliner and haphazardly draw black on my water-line. I run blush over my cheeks, and retouch my lips with lip gloss. I'm messily put together and have no time for anything else.

My phone vibrates again, a text from Sienna telling me

she's here. I snatch my phone from the counter as well as the lipgloss, and I run into my bedroom, my hands grasping at my bedside drawer. I reach into the box of condoms, pulling two out to stuff into my purse, and then I run out of my room, and then my place. I walk with purpose down the hall of my apartment, and down one flight of stairs, going straight to the lobby, and out the front doors. Sienna is parked in front of the entrance, her blue Honda a comfort to me. I open the door and jump in.

"Five minutes... One minute to spare," I shimmy my shoulders toward her.

I might have skipped a few steps but it's fine.

"You look hot too. I'm not surprised. You always pull it off," She says and I smirk. "Are those your jeans?"

The pants are baggier, yes, but they're mine, right?

"Um. I think so. Why? Do they look bad?" I'm out of breath from my sprint down the stairs.

"No they look really good on you, they just don't look like yours."

I run my hands over the material and furrow my brows. Hmmm.

"Wait a second," I press my lips together and unbutton them. "Check the tag."

I pull the waist up, loosening it more than it already is.

"I'm driving!" She keeps her eyes on the road.

"Who cares, it'll only take a second," I wait for a second and feel her chilled fingers graze my skin.

"Levi's, men's sizing."

My tongue swipes the inside of my mouth, pressing to the inside of my cheek. Oops. Realization blooms inside my head while I button the pants again.

"These aren't yours are they?"

I nestle myself back into my seat at her question and

buckle up once more.

"Do you know Jayden Cavilarro? He's on the lacrosse team," I ask.

Sienna nods at me, "Yeah, he has that big lion tattoo, right?"

She nails it right away. I knew she would know who I was talking about.

"Yeah, that's the one. We fucked last night and-" Sienna practically chokes on my words, but I continue. "I told him not to stay, and then we were kinda hanging out after, and this morning I woke up and he stayed so I got mad, and snapped and he ran out of my apartment, and I guess he forgot some things."

She replies by laughing so hard that her chest shakes, "You say he left some things like his pants aren't something crucial. Did he run out in his underwear?"

I try to replay the events in my head but come up short. I wasn't paying attention to him.

"I don't know, I told him to get out and he did. Maybe I scared him."

She nods quickly, "Yeah you probably did. You're intimidating."

"Well, they look better on me, and he can't have them back."

They really are comfortable. I look back toward the road instead of at the stolen bottoms.

"God, your sex life is like a book in itself. I fucking wish," Her eyes are amused as she looks at the fast moving asphalt in front of her.

"Men are simple minded creatures. If you want to get laid, make sure he's single, and it's easy from there."

Sienna shakes her head, her pretty naturally curly hair bouncing as she does, "I am not confident enough for that."

"You should be. You could literally get anyone you want Si, you're like the epitome of perfection," I boost her the way she always does me. I mean it too, every word.

"I know I'm hot. I know I could probably get anyone, but I don't want anyone. I don't do hookups."

I furrow my brows at her. She's got highlights in her natural hair. Her brown skin is dewy per usual. Dear god, I need her skincare routine. She's wearing dark brown lipstick to match her shimmery eyeshadow. Normally when she's on the field she takes out all her piercings, but right now she has her septum in. I could never pull it off, but she does so well.

"I know that's a lie, there's gotta be somebody. Everyone is attracted to someone."

"Not true, some people aren't," She's trying.

I can give her that, but she won't win with me.

"Okay you're right, some people aren't but I know you're not one of them," I fight back.

"Okay so maybe Lawson Bennet is the hottest person I've ever seen," She's correct about that.

I clap my hands together in excitement, "I fucking knew it... Perfect choice. He does have a nose ring, which is always a red flag, but he's only being used for sex so it shouldn't matter."

He's always up for a hookup or at least he's rumored to be. He has dirty blond hair, meaning he's not my type, but he's attractive, to say the least.

"Problem one, he plays football, and I hate football players. Problem two is that I feel like I would never have time... Not with school, and lacrosse... I don't do hookups. I'm bad at... at all of that kind of stuff," She spills.

I know she hates football players because of her shitty ex. Thank god that she dumped him two years ago. Even with that, she doesn't have the closure she needs to move on just yet.

"Well, you don't need that much extra time to have fun and see where things go. It doesn't have to be serious. I think you should at least try. I mean, I would. Lawson Bennet is hot and available. I've also heard that he's fantastic in bed. Hookups are easy!"

"You have bigger balls than I do but, I'll think about it," She promises.

She's not the kind of person that would say something just to get me to shut up. Sienna is incredibly hard headed. She will always do what she wants. I like that about her, she never puts up with bullshit.

The apartment complex we pull up to is a bit farther from campus. This place is far too expensive, and somewhere I would never be able to afford alone. A lot of the students here don't pay for their housing, their parents do. Leah Ashley is one of them. We aren't friends in the slightest. She only invites me to these because she knows I will get the buzz going about the event.

Sienna and I get out and walk inside the building together. The elevator takes us to the 10th floor which is the very top of the building. We've both been here plenty of times before. It seems to me that Leah is always throwing a party.

The moment we walk through the unlocked door my eyes land on the typical groups. The people on the couch, half watching whatever is on the TV despite having no sound on, and the other half far too infatuated with the other person to even come up for air. There's a group of rowdy boys, most of them football players in the kitchen. There are the wall huggers, cups close to their mouths which is normally what I am. Then there are the scattered talkers, some people bouncing, and some just standing still. Leah's place is giant, big enough that people could disappear together and no one would notice for the night. I've done it a time or two.

"Look who's over there," I point out Lawson, and Sienna only looks for a second.

"Alcohol first, then I will talk to him," She directs me to the kitchen.

"I like the way you think."

I open the fridge and grab a seltzer from the top shelf. Sienna goes straight for a handle of vodka on the counter. So that's how tonight is going to go. Hell, who knows, she might not be my ride home – she might be going home with someone else.

"You'll drive if I can't?" I nod right away.

"Or we can Uber. I've got you. That is if you even need a ride home. Who knows whose bed you'll end up in tonight."

She pours herself a shot, and downs it like a champ. She jumps up and down, shaking herself out. I watch her hair bounce as she prepares to talk to Lawson.

"How do I look?" She asks.

She's taller than me by a few inches. She's wearing a baby tee that's tight on her body and tight jeans. She's certifiably hot.

"Like you could conquer the world."

She nods once swiftly before brushing past me toward the lean football player.

He's got a bright smile on his face. He's with Griff, and I think Griff's girlfriend. Her name is Jade if I'm not mistaken.

Lawson's blondish brown hair is parted to the side and it's long, reaching right at his eyes. He has a single strand that hangs in the front. He's hot. She's got good taste, to say the least. I smirk as Sienna approaches him and all the attention turns to her. I don't miss the look he gives her, his eyes bright as he watches the pretty girl in front of him. He immediately engages in conversation, Griff and Jade seemingly disappearing into thin air.

My job is done, not that I really did anything. I walk through the crowded space, greeted by plenty of familiar faces. I engage in some small talk, despite trying to avoid it. The truth of it is, Sienna is the only true friend I have here. I have acquaintances. Bellamy is one of them, same with his roommates. There are familiar faces everywhere I turn, but no one knows me like Sienna.

Honestly, I prefer it that way. My mom was my best friend growing up, and she still is despite the hours between us now that I'm in college. She always told me to keep my circle small. To be nice to everyone, but not to trust all of them. Sienna and I aren't the type of people to go out of our way to make friends, I guess that's why we gravitated toward each other freshman year. I remember it like it was yesterday, I was helping out on the sidelines, wanting to be a part of any team that would take me, and she was yelling at the captain of the team calling her choice of play idiotic. She was right too, Sienna became team captain the next year.

I scan the party and I see Jayden. Images of last night begin replaying in my head. I ignore him at all costs. Not that I'm opposed to speaking to people I hook up with. I'm mostly avoiding him because I don't want to go through the awkward conversation about me wearing the man's pants to a party he's attending. He was also subpar in bed, and I've never been the type to spare a man's ego. If he suggests another hookup it's going to be shot down right away.

I continue to scan the crowd, and my eyes catch on pretty light eyes. I notice they belong to Bellamy right away. He's wearing a Van Halen shirt, cut into a muscle tank to show off his arms. He has on black pants again, and high top Converse. A normal outfit for Bellamy. My eyes slowly move over his arms, and my mouth starts to water. The most infuriating part about Bellamy is that he knows just how good he looks. Everyone does.

I feel his gaze, and I see it too. I raise my eyebrows at him. I raise my drink, and his lips pull into a smirk, that devilish dimple noticeable even when it's dark. There's a deep warmth that erupts in my lower abdomen when I see a smile as attractive as Bellamy's. It's a shock that my cheeks aren't flame red as we stare at each other.

I sip my drink, and out of nowhere, I see a soft slap connect to Bellamy's chest. I can't tell if it's playful or not, but I watch the scene play out in front of me from afar. Bellamy's brows furrow as he looks at the culprit of the slap. I see Leah Ashley say something to him, seemingly unhappy. I narrow my eyes at the two of them. He argues with her, and she shoots me small looks as she gets angry. I scrunch my nose and move away.

I've never been this annoyed at a conversation I'm not a part of, but there's a first time for everything.

That's something about Bellamy. He's definitely the dating type. Anyone can see that. I know the two of them dated but I'm almost positive they broke up months ago. The nosy part of me wonders why he still comes around her, but the other side of me knows it's not my business. Maybe there's still something there. Maybe they're trying to work through it. Who knows.

I walk back toward the front of the apartment and see someone I wish I hadn't. I try to turn before he makes eye contact, but it feels like slow motion as he looks directly at me. I've never wanted to vanish into thin air more than I do right now. I regret every choice I've ever made to lead up to this. I've never wished I wasn't born, but at this moment I do. That way I could have never met Dylan Brody.

"Kamryn!" Dylan yells over the music and chatter.

The only boyfriend I have ever had in my life that I would actually count. I should also add the "biggest regret" to that list. We broke up a little under a year ago. I don't miss him in the slightest.

"No," I shake my head, but he steps up to the plate despite my initial disgust with the thought of a conversation.

"Oh come on, it's been a while. We can catch up, let bygones be bygones."

I shake my head dramatically in his direction, "I would agree, but I hate you. So I would rather grab a blanket and pillow and take a nap on the freeway than talk to you right now... If I'm being honest."

I watch his smile turn to a frown.

"You're being dramatic. You know I love you, and I know you care about me. I hate that you have to lie in such graphic detail to convince yourself-"

"You're boring me... And I don't love you. I actually never loved you, at all. You were horrible in bed... And you also cheated on me. So I'm not sure where the love you're talking about is coming from," We've had this conversation before.

I wonder if he somehow forgot it from the last three times.

"I never cheated on you... She was like my work wife..."

I choke on laughter, and lies, my eyes wide as I glare at him, "Do you let all your work wives give you head or just her?"

"She didn't give me head."

"Why are you telling me a story I already know?" I question.

"Because you never let me tell it," He raises his voice over the music.

I don't let him tell me because I have proof. Vivid, camera footage proof. Sienna and I might have hacked into the security footage when I was speculating that he was cheating. I won't incriminate myself because that was in fact very illegal. But I know he cheated.

"Yes, because I like my version better... Because it's the truth. Because I'm truthful, and you are a lying piece of shit that wasted my time," I can tell the insults dig in deep.

His short stature almost shrinks even more. His eyes scan me and shoot straight back to my own eyes. He looks like he's about to piss me off even more.

"Those aren't your pants," He reaches toward me, his fingers starting to grip the belt loops of the pants I wear.

I slap his hand and take an exaggerated step away from him.

"Ew," I shiver at the thought of his hands touching me again.

There's shock on his face as he stares back at me, "Who's jeans are those?"

He steps toward me again.

"Mine," I step back.

"That's not true," He tells me as if he truly knows.

I don't know why he thinks for a second he has any right to know. But I think his reaction to my honesty would be far more entertaining than this conversation altogether.

"They belong to Jayden. He left them in my bedroom after I fucked him last night. They look good on me don't they?" I ask him, posing, and turning.

There's blatant disapproval of his features.

Dylan is around 5'9. He plays lacrosse. He's got patchy facial hair that fits him. He's not ugly, but he's not the greatest-looking guy I've ever been with. He was just a sweet talker, and I fell for that. Stupid of me.

"Do you put out for anyone who wants you?" I'm assuming he thought that would sting, but coming from him, it doesn't in the slightest.

"I dated you, didn't I?"

His jaw clenches, "I just thought you had a lot more respect for yourself than to let just anyone in your pants."

I nod my head at his words. "Fair point, but these actually aren't my pants as we established a few seconds ago... They're his."

I point to Jayden who isn't paying attention.

"You're so embarrassing."

"And you are making me feel like manslaughter is an option in the near future. Stop telling people we dated, and you can forget about it like I'm trying to," I turn away from him, walking in the opposite direction.

"Kamryn-" He calls out.

"Go fuck yourself, Dylan!"

I find Sienna, still talking to Lawson who seems completely infatuated with her right now. I smile at the interaction, both of them alone now. I find myself migrating toward the couch.

Bellamy Archer... I see him once again but he's alone this time, his hands on his large thighs as he sits. I approach, and he sees me, nodding at the incredibly small spot next to him. I plop myself down, angling myself to him, my legs dangling over his as I lean back into the plush sofa.

"Dylan Brody?" Hearing Bellamy speak my ex's name makes me cringe. I also hate the thought of Bellamy seeing the interaction I just had. "Did he just try to grab you? You look like you had it handled, but still."

I sigh, hating how perceptive this man is.

"Yeah, but it's not a big deal. He was trying to see my... You know what it doesn't matter. Are you watching me?" The football player looks at me, his eyes are captivatingly blue.

I could swim in them, that's how bright they are.

"I was actually, yeah."

My eyes flip down to his smirking lips. I can't go home with Bellamy Archer tonight. He's dangerous, and that's putting it lightly.

"Weird," I joke.

His hand is resting on my leg right under my knee, he squeezes, and looks at me, his hand slipping from my body. Instantly, I want it back on me, and I have to fight myself to not say it out loud.

"You okay?" The sentiment in his voice is prominent.

"Why wouldn't I be?" I shrug my shoulders.

"Because you two dated, didn't you?"

"If I decide to count it then sure..." I sigh.

"Decide to count it?" He repeats my words for an explanation.

"You're one to ask questions. I saw that little moment with you and Leah," I deflect, hating the attention.

"It's not my fault. She was talking to me. I was distracted."

I roll my eyes, "You're going to make me lose my invite to these things if you don't stop pissing her off."

I hold back laughter.

"She doesn't know you were the one distracting me," He says.

I sit up partially so I can really look at him.

"You might need tutoring in women if you don't think she knew what you were looking at. Don't be stupid," It's hard to keep myself from rolling my eyes at him.

"I mean I can look at anyone I want, can't I? Considering she's not my girlfriend?"

I watch his lips move, and do everything in my power not to let myself look at the rest of him right now.

"I don't care who you look at. She seems to think that you two are still dating though, doesn't she?"

He brings the red cup to his lips, and his teeth peek out from behind his lips as they curl into a subtle smile. My chest erupts against my will. He's just so hot.

"Are you jealous?" He asks, and I can hear just how amused he is by the thought.

I give him a testy look, and he slowly nods his head.

"Not the jealous type. Got it."

"You're so smart," I reach forward, and pat the top of his head in approval.

"I have a wonderful teacher, her name is-"

"You are the cheesiest, most corny, sarcastic-"

"You're doing such a good job boosting my ego Ryn, keep going," He fans himself, and I shut my mouth right away. "Oh come on, I was about to start writing them down for my resume."

I push myself off of the couch now. "I need another drink."

"Get me one?" He has a hopeful look in his eyes that I know I'm about to crush.

"Who said I was coming back?" I turn away from him, knowing and hoping for my sake and his own that he stays on the couch. He looks far too good tonight to be following me around. If he keeps it up I might find myself leaving with him, and that cannot happen.

CHAPTER FOUR

LIKE THE MOVIES BY LAUFEY

THE NEXT DAY ROLLS AROUND SLOWLY. SIENNA LEFT before me, she wasn't drunk, but I did see Lawson waiting by the door when she had mentioned leaving. I have no idea what happened if anything at all, but I know my best friend. She doesn't like to be asked, she likes to tell me when she feels ready, so despite how badly I want to know I leave my questions up in my brain for the time being.

I haven't talked to Bellamy since he drove me home from the party. He's never been a big drinker at parties, at least during the time I've known him. He said he wouldn't be late after I hopped out of his Jeep last night. Now that I'm up and awake I prepare myself for the few finals I have this week despite my hangover, and clean my apartment up. I'm not the neatest person, but since Bellamy is coming over for tutoring the last thing I need is for him to think I'm a total slob.

I wait.

And then I wait more and feel a sticky, hot annoyance boiling inside of me. Bellamy is late. I shouldn't be surprised, but I am. Considering I'm doing this as a favor to him, and not a normal tutoring session I would think he would at least try to be on time. He's never late for anything. Especially tutoring.

I sit on my couch, watching a Nicholas Sparks movie that happens to be playing on the TV, that I also happened to not be able to turn off. My heart thumps as the two characters kiss in the rain, my mind reeling at just the sight of it. They haven't even confessed their love for each other yet, but it's already so blatantly obvious as I watch them. They know it too, they've just never said it. The way the entire movie is set up makes me feel warmth in far too many areas of my chest. I reach forward, writing another thing on my list.

Kiss in the rain

I doodle a cute rain cloud next to the words I scribbled on the page as the film plays behind me. This list isn't my proudest moment. I've been drawing on it for a few weeks now, adding things here and there. When I have free time I enjoy spending it watching movies. Rom coms, of course. I always get too invested, and this was my way of stopping that. This is my way of proving this stuff doesn't exist in real life.

My mind snaps when I hear a knock on my door. I turn the volume down and make my way to the door. I squint to look through the peephole, only to see Bellamy. Never has just a glimpse of someone flipped my stomach over but Bellamy is truly a different breed. I swear the man isn't human. He's got to be some type of alien from planet scorching, burn your skin off, smoking, kill you with their looks, hot. That's the only explanation for this.

"You're late," I open the door to him. He looks me up, and down, his lips turning up into a smile.

"You're pretty when you're annoyed."

I roll my eyes at his senseless flirting. He steps through the entryway wearing black straight leg jeans that are loose on him. Clean white Nike's on his feet, and a Seattle Pike University athletics shirt on. Predictable Bellamy attire. His hair is damp, and curling up at the ends.

"Don't be mad at me. I figured you'd appreciate me coming to your apartment clean instead of gross from practice," He tries to make excuses, but my ears are already buzzing.

"Wow, thank you for being so disturbingly kind. I do have a question for you though," I walk backward toward my living room, making sure my eyes are locked on him. He's looking around my apartment until I ask him the question. Now his eyes are on me.

"Yeah?" He tosses his bag on the ground near the couch.

"Do you do anything besides tackle other sweaty men so you can throw balls?"

He chuckles at the question which only makes me smile.

"Actually, sweaty men tackle me... And yes I do other things as well... Either way, I'm not the only one who enjoys being around sweaty men all the time... And women too. You're on the field just as much as I am," He throws himself on my couch and smirks at the TV. "Nicholas Sparks, my favorite."

He picks up the remote, and I snatch it from him.

"No, we are not here to watch romance movies and hang out. You need to study," I click off the television, throwing myself next to him.

"You're hot when you boss me around."

I shake my head, "Stop flirting with me, get your notes from class out."

He doesn't move, "We could use your notes..."

"You didn't take any notes, did you?"

He shakes his head.

"Do you even care to pass?" I ask.

He groans, throwing his head back, "I do, but I figured you would take better notes so I kind of... Well, I just banked on you... Don't be mad, Hart, I just know how smart you are," He hides his failure with compliments, little does he know they won't affect me like he thinks they might.

"Don't call me Hart, and don't try to flatter me. You're an idiot," I pull out my notes, pushing things on my coffee table back.

"Good, we both agree that I'm an idiot."

"Get out a pen and paper. I have practice worksheets we're going to go over... I'm going to read off every pinpoint I have and you're going to tell me what you need to work on, alright?"

He nods, "You got it, teacher."

I smile to myself, thankful I can control the heat that comes to my cheeks. I'm not sure why the nickname is cute, but it is.

I start to go over the final and try to stay focused despite the different settings. Normally he's sitting across from me in the student center. I'm on the clock being paid by the school, and he's there of his own free will. We have plenty of space between us and plenty of room for me to think, and him to study.

Right now we're on my couch, and he's leaning over, right next to me, watching as I go over an equation. His body heat is scorching, and it's making me far more nervous than I'd ever admit.

My eyes peer over at him, and he's staring at the paper, his messy hair hanging over his forehead. It's not like all the girls that go after him are wrong for doing so. He's easy to look at, and he's surprisingly charming too. I noticed it far before now, but this is the first time I'm admitting it to myself. I would jump Bellamy Archer's bones if I ever had the chance because holy hell he's beautiful.

AFTER A COUPLE OF HOURS, our dynamic has changed. We're no longer stiff and rigid as we sit next to each other. He's slouched into the corner of the couch, and I'm sitting upright, my feet kicked up on my coffee table. I continue going over the study guide I've made for the two of us, and I point to the next spot, my eyes flipping to him. He's not looking at his notes, but straight at me.

I launch forward and steal his notes, noticing nothing written down from the past ten minutes of me talking. I flip my eyes to him, and then I narrow them.

"Are you paying attention?"

"Sorry, I got distracted," He looks me up and down, and he doesn't even need to try to flirt, it must just come naturally. When you look like he does I guess it has to.

"Are you serious right now? Bellamy, this is your last chance, there's no more studying after this," I try to raise the stakes, wondering if it will set in.

"Yeah I know, but I think I've got this covered... Now I mean, I've got it covered now."

"Good, you can go then."

His jaw drops, "Kicking me out so soon?"

I throw my notes to the side and stretch my arms and

back, feeling tight after sitting for so long, "You wear me out."

I fake a yawn and he laughs.

"I try my best."

I look over to the side at him, his eyes looking at me again.

"You said you couldn't tutor me yesterday because you were working, but the student center is closed on the weekends so..." He questions, and I nod.

"I work here at my apartment. Free housing that way."

He raises his eyebrows at me, a soft nod following.

"You really are smart," He compliments, and I smirk.

"I try my best," I repeat his words, and he smirks, copying the look on my face.

My eyes scan him, and I peer at his tattoo, not able to see the entire thing, but seeing wisps, and pretty markings, "What does your tattoo mean?"

"It means I look great naked," He tells me, and I laugh instantly, him following suit. "That was cheesy, I'm sorry... Um, I got it for my parents."

I nod my head. It feels so normal for the two of us to just sit here. It feels like we hang out every day, like this is a casual thing we do. I've tutored him for the entire semester so I guess that must make sense.

"What's this?" He asks.

I focus on what he's talking about. I see his hand start reaching forward to grab something on the coffee table, and everything moves fast. I reach quickly, trying to beat him, but I fail miserably.

"Nothing," I snap, but he's already got the paper in his hand, and he's standing up now, using his other arm to hold me back. I try pushing him, but he turns his head.

"Behave."

I keep reaching despite the warning. He's got almost an entire foot of height on me.

"What is it? *The List of things I've seen but never done?*" His eyes are scanning the long list. I made the list as a joke, more for personal entertainment than anything. "This is all cheesy romantic shit."

I stop trying to grab the paper now, my hands thrown down at my sides as I give up. He looks directly at me, his eyes looking for an explanation.

"It's stupid, and it's none of your business either, and I would like it back. Please."

His evil smile tells me he's not giving me that list back.

"Cheesy carnival dates, and kissing in the rain. Slow dancing in the street. Food fight in the kitchen, cloud watching..." He reads pieces of the list.

I cross my arms over my chest, anger bubbling inside, "You can stop at any point."

"I could but I like seeing you all worked up. I'll give it back if you tell me what it is," He raises his eyebrows.

"Do I have to?"

He waves the paper in his hand as a response. "Do you want this back?"

"This is blackmail," I argue.

"Not really."

"Yes, really."

"Just tell me what it is, Kamryn," He's amused and I'm annoyed.

A common dynamic between the two of us.

"I like romance movies, okay?" I confess, but he still doesn't hand it back to me.

"Okay? So do I, that doesn't explain this," He points to the list.

"So when I watch them they're all cheesy, and romantic, and I'm not. So I wrote down the things I've seen that I've never done in them. That's it, that's all it is, now give me the damn list so I can throw it away," I tell him.

"Aww come on Ryn, don't throw it away. This is gold. You're secretly a hopeless romantic."

My limit has been reached.

"Okay fine, you can make fun of me all you want, just give it back," I hold my hand out.

"No can do. First of all, I'm not making fun of you at all, it's adorable. Second, I'm keeping it, and completing it," His cockiness is prominent but not wanted at all right now.

I don't get embarrassed easily, but this? *This is fucking embarrassing.*

"Okay, take whoever you want on the dates I don't care, but give the list back."

He laughs, "Completing it with you. Obviously."

The attitude bounces around my living room. I'm the one laughing now.

"You should drop football and go into comedy. Now give it back."

"You do realize you're about 5 '4, and more cute than you are scary... Meaning I'm not going to listen to you."

I think my glare might be able to burn holes through him if I keep at it long enough. I guess we'll see, "Well, I'm not going to do the list with you. It was a dumb list."

"It's not dumb. Do the list with me," He pleads, and though I like the sound of him begging, I'd like the sound of the door closing behind him better.

"No! Did you get a concussion at practice? Are you losing it?" I press my body to him trying to reach the list. The warmth he radiates isn't alarming, but incredibly, and dangerously welcoming. "I'm not going out with you. Not now. Not ever."

My words contradict everything I feel inside of me right now.

"I'm not giving it back," His voice is matter of fact, as are the stern features on his already structured face.

"Fine, keep the list, but if you tell anyone it's mine I'll deny it. I'll see you tomorrow, now go away," I help gather his things, and shove them in his hands.

"And this weekend for our first date."

"I don't do dates. Especially not with you."

"That's offensive," He puts his hand on his chest like I've hurt him.

"Your ego will survive, I promise... If not I know a few cheerleaders who would love to stroke it back to health, which is a perfect job for them, not me, now go away so I can sleep," I point to the door.

"Fine, but this isn't over Hart," He grabs his backpack from my hand, the list still in grasp.

"My name is Kamryn, and it is over. Don't bring up the dumb list again," I raise my eyebrows at him, knowing good and well that Bellamy Archer isn't going to be intimidated.

"Sure," He loosely agrees and opens my door. "Thanks again Ryn," He winks. I close the door behind him, and press my back to it, slowly sliding down until my butt hits the cold tile flooring. This is what I get. I did it to myself.

CHAPTER FIVE

PERFECT BY ONE DIRECTION

I WENT TO BED EARLY LAST NIGHT JUST SO I COULD walk leisurely to class this morning. I'm not late. I'm actually early, for once in my life. I sit at my desk and pull at the sleeves of my sweater. I'm practically drowning in the material, but it's warm. I tend to get cold easily, especially in these classrooms that feel more like a hospital than a learning environment.

I look over the notes in my hands, not worried at all about this final. I know I've got it covered, but there's no harm in one last look. I see Vans walk past, my eyes still looking down at the paper in my hands. I know Bellamy is behind me now. He seems to always choose the desk behind me. We have never had assigned seats. There are always plenty of empty desks around the room. Despite all of that, he still chooses this specific chair every.single.day.

"How'd you sleep, Hart?" He tugs on a strand of my hair, starting to wrap it around his finger like he's done in the past.

I take my hair, and pull it over my shoulder, making it harder for him to touch.

My mind wanders to the list he now has in his possession, and I feel embarrassment burn through me and the
heat that flushes my cheeks. Luckily he can't see me. I'll
never admit it to him, but that list hasn't left my head since
the moment he walked out of my apartment. My mind reels
over what he's thinking about that damn list.

"It would have been better if you would have given me
my list back," I tell him, keeping my head down.

"Oh yeah, about that... I was thinking about the ferry
boat date first. That's a good first date, isn't it? You got it
from Grey's Anatomy, didn't you?" I clench my jaw.

Don't get angry, he's joking around. It's just a joke.

"Bellamy, you might have lost your mind if you think
I'm going on a date with you. It's not happening."

He taps his pencil vigorously behind me.

"Why not?" He asks.

"You don't get to know that. All you get to know is that
the answer is no, and there's no point in asking again
because the answer won't change," I tell him.

The rest of the class has slowly filed in, and our
professor is now standing at the front of the class, holding a
stack of finals.

"At least let me plead my case. Just once, and if you say
no again then that's fine, I'll leave it alone," He whispers
now, not wanting to draw attention.

"Fine, just shut up," I catch his smirk before I turn back
around. It would be very hard to miss at this point.

The tests come out, and my mind leaves Bellamy and
turns to equations, and math. Every question feels like a
breeze, my mind faltering on only a few, but coming right
out of it. I work hard, and diligently for what feels like ever,
but when I look up, It's only been about 45 minutes. I
check, and then double check and I'm the first one up, and

out of my chair, turning my test in to Professor Gallen, and he doesn't question it. I walk out of the class, my bag on my shoulder. I make my way down the hall, and outside, the sun hitting me as I walk down the steps of the science building.

"Kamryn!"

I clench my jaw, my eyes rolling automatically as I hear his voice calling after me. I turn slowly and face the tall football player.

"Don't look so happy to see me," He jokes, slowing his jog down as he meets me in the grass.

"Why are you out here? You should be taking your final."

"Yeah, I finished before you did... I was waiting for you to be done so I could follow you out here," He probably bombed it if he finished before I did.

"And how do you think you did?" I ask.

"Wonderful thanks to you, hey about what you said in class... Pleading my case, and all that..."

I cross my arms over my chest as I stare at the persistent but incredibly adorable quarterback in front of me, "Go ahead, but don't expect a different outcome."

"See here's the thing. I've only got about three weeks until summer session starts. Which means I've got three weeks to pack a lot of fun in, and that's what this would be. Kind of like, we date for a few weeks, and there are no strings attached, and that's all it is... You're an attractive woman, and we get along well, or at least I think we have these past few months of tutoring... I don't see why there's a problem," He makes the offer sound incredibly tempting, all I can do is shake my head, a soft smile on my lips.

I can't.

"Bellamy, you're a nester."

43

He narrows his eyes, "A what?"

"A nester. You date for a long time. You go out with people to find a girlfriend. You're super romantic and all mushy and I don't do that. I don't date. I hookup. I don't want to hurt you or-"

"You don't think I'm capable of casual?" I can't tell if he's actually offended, but I do know he sounds like he might be.

"You have proven that you aren't. You dated that one girl for the first two years you were here, and then you started dating Leah over the summer, and you two broke up, and ever since... Well, you've been single but I have serious doubts that you have hooked up... Have you?"

"Once," He shrugs his broad shoulders. "But that's not even a good point. Because I said there were no strings attached and I meant it. We wouldn't even really be dating. We'd be like... Fake dating."

I narrow my eyes, the idea sounding better and better which only annoys me. So I just need to turn him off of the idea of me, that way he'll change his mind. There's no way any of this would end well.

"My body count is 23, give or take a few people," I know most men would turn their nose up to that number.

Bellamy looks completely unphased though, "More experience. More fun. Do you really think the amount of people you've slept with bothers me?"

What in the feminist bullshit is this? As if he wasn't already hot. *Now he's respectful too?*

"It would bother most."

"Well, I'm a different breed," He tries to market himself to me, but I keep trying to give him a major ick.

"I'll always like my vibrator more than I'll like you."

"Honestly I like your vibrator more than I like me, and I like me a lot."

I work hard to hold my laughter in, knowing it would make it incredibly hard to drive this point through.

"I have a crazy ex that might kill you."

"I'd love to see him try," He sounds incredibly serious now, and the thought of Dylan against Bellamy is almost laughable when I think about it.

"I murdered someone once," I lie.

"And you didn't call me for help hiding the body?"

I'm officially out of ideas. I guess I have to let him down hard.

"I leave in two weeks to go back home to my parents... There's no time."

"I can make a lot of things happen in two weeks for you. Hell, give me ten minutes and I could make something happen for you," He shamelessly hits on me, and my jaw drops.

His smirk grows into a smile, and I hold the smile appearing on my face too, "You're making it so much harder to say no..."

He keeps smiling.

"But I'm still not going to do it. No. Not happening," I turn away. "You're cute Bell, and sweet too, but I never made that list so it could be done... I made it as a joke, more for personal use."

The smile never fades from his face despite the rejection I'm spoon feeding him right now. He shoves his hand in his pocket, his eyes locked on me.

"Alright, if that's what you want," He agrees, I'm not sure why I'm shocked by his response. "I guess... Well, I guess this is my last time seeing you before you leave then."

I stand still, wondering how he's accepting defeat so easily, wishing he wouldn't for some reason.

"I guess so," I agree.

"Alright then, safe travels. I hope I get to see you on the field next year, Ryn. You should try to join summer sessions," He holds an arm out, and I lean in.

He envelopes me in a tight hug. I half hug him back, still questioning why he's given up so easily. I look at him, my brows furrowed.

"What?" He asks me, and I shake my head, my eyes trailing to my feet instead of his face.

"Nothing. Have a good summer and good luck at summer sessions," The words taste bitter in my mouth as I speak them.

I walk away, leaving him in the quad as I walk back to my apartment.

What the hell just happened?

CHAPTER SIX

WHAT I LIKE ABOUT YOU BY THE ROMANTICS

Days later I walk out of a stadium style classroom and feel like I can take a deep breath. Every single final is done, and my junior year of college is now complete. Of course, I still have to wait and see what my final grade is but even if I bombed every final, which I didn't, I would still pass all of my classes. Meaning there's nothing to worry about for the last two weeks I'm in Seattle.

I enjoy walking on campus. I've made the most out of not having a car here. There's bus transportation for the campus of course but I'd prefer the fresh air, even when it's cold. Our campus is beautiful. It sometimes seems like Seattle Pike feels like it's its own corner of the world. Like nothing else exists outside of these classes, or the dining hall, or my friends.

My apartment is only a block away. Sienna said she'd be meeting me there, but knowing her, she's probably already inside, slumped on my couch with some rom com on. She's also probably helped herself to my snacks.

I begged Sienna to move in with me. She's a lot tidier than I am, and we both know it wouldn't have worked out because of that. We value our friendship over living together so we decided it was better this way. She lives alone now in her own place just like me, and she's close too. Close enough to walk if she wanted to.

I open my door to a sight I knew I'd see. Sienna is sprawled on my gray sofa, a bowl of popcorn in her grasp, her eyes trained on the TV. 50 First Dates is on the screen, one of my favorites, and one of hers too. I can't count on my hands and toes how many times the two of us have watched this movie on my sofa or hers.

"Finally!" Her voice is cheerful, and it makes me smile.

I throw my things on the floor, and launch myself onto the couch, practically on top of Sienna.

"We're done," I sigh in relief.

"Thank god. I'm sick of college."

The romance plays behind her words. My eyes are trained on it, my mind betraying me. I think about his eyes first, and then the rest of him. His smile, and his body...His offer.

Every part of me is contradicting itself when it comes to the thought of Bellamy Archer, and this stupid list. On one end, I should be happy that he left it alone. I should be happy that he just gave up. But I'm oddly unsatisfied with that fact.

The thought of doing this list with Bellamy brings up a million red flags. Mostly because Bellamy is a walking green flag. Green flag men are hard to find, and they fall incredibly hard. Especially for red flag girls like myself. I'm only a red flag because I'm absolutely not looking for a relationship in the slightest. It might be a bit presumptuous to place Bellamy in a category but I know I'm right. I know he can't do casual the way that I can. I know someone like him would end up hurt by someone who's not ready to date. Someone who might never be ready to date.

Opposites might attract, but they shouldn't when one of them is the human embodiment of a cinnamon roll, and one of them is a heartless bitch. If I hurt his feelings, everyone else might hurt me. It would also hurt me to hurt his feelings if I'm being honest. But that doesn't stop me from seeing the list on repeat in my head like an agonizing movie on loop. I can't shut my head up about it.

"So…" I want to bring it up to her but it's almost impossible to do it casually… Sienna is the type to freak out when I bring up boys in a non-sexual way. Especially boys with the name Bellamy Archer.

"So what? What did you do?" She asks me, and my jaw drops slightly.

"Who says I did anything?" I ask her.

"You did. You started the conversation with sooooo. That means you did something… Or you're thinking about doing something. Which one is it?"

I drag my bottom lip through my teeth, preparing myself to tell her.

"So remember that list I said I was going to make you? The one that was going to prove that things in romance movies don't ever happen in real life? Well, I was almost done making it, and I tutored Bellamy Archer in my apartment the other day, right?"

She sits up at the mention of Bellamy, her interest piqued.

"I'm listening…" She has a mischievous look on her face.

Knowing my best friend so well, she has to have a million and one crazy ideas swirling through her head right now.

"Well, he obviously grabbed the list-"

49

"Obviously," Sienna is smirking at me, completely relaxed on my couch.

She's eating every ounce of this up.

"He asked what it was, and wouldn't give it back, and then he suggested that he help me complete it, and I don't know why. I have no idea what his intentions with it are, but I said no. He asked again and again, and I said no every single time, and then he just said okay, and wished me a good summer."

She tilts her head toward me like she's waiting for something else.

"I don't see the problem..." She shakes her head. "So you're not into him like that... That's fine, and he's obviously a good guy, he's not going to try and force you, or make you go out with him."

I nod, agreeing with her partially.

"But?" She asks.

"But ever since I said no, and he said that's fine, I have not been able to shut up that stupid little voice in the back of my head, and I can't stop thinking about it, or him," It almost burns my tongue admitting it out loud.

"Okay, that's exciting. So when are you going to tell him? I have been waiting for this moment since the day you said you were tutoring Bellamy, he is-"

"No... No, absolutely not. I was telling you that so you could talk me out of it."

"Then you're shit out of luck because I was going to tell you that you should do it."

I cover my face with a throw pillow and groan into it as loud as I can.

"Oh come on Kam. What's the worst that could happen?"

I throw the pillow across the living room and sit up as quickly as possible.

"He falls head over heels in love with me, and I break his poor little heart."

I've never seen Sienna roll her eyes as hard as she just did.

"Okay, when I don't know what to do, I make a pros and cons list, so that's what you're going to do. So pros... I don't want you to talk, I'll tell you what they are. He's a quarterback which means he has quarterback hands."

"Quarterback what?" I interrupt.

"Quarterback hands... Oh my god, do you know anything? Not only him, but practically every football player has hot hands. You can't tell me you never noticed them," She says as I continue to shake my head, having no clue what she's talking about. "Okay, well, you're in for a treat. He probably knows just how to use his large, football player hands too... That's a very very big pro."

Sienna doesn't let up about the hand thing.

"I don't care about his hands. I care about the fact that Bellamy has never been the type to do casual. He's more like you, and I'm more like... Like his best friend Lawson who can't keep it in his pants," I shrug, and Sienna's eyes go wide.

"Okay, well... Did he says he wanted more than the list?"

I shake my head no to her question.

"No, he was the one who added casual, no strings attached," I sigh the words out.

"What things were on this list?" Sienna asks, and I rattle off some of the contents.

"I just don't know," I admit to her.

"Well, I do... He has made it very clear that he has no

intentions of anything more. He said no strings attached first. He's literally one of the most attractive men that walk this campus, and honestly, probably the world. You get sex, you get good experiences and fun memories, and you get to complete the list, and then go home... If anything more happens, that's not on you... You've clarified what you want. If he expects more. He fucked up, not you."

The turning in my stomach continues, nothing making it subside.

"I just don't want... I don't want things to be awkward or anything... What if I end up able to help the football team next semester? Then how am I going to act like nothing happened?" I truly don't think I'd be able to live with myself if this messed anything up for me being able to do what I love.

I want to work with the football team more than any other sport at Seattle Pike University. I'm in good graces as of right now with the coach.

"You've slept with at least five guys on the football team, and kicked them out after... If that's not going to be awkward, then why would this be? You're friends with him, it would probably be less awkward if anything. I seriously don't see a single con to this, I mean it... You know I would try my hardest to turn you away from anything I thought was a dumb idea, but this? This is genius."

I run my hands over my face, and harshly through my hair, "It was three football players... But either way, should I text him?"

"He's at drills... Or he's about to be. He wouldn't answer... I mean, you could just show up?"

"Drive me to the field?"

She's off the couch before I can even blink.

From the second we get in the car I start questioning my

mental state. I question exactly how I thought this was a good idea for even a split second. I know I'm sweating too. This will end badly. I have a gut feeling about just how poorly this is going to end. I nestle myself into the passenger seat, crossing my arms over my stomach as I panic mentally. I think I'm going to vomit. Profusely. Exorcism-type vomit all over this car, or possibly the football field.

"You're not backing out."

I open my mouth to argue but she doesn't let me.

"No! You always push me to do the things I want to do, and normally I don't get the chance to do the same because you just do whatever you want, but this is my chance... This is a good thing, and you're doing it or I swear I will... I don't know, but you can't back out now. We're almost there," Sienna states.

"What if he changed his mind?" I ask, and she shakes her head.

"Well, give me the list, let's just go over it, and see if this is really even worth the drama," She holds her hand out, and I cringe.

"He might still have it with him. He said he wanted to keep it," I explain, and she smirks.

"He didn't give you the list back... He still had hope. I bet it wasn't much, and you probably bruised his ego just a bit, but he's still going to be excited. I will put money on it."

I hold my hand out to her, "Okay how much?"

She rolls her eyes at me as she turns down the street, the stadium coming into view. I take a deep breath, blowing it out of my mouth, and then I close my eyes, pressing the back of my head to the seat.

"I swear if you throw up in my car..."

"I might," I feel my stomach churning.

This is not me, I never back down from a challenge,

ever, but Bellamy is like a Mount Everest sized challenge. This isn't going to end well, I already know it.

"You are being overdramatic. Stop being a little bitch, get the fuck up, and go tell him," She parks the car on the street, and I groan.

"Come with me."

"I am not coming, Lawson is on the field, and he-"

"I need you to come with me if you want me to do this."

She unbuckles her seatbelt, probably questioning our friendship while she does so.

"Fine," She agrees and gets out with me.

I know I'm being dramatic. I know that I need to put on a face right now and grow up, at least in front of him. I take another deep breath. Sienna and I get out of the car and meet around the front.

"I've got this," I tell her outwardly, but I know I'm telling myself more than her.

"Confidence is key," Her reminder goes in one ear and out the other.

For the first time ever I have no thoughts in my head as I walk through the entrance of the stadium, going toward the bleachers. I have no thoughts because I know if I had any they would all be telling me to turn around and go home. So I have no thoughts. None at all as I walk down the steps of the stands, my eyes focusing on a football team that's warming up, readying themselves for drills.

The cheerleaders are out on the field. I'm assuming tryouts are soon for next semester. I feel a few eyes on me, and I can see eyes on me too. People are probably wondering what the hell I want. Coach is talking to the boys, but slowly all their attention turns to me, and so does the coach's.

"Start your warmups!"

I catch Bellamy's confused look as he hesitates to move and start his warm up. Coach approaches me, and his eyes flip to Sienna who stands behind me. Now or never.

"Kamryn Hart, right?" Coach asks me, and I nod.

I've definitely introduced myself before and expressed my interest in the team. For once, I see he's listened. From what I've seen that's not a common occurrence with Coach Corbin. He doesn't like working with sports medicine students; he'd rather stick with professionals.

"Yes, coach," I smile, and he does too.

"What can I do for you, Hart?"

"I need to talk to Bellamy."

He narrows his eyes on me.

"You need my star quarterback? Right now?" He looks back at Bellamy, and then me once more.

"I know, I know... I'm sorry, but it will only be a second."

He doesn't look amused, but he also doesn't look pissed so that's a good sign in my opinion.

"I like you... I've been watching you on the sidelines at other games this season, and I promise if this was anyone else, I would say no... You better make it quick, Hart," He snaps his fingers toward the field, trying to get the attention of his players.

"I will!" I feel a different sense of nerves, knowing the coach has been keeping tabs on me.

The good kind of nerves. The second my eyes land on Bellamy, it's the bad kind again.

"Archer!" Coach Corbin yells, and I watch as Bellamy's attention snaps in my direction, and then his coach.

I don't hear what Coach Corbin says, but I watch as he hikes his hand back at me, and then looks over. He shrugs at Bellamy and walks away onto the field. Bellamy stalks toward me, his helmet removed now, showing messy hair. He takes out his mouthguard as he approaches, his height towering over me.

He's wearing a Hornets tank top that's tight fitting to his body as well as the normal football pants and cleats he always wears on the field. He's got a very thin layer of sweat on his large arms, one of them holding a football, the other holding his helmet. As he gets closer my eyes focus in on his hands, Sienna's words playing in my head, and my stomach flips at the sight of how fucking big his hands are. The veins of his arms, and the simple way his long fingers curl around the helmet. Quarterback hands are definitely a thing. They make Bellamy's appeal grow exponentially. Especially now that I have thoughts circling my head of exactly what those hands could do-

"Are you okay?" He asks and my heart warms.

I find it somewhat endearing that his initial instinct is to check on me.

"Not really," I speak to myself.

"What happened?" His eyes are scanning my features.

"I think I've lost my mind but... You've got two weeks," I lay it out on the table.

He questions me with his features, not understanding at first. His brows are furrowed, and his head is turned slightly to the side. I watch as his eyes widen ever so slightly. I watch everything click in his mind.

"Hold on..."

I stop him right before he speaks, "You have two weeks, the only rule is that there's no strings attached. Other than that, everything is on the table, do you understand?"

His eyebrows raise, and he smirks. He nods his head slowly, still not speaking as he keeps his eyes locked on me.

"I do... What made you change your mind?" He asks.

"She did," I throw my hand back to Sienna who I know is still behind me.

"I would hug you but I'm sweaty..."

"I'll just imagine it," Her tone is incredibly sarcastic.

"I'll text you?" He asks, I nod. "Are you serious right now? You're not fucking with me?"

I shake my head.

"I'm serious... So don't fuck it up," I turn away toward Sienna, and close my eyes, letting out a silent breath now that he can't see me.

I don't want Bellamy to know how panicked I am. I don't care if my best friend sees it though. She's seen me freak out too many times to count.

"I won't..."

I look over my shoulder, and he's watching me walk away. I look him up and down, my eyes catching on his hands again, my stomach tightening at the sight. I have no idea what I've gotten myself into but I think I'm completely and utterly screwed.

CHAPTER SEVEN

BABY BLUE BY LUKE HEMMINGS

When was the last time I went on a date? I couldn't tell you. Not a date that counts anyway. Not a cute date where things are planned, and I wear a cute outfit that I love and feel pretty in... I haven't gotten to that part yet. The dress, and the feeling of being pretty part.

I'm sitting in my bedroom right now, butt-ass naked, contemplating if a dress is too much.

I'm not nervous.

I'm not scared.

I've been around Bellamy all semester, and nothing has changed between the two of us even now that dates are added. I just don't know what he's wearing, and I hate it more than anything when I go somewhere and I feel out of place. That's the last thing I want. I pull up my phone, and text him, asking what he's wearing, and right away, he responds.

Clothes.

> Obviously, but what exactly are you wearing?

Are you hitting on me, or are you genuinely curious?

> Bellamy, you're already annoying me. I actually want to know.

Are you not ready yet? I'm almost at your place.

> You are doing everything but answering the one question I asked you.

HE'S USELESS. I get off the floor. Not without letting an animalistic groan out of my mouth. Then I walk through my living room, still naked. I go to the laundry room and flip through the clothes I have hanging up in there.

My mind is jumbled, and now I'm annoyed so all I do is stare, looking at my options. I reach for the baby blue dress that I haven't worn yet, and I take it off of the hanger, stepping into the dress. I leave it unzipped toward the top which I can't reach. The dress has pretty dark blue flowers scattered all over it. It reaches the middle of my calf and hugs me tight at the top, but underboob down it flows. I walk back through my apartment and grab a pair of strappy heels, ones that tie up all around my ankles.

There's a knock on my door, and I run to it, looking through the peephole first before opening it up. Bellamy stands in front of me. He's wearing a pair of light gray pants, and a black t-shirt, the t-shirt fitting him so well. The soft black material hugs his arms like it's his best friend in the world.

His hair is the same as it always is, messy, yet managed. The ends effortlessly curled. He's got a simple silver necklace on, and a few rings on his fingers, and now I'm staring at his hands, thinking about what Sienna said. *Quarterback hands.* I snap my attention away, looking into his pretty light blue eyes instead of letting my eyes linger anywhere else. Anywhere they shouldn't.

"Can you zip up my dress?" I turn before he answers.

I drop the shoes on the floor and move my long black hair from my back. The second his fingers graze my skin I swear every hair on my body stands up. Awareness spreads through every inch of me as I feel my body awaken just from the simplest touch. I react to him far more than I would if it was anyone else. What just happened is proof of that. Dear God, I need to behave myself.

"All done," He tells me, reaching his hand around my body.

He gathers my hair, moving it to my back once again, and then he turns me by one shoulder. His touch lingers and his stare is prominent. I look up at him hesitantly, no expression present on my face as I wait for him to reveal what he's thinking as we continue to stare at each other.

"Pretty."

I press my lips together, but they inevitably turn up into a smile. Bellamy normally throws comments at me that are senseless, and seem as though they're a joke. This, though it's simple, feels real. Like he truly means it when he says it. One word, only one but it hits my chest hard.

"Thanks," I turn around, not letting any of my thoughts be seen on my face.

I grab the shoes from where I dropped them on the

floor. I walk into my living room and throw myself down on the couch.

I hike my leg up so I can put the heels on, the material of my dress beginning to slip up my leg as I rest it on the table. I feel the air brushing my exposed skin. I'm not showing too much, but just enough.

I catch Bellamy's eyes, his hands in his pockets, his face, and gaze stuck in my direction. He looks like he was struck by lightning. It's not a bad look but it's one I don't know so I speak my thoughts.

"I'm sorry it took me so long. I didn't know what to wear because someone likes to keep things a secret," I snatch some of the unwanted tension from the air.

He might enjoy it, but I know I don't.

"I have to have some edge on you... I also had no idea what you were wearing. It's only fair, right?"

I roll my eyes as I switch feet. I try to move quickly as I put on the other shoe.

"Well, I don't care what's fair. I need to know from now on what the dress code is for every single one of these stupid dates," I lace the shoes with skill around my ankle and calf.

"As long as you don't call them stupid again. Speaking of..." He reaches into his pocket and pulls out the list.

The thought of him having it – keeping it, and looking at it – ties knots in my stomach and I hate the feeling. I watch as he holds it, ignoring his hands as I look, and see his eyes scanning the paper.

"We've got a lot to get done," He shakes the list lightly, his eyes sliding back to me.

"Yeah, and I know some of those things aren't possible right now, but it's fine. I guess we can just do as much as we're able," I stand and make my way to him.

He watches every move I take like he's never laid eyes

on me in his life. I move close to him, practically chest to chest. He's focused on me, more than he ever has been right now.

"Ready?" He asks and I nod softly.

He motions to the door, and then he opens it for me. We walk out together, down the hall, and to the elevator. As we move through my building, he's sure to open every door for me, and the moment we walk out of the complex he walks around me, moving me so I'm on the inside, and he's closest to the street. All green flags from Bellamy Archer, that's a fact. Not that I'm surprised.

"My car is right up here."

I walk beside him, a small distance between us as we walk, his arm barely brushing mine as we move together. I continue my pace down the street and feel his presence leave. My head turns and I look at him as he opens the door of an old beat up Jeep. I knew he drove a Jeep, but I didn't think this is what it would look like. One that looks like it's lived a lot of life. Been to a lot of places. The car is more loved than I am from the looks of it.

"This is your car?" I ask him.

"I've driven you before... And for someone without a car, I don't think you have much room to judge mine."

I walk back to him and shake my head.

"No, I'm not judging. I just expected something different," I know he's got money.

A lot of it too. His family is loaded. I guess it was shallow of me to expect anything at all from him. Especially that he'd have some fancy nice car. Oddly enough, this old beat up car fits Bellamy perfectly. I did think his reddish Jeep was newer than the one I'm now sitting in.

"What were you expecting then?" He closes the door behind me as I climb in.

He walks around the front of the car and gets in on his side. We both buckle, and he pulls away from the sidewalk, beginning our drive.

"Something newer... I don't know, at first, when I had no idea what you drove, I expected you to drive a sports car. Or like a fast car. A Mustang or something. Tesla. I don't know," I shrug again, the words feeling stupid as I say them.

He fits the Jeep, but damn would he look good in a Tesla or a muscle car.

"Doesn't your ex drive a Mustang?"

Did he just make me want to throw up already? Not even ten minutes into our first date ever?

"You know normally people you're dating don't mention your ex."

"Well, good thing we're fake dating, so I can."

I can tell Bellamy finds himself incredibly amusing right now considering the smirk plastered on his face. Though it looks good on him, it annoys me to my core.

"Yes, he did drive a Mustang," I don't want to tell him, but considering Bellamy's track record.

I don't think he'll let it go until I confirm.

"Yeah, I don't need a car to compensate..."

My jaw drops. He laughs, and I watch him carefully, my eyes focused on his face.

He's got pretty skin, smooth, and even. His lips are pink, and curve around his pearly white teeth perfectly when he smiles or laughs. The second he reveals his smile, he reveals a mark carved deep into his cheek. A deep dimple that softens every feature of his. Bellamy doesn't have hard stern features. He's got intimidating features. Because there's not a single flaw in the way he looks.

There's light stubble on his structured jaw, not patchy, or uneven. He has light eyes that focus on the road, only looking elsewhere occasionally, just like he's doing right now, looking at me. Bellamy looks perfect, and the way he looks at me might be more perfect than that. I look away, noticing the way he's gripping the steering wheel with both hands.

"Why are you gripping the steering wheel for dear life? Should I be scared?" I ask him.

"No, sorry," He apologizes for nothing, and moves one of his hands, resting it on the gear shift.

I look at his muscular hands, ring clad, wrapped around the wheel instead of around my throat, and I-

"I think I'm nervous," He announces, and I'm glad he stopped my completely inappropriate thoughts.

They were out of hand... *No pun intended.*

"Why would you be nervous?" I ask him.

"I'm taking a pretty girl on a date," He tells me, and I smile at the smooth compliment.

The word pretty is so superficial, but it sounds like butter when it comes from Bellamy Archer, and I don't think there's any way I could explain why.

"Oh, that. Well, you've taken plenty of pretty girls out, and if you get too nervous remember there's no pressure... Considering it's all fake," I alleviate the small bit of tension once again, reminding him and myself of this arrangement.

"You're right..."

Both of us start to relax. I feel far more comfortable knowing he was nervous. I don't know why that sends ease over me but it does. I guess it shows me that he's taking this seriously. My feelings somehow always feel validated if someone feels the same way I am.

"So this list... I've read over it a few times. I know you like romance movies. Where were some of the ideas from? What movies inspired it?" Bellamy asks me, and part of me is scrapping to remember what items I put on the list, but part of me doesn't want to remember so I don't have to tell him.

"I don't remember," I shrug, and he sits up, taking the list out of his pocket.

"Now you do," He smirks, his eyes dancing between me and the road.

I roll my eyes, and snatch the list from his fingertips, contemplating letting the list fly out the window and pretending it was an accident. Knowing Bellamy and how persistent he is, he'd probably turn around and walk the freeway until he found the list, even if it did risk his life.

"Which ones do you want to know?" I ask, looking over my doodles, and scribbled handwriting.

"Kissing in the rain?" He asks.

"The Notebook, duh."

"And romantic first time?" He adds.

"New Girl. Jess and Nick had a romantic first time and it was adorable and so sweet. I loved that episode," I explain.

"Your pretty bouquet?" He keeps peeking at the list.

The wind is rustling his hair as he drives making him look effortless.

"Big Fish. The field of daffodils scene is one of the most romantic of all time. I know a bouquet isn't the same as a field, but it's still the thought that counts. Plus no one has ever even gotten me a single flower let alone a bouquet," I tell him.

"What about the playlist?" He asks, and I shrug.

"I feel like one of the most romantic gestures is when someone hears or sees something, and they think of someone else. That's what dedicating a playlist to someone is. Hearing someone and tying it to someone else. In the movie Stuck in Love, Rusty says that Kate reminds him of the song *I've Just Seen a Face by The Beatles*. That line always gives me butterflies. So I took inspiration and put the playlist on the list," I say.

I love that movie so much. It's definitely one of my favorites.

"What about the New Year's kiss?" He asks, and I think of my parents, but don't want to tell him anything about them.

At least not my favorite stories about them.

"When Harry Met Sally. He confesses he loves her at the New Year's Party, it's romantic, and ... and I just think New Year's is special," I shrug, and he nods.

"Cute. This little list, and all your little doodles, it's cute," He compliments, and I blush.

It is cute, and not like me at all to do such a thing. When I do I end up in messes like this one.

He drives us the rest of the way, making jokes to me, and asking me questions that are easy, and simple. We talk like we did when we were distracted from studying. The drive is easy and quick.

We arrive at Elliot Bay, the ferry boats perfectly in sight. There are a few of them, lined together. Part of me gets incredibly excited, the feeling welling up in my chest. I push that excitement down, knowing this is fake. That this is for a list, and nothing more.

I reach for my door, starting to open it. A hand reaches across the car brushing my body, Bellamy's hand encloses mine and he closes the door. He has completely invaded my personal space as he leans over my seat. I look at him and his face is inches from mine.

He raises his eyebrows like he's wondering what the hell I'm doing. I'm staring at him wondering if his hand covering mine is making me hot or if it's just a hundred degrees right now. I swallow deeply as I'm face to face with him, noticing just how perfect he looks in high definition.

"Don't be rude. We're on a date. I open the doors, you look pretty," He chastises me, and moves away, but leaves the tension.

Bellamy gets out, and circles around the back of the car. I take a deep breath, and then he opens the door for me, holding his hand out, waiting to take mine. He helps me from the car and lets go of my hand right away, making me somewhat nervous at how jumpy he seems. We walk with no contact at all and continue toward the boats. He gets to the ticket kiosk, and I walk up first.

"One ticket please," I tell the woman behind the desk, and Bellamy once again leans close, invading my bubble once more.

"Two... Two tickets," He tells her, passing her a card with his name etched on it.

I open my mouth to protest, and then close it. I'm not used to this type of treatment. I feel like a fucking princess, wow. *Is this what healthy feels like? Is this how others live every day?*

"Don't look so surprised Ryn," He laughs as he takes the tickets and his card back.

"I wasn't trying to, I'm just not used to this," I say.

We walk together now as we talk.

"Dates?" His eyes are so soft, I can barely look at this man without my insides melting, what did his parents feed him?

"People paying for me on dates," I correct him, my eyes scanning my surroundings instead of looking at the man next to me.

"Not to bring him up again... But he never paid for

you?" Bellamy approaches the man on the dock first, handing him our tickets.

"No, we either split things, or I paid for both of us," I admit, already knowing he's going to hate that response.

"Ew," He disapproves as he scrunches up his nose, and I laugh.

"Why do you think it was so short lived?"

"Because you hate men," He answers, still not touching me once as we walk onto the ferry boat.

His answer is very funny and incredibly honest for a man, but it's not entirely true.

"Yes, but no. It was short lived because I hate relationships, not men specifically," I correct him.

"The list in my back pocket tells me differently. You're a hopeless romantic," He tells me.

"A closeted one. It's not even really a secret... I just like romance movies... Just because I like them doesn't mean I want them to happen to me. I watch horror movies too, that doesn't mean I want a ghost eating my face off."

The look on his face tells me everything I need to know. It's like he can see right through the lies. It's not a full lie, only half of one. I know I deserve to feel the things within the movies and books I love so much, I just don't think it's possible in real life, and if it is, it's far too hard to find. I'm not ready for the disappointment I will have to endure to find the close to perfect person. I don't want relationships anymore. And I definitely don't want the ghosts eating my face off either.

"You said that you know some of the stuff on the list won't happen," He points out.

We walk up the steps of the ferry boat, going to the upper deck. There is a good amount of people on board, but not as many upstairs. The deck is breezy and vast. A lot of space for the two of us to be alone. My nerves skyrocket once again.

"I did say that," My chest is buzzing.

"You know I will be making everything happen, right? With consent, and after I talk to you... I just want to make sure you know I have every intention of keeping it all on the list... Doing everything."

My shock is hard to hide on my face. I graze his features, trying to catch him in a lie, but he's telling the truth. My surprise sits in the air.

"You know sex is on that list, right?"

He gives a short nod as he motions for the two of us to sit down on a bench near the edge of the boat.

"I'm aware," He's completely calm and collected.

I hope I'm coming off the same way despite how fast my heart is beating right now. This man has lost his mind. No, correction. I have lost my damn mind.

"So no offense, but how do you expect to have sex with me if you won't touch me at all?"

His eyes are trained on the ground and his smile illuminates his face. His legs are spread as he sits, one of his hands resting on his thigh, the other hand resting on the back of the bench behind me. He looks up, his eyes catching mine. I watch as he looks between my eyes like he's searching for something specific as he stares at me. He reaches his hand up, his fingers tracing my cheekbone and moving upward to tuck my hair behind my ear.

Bellamy has touched me in passing. We've hugged each other goodbye. We've grazed each other's hands when studying but he's never... Never touched me like this. No one has touched me like this, and I think my heart just dropped so quickly it might be in my ass.

"I have no problem touching you Ryn, I just need to

know what you're okay with before I start assuming..." He tells me. "I just don't want to make you uncomfortable, especially not on our first date."

I'm not used to this. To a good person. To someone like Bellamy. His thumb traces my cheek, his fingertips behind my ear, holding me right where he wants me. Right where I want to be.

"I told you there are no rules... Everything is on the table... Everything except strings, those will never be attached," My words don't sound forced, at least I hope they don't.

I feel forced as I speak them though. It feels like I've never had a drop of water in my body my entire life, that's how dry my throat is right now.

"So if you're ever not comfortable with something you'll tell me?" His clarification somehow sinks my heart even further, mostly because I've never had someone talk to me like Bellamy is right now.

Hot, and respectful, I don't know if I can get over it. That is in fact the bare minimum, though. Maybe I should raise my standards...

"Yes, I will, consent king," There's a slight smile still playing on his pretty lips.

"Your sarcasm is highly unreasonable considering I'm being a gentleman," The boat honks its horn, slowly beginning to move. "Why?" He asks out of nowhere, I furrow my brows, and his hand slowly falls from my face, but slides over my shoulders, slowly pulling me closer to him.

"Why what?" His warmth is indescribable, and I'm infuriated by how good it feels.

"Why is everything on the table? Why are there no rules? Why did you say yes?"

"Because Sienna convinced me."

"You don't strike me as someone who does things they don't want to do."

"Because I'm not. I do want to do this. I figured it would be fun. And if you were willing then I'd have sex with someone I find attractive... And it would be a good way to end the rest of the semester, because we're friends, and we can have fun together," I explain to him exactly what I've explained to myself a million times to ensure I wouldn't back out.

"So you think I'm attractive?"

I roll my eyes and shove his chest.

"Do you have selective hearing?" I ask.

"Yes, I listen to what I want to hear that way I'm never disappointed," He tells me, and I laugh.

"You know there are tattoos on the list too?" I raise my eyebrows, feeling like this is a challenge. *There has got to be at least one thing he's not going to complete.*

"You know I'm the one who has the list, right? Meaning I know what's on it... And either way, I have tattoos, I don't care if I get another one. You're the one without any," He points out, and I get defensive instantly.

"You don't know if I have tattoos."

A low chuckle rumbles from his chest.

"Okay, do you have tattoos?" He entertains my statement and I sigh.

"No, but it doesn't matter," I tell him. "I've always wanted tattoos. I've just never really thought of anything I'd want on my body, you know?" I ask.

"I don't know, but I do understand. So you've never had anything important enough to get tattooed, yet you'll get one because of some list that you claim is stupid?"

Call me out, why don't you... *Geez.*

"Tattoos are memories. They don't have to be meaningful artwork as long as they have meaningful experiences behind them. I'll always remember this, even if I never talk to you again after it's over," I tell him, knowing we'll probably continue as mutual friends after all of this is said and done.

At least a small part of my hopes for that.

"I've always wanted to make this into a full sleeve... And I've wanted hand tattoos for the longest time," He tells me, and naturally, my eyes travel to his hands at the mention of them.

Which wasn't the smartest move considering my stomach dropped at the sight. There's something wrong with me... Bellamy is watching me, noticing how I notice him, and my eyes snap away from him.

"Good idea," I add casually, swallowing the ball in my throat.

"Yeah," The tone in his voice tells me he knows where my head is at, and there's nothing I'm going to do about it. "You know I have to get to know you and all that right?" He asks.

"Real dating means you get to know someone. We're not dating, meaning we don't have to get to know each other."

"Yeah, that's not going to work with me. I'm not going to ask your deepest darkest secrets, I just want to know more about you. You're favorite things... Small stuff. We've gotten this far, don't let me down now Ryn."

I feel his fingers on my skin, tracing small circles on my shoulder. It's oddly comforting, chills settling on my skin. I'm not sure if it's from the simple wind from the moving ferry boat or if it's from his touch, but I choose to ignore all of it.

"Okay, fine. If we're playing twenty questions on our

first date like kids, you better not ask dumb questions. I mean it," I tell him, and he smirks.

"Favorite romance movie? Romcom, or romance, or whatever... It doesn't matter," He tells me.

"I like comical ones the most... Like Easy A. That one is amazing. But out of the sentimental ones, I really love Stuck In Love and I love La La Land," I tell him.

"Oh come on... La La Land is not... No. I'm sorry, that movie is horrible," He sits up, the conversation serious now.

"Oh yeah? Why?" I shift toward him.

"Because the ending is god awful! That is a shitty way to end such a picturesque movie," He speaks his truth, and it makes me smirk, showing exactly how wrong he was about me.

"This is proving my point. Only hopeless romantics hope for a happy ending... It's just like real life, nothing ends the way you want it! That's just the way it goes. That's why I love the movie. It's real."

His arm falls, slinking around my lower back only to slide me closer to him. I move my hands up, still keeping some distance as I place my manicured hand on his chest.

"I just love how pessimistic you are..." He smiles.

"And I hate how optimistic you are," I fight back, my tone completely playful.

"You're a shit liar... Either way, my favorite romance is The Notebook. It's top tier... And even though the ending wasn't perfect, it was better than that stupid La La Land movie. And the Proposal. It's the best one. It's the best cast. And it has a wonderful trope too."

I scrunch my nose up. "You using the word trope feels wrong," I tell him.

"Don't be mad because I'm just as well rounded in romance as you are."

I get up, moving toward the railing of the ferry boat, but not too close. The sun is setting, the sky a million shades, all blending together perfectly. My eyes scan over everything, my ears listen in, the waves slapping the boat, and the simple sound of the engine too.

"It's your turn."

I feel him behind me, and then next to me. He walks to the railing, actually standing on the edge, holding on, looking at the water below him.

"Which of your tattoos is your favorite?" I ask, my eyes catching the ink that peeks from the black shirt.

"Well, this is a few pieces mixed into one big piece so I guess I really only have one in my head," He tells me, and I watch as he pulls up the sleeve of his shirt, revealing his bicep to me, my mouth watering on the spot.

I suck in a breath at the sight of the tattoo fully. It looks like a painting, angels, sculptures. It's incredibly well done, and beautiful. The black and white shading almost makes it look real.

"What's the significance? With your parents I mean..." I ask.

I instinctively reach my hand out, stepping close to him. I take his arm in my hand, touching his warm skin, turning his arm so I can see the half sleeve that must continue onto his chest. I can't see all of it because the piece is so big. He's quiet, so I look up at him. He's watching me as I touch him, his eyes stuck like glue on my face. He's very attentive in what he does, and how he watches me, and I'm not used to it yet at all. I feel like running away when I catch his eyes on me like they are now.

"Oh... Um, my parents passed away when I was in high school. They traveled a lot, they were big in business, but they had a company together so every deal was done together, every trip... I spent a lot of time with my grandparents growing up, but my parents always made it home for my games... They loved Italy... They loved art. Michelangelo, and all those older painters, and artists. That's why I chose this style, it's significant to them. Some of their favorite things all meshed into one," He tells me, his words directed to me as I carefully inspect the intricate ink on his strong arm.

He's incredibly open. More open than I could be and I appreciate that, but I'm unsure of how I should go about talking to him about it... If I should even acknowledge it at all...

"Wow..." I breathe out. Those are the only words I can form at the sight of the artwork etched on his skin.

Not only do I not know how to reply to him after what he just said, but I also can't stop looking. It's the perfect piece to be able to dedicate to someone else. It truly is one of the most beautiful pieces of work I've ever seen on someone's body. It helps that his body is so nice and sculpted... A piece of art itself.

I let my hands fall, and look up at him, noticing how close he is to me, and how close we are to the railing I have tried so hard to keep a distance from.

"It's your turn," I almost whisper the words, and he nods, his eyes still staring me down.

I wonder if he feels the tension between us or if I'm completely making it up in my head. I wonder if he knows that I want to touch him again.

"You hate romance... Is it because of Dylan?" He asks me, and I instantly glare at him, my eyes narrowing.

The tension leaves my body, and annoyance fills it.

"That has nothing to do with it. And it's none of your business either. What about you? Why did you and Leah break up?" I cross my arms over my chest, and he tilts his head.

"I didn't mean to piss you off Ryn... Either way, I just want to make sure someone else didn't ruin something for you that you deserve to enjoy," He's even closer to me now.

I look up at him as he faces me head on, his eyes looking down on me, his body right in front of me. My back is turned away from the water, and the railing. He leans forward, his hands grasping the railing, and simultaneously pushing my back against it too. He's pressing me to the cold metal, holding me in place. Our chests touch, and my heart stops.

"Are you going to tell me, or are you just going to stare?" I try my hardest to keep my lips pressed together, not letting an inkling of a smile peak out.

"I don't know, I like the view," He raises his eyebrows, a lopsided smirk forming on his lips.

"That was incredibly cheesy," I loved it though.

He's very good at this cheesy romantic thing.

"Isn't that the whole point?" I don't answer, still waiting on his. "Why do you think Leah and I broke up?" He asks me, pushing off of the railing, releasing me from his grasp.

I move, putting distance between me and the railing once again, "Because she hits you a lot and acts like everyone owes her something."

"I mean that wasn't the reason, but it is true... Leah broke up with me believe it or not. She said I spent too much time playing football and I didn't give her enough attention while I was on the field," He tells me, and I furrow my brows.

"On the field? While you're playing?" I ask, and he shrugs.

"She was cheering on the sidelines... She expected more

attention. Ryn, it makes no sense to me either, but I just let it go. She wasn't the greatest girlfriend. A week after she broke it off she started trying to start something back up, she told her friends she only broke up with me to show them she was serious... I don't know. She probably thought I'd beg her to stay, or something like that. It's all stupid... Dating her in general was stupid of me. We didn't fit well," His words relieve stress from my shoulders.

"So I'm not jeopardizing anything right now between the two of you?"

He chuckles, "If I was trying to get my ex back I would have never agreed to this... And this isn't some ploy to make her jealous either... I do that by speaking to you, I didn't have to take you out to do that. Leah and I are done... You don't have to worry."

I shrug and look down.

"Wasn't worried," I brush off his comment, walking back to the bench, an island appearing, the boat closing in on the port.

Even if he was trying to make her jealous he would never admit to that, especially not on our first fake date. That would be a horrible way to start all of this. I'm sure a part of him likes the thought of it. Making Leah mad.

"So if you found the perfect girlfriend, the perfect person for you, and she said the same thing that Leah did would that change anything? If Leah didn't break it off with you would that have changed things with you and how much time you dedicated to football?" I ask, wondering where his head is at.

I know how good he is at the sport, but how serious is he?

"No, nothing would change that. Football is the first love I've ever had, it makes me who I am. I'm not giving up who I am for another person. I won't do it ever, football comes first. If she or anyone else truly loves me they wouldn't make me choose," His explanation is mature, but also shocking.

For someone as obsessed with romance as Bellamy claims he is, he's far more obsessed with his sport.

"So you'd marry your relationship with football if you couldn't find the right person?" I ask.

"I'm already married to football. Whoever I find is going to have to join the marriage, and they're going to have to be okay with it," He shrugs and it's obvious he's set in this decision.

His dedication is intense, almost overwhelming. Leah was jealous of football. She seems like the jealous type too.

I'm the perfect person to make her jealous if that is his goal. Leah and I are complete opposites while also being the same in odd ways. Leah is stunning, blonde, with the perfect cute features. She's cute and sweet. We're different because Leah has a venomous side she doesn't show. I let mine reign free. She's the kind of girl you can bring home to your mother. I'm the kind of girl guys keep a secret from their parents. My black hair, and dark makeup as well as the showy clothes I wear are enough to send red flags flying. Leah has always been fake to me because Leah doesn't approve of my extracurriculars. Most of the cheerleaders aren't fans of me because of what I do in the bedroom.

I grab my bag and try not to think about his words but I can't help but ponder them. He follows me as the boat slows, and we move down the stairs, I hold onto the railing. He keeps me steady, his hand on my lower back as I step. It's safe with him. That's something I'm realizing. He makes every right move to make me feel comfortable. I realize there's so much intimacy in feeling safe in someone else's energy... and that's what I feel with him. It's an underrated feeling.

The boat comes to a stop, and the crew helps dock us, making the boardwalk for us to get off and go onto the island. We shuffle our way to the exit, the rest of the passengers moving too. Once we reach the exit there's a small gap between the boat and the boardwalk. Bellamy walks over the edge, and I look at the gap. He turns back before I even say a word and he holds his hand out. I look at his hand, ignoring the flip of my stomach, and I place my hand in his.

He leans over, taking my hip in his free hand, lifting me over the gap, making sure I put no effort in whatsoever. I watch him carefully now that I'm standing next to him. He just keeps on walking, his large hand swallowing mine whole as we continue onto the island. As much as I hate to admit it, this is the greatest first date I've ever had, and it's not even over yet.

CHAPTER EIGHT

CLOSER BY TEGAN AND SARA

He holds my hand the entire way as we walk toward the restaurants on the island, and he seems like he has no intention of letting it go. It's darker now, but the sun hasn't fully disappeared from the sky yet. He keeps me close to him as we walk, looking in shop windows, our words escaping only every now and then. There's still a bit of tension in my body, the feeling of his so close, but so far all at once.

He's bigger than me in every way. He overpowers me, but somehow I feel like we fit as we walk together. This is all very simple. Walking with him is simple, and I know the tension I feel is only in my head. But, the simplicity of it all is what makes my head spin, how casual and normal all of this feels. I have no doubt he feels nothing right now, he's just here, and he's enjoying his time... That's the difference between us.

"Is this okay?" He asks, nodding his head to a small pizza restaurant.

I nod my head, and he pushes the door open, a small bell sounding. He leads me through the door with his hand, letting mine go as I walk in. He follows behind, his hands moving over the tops of my bare shoulders and down my arms as he follows behind me to the counter. I lean back slightly, looking up at him over my shoulder.

"I'll take... Hawaiian but add banana peppers," I tell the man behind the counter.

The man working doesn't think anything of it, but Bellamy makes a short noise that makes me look back at him.

"What? You have a problem with my pizza prefer-ence?" I challenge him, and he looks at the man instead of me.

"I'll have pepperoni and black olives. A normal choice, unlike my date here," He nods to me, standing close behind me.

My back presses to his hard chest only slightly, and he looks down at me, a light smirk forming on his lips as his eyes glaze over my features. This is what butterflies feel like, exactly how he just looked at me.

"You're pretty," He tips his chin up at the compliment, and I smirk at him, wanting nothing more than to cover my face because I know how much I'm blushing right now.

I hate PDA but I completely forgot we were even in public for a second.

"You two are adorable," Both of us snap our attention to the old short Italian man behind the counter.

"It's her, not me... Here," Bellamy reaches into his pocket, pulling out cash, far more than what he owes. He puts his empty hand on my upper arm as he leans over me, handing the older man the cash. "Keep the change, thank you, sir," He smiles his famous, pearly white grin, and then walks away, turning me with him.

We sit, we wait, and then our pizza comes out.

The two of us don't take long to finish our food, and he's sure to help me from the booth afterward. He holds out not one but both of his hands for me. I look at his face, not his hands, and place mine in his. He lifts me out of the deep seat and pulls me toward him. Once I'm standing he lets me go first, his hand soon finding my back again, guiding me carefully until we're out of the restaurant. He nods his head, and I look back toward where the ferry boat was docked.

"Are we not going back yet?" I ask him.

"I figured we could knock two birds with one stone tonight..." He nods his head, and I look where he's nodding.

There's a bright neon sign, an arcade, and I find myself smirking.

"We're not really dressed for an arcade are we?" I ask.

"Outfits don't matter, let's go," He nods his head to the arcade, and pulls me with him, his hand grasping mine again.

He holds my hand as we walk into the arcade. He brings us to one of those machines that converts real money to a card so we can play games. His head is truly in it because we go straight to the games without a second to spare once the card is in his hand.

"You know I'd be fine with you just buying me a silly stuffed animal and-" I watch and shut my mouth as Bellamy lets go of my hand, and turns to me slowly.

His jaw is dropped as he looks at me with disapproving eyes.

"That is the most unromantic thing I have ever heard of. Do you even hear yourself right now?" His hands are now on his hips as he looks at me like I just killed a puppy.

"That's kind of the whole point."

He scoffs so loud I'm sure everyone around heard.

"No, the whole point is to be cheesy and romantic with

you... I'm winning this fair and square. If you're bad at arcade games just say that," He walks off without me now, ready to prove his point.

I follow behind him as he finds the basketball games, all lined up next to each other. I feel like I might have unlocked the inner child in him by putting this on the list. Though this is all for me, I can see now he'll get a lot of joy from this too.

"I'm not bad at this one," I stand directly next to him, my shoulder touching his arm right above his elbow.

"Not as good as me. I'm the quarterback," He boasts.

"Like that matters, this is basketball, not football. Though, I know it might be easy for you to get your sports mixed up..."

He swipes the game card, ignoring my insults. We start, our bodies brushing as we shoot hoops. We both get so into the game, we forget that it has to end. The timer goes off, and he looks down with a triumphant look until he sees that I scored more than him.

"Impossible," He furrows his brows, and I smirk.

"Hate to break it to you, but I spent almost every afternoon on the court this semester. I won fair and square," I swipe my hands together, dusting them off from my win.

There's no hiding the smile on my face now.

"So you'd be up for a rematch then?"

"I never said that. I don't do the whole losing thing, especially after I just won. Next game."

He takes my hand and he brings us to Skee-Ball, and I watch as he swipes his card. I just stand next to him, watching him as he takes the game ball in his hands.

You know, Skee-Balls aren't tiny. They are very normal sized balls... but a Skee-Ball in Bellamy's hand looks like a child's toy... And I really wish I hadn't looked because now I can't stop. I watch as he plays, my mouth basically watering at the sight of him playing a stupid arcade game. I'm not really sure how one person can make the most unattractive things attractive, but that's what Bellamy seems to be doing with this game.

"Do you want to play?" He asks, and I hesitate, wondering if he caught me staring.

"Oh... No. I'm fine, I can watch. You're just... Really good."

Good at holding small objects... Like my fucking throat.

"Do you want me to show you?" He asks, and I want to say no, but how else am I going to tell him I want to watch him hold tiny balls? I'm not going to.

I step forward, and he takes my hip turning me around, but he doesn't let his hand slip away. He keeps it rested there, gripping me loosely, his thumb pressed to my back, his long fingers wrapping around the front of my body. He leans over, scanning the card again, and then he bends down to grab one of the balls. I watch him shamelessly now, knowing he can't see me staring at his hands from this angle. He passes me the ball and then lets his hand cover mine, and I think my stomach flips a million and one times. I feel like my insides could win Olympic medals in gymnastics considering how many twists and turns they just did, holy shit.

"Are you okay?" He asks, and I nod, the back of my head brushing his shoulder. He brings my hand back and then forward again. "Let go," He breathes out, and I do.

Just like he had done before, the ball goes in perfectly, earning us 100 more points.

"Again?" He asks, and I don't oppose, mostly because I'm secretly enjoying the feeling of his incredibly large hand covering mine which is embarrassing to admit.

But I don't care. I need to tell Sienna that I hate her for pointing out his hands to me because I never noticed them before. If I had...

Well, I don't know if Bellamy would have lasted as a friend this long.

After a few more rounds of Skee-Ball, we move on. Making our way through the entire arcade, we play games until our cards run out. We take them up to the prize kiosk and put the tickets together. We wait at the ticket counter, looking to see just how many points we racked up, waiting to see just how big my new prize will be. The number continues to go up until it reads 10,232. We look at each other and Bellamy has a shit-eating grin before turning back to the guy behind the prize counter who looks like he hates his life.

"Whatever she wants," He tells the guy who doesn't even change the expression on his face.

He doesn't nod, or acknowledge Bell at all, he just looks at me, waiting for my reply. Fair enough.

"Which one do I get?" I ask Bellamy, looking at the plethora of giant furry stuffed animals on the top shelf.

They're all 9,000 tickets.

"I don't know, the big purple monster looks kinda like you," He points out, and I smirk, fighting a laugh at his insult.

I look up and see a giant dog stuffed animal, a golden retriever, and I point to that one.

"I'll take the dog."

The worker pulls out a step stool and climbs up so he can grab the animal. He takes it from its home and passes it to me, looking to Bellamy for an answer to where the rest of the points are going to go.

"Do they stay on this card?" He asks, and the guy nods.

"Cool... Stay here for a second alright?" He asks me, and I nod, watching as he takes the game card with the rest of our tickets, and walks behind me.

A young girl with blonde pigtails is walking with her mom behind us. Bellamy approaches the pretty mom, and smiles at the young girl, saying something to the mom first that I can't hear. I watch as she smiles, and nods her head, putting her hand on her daughter's back. Bellamy crouches down on one knee talking to the little girl. She smiles at him, her smile so wide it looks like it might be hurting her cheeks. She nods a few times, and he hands her the game card. He stands, making his way back to me.

"Thank you!" The mom calls out.

He just smiles at her, and then comes back to me, placing his arm over my shoulder. We walk together to the exit, and then toward the boat.

"That was sweet," I tell him.

"She kind of reminds me of my little sister," He tells me, and I turn my head to him quickly.

"You have a sister?" I ask him, and he nods.

"She's not so little anymore. She's four years and a couple of months younger than me. So she's 18 now. A senior... She was 12 when my parents passed..." He tells me, and I nod.

"What's her name?" I ask.

"Brianne. I call her B."

"That's a pretty name."

He holds me tight against his side.

"Why did you pick the golden retriever?" He nods to the large stuffed animal I'm holding in my hands.

"You said the purple monster was me. Well, the golden retriever is you," I shoot him a look based on yet another cocky grin on his face. "What?" I ask.

"You got a stuffed animal that reminded you of me," He boasts, his selective hearing coming into play. "Come on, we're going to miss the last ferry and get stuck here," He nods his head.

"My feet hurt, give me a break," I tell him, still picking up the pace to run with him.

We make it to the boat in time, but this time we don't go to the upper deck, we walk until we get to the bench closest to the captain's side. I sit down, and there are very few people on the boat now considering how late it is. There are pretty bistro lights hanging around the entire ferry, and there's a warm glow casting from them, highlighting every perfect feature Bellamy already had.

One thing I have learned for sure from this date is that I am more attracted to him than I had initially thought. Of course, I could see how good looking he was. I knew that from the start, but I didn't see it in the way I do now. There truly is no flaw in his outer appearance. He's the perfect man. He's perfectly tall and perfectly muscular. His smile is to die for. His teeth are without a flaw, and his dimple is incredibly sexy... Just like his tattoos, and his arms. I haven't seen him without clothes, but I imagine it's just as flawless. There's no denying I want him in that way. I have fully confirmed that now.

"Did you have a good time?"

I nod softly, "Did you think I wouldn't?"

He shrugs as he leans down, scooping my legs up so they're together on his lap. He unlaces my shoes one by one, unwrapping the straps from my calves and pulling them off of my feet. He keeps the heels next to him on his side of the bench and also keeps my feet where they are, propped on him.

"I hoped you would, but I also knew if I didn't make this

date perfect it would set me up poorly, and you'd never finish the list with me."

"Awe, how cute."

His hand rests on my bare leg, his thumb moving back and forth on my skin softly.

"You think I'm cute," He speaks out.

"Selective hearing," I chime in, and he shrugs.

"Always thinking happy thoughts."

I laugh, covering my face as I do.

The boat takes its time docking, and I reach over him for my shoes, but he pulls them away. He takes the shoes in his hands and stands up, reaching for me. I think for a second he's going to stand me up, and I want to protest, but he doesn't. He pulls me up in his arms, honeymoon style, not letting me lift a finger, or touch the ground at all.

"Now call me your knight in shining armor so I can live my fantasy out," He tells me, walking me toward the exit of the boat, physically and metaphorically having swept me off my feet tonight...

CHAPTER NINE

STARVING BY HAILEE STEINFELD

I LIFT MY HAND TO KNOCK ON THE DOOR AND BRING IT back down right away. I wipe my hands on my jeans, feeling the sweat gather. Dear god, he gives me nervous sweats, mostly because everything with him is so go with the flow. I never know what is going to happen. Also because he's in full control. I lift my hand to knock again, and the door opens this time. I'm faced with a very attractive, not as tall as Bellamy, but still tall Griffin, and his girlfriend Jade.

"Hi, you must be Kamryn," The pretty girl speaks.

She's got light caramel hair, and natural curls that frame her soft skin. Her skin is brown, but not as dark as Griff's. She does her makeup perfectly, I notice a pretty light pink in the corners of her eyes that highlights the dark color of them.

"Yes, and you're Jade right?"

She smiles, her lips curling over her perfect white teeth, "I am."

She shakes my hand, and I smile at Griff.

"Take care of Archer for me. We're out for the night.

See you around Kamryn," Griff pulls Jade along and leaves the door open for me.

"Bye!" I wave to the two of them, watching them walk down the long hallway.

I start to walk in the door without watching where I'm going and run into something hard... Someone hard, actually. I look up, horrified I'm going to find Lawson, but luckily finding Bellamy instead. I sigh in relief, and he smirks.

"So excited to see me..." He jokes, and moves me inside his apartment, kicking the door closed behind us.

"I thought you were Lawson, so I got nervous," I admit.

"That reminds me..." He turns away from me. "LAWSY!" Bellamy screams, and I flinch away from his loud voice.

I step around Bellamy, finally getting a view of his apartment. It's narrow, two stories. There's a catwalk above us that gives a view of the entire living room. The couch is large and dark blue and has no pillows... What else should I expect from three college boys? There's no tasteless decor though, which is something I can appreciate. I hear a loud crash from above, and out of the bedroom on the far right side of the catwalk above comes a dirty blonde idiot, falling out of his doorway.

"I'm up!" He yells and that's exactly what it looks like.

He just woke up, most likely due to Bellamy's screaming.

"Good, now leave," He tells him, and I swat Bellamy's arm.

"He doesn't have to leave," I whisper.

"It's fine Kamryn, I was leaving anyway. Your grumpy ass boyfriend knew that, he's just been an ass all day," Lawson says.

90

I nod my head and look at Bellamy.

"I haven't done anything," He argues.

Lawson shuts his door behind him, and walks across the catwalk toward the stairs, still having not brushed his hair.

"That's not true. He had us clean the whole apartment the entire day, he even made me clean my bedroom!" Lawson complains like a child, and I smirk. It's obviously Lawson isn't as put together as his friend. I find it oddly charming though.

"Well, I didn't want it to look bad," He defends himself, which makes my smirk turn into a smile. I watch as Lawson slides on his shoes, and walks past us, pushing Bellamy away from him. "Going to pick up Sienna?" Bellamy asks and Lawson shoots daggers at his roommate.

"No. I'm not seeing Sienna at all..."

I have no idea if he's lying. Sienna hasn't said a word about Lawson to me.

Lawson's eyes move to me, "I'm happy you're here, but don't fuck on the counter, or the couch. Bellamy, you have a nice bed, please use it."

He speaks to both of us, and I just stare at him, not surprised at how blunt he is. College boys, they're all the same. Except for Bellamy.

"You know we're not really dating...right?" I ask as he opens the door.

"Yes, I'm very aware of that," He nods and then walks away, closing the door behind him.

I look at the closed door, and I'm turned away, and toward Bellamy, the first time he's touched me today and held on.

"What did you tell your friends?" I ask him, not offended that they know, but curious.

"Exactly what happened between us. The arrangement,

all that. So they know what we are," He tells me, and I nod. "Did you not want me to tell them?"

I shake my head instantly.

"No it doesn't bother me, I was just curious."

He keeps hold of my shoulders.

"Alright. So, I know we're still trying to get used to this... arrangement, so I figured we could cook together. That way we're more comfortable with each other for the next two weeks, you know?" He asks me, looking me up and down now.

I'm wearing a pair of loose white track shorts that reach the tops of my thighs and a large SPU lacrosse t-shirt I got while working on the field this year that's halfway tucked in. I kick off my Air Forces, leaving myself in white socks, but losing some of my height as I stand in front of him. He's wearing loose gray sweatpants and a dark blue compression shirt that shows off his arms well. Both of us are very relaxed, and I'm glad I dressed down.

"I'm comfortable with you."

He reaches forward, slinking his arm around my lower back, pressing my body into his muscular torso. I hold onto his forearms, creating friction, and tensing up, not expecting the sudden gesture.

"Are you sure about that?" He asks, his hair flopping onto his forehead as he looks down at me.

His hair normally has some product in it, I guess. It normally doesn't look this casual... I've never seen him this casual in general. He somehow looks better which shouldn't be possible.

"I am, I just wasn't expecting you to touch me yet."

He loosens his grip, but I stay in his arms, not moving away.

"Well, expect the unexpected from now on, got it?"

I nod, noticing the light smile on his lips.

"Got it. Expect the unexpected with you," I agree.

He moves away from me and turns around a corner. I stop right when my eyes come into focus. There's a spread out kitchen with beautiful marble countertops, and I don't even want to know how much each of them is paying for their share of this apartment. I keep my eyes open as I look around at everything, the high pretty ceilings. I can't stop looking at everything.

"Did you just come from the gym?" I ask him, my hand dusting over the counter.

"The field. I was running drills," He tells me.

"Is that where you always are?" I take my eyes from the kitchen and look over at him as he stands behind me, taking things out of the fridge.

"Yeah, most of the time. I love it. It's not really about working out and staying in shape. That's a plus. I just enjoy the game, and if I don't practice, if I don't constantly work on it, I'll never continue in the NFL and everything else," He closes the fridge, and opens a cabinet above him, easily reaching to the top shelf to grab a box of spaghetti noodles.

He reaches down underneath him, taking pots out of the lower cupboard.

"So you really are playing because you love it... Not because of free college, or because it's what your parents wanted?" I ask, and he shakes his head.

"The sport reminds me of my parents a lot. I started football because of my dad but I continued because I love it. I love the attention, of course, the sound of people cheering for me, and all the love in and out of school. But I just love the game. I had the grades for free college. I didn't need football," He tells me, and I furrow my brows.

If his grades were that good, then why does he constantly need tutoring?

"I guess college practice is a bit tougher. Harder to keep your grades up, right?"

He looks at me quickly and nods, looking away almost as quickly, "Yeah. Coach Corbin is a pain in my ass. And you're going to be a pain in my ass if you just stand there and watch me cook instead of helping me. I know I look good but-"

"You are so full of yourself. The only way you'd stop me from helping is if you were naked in the midst of your kitchen."

He raises his eyebrows, a lopsided smirk forming on his lips, "Oh you are so bluffing right now." The words sound like a laugh when they fall from my lips.

I roll my eyes. Bellamy slowly lifts the hem of his tank top, my chest burning instantly at the sight of his chiseled stomach. Right away he drops his shirt before showing too much.

"No, I've got to leave something to the imagination," He tells me, and I stare at him, watching as he turns the water on, filling the pot.

Bellamy starts everything and turns some music on. The two of us are now standing side by side, individual cutting boards next to each other. He cuts fresh basil, and I cut up garlic for the sauce. I watch carefully, his hands cutting the basil perfectly. His fucking hands. They're clean, no rings today, but they look just as good. He finishes cutting, and walks around to the other side of me, washing his hands. I peek to the side, watching him do that too, making sure he sees nothing as I do so.

"I'll take over, can you put the pasta in the water, and

get the sauce started?" He asks me, holding his hands out for the knife.

I look, and swallow deeply, passing him the sharp object, wishing I could shove it in my eyes for staring so deeply at an outer extremity on a man that truly means nothing... Or at least it should mean nothing... Here I am though, sweating over his fucking quarterback hands once again. I look at his eyes, seeing them narrow as I hand the knife over, his lips twitching, threatening a smile.

"Sure," I nod, walking past him.

I see the water begin to boil, and I take out the noodles, letting them slide into the large pot. I cover it and reach toward the stovetop. My hand is covered by his right away, and I fight the urge to groan as he turns the heat down only slightly for me.

"Sorry... Didn't mean to intrude."

I look away from his hands, and look up at him now, watching his face as he watches me. I look away from him again and grab the premade pasta sauce. I twist the top, knowing I'm making the worst face known to man as I try my hardest to open the damn sauce.

"Can you... Open the jar?" I pass it to him as I struggle some more.

"Sure," He agrees simply, taking the jar in his hands, opening with ease, but his muscles still flex. The veins prominent in his hands and arms I look away, reaching for the jar, but he moves it away from me, holding it up and behind him. "Uh-uh. Hold on a minute..." He hesitates, his eyes catching mine.

"What?" I ask, crossing my arms over my chest.

"What's your deal?" He asks me, and I shake my head.

"I don't have a deal, what are you even talking about?" I ask him.

"You do have a deal. With my hands or something... What's the problem?" He asks me, and embarrassment settles throughout my entire body.

"There's no problem, give me the jar," I hold my hand out, ignoring his heated question.

He doesn't know it's heated. I do though. I know just how heated it makes me feel. He puts his hand in mine, and I groan, slapping his hand down.

"See?" He asks, and I cross my arms again. He sets the jar down on the counter behind him.

"I see nothing. Aren't you supposed to be doing something? Cutting? Being useful?" I ask.

I start to turn away, but before I can there's a soft, and incredibly large hand holding my jaw. The feeling just his hand gives as he holds me exactly where he wants me is enough to send me into orbit. I stand incredibly still, my eyes fixed on him as he stands chest to chest with me, his hand still grasping my jaw. Not tight enough to hurt, but the perfect amount of force to have me at his will.

"How about I cut... to the chase here," He speaks softly to me, looking down at me with expecting icy blue eyes.

"That was not as smooth as you think it was," I insult him, and he lets his grasp loosen, his hand slowly moving down my neck, chills rolling over every inch of my body as he now flips my hair back over my shoulder.

He lets the same hand move down, and grasps my hip, pulling me forward, alleviating the little space that was left between us. There's no room to move, the friction of our bodies sending shockwaves up my entire body. His opposite hand now moves to my face, cradling my cheek into his hand. My eyes flutter at the touch out of instinct, his thumb tracing over my cheek, my lip shaking at the touch, an unusual reaction from me. This is a lot. His touch is loaded with so much when it shouldn't be at all.

"Is it okay if I get this part out of the way, Ryn?" He asks softly, and despite what I had said, telling him how un-smooth his last move was. This is all smooth, very, incredibly baby's butt smooth.

"Uh-huh," I mumble, my words catching in my throat, and I mentally scream at myself, wondering why that of all things was the first thing I could get out.

"Uh-huh?" He asks, his chin tilting up, his eyes hazy and cool as he looks at me. He brings his other hand up slowly again, caressing my other cheek now. "So eager, aren't you?" He jokes.

I roll my eyes, the burning, wanting, need in my chest exploding all at once. Desire clouds every ounce of my judgment. Curiosity finds itself in every corner of my mind on if his lips feel as good as they look.

"Can you just kiss me?" I ask him, and he does.

He wanted to wait for me to say it. For me to ask. For me to confirm with my words he is what I want, and he is right now. Dear god, it feels so innocent to be kissing him because I know that's all this will be. Just a kiss.

But the way he presses his lips to mine. His body to mine, his hands to my face. I want everything all at once right here, right now. *The counter is fine, and so is the floor.* I tilt my head to the side, kissing him harder, standing on my tip toes now to reach the man in front of me. One of his hands moves from my cheek to the back of my head, threading through my hair, only to pull me closer to him. He feels every ounce of heat I do. He wants to be just as close as I do.

I pull him down to me by the back of his neck, angling him closer to me, giving me every bit of access I can have right now. He leans into me. His hand is moving once again, this time feeling its way down to my hip, gripping me tightly as he pushes me, and guides me back.

I can't move. I don't even think about it because I don't want to.

Bellamy takes every ounce of control from my body and makes it his own. He uses it all, he overpowers me in the best way. His other hand is still threaded through my hair, and I take his lip between my teeth, nipping him softly, pulling it through my teeth. He breathes out, and I feel a tight pull on my hair, my head tipping back at his will, moving away from his lips. He doesn't let himself slow down, his lips continue kissing me, everywhere but my lips, my jaw, my neck, and the moment his lips meet right under my ear, a soft bite, and then another harsh kiss mixing with the tight and pleasurably painful grip he has on my hair, I can't help but let out the slightest moan. He pushes into me harder, my lower back hitting the cold counter.

"Fuck," He groans into my mouth before he kisses me again.

He's taller than me, far too tall in these moments when the two of us wish we could be as close as possible. In sync, we move together. With as little effort as possible, his large hands move to the back of my bare thighs under my shorts, and he's lifting me up. He places me on the counter and places himself perfectly between my legs.

Bellamy Archer is a god on this campus for plenty of reasons, but I can worship this man for one specific reason... The way he kisses me. Like I'm the only thing that's ever existed to him.

His hands are grabbing the tops of my thighs now, moving up to rest the bend between my thighs and my hips. His thumbs dig into the crease of my legs sending butterflies swarming through my entire body. He presses himself harder, his hips sitting between my legs. Just one movement gives me a single taste. Just one single movement makes me want him in every single way. He's hard. He's big. He wants me, and... we hear a sizzle, and pull our lips away from each other, looking over our shoulders. Bellamy reaches behind us, not removing himself from me as he turns down the heat on the stovetop, stopping it from overflowing anymore.

"Didn't mean to get carried away..." He speaks softly, his thumb drawing over my bottom lip.

I hold his wrist, my eyes scanning his features, now more than ever feeling comfortable with him. I get what he meant before. How he said we weren't completely comfortable yet. Now, after that kiss... There's more tension, but more comfort as well. There's ease with him... So much ease. I shake my head in response to him.

"It wasn't just you. You're a great kisser," I tell him, and he raises his eyebrows, a dimple curling into his cheek.

"Am I?" He asks, and I push his chest back, breaking us apart.

I remove myself from him and off the kitchen counter as well, ignoring how easy it was for him to lift me like he did. The image replays in my head a hundred times over. Like a movie. This, all of this, is just like a movie.

"Don't act like you were unaware," I make my way back to the pasta sauce with an ache in my lower abdomen and my damp underwear.

Fuck Bellamy and his stupid quarterback hands...

I get to work, and the two of us continue to make dinner until it's all finished. We plate our food together and sit down at his dining table. The wood is dark, almost black, and it matches the rest of the interior.

Another thing that I realize with Bellamy is that we

don't have to constantly talk. He's here, and I'm here. He speaks when he feels like he needs to and I do the same thing. Normally I would feel uneasy in silence, but with him, it doesn't feel awkward, or too still. It feels fine, which is comforting. I don't have to talk constantly to entertain him. I knew this from when I would tutor him. I'd give him things to work on, and I could study. Sit in silence with him and not feel awkward like I did with some of the other students I tutored. *He's just easy.* I guess if I was going to do this list with anyone, he's really the perfect person. I'll never admit that to him though.

The two of us eat, and we play out our dumb scene with one meatball. It's as cheesy, and cringy as I imagined it would ever be, but he's cute so it makes up for it. Bellamy doesn't push with conversation. Most of it comes naturally from him, and it feels natural to me. I'm an open book either way, I just normally don't talk much when it comes to the other sex. I keep it strict, and to the point, so it's nice getting to talk to him about something other than schoolwork, or football.

"What did you say your parents' names were?" I ask, jumping out of my thoughts, and back into the conversation.

"My mom's name was Amanda, and my dad was Chris," He gives names to the faces I've made up in my head.

Our knees touch under the table, and the air between us is soft and calm.

"When they passed away how did you... I mean when you found out were you..." I hesitate, not knowing how to ask the question but wanting to be able to formulate the words.

I'm not good at this part. The casual talk about traumatic pasts, or sad things. It's not an easy conversation to have even with someone you're incredibly close with already, but I'm just learning to be close with Bellamy. I'm just starting this journey of being more than an occasional friend.

"We got a call when they were away. I remember not believing it at first. I forgot every day and would wait for them to come home from their work trip, but they couldn't. It was really... It was really hard. It's not something anyone ever should have to go through. I just knew I had to be there for my sister, and that's what I did."

His face changes when he talks about his sister.

"You two are close?" I ask, knowing he's told me small things about her before now, but nothing crazy.

"She's my best friend, and I'm hers. I went to therapy with her. We went to sessions together, and I did sessions on my own as well. She's still in therapy to this day, I don't know if she'll ever stop. I got more time with my parents than she did though so I... I don't get it but I do at the same time," He explains, and I nod.

I don't know what I would do if something happened to my parents. My heart hurts for both of them.

"At least the two of you had each other," I add.

"I was about to quit football. The season was going to start, and I couldn't imagine playing without my parents being there. I remember getting sick to my stomach at the thought of playing the sport, and still loving it when the people who made me love it weren't there anymore. Bri was the only reason I kept going. She asked who she was supposed to cheer for if not for me, and we helped each other through that. It's been a long time, and we'll never get over it, but we're stronger because of it I think. We're as close as we are because of it too. I don't think I'd ever forgive myself if anything happened to Bri," He explains, and I fight the urge to let my lip pout at how sweet, and heart filled his words are.

"I'd love to meet her one day..." I don't know why I say it.

Mostly because that's only a thing real couples do, and we are anything but a real couple. I have no reason to meet his sister. Not in the slightest.

"She'd jump for joy if I brought a friend over that wasn't a guy," He laughs, defusing the situation for me, and I could kiss him just for that.

He's good at doing that. Easing things, and relieving tension. I, on the other hand, am the one who creates that tension.

"Your parents would be proud of you. Proud of all the stuff you've accomplished in college," I know my words probably don't have weight considering how new all of this is between us, but I hope it's decently good to hear.

I hope it lifts something inside of him because he's too kind to feel this kind of hurt. I wish he didn't have to.

"I always imagine how happy they'd be to see how... Not to sound full of myself, but how good I am on the field now compared to how I was back then."

I shake my head at his words and instantly jump into the conversation.

"You don't sound full of yourself. Your stats this year were absolutely insane Bell, and besides that. You threw a perfect touchdown pass every single game. Your year to year stability within the team is what keeps the group together I think. Since your freshman year, you've outshined every..." I trail off when my eyes catch his.

They are lit up, bright like a Christmas tree.

"Sorry," I stop myself, feeling my cheeks heat up.

So I'm a football fangirl. I like to know my shit when it

comes to the team I've looked up to since I was a sophomore in high school.

"You're so adorable when you talk football stats to me. You know more about my stats than I do, don't you?"

I shrug in response to his question, "I just like to keep up with it. I kept up with you guys, all the important players, watching for injuries, or tendencies so when I hopefully work with you guys I'll already be ahead."

I tell him the truth, knowing I've been to every game since freshman year, and watched the ones on TV that were away games.

"You've always wanted to come here? To Seattle Pike?" He asks, and I shrug.

"Since my dad and I bonded over football so much growing up, and my mom was a fan too, they got my tickets to see a game back when I was in high school. I fell in love with the campus, and the energy within our stadium. It was all I could think about for weeks, and I knew I wanted to come here. I got a scholarship, and it paid for almost everything so here I am. Younger me would be proud," I smile to myself, and Bellamy is smiling as well.

"Your love for the sport makes you so much hotter," He ruins the cute moment between us, and I roll my eyes, my smile not leaving my face.

"You're gross," I laugh, finishing off my food, and pushing it in front of me.

I like his so called gross banter though, it makes my stomach heat up. I'll never tell him that though.

"I'm charming, not gross... Now we move on to dessert," He tells me, stealing my plate from in front of me the second I'm finished.

"Hey! I can clean off my plate myself," I tell him, hating the thought of someone cleaning up after me.

"How do you feel about brownies?" He asks me, ignoring my protests with my plate in his hand.

"Brownies sound delightful. Why don't you get the stuff to make them while I clean off our plates?" I ask him, and surprisingly, he doesn't argue.

He passes by me, his skin brushing mine, making every hair on my body stand up. I wish I had control of myself. I obviously have enough considering I haven't started taking his clothes off yet, but still. My body doesn't know what's going on. Neither do I if I'm honest.

There's so much desire built up, and I have no idea what's going on inside his head. *Does he have the same reaction? Does he want me, or does he just want to complete the list?*

"Why did you want to do this with me?" I ask, moving the sponge over the plates, hand cleaning them instead of putting them in the dishwasher right away, distracting myself, but also being thorough.

"The list?" He asks from behind me.

"Yeah," My eyes are on the dish, not him.

"I don't know. You're fun to be around, and it gives me good ideas for the future I guess... And you've tutored me all semester, and I never got to repay you for helping me pass."

I smirk to myself, knowing he can't see my face right now.

"You know the student center pays me to tutor you, right?"

"That's them, not me."

"Well, I would've taken payment in cash, check, Venmo, or Paypal," I joke.

"Payment in orgasms is better, don't you think?"

I choke on quite literally nothing. The air in my lungs

ceases to exist at the statement I didn't expect to come from him.

"That's a pretty confident statement," I finally turn around to face him.

He's standing there, his back turned to me. He's in the process of getting everything situated to make brownies.

"I'm fully aware of that... And my capabilities."

I feel my cheeks heat.

"Are you going to help me, or keep staring at my ass?"

My jaw drops, "Your ass doesn't even look good in sweatpants, don't get a big head," I invade his space now, coming close to him.

"I already have a big head Ryn. I'm the star quarter-back... Remember?" My eyes roll at his not so subtle narcissism.

I steal the bag of brownie mix from him, ripping it open with my teeth. I pour the bag into a big mixing bowl, a puff of brownie dust coming up around my face. Bellamy stands incredibly close to me, cracking eggs, and pouring ingredients into the bowl.

"Do you have a whisk?"

He opens the drawer, passing me what I asked for.

"Of course I have a whisk," He leans back on the counter, and I hold the bowl in my hands, and start whisking the contents. "You're not doing it right," He pushes himself from the counter.

"I'm mixing brownie batter, how could I be doing it wrong?"

He's got a boyish grin on his pretty face as he moves forward toward me. He puts his hands over mine and starts moving my hands, whisking the contents harder, and faster.

"You have to put a little elbow grease in there."

Brownie batter starts going everywhere but the bowl, the splatter hitting not only the counter but me too.

"Bellamy!" I yell, unable to take my hands from his, or stop the movements he's creating. "You're making a mess!" I laugh now, watching the smirk on his lips turn into a smile.

I move back, and turn away from him, realizing that he had no intentions of actually making brownies. I think back to the list. *Cute kitchen food fight where we cook together.* This was on the list. And although I made it, I seem to forget that's what we're doing.

I put my hand in the bowl, and turn, reaching up to his face. I smear batter on his cheek, and down to his jaw. He just stares at me, his pretty bright eyes completely amused right now as he stares. I wait for him to make a move, knowing he has a full advantage over me. He moves quickly, taking an egg from the open carton and smashing it right on top of my head. My jaw drops. My glare burns through him.

"You asked for this," He tells me, and the war starts, both of us slinging batter and whatever else we can get our hands on.

The kitchen turns into a mess quickly, and so do Bellamy and I. I can't hear anything over our laughter, but it all goes still the second he pulls me to him by my lower back. I'm once again pressed to his hard chest, he's got brownie batter coating his cheeks as he stares down at me.

"You've got a little something... There," I motion to his whole face and watch a slow smile hit his features.

He's the most attractive when he smiles. Because his smiles are always genuine. When he smiles it makes me feel like I'm getting punched in the stomach because I don't think I've seen anything more purely perfect than his smile. I've got a thing for boys with pretty smiles, and Bellamy's is the prettiest.

"You too..." He takes his pointer finger and swipes my cheek, collecting batter.

He brings his finger down to my lips and I take the batter, my lips curling around his finger. I watch his face change instantly, and I internally groan at the way he grips my jaw, just the same as before. He kisses me quick, not the same as last time, but still just as hard, and full.

He pulls away, and runs his tongue over his lips, "You taste like chocolate."

"I wonder why."

He releases me. I look down at myself, my white shorts ruined, his clothes stained too.

"Dear god if anyone passes me while I walk home I'm going to get so many stares," I laugh to myself.

"Yeah, you're not walking home this late... You can shower here. I'll drive you home," He tells me, nodding his head behind me. "Come on," He starts walking, and normally I would protest, but my clothes are covered in brownie mix, there's a cracked egg in my hair, and I don't want to be like this any longer than I have to.

That was a cute idea for the list, but I never intended to do it. They never show the cleanup in the movies. At least it wasn't my kitchen.

"I'll help you clean up and then-"

"Don't worry about it... Here," He opens a door that's right past the living room, and I realize now it's his bedroom.

He has a nice bed, a giant bed that probably feels like the softest cloud in the world. Everything is simple, dark gray sheets, and a white comforter. His bed is made, and his room is decently clean, football jerseys framed on the walls, and photos on his nightstand I can't quite see from where I am. He has a giant mirror in the corner of his room that reaches the floor, and a TV mounted on the wall across from his bed. Under that is a dresser, and a pile of shoes next to that. It's lived in, but still clean.

"I want to help you clean up," I tell him, and he turns to the left, going to the dresser.

"How about you stop worrying and take a shower?" He asks and hands me a shirt and sweatpants. "Change into this. There are clean towels under the sink and on the rack."

He walks around me and to the bathroom. He opens the door, and flips on the light, revealing a pretty big bathroom for an apartment. It's the same color scheme as his bedroom, gray white and blue and it's just as clean. I don't know why cleanliness is such a shock to me... I guess I've been in far too many frat houses.

"Thank you," I walk in, and turn over my shoulder to look at him. He's leaning against the doorway now, his eyes set on me.

"If you need anything you can just yell. I'm going to change too," He tells me, nodding his head. He doesn't close the door, he just narrows the view a bit.

I leave it open, knowing just what I'm doing. I lean into the shower, turning the water all the way up to the hottest setting it can go. I look in the mirror, a perfect view of his bedroom, and him now. He's removing his shirt, and I'm doing the same. I remove my shorts too, and he's looking back now, his eyes set on the bathroom, looking into the mirror at my reflection. His eyes are bright and lit up. I smirk as I reach around, removing my bra too, not showing him anything but my naked back. He knows I know he's watching me, he's looking into my eyes now.

"Enjoying the show?" I ask.

"I'm enjoying the fact that you're comfortable enough with me to have a show at all," He calls out to me.

I get a good look at his carved chest, the perfect muscles, his tattoo that I could look at for hours, and the sculpture of his body that I know he's spent a lot of time perfecting. I slide my underwear down my bare legs and pull the shower curtain back, a smirk on my lips. I don't have him in my sight right now, but I am imagining him, every muscle of his in my mind as I step into his shower. Tonight has been... Interesting, and very eye opening to just how attractive Bellamy Archer is... I don't think I've ever felt such a deep want for someone physically but right now I can feel it burning through my stomach.

CHAPTER TEN

I THINK I LIKE YOU BY THE BAND CAMINO

I'M WEARING HIS SHIRT. THE SHIRT HE GAVE ME ON OUR last mini date that I have no intention of ever giving back. To be honest, the shirt he gave me is one of the comfiest shirts I've ever worn in my entire 21 years on this earth. It's one of his Seattle Pike University football shirts. Probably from years past. It has the Hornets on the front and on the back is his last name Archer, 03, his jersey number on the field. Bellamy told me to dress comfortably and to bring a change of clothes for something casual as well as my stuff to get ready. I have no idea what he's got planned today. I walk out of my apartment building and there's a red Jeep, top down, waiting for me.

"Hey Ryn," He speaks to me as I climb into his car, sunglasses resting on the bridge of his nose, his smile blinding.

He's wearing workout clothes, and I tilt my head.

"What are we doing?" I ask.

"From the list, we'll be doing a movie date where I slowly make a move on you. I promise it'll be a great one, but I thought you could help me first," He tells me, and I look to push my own sunglasses up, pushing my hair back.

"I didn't sign up to work out," I tell him.

I don't mind working out. I actually enjoy running often, but I didn't plan for that today.

"I would never expect you to... I said help me, not participate," He slowly pulls away from my building and into the street.

He doesn't hesitate to reach over the console, his hand resting on my bare thigh, his finger already drawing circles on the soft skin.

This man is going to end me. He's constantly touching me, and my body is very aware when it comes to Bellamy. It's more intense because with him I've waited for sex. I've waited to cross that metaphorical finish line because of the list, which is very unlike me. Though this is a form of hooking up with him, it's very different. It's different because he treats me like a human being, and I treat him with a lot more respect than my previous hookups. Usually, in the end, I'm looking for one thing. With this, of course, I want that same thing, but I'm also somewhat wanting to complete the list with him.

He drives us, music playing over the wind that pours through the topless Jeep. Once we're pulled into the parking lot of the football stadium, and the car is turned off he reaches into his backseat and pulls out a giant duffle bag before exiting the car. I wait, knowing he'll say something if I even try to open the door for myself. Bell moves to my side, opening my door for me, giving me a hand. I hop down, directly in front of him.

"This..." He tugs on the rolled sleeve, his attention on the shirt that I'm wearing. "I like this... On you," He tells me, approving of my outfit.

"It's cuter on me I think," I tell him.

"So you admit it would be cute on me?" He asks, and I roll my eyes. "Selective hearing always works in my favor," He slings his arm over my shoulder, his height towering over me.

He walks me straight into the stadium, keeping me right by his side.

I see a group of girls, all of them walking up the stairs, matching shirts on their bodies. I recognize some of them, others not so much. It's the cheer team. I feel eyes on me instantly, and I would move, but I have a feeling Bellamy wouldn't let me. I shouldn't care what they think though, none of them matter in this regard. None of them know Bellamy or me, or what's going on. My mind spins, wondering what they're thinking. What are they going to go and tell their other friends, or boyfriends? I wonder how real this looks to people that aren't our friends. I wonder if they think...

"Hey Bellamy," I hear a few girls speak out flirtatiously.

Some even say hi to me, their voices not as kind... but there's one that doesn't say a word. I don't know how I forgot Leah was on the cheer team, especially because she's now probably the captain considering she's going into her senior year. Leah's eyes are sharp, not looking at him, but me. She looks angered and oddly hurt.

"Hey, ladies. Practice went well?" He asks over the group as we start to pass.

"First boot camp of the summer actually. Tryouts start next month, all the new freshmen don't start boot camp until a week before," Leah speaks, her voice not as pointed as her stare.

"Cool, hope it went well," He tells them and continues walking.

I look over my shoulder, and Leah is doing the same, her eyes glaring down at me. I look away, turning back to the front, not liking the thought of her being jealous over something like this.

Something fake.

I also don't like her claim on him in the slightest. She broke it off with him, why does she care what he does with his time? Why does she assume she has any control at all in his life? She's the type to try and ruin a good thing, I can tell just by the way she looked at me and Bell. I'm the protective type over my friends. I'd consider him my friend at this point, and she acts like it's her job to keep tabs on him. I understand being hurt, being broken up with, or wanting your ex back, but Leah takes it to another level. At the end of the day, if he's moving on, it's not her job to sabotage that. It shows me, and probably him, that she never really cared about him in the first place.

"Ignore her Ryn."

I look up at him the second we step onto the turf.

"It's hard when she's shooting daggers at me. Especially since she has no reason to," My voice is soft despite my words being serious.

"You have what she wants," He drops his duffle bag on the ground between us now.

"Not actually," I tell him, and he steps forward, over his bag.

He curls his finger under my chin, tilting my face up to him, "You're wearing my name on your back, and walking onto the field, my safe space with me. It might be fake to us, but to everyone else except our friends, it's not."

Reality rushes through me at how right he is. Leah thinks he's choosing me. She's noticed since the party. I don't doubt she saw me when I came to the field a few days ago to tell him I'd do the list with him. I don't feel one ounce of regret agreeing to this. *Not yet anyway.* But I wonder if I should feel bad... For Leah, or anyone else we're fooling.

"She was probably just telling me because she knows my sister is coming here next semester as a freshman. She cheers, and she's really good. Leah knows that," He shrugs, and I nod.

"Yeah probably..." I agree, wanting this conversation to end.

I don't need to worry about Leah at all.

"Put your hair up," He tells me, changing my thoughts again.

"Why?" I ask.

He pushes my hair back for me, his hands grazing my skin, sending flames through my body.

"Because I want to see your pretty face," He jokes, and I raise my eyebrows waiting for a serious answer. "Because it'll be easier for you. I can braid it for you."

"I don't have a hair tie," I tell him, and he pulls one off of his wrist.

"I do, turn around," He tells me, and I do.

He runs his large hands through my hair, pulling and twisting.

"How do you know how to braid hair?" I ask, knowing he's not even doing a simple braid, he's doing French or Dutch, something most men wouldn't know anything about.

"My little sister didn't have a mom as she grew up... My grandma is an amazing woman, but my sister wanted our mom, dad, or me... So I learned what I had to."

My heart melts, and breaks all at once, thinking of the two of them growing up without a mom or dad. Especially a young girl like Brianne.

"You're a really good brother..." I never saw it firsthand,

but by the way he treats me, and the things I've learned thus far about his family I can just tell.

"I try my best," He tells me, still working his fingers through my hair as he braids it back. "Do you have any siblings?"

My chest vibrates. I don't know why it feels intimate when someone wants to know something about me. Not someone, but Bellamy. Because I know he's the type of person who's actually going to remember what I say. He's actually listening to me.

"No... My mom couldn't after me. They always wanted more, but they couldn't. I was like a miracle to them," I use the words my mom always used.

"How fitting."

My smile is quick after that one. Bellamy is smooth, he knows just how to talk to me, and I don't know who taught him, but he's doing great.

He finishes the braid, and ties my hair, flipping the tail over my shoulder, "I know you've got a strong voice. I brought you here because when I train by myself I get a little lazy. I figured you could help me with my form, with everything I do. Yell when I need to step it up, considering I know you love football."

I feel my stomach heat up.

"You know I love it. So you want me to help you train?" I know he's giving me insight into the game, to the team, and I also know this could help my reputation with Coach too.

Bellamy is the star after all. I feel a tug on my heart at the thought of this gesture. One he'd probably brush off, and pretend isn't that big of a deal when in reality it is. If Bellamy can trust me with his training on the field, the coach will listen to that. This list was silly and stupid, but he's going above and beyond to show me that he's a really, really good guy.

"That's the idea... Every few days. Can you wrap me up first?" I nod without a second thought.

"Yeah, where's your tape?" He reaches into the bag, bringing it out.

He tosses me the roll, and I catch it, coming over to him. He holds out his right hand to me, flipping it up to the sky. He gets taped often from what I can see. He seems to be used to it. This is the hand he throws with. I start where I usually do, my eyes fixed on his hand. I can feel his gaze on me, and when I look up at him, I can see his smirk easily.

"I don't want to hear it from you, I'm being professional right now."

He knows. He always knows when he's affecting me and normally that would annoy me. But he's so hot. That's such a silly way to put it. It almost makes me feel childish saying it to myself, but it's so true. He's just that attractive, to the point where I can barely look at him sometimes.

"This is what you want to do for a living and you can barely keep your cool."

I fight the urge to argue. I've never had a problem with anyone's hands I've worked with or on while being on any field or court... Bellamy's hands are very large compared to most. It's just different. This isn't a normal thing for me, but he doesn't need the ego boost knowing it's only his hands.

"I'll manage," I turn his hand over to look over my work. I bring my mouth to the tape and rip with my teeth, something I normally wouldn't do, but I can since it's just us. I wrap each wrist, and then his fingers as well, making sure to do a good job on each. I finish and look at him. "Anywhere else?"

He shakes his head, his eyes looking at me like I'm the

most important thing in the world. Having Bellamy's attention, his full attention... It's intimidating, to say the least.

"Nope, you got it," He flips my chin up before backing up. "Thanks, Ryn," He smiles a wide smile, and I press my lips together.

He starts with simple stretches, and I do them with him, following his movements, easily making him laugh. He tosses me the football, and I toss it back, the best I can. I'm fit, but I'm not Bellamy, no one is.

He truly amazes me with his strength, with how far he can throw a football. I'm not easily impressed considering how much of the sport I watch, how much of all the sports I watch on the TV or in person. But Bellamy has always impressed me, even when I wasn't tutoring him, and he was just a person on a field in front of me. I barely knew him at all until this year, just of him. Just of his talent on the turf.

"What team?"

I shake my head at his question, using all my strength to throw the ball back to him, "That's a loaded question. What team for what?"

Bellamy's arms flex as he preps himself, then he throws the ball straight back to me, a perfect spiral. This is a test of my mental strength as much as it is my physical strength. Bellamy looks better on the field than he does anywhere else, he's comfortable. He's sexy, he's showing off his skills, and his body. I push past the intrusive thoughts and continue on.

"What team do you want to do this for? What team do you want to work with for the rest of your life?" He asks me as I catch his pass, moving back a bit at the impact of the ball hitting my chest.

I'm going to have bruises from this damn ball.

"That's not an easy answer. I want to be close enough to

my mom and dad... But I don't love the Washington Commanders as a team. Ideally... I love the 49ers as well as the city of San Francisco, but I also love the Raiders. If I had nothing holding me back at all, the Giants. New York sounds exciting," I tell him. "What about you? What NFL team is your dream?"

His amusement is prominent across all of his features. I wonder if he could ever talk about football with any of his other girlfriends or if they ever cared. Not that he's really my boyfriend, but still.

"Well... I'm also not the biggest fan of the Commanders, but I love the 49ers. I love the Broncos too, or even the Packers. I'm honestly shocked you're a Giants fan. Can't say I love the team, but I love the city. But if I had to pick one, nothing holding me back either I think I'd pick the Miami Dolphins, that was my dad's favorite team, and I love the beach, the warmth, and the ocean. Miami sounds exciting."

We both know there's hardly any way of knowing who or what team you could play for, it's fun to dream, to wish, and to hope. Truly, I'd work for any team that was willing to have me, even if it was The Commanders.

"I like the drive the Giants have. My dad and I watch them together, and we love them so I guess we have that in common, wanting to work with our parent's favorite... Though I don't really like the Dolphins colors."

He gasps at my words, and I smirk at the small dig.

"I think you'd look great in Giants colors Ryn," His mouth twists into a smile that makes my stomach tighten.

Imagine one day the two of us worked professionally on any team... Or even on the same team. The thought warms my chest. I feel like there would be a very big sense of comradery if that were the case. It would feel more like home to know a familiar face on my dream team.

"So I know you really like football. I did think you were only interested though because of your major... I'm seeing now that's not the case," He throws the leather ball my way, and it hits my chest as I catch it.

Dear god, is his arm made of steel? I throw a perfect spiral back to him.

"I really like football, not just because of my major," I say. "My dad was always watching during the season, I know I told you he took me to college games and stuff. When I was old enough to understand the sport I started watching it with him. We would yell at the TV together every game, and we had our own touchdown dance just like the players. The games on the TV were an event. I was home and seated for every single one right by him. When our favorite teams would come into town he would do his best to get tickets even if they were in the back row."

"So your dad got you into it. But how into it are you really?"

"I mean I loved it so much I chose to go into sports medicine with hopes of working with the NFL. You know I know stats. I know players. This sport is just different than all the others because the fans are different. The excitement at the games and everything that comes along with it. Football has more high stakes and that's why I love it the most," I throw another perfect spiral throw toward the quarterback in front of me.

"So potentially we can watch games together this year when the NFL season starts?" His lips form a lazy grin.

His dimple is prominent on his smooth face. We won't be fake dating next year, but he has obvious hopes we will still be friends enough for that. I can imagine myself watching football with him during the colder months. I'm sure Lawson would be there too. But I have no idea what's going to happen leading up to the school year. I can't make promises for that kind of thing. Not now anyway.

"Aren't you supposed to be working hard, not chit-chatting, and tossing a ball?"

He nods at me, waiting for me to pass it back.

"I just love seeing the way you throw, it's kind of turning me on."

I roll my eyes, coming in close to him now, relieving the space we have between us.

"On your back, workout, get your body warm, then we'll do drills."

He smirks, dropping the football, and also dropping to his back.

"Fifty, go," I tell him, and get on the ground with him.

I place my knees on his feet, and he starts his curl ups, coming all the way up, his face incredibly close to mine.

"You come that far up every time, you get something on fifty," I try to encourage him though I'm almost positive he's going to come that far up every time even without an incentive.

"You're underestimating me," He talks as he works out, not breaking a sweat.

He's incredibly skilled, and fast despite how far up he's coming, and before I know it he's at fifty, and he's already kissing me as he makes it up from his last curl up. He lays back down, his lips separating from me, and I put my hands on his knees, looking down at him.

"How did you know that was the something I was going to give you?"

"That's what I was hoping for," He shrugs and gives a golden smile.

I stand up, not letting myself fold, and show the smile I have loaded behind closed lips. I hold my hands out for him and help him up. He walks me through some of the normal drills he does, and I help him through them, watching as he keeps his stamina up through all of them. He starts to sweat, the sun beating down on both of us, and I watch as he brings the hem of his shirt up to wipe the sweat from his face.

"You can take it off," I say. He just looks at me, his hands on his hips as he catches his breath. "Your shirt. If you normally don't work out with one on, then take it off. Don't change your routine because of me," I tell him, and to my surprise he actually does.

My eyes catch the tattoo, noticing just how defined his chest, and torso actually are. He was too far away when I was in his bathroom, but right now he's up close and personal. Talk about perfection. He really does look like one of those sculptures, his body could be fake. If I didn't know any better I'd reach out just to make sure he was real.

"Ready?" He claps his hands, snapping me out of my unnecessary fantasy.

It's not normal to want someone this bad, it's not normal at all.

"Water, then we'll go," I bend down and toss his bottle to him, grabbing my own while I'm down here.

"You know you make this a lot more fun, mostly because you're actually into it... Are you enjoying this?"

I nod, gulping my water.

"I am. The field, football, and helping like I am, it's what I've always wanted to do. I love this," I motion around me. "Enough talk. Let's go."

I crouch down, and he does too. I count down, and we start more drills for him. He continues working, and I watch as he starts to sike himself out, his body beginning to tire out.

"Come on Bell. Don't slack on me now!" I yell, and he snaps his head up. "Come on Bell! Let's go!" I keep yelling, and he keeps it up, continuing through the drill until it's done, and then he makes his way back to me.

"If you want me to focus, you can't call me Bell, got it?"

I tilt my head, the lightest smirk on my lips.

"Sure, whatever you say, Bell," I walk past him, and pat his ass that's just as muscular as the rest of him. "One mile, both of us, then we'll go back to your place, and get ready for the date alright?"

He looks down at me, wiping a towel over his face, collecting the sweat.

"Both of us?" He sounds surprised.

"I'm dressed for the occasion, so yes, we can run a mile together."

He shrugs his shoulders and drops his things.

"Then let's go," He starts right away, leaving me in the dust behind him, I catch up to him, and we run around the field on the sidelines together. After we finished our mile we were both coated in a thin layer of sweat, but from the way he smiled, and gave me a high five I could tell we were both feeling pretty good.

We gather our things and make our way back to the stairs. He crouches down before we make our way to the top, and I jump on his back, letting him give me a ride all the way to his Jeep. Once we're in, he drives us back to his apartment and we freshen up. He takes a shower, and I fix my hair and makeup. I change into a pair of cut off shorts and a white sweater that hangs off of my shoulders.

Now I'm laying on his bed, and I was right, it really is the softest bed I've ever been in and I hope one day out of the next twelve I will be invited to sleep here, and I strictly mean sleep. Because I know it would be the best few hours of my life.

Bellamy's bathroom door opens, and he walks out in a towel, and my eyes scan him. He lets his gaze rest on me as I lay on his bed, and he grins at the sight before opening his drawers, facing away from me. He grabs a few things and then walks past the dresser, and opens the door to what I assume is his closet. He steps inside and closes the door behind him. A couple of minutes later he returns, fully clothed now. I look at him, and he's wearing a pair of jeans and a shirt that doesn't hug his body for once. It's a bit over-sized on his torso, but still somewhat shows off his muscular arms. His hair is messy, and almost fully dry, but still damp. He's glowing.

"Ready?" I ask.

"Shoes, and then I will be," He tells me.

He throws his towel in a hamper, and then I follow him out of his bedroom, and into the living room where Griffin sits alone.

"What are you up to Archie?" Griffin asks. He wasn't here when we had gotten back, we must've not heard him get back. Griff's eyes land on me, and he smiles. "Never-mind," He speaks out, realizing what's going on.

"We're going to the movies. Can I borrow your car?" He asks his friend who seems to understand why he's asking.

"What's wrong with your car?" I ask Bellamy.

"Nothing."

Griff tosses the keys to his Bellamy. "Archie's got some-thing special planned, don't make him ruin it," He has a giant smirk on his face, and I narrow my eyes.

"The two of you aren't up to any good," I cross my arms, and Griff shrugs.

"I think everything we do is good, but that's a matter of

opinion. I'm taking your car to the meeting then, that's fine?" He asks and Bellamy nods.

"Of course, just don't fuck it up," Bellamy says and Griff nods.

"As long as you two don't do anything gross in the back-seat. No funny business," He warns us and I scoff.

"Why do your friends think I'm just going to jump you on every surface?" I ask Bellamy, knowing Lawson warned us of the same thing.

"It's not you we're worried about," Griffin defends and Bellamy tosses up a middle finger.

"We're leaving before you get on my nerves," Bellamy nods his head to the door, and I follow him, still wondering about the car, but knowing I won't get an answer.

I had no idea I agreed to do this list with someone who would do his best to add so much to it. Bellamy is not a bare minimum type of guy, and that's all I've ever known in my past. That thought alone is scary because I love knowing that he's putting this effort in. I love knowing he's got his mind on this at all times. I love knowing I'm at the top of his priorities for the next two weeks.

CHAPTER ELEVEN

USE ME BY BLAKE ROSE

I DON'T KNOW WHAT I EXPECT WHEN WE WALK INTO the parking lot, but a black Raptor wasn't it. It's an incredibly nice truck, and I'm not surprised. Griffin comes from a very established family, his parents are well known lawyers. Griffin also got drafted by the Raiders a couple of months ago. No one was surprised, we all knew he'd be one of the ones to get drafted and play professionally. He not only came from money, but I know they wrote him a huge check for signing on. Bellamy opens the large door of the car and gives me a hand so I can get in.

"Come on," He gives me a soft pat on my ass as I climb in, and he closes the door behind me.

He goes to the other side, climbs in, and starts the car, the engine purring loud. He takes his normal stance, his hand on the wheel, and another on my thigh. It feels like it's almost instinct for him. Like he reaches out because he needs to. His thumb moves mindlessly over my thigh, and I'm hyper aware of the sensation it brings to me, the simplest touch.

"Why do we need another car to drive to the movies?"

Finally choosing to ask the question that's been in my head since Griff tossed Bellamy the keys.

"Because we do. It's not important," His voice is light and full of lies.

"It seems pretty important to me," I add.

"Oh really? Well, maybe you're a bad judge of character," He shrugs his shoulders, and I scoff. "You *are* a bad judge of character, you dated Dylan."

"That's not a fair judgment!" I yell, turning my entire body to him.

"It is, especially considering you haven't dated anyone else since."

"I haven't dated anyone else at all. Ever."

He almost stops the car at my confession.

"I'm sorry, what do you mean?"

I shrug, turning forward, and crossing my arms over my chest. I turn my legs to the other side of the car and look out the window.

"Oh come on, not the turning your knees thing, don't be mad at me..." He pleads.

"I mean I have never dated anyone. Dylan was, and is, and will be my only real boyfriend," I keep my knees turned toward the passenger side door.

He's trying to understand me, I get it, but I hate that he keeps mentioning someone I consider a mistake.

"Then I am going to judge you because if your dating history was going to be a one and done deal, Dylan Brody should have been your last choice."

I instantly wonder what his thought process behind judging my dating history was. I can't make sense of it.

"Well, it didn't last long so it didn't count."

"It counts... Why did you two break up anyway?"

"Why do you feel the need to know?" I turn my face to him, but not the rest of my body.

"You asked about Leah... I told you."

I'm being too harsh, and I realize that right away. I was curious, and he easily let the information out. I don't owe him anything, I know that, but still. Bellamy makes me feel comfortable. His energy has always been easy, and safe. He's not asking to be an ass, and I know that.

"He cheated on me. It was a girl he worked with. I had no idea she existed. And before you ask, I know he looks like a piece of shit douchebag, but he was good with words, and that was that. He sweet talked me and swept me off my feet then dropped me flat on my ass, and ruined everything. So I learned my lesson. He was also horrible in bed, and had a very average sized penis, so you can tell all your friends."

The embarrassment I feel for even having to admit I was with him is so harsh.

"I'm sorry he cheated on you. I'd punch him if you wanted me to," He tells me.

"I'll think about it," The image of Bellamy punching Dylan square in the nose is an appealing thought, but is violence ever the answer?

Well, sometimes.

"I'll put it in my schedule whenever you decide, but it has to be after the next two weeks though, I'm busy," He lightens the mood.

I notice how much I've relaxed again, my body turning back toward him. His hand finds my thigh like it had before, and I let him, finding comfort in the gesture. The sun has sunk low in the sky, and it's practically non-existent at this point. Today was good, and I'm almost positive I'm tired enough to fall asleep if whatever movie we're seeing isn't good... Or the move he makes is boring. Either way.

We've driven far longer than any route to any movie theater I know of, and by the time I start getting curious, Bellamy turns, pulling onto a gravel path, and up to a ticket booth. He rolls the window down and shows the person working his phone which I'm assuming has a ticket of some sort on the screen. Right away I sit up, looking in front of us. The second I see the giant screen, and the other cars pulled in, facing the screen I push myself up and lean on the console.

"A drive-in movie! Bellamy, this wasn't on the list, I've never been to a drive-in movie before!" I get excited right away and clasp my hands together.

I notice the smile on Bellamy's lips, and a bit of excitement now visible on his face.

"I figured I'd add a few tweaks... I made your list better, by adding me and my smart brain."

I ignore his narcissism, my excitement is far too heightened right now.

"What movie is it?"

He pulls into a spot between two other smaller cars. We're facing away from the screen now.

"The best rom com of all time," He opens my door for me and helps me out.

He leaves the windows open, and the car on, the radio turned to the right station.

"Is it The Proposal?" I recall what he has said before.

I look up at him, noticing the smirk of approval as well as his nod.

"Of course it is," He turns me around, and puts his hands on my shoulders, pushing me softly as we walk to the back of the truck.

The car is jacked, and too far off the ground for me, but not Bellamy. He opens the tailgate and reveals a makeshift pallet in the bed of the truck, plenty of soft blankets, and pillows. I don't even get a chance to look at him before he lifts me by my hips to get up on the bed of the truck. Thank god he did because if not I would be making a fool out of myself trying to jump up here.

We nestle in, both of us getting situated right next to each other, a blanket over the top of us. There's still distance between us. The bed of the truck is low, the sides coming up high enough that we can't see the other cars around us when we're laying down fully. It feels like it's just the two of us here watching the movie. The sun is almost gone and the large screen finally comes to life.

"You know you're kind of good at dates," I don't have very much experience, but this is what I had thought they'd be like when I was younger.

High school dates were superficial. Using your parent's money to take your girlfriend or boyfriend out. Going to the movies and getting dropped off, or having a curfew. Those are loose memories in the back of my head. When Dylan took me out it consisted of going to Applebee's and him trying to hook up with me in the backseat of his car after he made me pay for my part of the date. I could gag at the thought. Why did I even let that go on as long as I did?

"You sure you want to boost my ego? We're only on number three."

"More dates than Dylan ever took me on."

"What a douchebag, you know-"

"Shhhhh. The movie is starting," I point in front of us and start to feel the awkward tension between the two of us, the distance, and space.

I turn my head only slightly so I can see him, and then I turn back, looking at the large screen in front of us. He's comfortable. Or he looks comfortable right now and is faking it the best he can. I, on the other hand, am not comfortable. I'm physically desperate. The bed he's made us is sleep worthy, but him being so close yet so far is already driving me crazy and it hasn't even been five minutes. I keep my eyes forward, but am mentally on the edge of my seat, waiting to see what move he makes. We aren't laying fully. Just leaned back, and reclined, closer to lying than sitting but somewhere in the middle.

"You look like you're about to have a heart attack or something," He whispers despite how loud the sound system is around us.

"You're making me nervous," I admit, talking louder than he did. No one around us can hear anything, I'm sure of that.

"I didn't know I had that kind of power over you Ryn."

I don't have to look to know he's got that same award winning smirk on his face. I ignore him, and I feel him shift, and then I feel a warmth cast over my shoulders. If this was supposed to be cheesy it wasn't at all. It was incredibly smooth. His arm is over my shoulder, pulling me into his muscular body.

"Relax Ryn," He whispers, his lips brushing the side of my head.

I am relaxed now, my hand on his chest, and my body pressed to his, the movie in front of us casting a very pretty glow over the two of us.

As soon as the relaxation comes, it leaves. His hand is traveling up and down my back, his fingers drawing over my spine, and on my side, like he's trying to feel the curves of my body as I lay against him. There's tension but not the awkward kind anymore. Not for me anyway.

I don't know if he's doing this on purpose, but I'm about to make his comfort a personal hell. I slowly move my leg over his, cuddling my body to his tighter, playing my cards right as I push my body against his. I rest my head against his chest and press my hips forward, playing it off like I'm trying to find comfort when I'm actually looking for something completely different.

"The move I make next isn't going to be romantic or cheesy if you don't stop," He speaks out, louder than I had expected.

I don't stop, my hips grinding against him now, and he sighs. He threads his hands through my hair, and tilts my head to him, and away from the screen.

"There's a movie, don't be rude Bel-"

He's kissing me now, his hand threaded into my hair, and keeping me right where he wants me. I kiss him back, leaning up and into him, my body now angled on top of his. I press my hand on his hard chest, trying my best to stabilize myself. The more he leans into me, and the harder I press into him the more I realize there's no way to stabilize myself when it comes to Bellamy Archer. The attraction is far more than I ever had imagined at first.

I know how it makes me sound. I know how it makes me feel although it shouldn't. But kissing never brings anything more than a small burn in my chest, a bit of curiosity. It's never what makes me want more, and even further than that, I never want more, because most men know nothing about what they're doing when it comes to women.

But this, the skillful way he moves his lips against mine, and the way he holds me against his carved body doesn't send a small burn, it ignites my entire body. It burns me up and turns me into ashes right on top of him. I'm no longer human when I kiss him, honestly, I'm not sure what he makes me feel like, but I know it's good, and god it's dangerous because I would probably give anything to feel his hands on my skin.

"Ryn..." He pulls away from me, but I kiss him again, not letting him get a word in, no comments, no concerns.

I don't want to hear them, all I want is his body against mine. *Fuck the movie.*

"No time for common sense right now," My lips brush against his as I speak.

"But-"

I kiss him, locking my lips with his, creating friction as I roll my body onto his. I feel a groan rumble from his chest and into my mouth. I know my judgment is a bit clouded by his quarterback hands and incredibly sexy body, but I don't care. He uses his strength to pull me back from him.

"Bell..." I whine as I look at him, my chest against his as I lay next to him.

"Don't Bell me. This isn't... I just don't want you to regret anything. Or to think I'm using you because I don't need-"

"I know you don't. You've made that very clear, and I don't need it either but to be honest, I really fucking want it," I tell him.

"What exactly do you want?" His voice is incredibly suggestive, and curious.

I look into his eyes the best I can. The only light is coming from the screen behind my head, but neither of us seems to be paying attention to it. He's amused, he's slightly smiling at me, his eyes caught on mine.

"Come on Ryn, I wanna hear it from you."

"First of all, I want you to keep kissing me. And I want you to make more of a move than that."

He reaches forward, pulling me down to him slowly. He guides my lips back to his, and as soon as I'm pressed to him again, I can feel his smile. He's slow in the way he kisses me, agonizing, but delicate.

Every movement is meant to happen just the way it does. He's captivating me again with just one thing and I'm still shocked as to how. I'm holding myself up over him now, my arms somehow ending up on each side of his body. He reaches around my waist and pulls me down by my lower back, crushing my chest to his so we're closer. I gasp at the feeling of his muscular body so tight against mine, and before I can feel it all, the two of us are moving.

I open my eyes and feel the rush of wind around the two of us. He's only got one strong arm around my back, but he's managed to hold me to him and switch spots with me. He's over me now, and his hand is slipping out from under me. He looks at me first, like he's trying to read me, but before he finishes he's blurring my vision, and kissing me all over again. His lips are stronger, and more controlled than before.

"What do you want?" He asks against my lips, his breath heavy as he asks, and kisses me harder.

"I want you to touch me," I tell him, and kiss him this time.

I feel his hand against my cheek, grasping me that way. He's doing it on purpose. He's pushing me.

"Like that?" He asks, and I can hear the amusement in his tone.

He doesn't kiss me again, so I open my eyes and look at him. I see an incredibly sexy, but infuriatingly annoying smirk on his face. His dimple is carved deep into his cheek, and I feel like half of me wants to kiss him, and the other half wants to punch him.

"No. Not like that."

"Then tell me what you want from me," He nods his chin up, his smirk only growing.

I take his hand from my face and watch his expression change as I slowly move his massive hand down my body until it's resting over the button of my shorts. His hand curls around the waistband of my shorts, and I feel his fingers brush my skin as he does.

"Touch me," I tell him and watch the amusement change on his face instantly. I can tell it's partially nerves, and another part is lust, the lightness of his eyes darkening as he looks at me. "Go ahead."

He hesitates.

"You're sure?" He asks, and I smirk.

"I told you to make a move didn't I?" I ask, and he tugs the waistband of my shorts, moving me upwards.

I catch myself and prop myself up directly in front of him, our lips centimeters from each other.

"You don't get told no very often do you?" He asks me, and I shake my head. "Good, because I never plan to," He speaks softly and kisses my lips again.

I think he's a wizard, or maybe it's the magic of quarterback hands but he somehow gets the button of my shorts undone with one single hand. He unzips my shorts and keeps his lips attached to mine as if his life depends on it. He takes my shorts by the belt loops and tugs, pulling them down right away. I don't know if he has more experience than I thought, or if he's just faking it, but whatever it is I want more. I can't catch my breath at all with him because the second I feel his fingertips brushing the soft skin under the lace of my underwear I'm gasping.

"You're sure?" He asks one last time, pausing his movements.

"A thousand percent sure," I breathe out, and he moves, his fingers slipping down between my legs.

He brushes them up my center, and rests them on my most sensitive area, making my eyes flutter closed. Wow. *He actually found it on the first try.*

He circles slowly, and I moan out softly, knowing the two of us are very much so in a public place. The movie blares behind us, but I can't even comprehend the words coming from it. All I can think about is the perfect way his fingers move against my heat. Dear god, I didn't know men like him existed outside of books and movies.

"More?" He asks, his voice teasing me, and I know he's got all of the control.

So I decide against being sarcastic and decide to answer the way I know he wants me to.

"Please," I whisper.

I feel his fingers slip down once more, finding their way inside of me, curling right away as they move and I gasp at the feeling. He's moving slowly in and out, working me up, and I know he's doing it on purpose.

"Fuck," He breathes out, and I look at him to see him pressing his eyes shut. His lips part as he works me with his long fingers. He's getting off on touching me, and suddenly I'm even more turned on. "You're so wet," His eyes open again, catching mine.

"You're a good kisser," I breathe out.

"Didn't know I was that good," He smirks, his ego boosting more and more with every second that passes.

He slams his fingers deeper, catching me off guard, sending shockwaves of pleasure through me, and I moan louder. His thumb finds the sensitive bundle of nerves, and this time he catches my moan in his mouth, trying hard not to cause a scene. Thank god the truck speakers are so loud or else we would have been kicked out already.

This feels like a movie in itself the way he's making me feel right now. He moves faster and harder. Just like his lips, his fingers are precise, and fucking magical because with every movement I feel warmth, and pressure building within my body. My stomach is heavy as he kisses me, and pumps his fingers into me.

"Fuck, just like that," I tell him, feeling him curl his fingers at a fast pace.

He circles his thumb, keeping a perfect rhythm, and I feel white hot pleasure burst from my stomach, and down my legs, through my chest. Into my mind. Everywhere I feel it. I moan out again, not caring what kind of scene I'm making at all. I don't care if everyone in the world is looking right now, I'd tell them to take fucking notes. He doesn't stop, he slows down, and he works my orgasm out of me, and I could fuck him for that alone.

"Is that what you wanted Ryn?" He speaks close to my face and plants a small kiss on my lips as he removes himself from me.

He pulls my shorts up and buttons them for me.

"Precisely," I tell him, my breath is still uneven. "You should put that on a resume or something," I speak out and hear laughter next to me.

"What exactly?" He asks me.

"Orgasm extraordinaire," I tell him, knowing I'm getting ahead of myself.

I don't know if I should be excited for anything else but considering all he had to do was use his fingers to make me come, he must be good with every other part of him too.

"I'll get right on that. Now stop seducing me, and watch the movie," He tells me.

He pulls me back into him, not letting me move from his rock hard body. The muscles on his chest and torso aren't the only parts of him that are hard.

"But you're-"

"I'm going to be hard for the next three days thinking about that Ryn," He tells me, and I feel my cheeks heat up at the thought of him getting off on that, thinking of me like I just was. I'm glad it's dark. I'm glad he can't see my face because I will never admit to that. But some things are better left unsaid.

CHAPTER TWELVE

TIGHTROPE BY ZAYN

I WAKE UP IN MY OWN BED, ROLLING OVER ONTO THE soft comforter. The sun is just now waking up, just like me. I'm surprised I'm even awake this early considering how late the two of us managed to get home last night.

Last night.

My mind reels over everything that happened. Him kissing me. Touching me. My cheeks heat, and I grab the pillow next to me, covering my face. Fucking hell, Bellamy Archer lives in my head rent free. I don't think I've ever been one to blush about the night before but it's impossible not to when I think of what happened.

Not only was he physically good but he also seemed to genuinely care which was very different for me. He did what he should, a step that most guys skip, and that's asking if I was sure. If I was okay with things. He kissed me like he meant it, and he sure as hell touched me that way too. I know that stuff wasn't on the list. I know that we're doing it because we're both physically attracted to each other, and that boosts my ego even higher than it was before.

I've got plans with him once again tonight. This time

he's told me it's not a double date, but a triple date. Something I've never been on, mostly because I don't go on dates at all, but that's beside the point. He said to look "as good as usual," which only made me roll my eyes.

I plan on looking better than usual. He said we'd be going into Seattle tonight, and I love going into the city. I love Pike Place, and the pier too which is my first guess as to where this triple date will take place. I pick up my phone right away and dial Sienna. I've got to see if my thoughts are all in check despite the lack of information Bellamy has provided.

"Good morning," I hear her voice on the other end of the call. "Actually, is it a good morning? You never wake up this early," Sienna isn't wrong in the slightest. I laugh at her comment.

"It is a good morning. What are you doing today, or tonight? Bellamy mentioned a triple date, I'm assuming Lawson is going," I ask, knowing I'll need her help with my outfit.

She hesitates to talk at first, and Sienna is never at a loss for words with me. She clears her throat, and I wait for a response.

"Lawson did ask me to go out tonight, as friends, of course."

I sigh in relief at the fact that she's going but question why she tacked on the friend bit. She said Lawson was hot, and she said she wanted him, so what's the holdup? I know she didn't come home with me the night of Leah's party, but the question I have is, did Sienna go home with Lawson, or did she go home alone? Sienna is the type of friend to always tell me things when she's ready, the do it yourself type. I can ask questions all I want, but if Si isn't in the mood, or sure of her answers, she's quiet as a clam, and I have to wait for all the juicy details.

"As friends?" I pry, and she groans.

"Yes, as friends, friends, strictly friends," She cuts the questions off, and I smirk at her frustration.

Definitely not friends, but this is obviously a conversation for another day so I don't ask anymore.

"Well, I'm glad you'll be there. This is one of the dates on my list. Bellamy invited everyone... When you figure out your outfit, can you send me pictures?"

"I always do. Speaking of Bellamy, how is that going?" She asks.

I feel my cheeks heat up again, thankful she can't see me. She would know right away if she saw my face right now, "Better than anticipated considering I haven't ended it yet."

She chuckles at me from her end of the phone.

"I guess that's true. I'm honestly a little proud you've made it this far. Has he kissed you yet? Used his quarterback hands on you?"

I think about his hands and instantly break out into the sweats. Nervous laughter travels between us.

"Well..."

I hear Sienna yell at my answer which wasn't really an answer. I pull the phone away from my ear at the sound of her squealing.

"Is he good!?"

I manage to make some words out and know she's never shown much interest in any of my other hookups before Bellamy, probably because this is a bit more than a hookup even though there are no strings.

"Phenomenal honestly," I admit. "He took me to the field yesterday too. He had me help him work out. We ran together too. Leah actually saw us, she wasn't too pleased."

"I could not give a single fuck less about what Leah has to say about you and Bellamy. I'm just glad you guys are comfortable and that this is going well."

"I'm shocked. But either way, I'll see you tonight."

"I'll send you pictures! I'll see you later, bye."

I hang up the phone after her words, pushing myself up from the bed. I felt really good yesterday after that run. So I get out of bed, and go straight to my dresser, grabbing track shorts, and a large school shirt to throw on over the sports bra I already have on. I go into my bathroom, put on deodorant, brush my teeth and my hair. I pull it up on top of my head, and go back into my bedroom, finding socks and shoes too. I make my way out of my apartment and jog to the bus stop. The bus has a stop right next to the field.

As soon as I see the stadium come into view I turn my music up, and once the bus stops I get off and go straight for the stairs. I make my way into the stadium, my eyes settling on the bright green field, the navy blue and silver Hornets paint is brighter this morning than yesterday. The dew is making it glisten in the sun.

My eyes catch movement I hadn't seen before. A person. The second I see his muscles, the tattoo. The lack of a shirt... I stop in my tracks. I watch as he sees me out of his peripheral vision, his head turning and his smile very apparent as he looks at me.

"What are you doing here this early Ryn?" He yells out to me, and I smirk at the nickname.

"I wanted to come and run."

"Get your ass down here then."

I jog down the stairs.

"Help me stretch?"

He nods, pulling me into a gentle hug against his bare chest.

"Always. How'd you sleep?" He asks softly as he makes his way behind me, the two of us falling into a comfortable setting like we have the past few days we've spent together.

～

AFTER THE RUN Bell and I shared he drove me home, and I showered and took a really long nap. After that I managed somehow to untangle my hair, and get myself ready from the neck up... Everywhere else is questionable.

I stand in my closet now looking at everything, knowing he'll be here soon. I flip through the clothes, ignoring all of the ones on the floor. I have no idea what to do, mostly because he hardly gives me any details on where we are going, and what my dress code should be. He says city, and I say, bar or shopping? He doesn't understand why it matters. *Figures.* There's a knock on my front door which makes me sigh. I grab my phone and call Bellamy.

"Hello?" He asks.

"Are you outside my door?"

"Considering it's time for our date... Yes."

"Great, funny story. I'm not ready so I need you to come in here, take a right, and then come into my bedroom, and help," I tell him, tucking the phone between my cheek and my ear as I flip through the dresses that hang in front of me.

"How are you not ready? I gave you hours."

"Well, now you know I need days. Get in here," I urge him.

"I'm here, calm down. Also, you need to lock your doors. Also, where are you?" He asks, his voice growing nearer and nearer the longer his sentence draws on.

"In here," I kick open the door, and toss my phone way too far, watching it bounce on the bed.

His eyes scan over me, and he shakes his head as he looks away, his large hand covering his face as he rubs it with a sigh.

"Clothes are necessary for a date," He tells me, his eyes on my face, not my exposed body.

I'm wearing underwear and a bra. He's had his hands all over me, and if things go to plan then he's going to see me like this anyway... If I remember correctly he already saw me naked before I got in the shower the other day. Maybe this is far too forward, but I've never been a modest person. I'm sure he at least figured out that much.

"Yes, I know that, but you never tell me what we're doing and then I stress... So which one?" I hold out the two dresses I like the most right now.

A simple black dress, sleek, tight. Small slit on the thigh. I then hold up a yellow sundress, very simple, but bright, and pretty. It's also tight fitting with the most unique floral pattern. Both are casual but different.

"Yellow," He nods his head and leans back on his elbows as he stares at me.

I shove the black one into my closet and walk into my bedroom with the yellow. I take it off of the hanger and step into the sundress. Once it's on, I start to open my mouth, but he's already standing up. He reaches for me, zipping the dress from behind, his fingers grazing my skin. I'm burning up instantly.

"Thank you," I scurry away from him, and scramble to grab shoes from the floor.

I hold up a pair of white heels and the pair of Dr. Martens I wear with just about everything.

"Do the boots. I like it when you're short."

"Well I like it when you stop talking," I tell him, frantically throwing the white heels on the floor.

I grab a pair of socks from the dresser in front of my bed and throw myself down on the mattress once they're in hand. Bellamy closes the drawer, and I shove the socks, and shoes onto my feet. I watch as Bellamy holds his hands out, I kick one of my feet up, and he begins tying my shoe for me as I tie the other.

"Did you just use bunny ears to tie your shoe?" He asks me, and I ignore him, knowing he's just going to make a joke.

I stand up, and he looks down at me, his eyes scanning my features. He looks like he's in a haze, his mind lost as he stares at me.

"What?" I wonder what he's thinking.

What's behind those glossy eyes? He tosses my black hair behind my shoulder, and turns me slightly, walking me forward to the mirror that sits in the corner of my bedroom.

"You're a dream in yellow, don't you think?" He asks me, looking at me in the mirror as he stands behind me.

I look at myself, and up to him, feeling a smile creep onto my lips. He bends down, pressing the simplest kiss to my temple, and then he nods his head.

"Let's go Ryn. Your room stresses me out," He pulls me by my hand.

I follow along, grabbing my phone, and my bag with my free hand as we walk.

"My room isn't any of your concern."

"It is. I'll even help you clean it... but dear god, please clean it," He laughs, and I ignore him.

I like my mess because it's mine.

We walk down to the car, and like a routine, he opens my door for me and helps me in. As soon as he climbs into the car, his sunglasses are on, and his hand is resting on my thigh, his fingers already twirling on my skin, drawing aimlessly. We drive for a while, and the city comes into view shortly, the heavy buildings starting to glow as the sky melts into the shoreline. I look at everything, watching as skyscrapers pass by, and people do the same. He drives closer to the coast, and then I figure it out.

"Ferris wheel?"

"Among other things... Yes," He tells me finally, and I'm glad I didn't go with the heels now.

He makes his way to the parking area and gets out first. He opens my door for me and helps me from the Jeep with ease. He takes my hand in his, and we walk together, our shoulders brushing as we walk. The closer we get the more the group comes into view. I see Griff with Jade, and Sienna with Lawson, the four of them socializing, their eyes on us as they talk.

"Finally!" Lawson calls out to us when we're close enough to hear.

"Sorry, Cinderella wasn't ready for the ball," Bellamy jokes, and I shove him to the side with my shoulder, our hands still connected.

He doesn't budge, just squeezes my hand one, two, and three times. I look up at him, and he's already looking at me, smiling.

"Well, he never told me where we were going, so I was in a crisis," I tell them. "Sorry," I apologize and watch as Griff shrugs.

"Not a problem. Let's go," He nods his head, his arm slinking over his girlfriend's shoulders.

Jade wears a dress like me but hers is a pretty pink that compliments her skin well. Sienna is wearing shorts and a pretty white shirt that hangs from her shoulders. She and

Lawson walk close to each other but don't touch at all. I watch Sienna and Lawson, trying to decipher how untrue the friend comment was. They don't seem friendly at all, to put it plainly they look like they dislike each other. Part of me wants to jump in a Ferris wheel pod with her and make her tell me, but my better judgment tells me to wait it out.

I look up at Bellamy, and he presses his lips together into a sweet smile. Even when I'm doing nothing Bellamy seems to always look at me like he appreciates me. He seems to always have his eyes on me. Even when he puts his attention elsewhere I can tell he's still trying to focus on me, make sure I'm comfortable, or okay. Making sure I don't need anything from him. He's attentive and caring. He makes that obvious. He's really, really good at faking it, and that makes me feel more comfortable to ease into this.

"We're going to the Ferris wheel first?" I look in the direction of Jade who asked.

She and Griff are looking at Bellamy and me as we walk. I look at Bellamy too, not knowing the answer either.

"Yeah, if you guys are cool with that."

Everyone agrees, and we approach the pier, all of us walking down, and passing people as they leave. We approach the line, and stand in it, waiting with one another.

"So, are you two..." Jade starts, pointing to Bell and me.

"No."

She narrows her eyes at my quick response, turning her head to look at Griff.

"It's fake," Sienna says and the boys nod.

"So you two aren't actually dating? You're... Fake dating?" Jade asks, and I nod. "Explain," She smiles, and Griff does too, extending his arm over her shoulder.

"I'd love to hear your version of this story, Kamryn," Griff speaks out.

"Wait, me too," Lawson chimes in, keeping the same smooth, cool attitude.

"I've been tutoring Bellamy, and he came to my apartment, and snooped through my things until he found-"

"I was not snooping. The list was sitting on your coffee table begging to be found. I think she placed it there. She wanted me to find it, and beg me to do it with her," He argues, and my jaw drops.

"This is why you aren't allowed to tell the story because that is not what happened. I made a stupid list, for research purposes of course, and then Bellamy came over so I never put it away. It was just there, and he found it," I look up at him, and notice his smile.

"What list?" Jade asks.

"Her list of things she's seen but never done," Sienna finishes for me, and I nod.

"It was never meant to be seen by anyone but me or Sienna. We were watching a movie, and I told her romantic shit like what happens in those movies doesn't happen in real life... Because it doesn't, it's all fake. She proceeded to argue with me and said it could be possible. I made the list to see if she or I had actually done any of that stuff, and before I could give it to Sienna, Bellamy-" I try to explain, but Bellamy cuts in.

"I'm just a good person, and she begged me to do the list with her so I said-"

"That didn't happen. He annoyed me and I said no, and the only person we have to thank for me saying yes is Sienna. She's reasonable and level headed, so when I told her about what happened, I thought she'd say not to do it, but then she told me to do it. When the sane one tells you it's a good idea, there's really no arguing," I look over to Sienna after I finish, and she grins from ear to ear.

"At your service," She winks at Bellamy, and I roll my eyes.

"You're never allowed to tell that story, you lie far too much," I point at Bellamy, and his amused smile brightens.

He hangs his arm over my shoulder, pulling me into him as we move up into the line.

"Well, for people who aren't actually dating, you two are very... good at faking I guess," Jade tells up, and my smile turns awkward as I laugh.

I can't help but think of Bellamy's friends, and question what they think of me. I've never been too keen on worrying about others' thoughts about me because they could potentially hurt my feelings, and I don't have time for that. But I do question what they think of this arrangement. Of me, and their best friend. Did they encourage him like Sienna did me? Did they tell him he was crazy? Did they high five him when he told them that I agreed, or did they warn him to be wary of me? Questions swirl in my brain, but I fake a smile.

"All comes with the job," Bellamy brushes her words off, and we continue talking, but I'm focused on the sinking feeling in my stomach.

I manage to move from Bellamy's arm around my shoulder, leading the group to the front until we get to the ticket booth. Bellamy pays for the two of us, and then we're off. Bellamy and I escape into a pod, and we're sitting, away from everyone else.

"Ignore them," He comes close to me, sitting down just like I did.

"I am. I don't know what you're talking about," I brush his words off despite the odd feeling in my stomach.

"I could see it the second Jade said what she did... You curled up, you went somewhere else. It's not a big deal. I told you I was going to do a good job, everything is the same as it was, there's no change."

I nod, agreeing with him, and believing him too.

"Do your friends... I mean do they care that we're fake dating? Do they even like me?" I ask, not sure why I even care in the first place.

Of course, I want to work with the football team. I want all of them to like me, but it's more than that. I can't place it, but I know it's more than just wanting some players to like me.

"They think you're cool. They also think it's good that I'm stepping out of my normal... tendencies," He steps over the word, and I raise my eyebrows. "The fact that I don't do casual. As you called it, being a nester. They think it's good for me, that you, and the list is good for me. Why are you worried? Do you think they're out saying shit about you? Because they wouldn't do that. Not to me, or you."

He defends his friends and tries to ease my mind, but I continue my stream of concerns that lie far past just his friends. Concerns I didn't think much about before agreeing to do the list.

"I just don't want anyone to get any ideas," I know I don't have an impeccable reputation as it is... but everyone knows I'm not the dating type.

I have no idea what this will make others think. Part of me fears an expectation from others... Especially if people find out all of this is fake... I just don't want to put myself in any danger.

"Well everyone already has ideas," He admits.

"Yeah I know, your ex wants my head," My laugh is filled with annoyance.

"Too bad she can't have it. I don't really care, we can

know, no one else has to. It's easier to live life without giving a damn about other people's opinions, Ryn."

"It's just easier said than done," I look up at him, and he shrugs.

"I just don't know why you care about the opinions of others, if you know it's easier to not care then just don't," He speaks like it's easy, and I furrow my brows.

"That's like looking at someone with depression and telling them to just be happy. It doesn't really work like that Bellamy. I just don't like the idea of people seeing me as..." I stop, and he raises his eyebrows.

"As what? The dating type? Or is it the fact that they'll see you as mine? Do you think people won't want to sleep with you after this? I can promise you that won't be the case Kamryn," His voice is a little more pointed than I've ever heard it. His comment somewhat hurts my feelings, but I know he doesn't mean it the way it sounds.

I press my lips together and sigh, "It's not that. I just hate the thought of being asked about this, or the thought of people knowing this was all an arrangement. I don't want other people to think I'll be making any more lists, or doing any fake dating or... Or anything of the sort."

He sighs and throws his arm over my shoulder, pulling me into his side.

"No one has to know that it's fake, or they can. No one needs to know anything we don't want them to Ryn. The best part about all of this, is we're in control of all of it. We decide what other people know. I'm sorry for what I said. You have every right to be nervous about this, I just want you to try let all of it go," He tucks my hair behind my ear, and grins at me.

"Okay fine, have it your way. I don't want to talk about this anymore," I keep my arms crossed, and turn my face away from him, still uneasy about the topic, but wanting to move on from it.

I don't want to ruin this date, even if it is fake.

"Then I'll say something else, and we'll stop talking about it," I nod, waiting for him to come through on that promise. "You said you didn't have any siblings right?" I shake my head. "Was that ever lonely?" I shake my head again.

"No, my mom was... Well, she is my best friend. She and my dad are... Honestly, I couldn't even explain it. They're just perfect I think."

I know no matter how hard I try there won't be words for them. There never has been.

"Are you and your mom not as close anymore?"

"We were inseparable before I left for school. I still talk to her as much as possible. We're close in different ways now that I'm a few hours away. It's just hard when I don't live in the same house as her. But she has my dad, and she and my dad are fine on their own, especially with the way they love each other. They're best friends."

"You talk about the two of them like they hung the moon," He's not accusing me, he's interested in knowing more.

He's got a smile on his lips as he says the words.

"Because they did for me. My parents are just normal people to everyone else and that's fine, but I mean it when I say they really are the best people I'll know. They always cared about me and everything I did. They were the perfect example of a couple growing up. Mom and Dad had date nights every week while I stayed with Grandma. He would always take her somewhere new. My mom is always smiling, but she smiles bigger when he walks into the room. And my dad. He really would do anything for my mom. She says he's been that way since before they got married. He's been that way since the day he met her," I relax my body into his, practically melting in his warmth,

"So if you're parents are just like the movies, then why don't you think romance is possible in real life?" His question makes me think.

I guess it's a fair question, one I've never posed to myself, but I recognize the answer right away.

"Because they're the only example in real life that I have. Besides, my mom told me all the horror stories of her horrible exes too. Cheaters, narcissists, and assholes. It took her a lot of tries to get it right and find my dad. Do you know how many Dylans I'm going to have to go through to find a guy like my dad?" I ask, and he nods to my answer.

"Fair point," He's quiet for a second. "When did they meet?" He continues, and I don't think anyone has ever cared about where I come from besides Sienna.

"My mom was twenty and my dad was twenty four," I tell him.

"And when did they get married?"

"1995. They had a spring wedding, and it rained all day but my mom didn't care, neither did my dad. They were happy. My mom always told me rain is lucky on your wedding day."

"I like how passionate you are about the things you love..."

I feel my cheeks heat up. I look out, noticing how much higher up we are, far too high for my liking.

"You get the same way."

"Not like you," He argues back.

"Yes, exactly like me. When you are talking about football, even romance movies you get excited and chatty... You're the same way."

"I like what I like," He replies. "I like running... I like it a lot actually. I like driving home because the ride is nice. I like cats, and I like dogs. I like strawberry milkshakes. I really really like The Notebook, more than even I can comprehend. I think it's the best movie of all time. I can't say I like football because I don't, I love football."

"And what other things do you like besides Romance movies? What other things do you love besides Football?" I question, needing to know the things that make him who he is, just like he's learning the things that make me who I am.

"I love my sister. Brianne, I've told you she's my best friend. I visit her once a week. I actually really love cooking, it's fun, and it's relaxing. I like cars. I don't work on them, I'm not knowledgeable on that, and I don't have time to be, but my dad loved cars, so I learned a lot about models, and makes, and that kind of stuff. The Jeep I drive was his, and it was a lot nicer when he drove it. It's more loved now. I love my Jeep, that's another thing. It's my prized possession," He tells me, and I see the way his eyes light up when he talks about his dad. Someone he very obviously looks up to.

"Did your dad play?" I ask, and he nods.

"He was amazing in high school, but he tore his rotator cuff, and that was enough for him to not want to play anymore, but it's what made him and my mom meet. She was a cheerleader, and he was a football player, the picture perfect couple."

I think about him, and Leah again, my mind trailing back to his picture perfect cheerleader, and him, the American dream quarterback. My heart stills at the fact that I'm jealous when I have no right to be. I shake the thought.

"Will you keep your Jeep forever?" I ask, and he nods.

"Until the old thing falls apart. Stop interrupting me, let

me talk about the things I like," He pokes fun at me, and I smirk, leaning into his warmth, feeling the vibrations from his chest as his deep voice continues. "I like music, not as much as you do, but I do like to listen to it no matter what I do. When I'm working out, or when I'm doing school work," I furrow my brows at him.

"You never listened to music when I tutored you," I challenge him.

"Because you were teaching me, I was in your space, and you didn't listen to music when you worked so neither did I. You didn't pay much attention to me in Professor Gallen's class because you were always so focused on him, but I always had an earbud in. It helps me concentrate," I hadn't ever noticed that.

After we would chat before class I wouldn't turn to him again, I'd keep my eyes on Gallen, and leave before anyone could talk to me.

"What kind of music?" I ask, wanting to hear him talk more.

"I like some of the things you like, Harry Styles and Taylor Swift because of my sister. But I really like a little bit of everything. Rock music, like Foo Fighters, and Metallica. My dad always listened to alternative music. I love Greta Van Fleet, I think my dad would have really liked them too if he was still here. When I work out and play I like to listen to Drake. I listen to country a good bit too."

I scrunch my nose up to that.

"Country music is good. Chris Stapleton and Kelsea Ballerini are awesome. And don't forget that Taylor Swift used to be country too, don't think I've forgotten that. I think if you gave it a chance you might like it," He nudges me, and I shrug. "Back to things I like. I like bubble baths, I don't care what anyone thinks, they're soothing, and I have a big tub. I like those Pink Drinks from Starbucks... I like you..."

I look up at him, thinking he'll be looking down at me right now, but he's not.

"That was smooth..."

He smirks, shrugging his shoulders once more. He's got the perfect lopsided grin. The kind that's perfect because it's crooked and imperfect. He's pretty when he smiles. He's pretty when he does anything. Pretty isn't the word I'd use when talking about men most of the time. I'd probably use the exact opposite, but I think it's the best way to describe him... He's a pretty person, especially now, at the top of the Ferris wheel. Washington is behind him, the sunset too. I can almost place him as a handsome shadow now that the sun is pouring in around him.

"Alright, let's get this over with," His tone is full of sarcasm, and I roll my eyes.

He takes a soft hold of my jaw, tilting my chin up, and then letting his hand slide down my exposed throat. He curves his hand around my jawline until his fingers are touching the hair behind my ear.

"Don't sound too excited," My lips are dangerously close, almost touching his.

"I can't have you getting any ideas, can I?" He asks, and then he kisses me again.

Our lips mold together, they fit with one another, and with every move he makes it feels more perfect. There's no way to be physically closer to him, but god do I wish I was.

It's hard to think when I'm around Bellamy because every time he kisses me, every time his lips come close to brushing mine it feels like I lose every bit of sense, and knowledge I've ever learned. I break the kiss this time, knowing that my senses are far too jumbled, and we are way too high in the air for that kind of feeling.

"Cross it off the list," I tell him, an electric feeling still radiating in my stomach after that kiss.

"Already done Ryn," We settle into each other again, the two of us sitting closely with no intention of moving until we're back on the ground.

CHAPTER THIRTEEN

TATTOOS TOGETHER BY LAUV

WE WENT FOR MILKSHAKES AND CHECKED OFF YET another thing from the list with everyone. The other couples left before Bellamy and me. We ended up getting a basket of fries to share before we wanted to leave. We got home extremely late, and I was scared for my life when we were driving home. Bellamy truly isn't a bad driver, but when the man is tired it's like he never even legally obtained a driver's license and I'm not being over dramatic.

I made him sleep on my couch. Now I regret that because I'm staring at my bedroom door, wondering if I should walk out into the living room or not. I'm also contemplating if I should have just let him sleep in my bed. I mean... He could have. I wouldn't have minded, but I also hate rejection, and the thought of him telling me no, and that he'd rather not made my soul leave my body for a few minutes so I didn't even ask.

What happens if he's not awake? What if I wake him up? What if he's left my apartment and I had no idea, and he's gone, and I'm overreacting? Even if he's here I know I'm overreacting because this is my apartment, but still. The thoughts swirling around my head are enough to make a grown man cry. Okay, maybe not. But again, it doesn't matter.

I take a deep breath and reach for the door, knowing if I think about it too long I'll stay in my bedroom all day. I'm wearing a t-shirt, no pants, and a pair of socks. My hair is in two long braids and is probably messy but I don't care. I look at my couch and see Bellamy Archer, awake, and cuddling the stuffed golden retriever he won me a few days ago as he watches The Notebook on the TV.

"Good morning," He chirps, and I find myself smiling at the scene in front of me.

He opens up the blanket he lays under, and nods his head. The stuffed animal is discarded on the floor, and I don't hesitate to scurry toward him. I jump on the spacious couch, and he closes the blanket around me, capturing the warmth around us. His arms are also around me now, resting around the front of my stomach. He pulls me back, crushing my body to his, and I realize right away he has no shirt on, and no pants either.

He's only in boxers. I don't panic, not outwardly at least, but inside I feel like I might combust. My body might light up, and burn altogether due to the thought of being pressed to him like this with no mental warning at all. There's no turning back now.

"You're so warm," I speak out as his other arm rests under my body, now curling around me to pull me even closer.

He spoons me. My back pressed to his chest, his arms tight around me.

"And you're freezing... Are you cold blooded?" His voice is deep, and gruff in the morning. Hot.

"Yes, I'm secretly a snake."

He only holds me tighter.

My mind wanders to the last time the two of us were on this couch. I was tutoring him, we had never touched unless it was in passing. Now we have, we are right now. Now I can't look at his hands without shaking in my fucking boots.

There's a lot that has changed between Bellamy and me. I feel more comfortable around him. There's not as much annoyance sitting between us. I feel like I could probably talk to him if I need something... Or someone. I don't know how to explain it except for the word comfort. He's like a human form of comfort.

"What do you want to do today?" He asks as I feel his chest rise and fall behind me, against me.

"Isn't that your job to know that?" I look over my shoulder at him.

"Normally it would be, but I haven't planned anything for today," He admits.

I turn my full body toward him now, disconnecting his hands from me. We face each other, and I get a good look at his face now. He's got hazy eyes, they're more gray than blue in the morning, but still pretty. His hair is messy and sloppy. He's cute this early. I could quite literally cuddle up to him, and go right back to bed I think.

"Well, then get to planning. You're the one with the list, not me," I tell him, and he groans, and pushes himself up.

I sink into the couch as he moves over me, holding himself up with one arm as his other reaches toward the coffee table in front of him. He grabs his wallet, and then falls right back down next to me, opening it. I see a picture, it looks old. I take his wallet in my hands, looking at the photos he has inside. There's a picture of him and his two roommates. Then there's a picture of a family. Two younger kids, and two incredibly beautiful parents.

"Who is this?" I'm pretty sure I already know, but I don't want to assume anything.

"Me, my mom, my dad, and my sister when she was really young," He points to everyone in the photo.

It must have been Halloween because everyone is in a costume. Bellamy's parents are firefighters, and he and his sister are dressed as Dalmatian dogs. I smile at the photo and the young Bellamy.

"This is such a cute picture," I pass his wallet back to him.

"You think that's cute, you should see my other baby pictures," He opens his wallet, and pulls out a folded piece of paper.

He unfolds the paper, revealing my list, and I don't know why the thought of him carrying around that silly list makes my stomach heat up, but it does. He holds it over us, and my memory is instantly refreshed.

☑ ~~Ferris Wheel Kiss.~~
☑ ~~Win stuffed animal at an arcade.~~
☑ ~~Spaghetti with only one meatball.~~
☑ ~~Cute kitchen food fight while we cook together.~~
☑ ~~Sharing a milkshake with one straw.~~
Slow dance in the street.
Carve our names into trees.
Make me a playlist.
Romantic first time.

Buy me the prettiest bouquet of flowers you've ever seen.

☑ Ferry Boat date.

☑ Seeing a movie and you slowly making your move.

Romantic New Years Kiss.

Get tattoos together.

Defend my honor.

Midnight Beach Trip.

Cloud Watching.

Go to a karaoke bar where I sing horribly, but you watch, and look at me like I'm the best in the world.

Kiss in the rain

THE CUTE CHECK marks warm my heart just the same. I look at the list, feeling somewhat embarrassed as I do, but ignore the sinking feeling as soon as I feel it. It's far too late to be embarrassed around him. It's especially late in the game to feel embarrassed about this list.

"What about tattoos?" He asks and the sinking returns.

"You seriously would get matching tattoos with me?" I barely believe him.

There's no way he's serious. Also knowing my mom might have my neck if she knows I got a random tattoo with some random boy she's never heard of in her life. She knows how I've felt about tattoos, and not being sure what I wanted. She would kill me.

"Hell no. I don't want to get matching tattoos. That's no

fun. I want you to pick a tattoo out for me, and trust me to pick one out for you."

My laugh is so loud it shakes my chest.

"You want to pick out my first tattoo ever... And I would have no say in what it is?" Just making sure I heard him right, I think I might have gone crazy or misheard, that must be it.

"Um... Yeah," His smile is prominent on his face, and incredibly charming too. "Come on, just trust me."

He smiles with closed lips now, and I feel nervous energy rolling through my body. I trust him, somewhat... But to let go of it all, to give in fully is tough for me, especially considering how new this all is. It's new but it feels like it's been going on for weeks on end which makes this even scarier.

"I trust you with a lot of things, but-"

"Like what?"

"Um... My body... And... and this list. I trust you to drive me places. And to stay in my apartment. I don't know, I trust you but-"

"If you trust me to make you feel good... and to sleep at your place... Then I think you can trust me enough to know I would never permanently put something on your body that you would hate..." He sneaks his arm under my waist, pulling me close to his chest.

I press my hand to his bare chest, stopping him from pulling me too close, "And you trust me? To let me pick something out to put on your body forever?"

He shrugs, "As you said before, tattoos are memories, right? I don't care."

I did say that before, didn't I? He's right. Tattoos are memories, and this is a good memory, all of this, but... Well... I guess there's no but. He's right.

"Do you get to choose where it goes too?"

He nods, "If you're okay with that... Or any of this... We can cross it off the list if you're not comfortable Ryn... That goes for any of this stuff, if you change your mind we don't have to," He motions to the paper in his other hand. I shake my head right away.

"No. I'm okay. Let's hurry up though so I don't change my mind," I start to get off of the couch but he holds me tight against him.

"Hey slow down..." His voice is playful which makes me look directly at him. His stare is intense when he's looking straight at you like this. It's like no one else exists in the world. I freeze in place. Bellamy's hand moves forward, holding my face. "You're pretty in the morning,"

He compliments me so easily, and I rest my face in his hand, letting a small smile ease its way on my face. Butterflies are flying wild in my stomach right now. I'm not used to the feelings, but it's... it's warm.

"As opposed to every other hour of the day?" I ask.

"Not what I said... I just thought I'd point out that you're especially pretty when you wake up."

"Okay, enough flirting. Let's get tattoos," I push off of him.

He doesn't hold me back from moving, and I'm glad he doesn't this time. I get off the couch and walk toward my bedroom, seeing him sit up.

"Go get ready. I'll let myself out, and be back in a little while to pick you up okay?"

I start to go into my room and stop myself in the doorway.

"Hey, when you come back could you-"

"Yes, I'll come back up and help you pick out an outfit, now go, you take forever," He urges me away, and I smile, liking that he already knew what I was about to say to him.

I'M JUMPING into a pair of loose fitting jean shorts when I hear a knock on my door again. I run to the door in shorts, and a bralette, my hair damp and hanging down my back. I stand on my tiptoes to look into the peephole, only to see Bellamy, leaning against the wall outside of my door. He should be proud I'm locking my door now. Even though the only reason I left it open in the first place was because I knew he'd be coming over, but he's anal about it even with that excuse.

I open the door, and he's wearing black shorts, and what looks like a vintage football t-shirt. The Packers are on his tee. One of the teams he mentioned that he loved. He looks casual but fit. He looks good as always. He looks me up and down taking in my lack of shirt and smirks to himself, walking past me and into my bedroom as I close the front door.

"Okay I just need you to pick a color," I tell him, running into my bedroom after him. "Yellow or green?" I ask him.

"Yellow, easy," He gives me the answer like it's second nature, and he's already thrown himself across my bed.

I go back into my closet and take the yellow cropped t-shirt off of the hanger. I walk back out and pull it over my head, adjusting myself as I look in the floor length mirror.

"Have you thought about what you're going to be tattooing on my body?" Bell's voice echoes behind me as I look at myself, I can see him looking at me through the mirror too.

I nod instinctively not wanting to cause panic. I have no fucking clue what I'm going to tattoo on him, literally not a single idea has crossed my mind. But it's not a full lie. I have been thinking about it.

"What about you? Do you know what my first tattoo is going to be?" I ask him.

"I do. I thought of it before you had even told me you were okay with the idea..." He tells me, and now I feel even more pressure.

He's been planning this, thinking about it, and I'm about to have to pull something out of my ass.

"Nothing inappropriate. If I open my eyes to a penis tattooed on my body, I'll have gained one and you will be losing one," I warn him.

"I would never do that to you. Griff, maybe... But not to you," He winks at me as I reach down to the ground to grab my Dr. Martens.

I slide them over my feet, my socks peeking out over the top of them. I tie my shoes, and Bellamy is practically dragging me out of the door, and downstairs to his car.

He keeps his large hand spread over my thigh the entire drive, drawing eager circles over my skin showing me that he might be a bit more anxious than he's letting on. I think long and hard about what tattoo I want to give Bell. By long and hard I mean as long as it takes us to be parked in front of the tattoo shop he's chosen.

It's the middle of the week, and we're a bit outside of the city so when we walk inside there's hardly anyone in the shop. I hear the light hum of a tattoo gun and the sound of music. Bellamy takes my hand in his like it's instinct, and he leads me forward, and up to a large glass counter. Inside are piercings, and jewelry. I look around at the walls, hoping for

165

a very last minute bit of inspiration, something that sparks my interest.

"Are you sure about this?" My eyes continue to scan everything surrounding us.

"One hundred and ten percent sure. I don't care what you choose, as long as it's not inappropriate. You can put it anywhere on my body... With very very few limits."

I have an idea but no image of it in my head. My eyes catch on a simple drawing, it's classic style, of course, with no color. It would match his other tattoo well, and it fits him, and it fits what I was picturing in my mind. My mind reels at the significance of it to me, and what it would mean to him. It makes me smile, the thought of how cheesy it would be but also perfect. He squeezes my hand, and I look down, my eyes looking at his hand that completely covers mine.

"Okay, never mind, I don't have doubts anymore," I confirm.

"Are you sure?"

I nod eagerly.

"What can I help you with?" A man asks, approaching us on the other side of the counter.

"So she's picking out a tattoo for me, and I don't know what it is... And I'm doing the same for her."

The man raises his eyebrows, looking completely unsure of the two of us.

"Did you lose a bet?" The man is burly and large, and covered in tattoos. I stifle a laugh.

"That's what it feels like doesn't it?" I joke.

Bellamy rolls his eyes. "She didn't and neither did I."

I smile at how defensive he is. He's an easygoing person, though he's persistent, he's normally relaxed. I do watch and notice the small times, the little instances where he reaches for my hand, gets protective and turns into the scary boyfriend – not the easygoing one. Fake, of course. The scary fake boyfriend. Right now is one of those times, he's very stuck on not wanting others to know what we have going on between us. He likes it being between us, and our group of friends, and I do too. Not that these tattoo artists truly care what Bellamy and I are.

"Alright, I don't care. I'll do hers. I'll grab another artist for yours. You said this is some kind of secret? She can't know, and you can't know?" He asks Bellamy, and I watch as he nods.

"Exactly."

I realize just how dumb this sounds now that we're saying it out loud.

"It's none of my business," The artist speaks like he's reminding himself as he walks away from the two of us and down a hall.

He comes back with another guy, and Bellamy and I separate, going with the other's tattoo artist, explaining the pieces we have chosen for each other.

I point to the wall, pointing out the artwork I had seen and loved. I give him a size reference and tell him where to place it, my stomach filling with butterflies at the thought of my own tattoo, and the one Bellamy is going to walk out of here with.

"Are you two fine to get tattooed at the same time?" The first guy we spoke to asks.

I hesitate for a second, not scared, but a bit apprehensive. I've never been tattooed before. I know I'll be fine, but there's a bit of fear locked inside of my chest, buzzing there like a swarm of bees.

"Can we be in the same room?" Bellamy's eyes are on

me as he speaks, obviously noticing my apprehensive feelings.

"Whatever," The guy speaks, and nods his head.

"You can't look..." Bellamy warns me.

"Neither can you."

The two artists get both stations set up, and sit us down. I turn my face away from the artist and notice Bellamy doing the same, looking directly at me. I smile and wave with my free hand. We're close, but not close enough to touch.

"You ready?" The artist asks Bellamy.

"Go for it," He tells the guy.

The tattoo gun buzzes, and I watch as the artist preps himself, and gets started. Bellamy doesn't flinch at the touch of the tattoo gun on his skin even though the area is so sensitive.

"Nothing?" I ask.

"I thought my hand would be worse... Also, I should have known you'd choose a hand tattoo."

I might punch him later for exposing me in front of two strangers. Let's hope they don't pick up what he just put down.

"It's a cool place for a tattoo," It starts to sink in that I might actually be crazy.

I'm getting a tattoo... With Bellamy Archer. My fake boyfriend. Someone I might not speak to in two weeks. The thought upsets me, it unsettles me slightly thinking of not talking to him at all. I shake it completely. We'll still be friends after this... Right?

"Ready?" The tattoo artist has his eyes locked on me.

I nod and smile at the man, "As I'll ever be."

I hear the buzzing and I close my eyes. Bellamy chose my forearm. Right under the bend of my arm. I could feel the artist sterilizing my skin. I'm anxious to see what it is, to see what he decided for me. I tilt my head up to the ceiling, waiting for the pain. The second the needle touches my skin I'm thrown off. It doesn't feel good, but it doesn't hurt. It's just... uncomfortable.

"You good?" The artist asks me.

"Fine."

"It's her first," Bellamy exposes me once again, and the artist practically snorts he laughs so hard.

"No shit? It's your first tattoo, and you didn't even choose it?"

I don't look at him, mostly because I don't want to see the tattoo.

"Nope."

"You must really trust your boyfriend."

Despite the weird feeling I get at the word boyfriend I still laugh softly. Jade mentioned us dating, and it left me feeling unsettled mostly because I didn't want Bellamy's friends to think badly of me. I'm not one to care about opinions, but I seem to care about theirs. I like them, all of them a lot. But hearing the word boyfriend from a stranger, I don't mind as much. Mostly because I know this person won't remember me tomorrow, or the next day. I'm minuscule in this man's life, this lie won't mean a thing to him. To Bell's friends? It does mean something to them. Even if they aren't involved, this list means something to the whole group.

"You have no idea..."

"How does it feel?" The artist asks.

"Kinda like losing your virginity," My mouth speaks before I have a second to even think about what I'm saying.

A chorus of laughs comes from the entire room.

"Never heard that one before," Bellamy's artist speaks out.

I look at Bellamy who has a bit of pink in his cheeks, and a smile on his face, "Are you going to elaborate on that one Ryn?"

"It hurts, but not like I thought it would. It's more uncomfortable, and dull," I tell all of them.

"I guess that's better than the alternative," The tattooer speaks out, and I lose focus on the way it feels, my eyes landing on Bellamy instead.

I watch the walls around me, my eyes drifting to anything that isn't my arm, and then the buzzing on my side of the room stops.

"Alright, you're all done. Do you want to look now before I wrap it up?" The guy asks me.

I didn't think he'd be done so soon, but part of me is relieved that the tattoo is smaller considering it is my first. I look at Bellamy, wondering if we're going to look together or once we're each finished.

"Go ahead," Bellamy agrees, and the artist then nods his head to the mirror in the room.

I stand up from the tattoo chair and go to the mirror, extending my arm. I look to see a simple tattoo. It's four numbers. A year. 1995. The year my parents got married. My heart fills up so much that I feel like it might rupture in my chest as I look at the four little numbers. I stare at the tattoo, practically frozen in place, scanning the small patch of ink on my forearm. It's perfect. It's me. It's meaningful...

"The suspense is killing me, I can't tell if she loves it or hates it," My artist speaks, and I snap out of my feelings, suppressing the small urge to cry that's building in my chest.

If I'm going to cry it will be in my room all by myself without an audience.

"I love it. It's actually perfect," I tell everyone, but my eyes are on Bellamy.

"For your parents. I figured a good first tattoo would be one for people you care about."

He motions to his older tattoo, and I really would hug him if I could right now, even though that doesn't feel like enough to show him that I appreciate him for not picking something stupid.

He listened... and remembered which is something I'm avoiding thinking about altogether because I hate the way it makes my chest swell. I hate the way it makes my mind feel too. I swear every judgment turns to mush at the thought of him being attentive the way he is.

"Thank you... I love it," I thank him, and turn to the artist too.

"No problem," He shrugs, and then he pushes a rolling chair over to me while he sanitizes his station.

I sit, and he cleans off the tattoo and takes a photo for me. He wraps it up after and leaves me sitting next to Bellamy. I get on my phone, and send the photo to my mom, and Sienna, knowing both of them will love it, and also be a bit shocked that I actually got a tattoo. At least I hope my mom loves it, especially since it's technically for her.

"How are you holding up?" I ask Bellamy, looking at him, placing my hand on his forearm, sliding it down till I'm holding his free hand.

"The hand hurts more now, and far worse than the arm, but it's still alright... I am curious to know what the hell you picked," The realization hits me that he picked something incredibly sentimental for me, and I didn't do that at all.

I picked a placement because I thought it would be

hot... The tattoo, I picked it because of something he had said, because of what the two of us are doing, but it still doesn't compare to what he chose for me. What if he hates it? I guess it's too late now.

We wait together, and I watch as the artist works. He's incredible at what he does, and the tattoo is looking even better than what I had seen on the wall. Bellamy keeps my hand in his other hand, running his thumb over my skin, his head tilted back as we sit together. He goes between looking at the ceiling to closing his eyes, and taking deep breaths. I can tell this spot isn't fun for him, and now I feel kind of bad. After around an hour the artist backs away.

"All done... Take a look," The tattooer starts cleaning up his station, and I turn Bellamy's face toward me, feeling anxious.

"Okay, before you look just know it's not as... Sentimental as what you gave me, but it looks really good... And it's hot too."

He smirks, shaking his head.

"I told you I don't care," He tells me, and turns his head, looking down at his hand, and revealing it fully to me too.

Two American traditional style birds, shaded perfectly. One on his hand and one right above it, closer to his wrist. The birds look like they are trying to reach each other. They look like they belong together on his skin, and dear god, they bring attention to his hands. As if they didn't already get that.

"I thought that because of your favorite movie and the two of us are doing what we're doing... I don't know," I shrug, trying to explain the tattoo, and I notice the smile on his face.

His eyes haven't left the ink. He continues to stare, and I feel like I might throw up.

"If you're a bird I'm a bird?" He asks, repeating the quote from The Notebook while looking at me, not losing the wide grin on his face.

"Yeah, exactly," I tell him.

"It's perfect and the placement is too. I love it Ryn. I told you I've always wanted one on my hand anyway. I'm glad it's this," He stands up to look at it in the mirror in full.

I stand next to him considering he didn't let go of my hand. We both look at his tattoo and then at each other.

"I think this was a really good idea," I say.

I don't know where the confession comes from. I would consider myself impulsive, but not this impulsive.

"Yeah, I'm full of them," He moves back to his artist and lets him clean the tattoo, and cover it, just like my artist did for me.

"Actually this was all my idea, you just helped," I remind him.

"Minor details," He brushes me off as the artist finishes wrapping his hand.

The two of us walk to the counter, and Bellamy insists that everything is being paid for together. He pays for both of the tattoos and tips excessively as he always does. He holds my hand the entire time we are in the shop and even when he walks us outside, and to his car. He walks me around to the passenger side and reaches for the door, but I turn him around, and away from the car. The urge I have is one I would have to fight incredibly hard to stop so I just let myself go without letting myself explain why.

Bellamy turns toward me, and I use both of my arms to reach up and hook around the back of his neck. The skin is stiff around my new tattoo but I ignore the uncomfortable feeling. I stand on my tip toes, and I ignore every warning in my head to back away.

For the first time since we've been doing this, I make the move. I kiss him. I do it softly. I brush my lips against his, barely able to reach them in the first place. I had told myself a hug wasn't enough when we were in the shop, it didn't feel personal enough. Now that my lips are on his, and there's still an excessive amount of pressure built up in my chest I don't think this is enough either. I don't understand the feeling inside of me. I don't know if I like it either.

It only takes him a second to relax his body, giving me better access to his lips, making it far easier for me to kiss him. His hands rest on my hips now, his back now pressed to the door of his Jeep as I press all of my weight into him. The kiss takes over my mind, swarming me with so many thoughts I'd never speak out loud that I make myself pull away. My calves burn as I stand back on the ground, and not on my toes. Bellamy follows me down, stealing another kiss from my lips before turning back to the car and opening the door.

He doesn't ask about the kiss. I know it was out of character for me. I've never kissed him, only let him kiss me. I've never been the one to make a move on Bellamy, but I couldn't hold myself back. Now he's silent. He just lets me in the car and gets in on his side.

I have no idea if we're heading back to my apartment. I have no idea if we're heading to do something else on the list... I have no idea if we're doing something completely random. I do know that whatever we do, I'd like to spend the rest of my day with Bellamy Archer.

CHAPTER FOURTEEN

HEAVEN BY NIALL HORAN

WE WENT OUT TO LUNCH, AND EVER SINCE I KISSED Bellamy he seems to be off. Maybe distracted is a better word? He's been checking his phone, and acting like he's somewhere else mentally. Part of me is telling myself I'm reading into it way too much, but the other part of me. The insecure part of me tells me I did something completely wrong. Maybe he really doesn't like his tattoo? Or I'm a bad kisser.. Or maybe he just doesn't feel as into this as he did before? He pulls back up to my apartment complex, so I turn to him over the center console.

"Hey, Bell..."

He looks away from his phone to look at me, his features strong, and his eyes light, "What's up?"

"Did something happen? Or did I do something wrong? Because if you hate the tattoo... I'm sorry, I thought-"

"What are you talking about?" He drops his phone instantly in his lap, focusing fully on me now.

"I don't know. After we left the tattoo shop you seemed like you were upset, or distracted," I tell him. "I was just making sure I didn't do anything... Or that you still wanted to do this because you're always telling me if I want to stop that we can, but the same goes for you. If you don't want to finish the list we don't have to. I mean you don't need me to-"

"Respectfully... Stop talking," He interrupts me, and I shut my mouth right away. "You're cute when you get all worked up... I didn't mean to make you feel that way. First of all, you've never kissed me before, and it made me feel good because it makes me know that you feel comfortable with me. Second of all, I have been distracted... Let's just go upstairs and I'll explain."

He nods his head and gets out of the car. He walks to my side, opening the door for me. He takes me by the hips and helps me from the Jeep.

I don't say anything but I feel somewhat relieved at his words and his confession about me kissing him first. Part of me is still anxious at the thought of Bellamy waiting to tell me the rest until we get upstairs. There are words left unsaid but I don't know what they are so I wait nervously, and- my eyes catch Lawson, and Griffin walking from the front doors of my apartment building, and confusion hits me like a wave.

"Bellamy, why are your roommates walking out of my apartment right now?" The two of them don't see us, but I'm positive it's them.

"Because they can't do anything right," He doesn't say anything to them, they don't even notice the two of us as they leave.

Bellamy doesn't say another word as he leads the two of us up the stairs and to my door. He kicks my doormat to the side and picks up a key that I had never put there. I furrow my brows and press my lips together.

"How did you... I've never put a key under my doormat before."

"Well I might have stolen your key when you were sleeping, and put it there before we left... And told my friends to put it there for us when we got back."

I shouldn't be mad, right? I mean there's a reason for this I assume, but still.

"Invasive! Why were your friends inside my apartment?" I throw my hands up, and he doesn't react to my initial annoyance, he just unlocks my door and opens it.

He holds the door open, and my jaw drops. This must have been what he was distracted by. It has to be. I would be distracted if I was going to set something like this up.

"I don't know if you remember... But I have a list to complete," His words are like white noise as I walk into my apartment which looks like it was transformed into a flower shop.

Okay, that's a bit dramatic... But really, there are bouquets of yellow and white daisies everywhere. It smells wonderful too. They're on the tables, dining table, and the coffee table. They're on the island in the kitchen too. I've never been particular about the type of flowers I like. Daffodils have been something I think of because of Big Fish. But daisies, all the daisies surrounding me make me feel more than that movie ever did.

"The list said the prettiest bouquet. Singular," My eyes are still on the flowers around us, I don't know if I'll ever be able to look anywhere else.

"Well, we've already realized I have selective hearing, and I couldn't pick just one. This is better anyway."

I just stare. I don't know what's happening but I feel an overwhelming sense again. The pressure inside my chest builds, and I push back the initial want to start crying. It's just flowers... This really does look like a scene from a cheesy romance movie.

I always feel like I'm in a movie when I'm with him, and I know that's the goal. But damn he's... He's going above and beyond, and I knew that before right now but he really is... He's doing everything I wrote but somehow making it better. It's hard to comprehend someone caring enough to make this silly list happen.

"This is so sweet..." I walk ahead of him to look at all of the flowers. "And your friends did all of this?" I turn around, standing in the center of multiple bouquets, surrounded by them.

It makes my heart scream. Part of me thinks of my childhood when I'd watch Gilmore Girls with my mom. That one scene with all the daisies. It's not the same but... It's so close. My mom would be in love with Bellamy if she had any idea he did any of this for me.

"They did... They did good too, even though they messed up the surprise," He motions around the room, then looks directly at me.

I watch as Bellamy takes out his phone, and I pose for a picture the second he holds his phone up. He walks forward, and I watch him as he does, not knowing how to feel or what to do in this situation. There's no "how to" book in this type of scenario because this shit doesn't happen, at least not until Bellamy Archer walked through my door. He has to know how I feel right now, there's no way it's not written all over my face.

"How did they mess it up?" I ask him, seeing just how perfect the scene around me is.

"I figured they would just use Griff's truck for all the flowers... Turns out it's in the shop. So they took longer than expected. So they had to use Lawson's car. Well, he drives a stupid Mazda, and it's tiny. They truly almost ruined everything. They were supposed to be done an hour ago."

I shake my head, an even bigger smile on my lips at his explanation. I look around, continuing to look at the pretty flowers, my heart beating out of my chest.

"My sister used to love the show Gilmore Girls, and when I read your list I thought of that one scene-"

"A thousand yellow daisies," I interrupt, looking at his pretty blue eyes, and he smiles instantly.

"Exactly... Well, not exact, it's not a thousand but-"

"It's perfect. I don't know what to say," I look up at him as he stands in front of me.

"How about you don't say anything because you don't have to?" His hand slowly rests on my cheek, softly cupping my face.

"What do you want to do the rest of the day?" I hesitate.

"If you don't want to do anything. I can go hang out with the guys, and give you some time to yourself, just whatever you want," He suggests.

"No," I speak a bit too eagerly. Bellamy raises his eyebrows, a smirk playing on his lips. "I mean, if you don't want to stay you don't have to... But you can. We can watch movies... Order food... Or something else..."

I make it apparent I'd be fine doing absolutely anything right now with him. I probably sound like a babbling idiot but I really like spending time with him.

"I'll stay if you want me to..." There's an awkward silence that drifts between the two of us, so I turn away from him and walk toward my bedroom.

"Is that a yes?" I leave the door open behind me.

"Obviously!" I yell. He makes his way into my bedroom,

and I kick my shoes off and jump onto my bed, the door still wide open. Bellamy stands at the foot of the bed, his eyes on me as I find my way under my comforter, and out of his line of sight.

"Are you waiting for a formal invitation?"

"I'd like one, yeah," His smart remark only makes me roll my eyes.

He starts to kick his shoes off too.

"Bellamy, would you please for the love of all things good... Get your ass in my bed?" I ask him and watch as he crawls into my bed for the first time, making his way to me.

He crawls under the covers, not hesitating to pull me directly into him. I grab the small remote from my bedside table, and he snatches it from my hands, turning the TV on, and instantly going to Netflix.

I watch as he scrolls through the romantic comedy section, inevitably clicking on one of my favorites. I've never told him it's one of my favorites. 27 Dresses starts on the TV, and the quiet day has turned perfect in seconds. My cheeks flame at the thought of the vases of flowers in my living room right now. I smile to myself, my body closing in on Bellamy's. I rest my head closer to his chest, my ear pressed down enough to hear the steady thrum of his heart.

"Do you like this movie?" He asks since can't see my brimming smile.

"I absolutely love it. The karaoke part of the list is from this movie. I love the scene where they're singing together in the bar," I move my leg over his body as I talk.

My body meshes with his within the first five minutes of the movie starting, and quickly I realize that watching movies with him might be the hardest thing I've ever done, well next to the last movie we watched together. I can't focus on anything.

I don't procrastinate. I'm a good student and an even better teacher. I don't like letting my mind slip up when I'm supposed to be focusing on something, but the feeling of his hard muscles underneath my body, the warmth of his skin grazing mine, and the sound of his heart inside of his chest practically begging to be set free. I can hardly recognize what's on the TV in front of me. My heart is beating so loud I feel like it's drowning out every sound in the room.

Bellamy moves his hand under the covers, and I feel it on my leg, right over my knee, slowly moving up my thigh. His hand moves up my leg slowly, grazing my ass, and moving back down to my upper thigh, resting there. His fingers trace slow circles, and I feel my heart pick up, and I can hear his beating faster just at the touch of my skin to his.

I don't beg. I don't make it known how badly I want, no *need*, physical touch from any man... But I would beg Bellamy to touch me if it came down to it... Right now I'm thinking about it all as his fingers toy with the hem of my shorts, dangerously close to my ass. I wait, wondering what to say or if I should say anything at all. I wonder if I should just move onto him, kiss him... Touch him...

There's an unease about all of this with me. There's no hesitation to actually do things with Bellamy. I want to do everything but I fear the unknown. I fear rejection... And most of all I fear just how comfortable all of this feels with him. I would feel comfortable asking him for something, I know he would joke with me, and I know he would try his hardest to make me feel good in every sense. I don't know why I'm uneasy with comfortability but I am.

Hookups are never comfortable. They're awkward and mixed up. This is a hookup on the next level. This feels like a friendship, but more. It feels like. I don't know... I don't know what anything feels like besides the feeling of his massive hands inching closer and closer to my ass... He's eager yet smooth with the way his fingers graze me.

"I want you..." He speaks out, and I've never been so relieved to hear any words come from anyone's mouth.

There was a silent tension that neither of us wanted to break, but I'm so fucking happy he did.

"Oh thank god," I speak out, and before I can turn myself over, he's gripping my thigh tight, and pulling me up.

I'm straddling his lap now, and he's staring at me with desperation in his eyes. I fight the urge to let my eyes roll back at the sight of him like this, wanting me like this.

"I'm going to need you to come here," He speaks out, and I lean forward only slightly, but it's enough for him.

He reaches up, his hand gripping the back of my neck, pulling me down to him. His lips captivate mine, overtaking me in the most pleasurable way possible, every sense in my body shattered, and thrown out the window. He brings his free hand up my back, slipping it under my shirt to hold me in place. He leans up into the kiss, hunger present in every movement he makes. He sits himself up fully, his back now pressed against the headboard of my bed while I stay on his lap.

He takes me quickly, flipping the two of us so I'm under him, and he has all the power over me. He brings his lips down to mine, feverish and wanting as they kiss me. The desperation is prominent every time our lips meet, and it sends waves of heat and pleasure down my spine. Kissing him is always an experience. It has been everywhere I have done it, but kissing him in my bed, it's a different kind of pleasure that I didn't know I'd feel.

"Everything is on the table?" He asks with his lips against mine, and I nod as his fingers push the shirt I wear up my body exposing myself to him.

"Everything," I breathe out, wondering what thoughts are crossing his mind right now, knowing all of them would be far too dirty to speak out in a crowded room.

His hands are grazing my skin, teasing me, clouding my head, pulling at every want I've ever had inside of me. It's easy to let my head reel with him, to let myself lose all control, and let him do anything and everything, especially with his fucking hands... Especially considering he's learning what makes me tick. He's learning my body, and what I like. What I want. What I need. He makes it easy to lose control. But right now I want control. I move my hand, sliding my fingers under his waistband so I can hook my hand around it.

"Ryn..." He breathes out, my name turning into a mumble against my lips.

I push him back, my eyes locked with his, looking for approval.

"Are you sure?" He asks.

His eyes never leave me. His concern for me sends shockwaves through my body. His hesitancy and worry for me only heighten the lust I have for him.

"Positive.." I nod my head, signaling him to move.

"But-"

"Shut the fuck up, and let me get on my knees for you," I never thought I'd be saying those words to him.

He looks at me, eyebrows raised. His shock only stands for a moment before he moves, listening to my words. I know now that I want to know the same things he does. I want to know what makes him tick. I want to know what makes him gasp, and moan, and I want to learn what makes him feel good. I want to learn his body as if my life depends on it. I follow him from the bed and lower myself down in front of him, not looking at him, knowing I might lose it if I see him staring at me.

I'm not the shy type, especially when it comes to my sexual wants and needs... But when Bellamy looks at me the way he does I feel like I've never been looked at before. His gaze is hard, strong, and intense. It locks me in place and shoots my nerves in every direction.

I wrap my hands around his waistband, slowly pulling down. I reveal his length and instantly feel warmth hit my abdomen at the sight of its size. I squeeze my thighs as I take him in, looking at Bellamy Archer in full. Dear god, he's going to fucking destroy me, and I'll be happy to let him.

I take him in my hand, not hesitating to do so, and I look up just to see him dissolve into pleasure with one stroke. I use my tongue to remove the precome that drips from the tip of his cock. I hear a tiny gasp leave his lips, and instantly crave more sounds from him, just like that one. I take him in my mouth, my lips wrapping around the soft flesh, my hand still working him as well. A guttural moan leaves his lips, and I move my tongue swirling it around his length, feeling everything between my thighs as I fuck him with my mouth.

I open my mouth, gasping for a breath as I move against him, and I look up at him, my eyes finally locking with his. He stares down at me, watching me while I take him, and I see every ounce of the pleasure I am causing him inside his blue eyes.

I see all of the wanting he has, I see the hunger, the need. I see it all and I bat my eyes despite the burn in them. I take all of him, feeling his length in the back of my throat, tears threatening my eyes. I brush my tongue against him, pressing down, flattening it as I get closer to the tip, his most sensitive area being stroked as I pleasure him. He moves his hands threading them into my hair, pulling it back, tugging tightly on the strands, and I moan against his dick.

"Kamryn, don't fucking do that," He speaks harshly, but the intensity of his voice makes me want to test him further.

I go deep once more, a few tears actually slipping from my eyes this time. I moan again, the moan vibrating from my chest as I wrap my lips around him, bobbing my head, pressing my tongue, and swirling it too. I watch as he unravels under me, every bit of his composure shattered into a million and one pieces right in front of my eyes. His body is covered in chills, and I feel him empty himself in my mouth, the warmth down my throat as I take it. He's pulling tighter on my hair now as he releases, and I have never been more fine with an action.

I slowly draw my tongue up his length one last time, removing him from my mouth, still pumping him in my hand as I look up at him. He's lost in feeling right now, his head tilted to the ceiling as he looks away from me. I take a few staggered breaths, trying to return my breathing to normal after that. I take his pants, and pull them up for him, standing up now, bringing myself to him, and he looks down at me, his eyes hazy.

He stares at me, his eyes shifting between mine, and then his hand is clasping my jaw, holding me in place so I'm looking up at him. He brings himself down to me, and he kisses me hard again, flooding my stomach with warmth, my thighs clenching from just one kiss. He takes me to another world with his lips, and I pull away before I'm drawn too far in, and can't find a way out.

"You're going to ruin me if you keep it up."

I can't help but let my smile show.

"Don't boost my ego too much," I joke, and he nudges my chin up again so I'm looking at him.

He wipes under my eyes, taking the very small bit of tears that slipped out, "Are you alright?"

I'm confused by the question at first, "Yes... Why wouldn't I be?"

"I don't know... That's why I asked. I was just checking. Just making sure you're okay. That everything is okay. You're fine? That was fine?" He asks, and I nod.

"I started it. I wanted to," I remind him.

"I know that. But sometimes people change their mind or do things, and regret it. Sometimes things are too much, and I just wanted to make sure."

I feel that same warm feeling in my chest that makes me want to take his clothes off. I'm not sure why that's my first instinct when I get mushy feelings in my chest, but it is.

I just stare at him, words lost in my throat at what to say.

"Come on, I think I should take the wrap off of your tattoo, it's been over an hour," He tells me, and I look at his. "Mine stays on for a few days. it's in a sensitive place. It's like a second skin, yours comes off now since your tattoo is smaller, and in a more covered spot. Come on." He nods his head to my bathroom, and I follow him, my mind still spinning at his concern for me, and his understanding of my wants, needs, and consent. That's a normal thing to care about but it's not something most people do.

He walks me into my bathroom, and grabs my hips, placing me on top of my counter. He holds my arm out, taking concern over my tattoo before his own. He unwraps the plastic around it, and I feel a little sting as the air hits the sensitive skin. I look at him, watching as he takes care of my tattoo like it's the most important thing in the world to him at this moment. My chest is warm at the sight, and I think of this, doing this with him, on the field, or off the field. Wrapping his wrists like I had the other day or taking care of him when he needs it before a game. I think of next year. I just think of him, and us, and this.

"What happens next year?" I hate asking.

I hate sounding desperate, but I shouldn't keep these thoughts to myself.

"What do you mean?" He grabs a washcloth from the counter and wets it under the faucet.

"With us, after all of this fake dating... and the sex, and everything else?"

"Um... I don't know. We don't have to speak if that's what you want. Or we can do whatever... Whatever is easiest for you."

It feels like the question makes him uncomfortable right away. He's hard to read sometimes. Right now is one of those times.

"What do you want?"

"Um... I don't want to not speak to you. I really like talking to you, and hanging out with you... I like being around you. Take away the sex part, and all the making out, and I think we might be really, really good friends... I don't know."

Instant relief washes over me, "I'd like that too. I feel the same."

"So we can be friends... After all of this, we can settle on friends."

I nod, knowing that's exactly what I want. I think not having Bellamy to be around every now and again would be hard for me. I've only ever genuinely spent time with him this week, and I love it far more than I thought I would. He's good company. He's a good person. Friends is a word that leaves a bitter taste in my mouth. Kissing him is fun. I'm sure sex would be even better. But friends is... It's fine.

"Good..." I agree, making it apparent to him that I'm on the same page.

But inwardly, it feels like I might not even be reading the same book.

I have no idea why either.

CHAPTER FIFTEEN

CEILINGS BY LIZZY MCALPINE

I RUN AS QUICKLY AS I CAN FROM THE FRONT OF MY apartment building, knowing Bellamy expects me to be upstairs half dressed. Not this time. Before he left my apartment last time I forced him into sharing his location with me, and I did the same, that way we could keep track for the next week or so. We'll be spending almost every second together but still. I watched his little avatar on my phone move closer to my apartment so I rushed, mostly because I knew where we were going tonight.

I run up to the car and grab the door, open it, and jump inside the beat up Jeep. Bell watches me from outside of the car, having just stepped out. He stares for a second, everything finally clicking in his head. He shakes his head, a grin on his lips.

He opens the car door on the driver's side and looks me up and down, and shakes his head once more, climbing back into the car. He's wearing black pants, and a yellow button up, partially unbuttoned with necklaces dangling on his chest. The sleeves of the shirt are tight and cuffed on his muscular arms. I watch as his hand moves forward, tilting my face up to look at him.

"My eyes are up here Ryn," He doesn't hesitate to use sarcasm and shows the ego that's always breaking through his surface.

He leans in, bringing my lips to his for a quick kiss before he backs away, and moves away from his parking spot, "You beat me to the car, that's a first."

"Why do you think I wanted your location?"

He scoffs, "I'm unsharing it then. I like coming upstairs to get you."

I'm the one grinning now, "Maybe it was a one time thing. We'll play it by ear."

I know just as well as he does how incredibly rare it is for me to be early. On time, yes. Early, not a chance. Sometimes, like today, I'm lucky.

We settle into the normal comfortable stance, and I pull my legs up, crisscrossing them in the passenger seat. My hair is in long waves down my back, pieces gently blowing around me from the circulating air that comes from the cracked windows. I look over at Bellamy as he places a hand on my thigh.

"You look absolutely stunning Kamryn," He speaks over the radio, and the wind but his voice carries over to me.

I'm wearing a dress once again. It's low cut and has buttons starting at my chest that go all the way down to the hem that rests right in the middle of my thighs. The dress is tight on my chest and flows out as it goes down. It's white with red flowers littering the entire thing. The compliment feels natural to me as it falls from his lips. Even so, it still makes my stomach do a million summersaults.

"Why thank you... I tried exceptionally hard to look this good today. You should be appreciative, but don't get used to it," I wag a finger at him, and he shakes his head, his eyes on the road now.

"I already am... You always look good," He says and I smile, sitting quietly next to him. "I'm serious. You always do. When you'd come into class you always had something like this on... Your hair was always nice... And on the field or court, you always look so pretty but in a subtle way. I was never there to see you, I was there to see a game, but I always caught myself looking at you. Always."

This confession is completely new to me. My heart is beating faster with every word, and I don't know if I like the feeling.

"And these dresses... It feels like you've been in them every chance you've gotten since this started. They drive me insane."

Heat dances up my chest, and claws up my throat, "Maybe it's on purpose."

He shakes his head instantly, "I know it isn't... If you knew the power you had when you wore these little dresses... You'd have used it all by now. I mean that."

I shut up right away, not caring to make any smart comments back. I don't know what's gotten into him tonight, but I feel a pit in my stomach at his honesty. His fingers swirl on the exposed skin of my thighs, and part of me regrets the dress choice tonight. It's getting me into danger because if he wants me, god knows I want him... I can't think of that right now, or the power he's claiming I have because it will go straight to my head. I decided right away to change the subject.

"Are you good at babysitting?"

He laughs instantly.

"Why do you ask?" He glances over at me, his hair

moving a bit, its soft nature making it lose its shape with the wind whipping through the car.

"Because I plan on having fun tonight... Too much fun equals a babysitter," I tell him.

"I can be a wonderful babysitter babe. Kind of hard to believe you'd even have to ask me how I'd feel about taking care of you."

My stomach drops once again as he squeezes my thigh. Once again I wonder what's gotten into him. A large wave of confidence seems to have settled somewhere inside his head. He's always been confident around me, but he's timid too... Maybe he's just realized how comfortable I am around him, and that's helped. Or maybe he's faking it. Whatever it is, I'm not going to complain.

Bellamy pulls into the karaoke bar, and I wait in the car after he parks, knowing he'll throw a fit if I don't let him open the door for me. He does and helps me from the car. I hop down in front of him, looking up at him, having more height now that I'm in platform Docs. He's still taller than me, looking down on me from where he stands. He takes my hand and spins me around, walking me forward. He lifts me up onto the curb and joins me on the sidewalk. We walk a bit down until we finally reach the front of the bar.

The minute we step through the doors, there's a pool of people, everyone seated around the place, a stage set up for the karaoke that should be starting any second now. Bellamy's hand connects to my lower back as he walks me in, and seats us at a table right next to the stage. He pulls my chair out for me, and sits right next to me, not across. He curls his arm around my leg, his hand on the inside of my leg close to my knee as he sits next to me.

"What do you want to drink?" His lips tickle my ear as he whispers.

"Tequila sunrise," I tell him, and he doesn't hesitate to get up, and go to the bar.

While he's away someone takes the stage, Hungry Like The Wolf plays over the loudspeakers. I laugh at the confidence, seeing how much fun the man is having on stage. Bellamy comes back, and everyone is cheering for the loud stranger. He's probably decently intoxicated, which is the only thing that is going to get me on that stage. I'm not an awful singer... But I chose sports medicine for a reason.

"I hope you know I will not be singing on that stage..." He whispers in my ear once again, and I laugh.

"I didn't think you would," I talk over the music, and he leans in closer.

"I do have a plan though... If you want free drinks. But you really have to go for it with me."

"I'd probably agree to almost anything if it meant free drinks," I admit.

"That's concerning."

I shrug with a smile on my lips. He leans back into his chair, spreading his legs, keeping his hand extended over my thigh. He still draws on my skin, back and forth in a comforting fashion.

A smirk rests on his lips, a drink in his hand too. He's not irresponsible. I'm sure he'll stop himself at one, just like I would if I was going to drive tonight. Good thing I'm not.

A few more people go on the stage, and I feel a leap of confidence push me forward. I leave Bellamy, and go to the MC, flipping through the books of karaoke tracks they have, deciding on a good one. I write down my name on the slip the MC gives me, and my song choice, and he takes it. I make my way back to Bellamy and wait for a few more songs before the MC calls my name over the loudspeaker.

"Get your acting chops ready," I say.

The list specifically says *Go to a karaoke bar where I sing horribly, but you watch, and look at me like I'm the best in the world*. He better stare at me the way I imagine or I'll sing all night long until he does.

"I could say the same for you."

I don't understand his statement, but I ignore it because it's my turn to take the stage. The backtrack to Wannabe by the Spice Girls starts, and I instantly put my entire heart and soul into this silly little song. Everyone in the crowd does exactly what they've done for everyone else, and starts clapping and joining in on the singing. I don't feel as nervous as I thought I would singing in front of all these people, especially considering just how mediocre I am at singing. I look down at Bellamy as soon as the chorus starts, and he looks at me like there truly isn't anyone else here, no distraction in his eyes. I hesitate the minute I see his stare.

"Keep going!" He motions with his hands and mouths the words to me so I do.

He crosses his arms over his chest, leaning back into the chair he sits in, looking as good as ever as he smiles at me. He really smiles, his lips curling around his teeth as he shakes his head, a laugh blooming from his chest.

He covers his face as I point at him, singing the words to the song, and I feel my chest warm up as he does. His smile is doing something to me that I can't tell if I like or not. I keep singing, wishing I might have picked another song because of this stupid rap, but glad Bellamy always under-stands the assignment when it comes to this list. He hasn't slipped up once.

I put the mic back on the stand as soon as the song ends, and I watch as Bellamy stands, clapping his hands. I start to move toward the lip of the stage to exit, but Bellamy surprises me, joining me on the stage. Confusion is an understatement. I look to the side at him, stepping back as he steps up to the mic, bending down to it considering I adjusted it for my height. He waves to everyone who has now gone silent.

"Um... Hello," He waves, and silence is still washed over the once loud bar. "This is my girlfriend Kamryn... I've been dating her for four years now... We're high school sweethearts... Give her a hand," He motions behind him toward me, and I have never been so confused in my life but I smile at the cheering from the crowd.

He just blatantly lied, and he looked really good while doing it.

"She's pretty, isn't she? Can I ask all of you for a moment with her... She loves karaoke, and she also loves me, and I love her, so I figured this would be the perfect place for this. Is that okay?" He asks, and I'm not only confused but instantly nervous.

Him saying it, saying he loved me did something to my stomach, and now my ears are ringing. All of this is some joke, he's playing everyone, but it sounded... The crowd cheers, and Bellamy pulls the mic from the stand and puts it behind his back so he can lean into me, his lips against my ear.

"What are you doing?" I whisper first and feel his lips curl into a smile.

"I told you to just go with it. You trust me don't you?"

"Always."

He backs away, completely shocking me as he gets on one knee right in front of me. I don't hesitate to cover my mouth with both of my hands, genuinely shocked at this moment. I know he's joking. Everything is clicking in my head. Fake proposal, free drinks. Bellamy Archer is not only hot, but he's also a fucking genius. Everyone around us is cheering and whistling now, excited as Bellamy brings the mic back to his lips, his eyes locked on mine.

"Kamryn Hart, you always know how to have fun, and to just go with it. You never back down from a challenge, and you really have put up with far too much of my shit already in what feels like the short time we've been dating," He winks at me, and I laugh, watching as he reaches into his pocket.

Confusion washes over me again when he really does pull out a ring, it's not an engagement ring obviously. But it is pretty, dainty, and small. The tiny jewel is an amber color, it almost looks like a cat eye.

"Will you marry me?" He asks, and I nod, pretending to be awestruck by him. Everyone screams, and Bellamy stands up, wrapping me in a hug that could probably win him an Oscar. What a performance.

"You have a fuck ton of explaining to do," I whisper in his ear as he hugs me, and I can feel a rumble of laughter as I'm pressed to his chest.

"I'm very aware," He slowly lets me slide away from him.

He leans down, kissing me softly, and we move from the stage. There's chatter throughout the entire place, and I can't help but notice all their eyes on us. He doesn't let his hand slide from my side as we get back to our table. The second we sit down a waiter approaches with two drinks.

"A couple at the bar sent these over."

I smile, taking the drink. *Absolute genius.*

"Thank you so much," I tell him, and I look at Bellamy who has a smirk on his lips.

The waiter walks away, and my jaw drops.

"Told you," He brings the drink to his lips, basking in

his master plan, and I drink my drink as well while also looking at my hand.

The ring is incredibly beautiful, but I can't shake the questions. Did he have this planned? Did he know he'd do this, or was he just going to give me the ring? Is it even meant for me? I have no idea...

Bellamy only has one, and I only have a few drinks, but plenty of water. The mixture of great singers, and tone deaf people who are trying their best is unique, but incredibly fun for us to watch. Part of me has a hard time focusing on the singing from the way he runs his fingers over my hand, my fingers, and my arms.

Bellamy seems to always be touching me, reminding me he's here, right next to me. It's incredibly comforting. I look over at his smiling face, feeling warmth crawl up my throat as he smiles in my direction. He's cute. There's just no other way to put it... But there's a duality, because the minute he's on the field, or removing his shirt, cute is the last word I would use.

"Are you ready to head out?" He leans over the table to ask me, and I look out of the tinted windows of the bar.

It's later now, and in perfect Washington fashion, I can hear a soft patter of rain on the tin ceiling of the karaoke bar. It doesn't sound harsh, but just enough to make our clothes damp, and our hair frizzy. I turn back, and nod. He takes my hand and we stand. Bellamy opens his wallet and leaves cash on the table which is very common from what I've noticed. Another thing I've noticed is just how much I loved being here with him. This night has been something different...

"It's raining," I exclaim even though we can both see the droplets hitting the windows.

He holds my hand now, walking me to the front of the bar.

"I guess I should have parked closer... I can pull around... Unless you don't mind the rain."

I smirk at him, raising my eyebrows. It seems he might have forgotten about the list altogether because that was a very big task on it. Though in so many ways, I'm not looking forward to it. To be rained on, to get soaked just for a kiss that could happen indoors... But I made the list, didn't I?

"I don't mind the rain," I lie to him, and he opens the door for me, revealing the rain drenched sidewalk outside of the crowded bar.

I've hated rain since before I could even remember. It used to upset me as a kid. The only good thing about rain is the romance, and I had never experienced that so it made me hate it even more. I'm not sure what it says about me that I hate the rain and live in one of the rainiest places, but I do. The street is empty of people but scattered with cars rushing past, eager to be somewhere else. Bellamy holds my hand, both of us still covered for the time being.

"Ready?" He asks, and I nod.

"Ready!" He pulls me, trying to move quickly, but I slip my hand from his.

He turns back from me as I stand on the sidewalk, if I'm going to be rained on, I'm going to do it right. I spin around, and I look at him again. For once, trying my best to not mind the rain, putting up with it. Liking the feeling of being stared at by him. I lift my hands up to the sky, and look up too, feeling the cold rain stick to my skin.

"Are you crazy?" He asks over the rain, raising his voice as it starts to rain harder.

"A little!"

He runs back to me and takes my arm. He hoists me up

and onto his back, and runs, both of us fully drenched now from the rain. He moves quickly down the sidewalk toward the beat up Jeep, and I laugh at the feeling of chaos but also comfort meshing in my chest. Bellamy slows down, and I jump from his body. He turns around, and reaches down, his hand connecting to my lower back to pull me into his gravity. Our chests crush together, and then he looks at me, taking me by surprise. When I expected his lips, I received his eyes, and my breath caught in my chest.

It feels better than I thought to be in the rain like this. To be feeling so many things in my chest, and my mind, and all over my body too. It feels like a movie. Like a cute scene I wrote about on a list I never wanted to complete. Thank god I am.

Bellamy has wet messy hair hanging over his forehead as he stares down at me, rain falling over him. His shirt clings to his body just like I do. Just like my dress to my body. My shoes are now filled with water, and puddles are forming around us. I might be imagining the feeling of his heart beating, but I swear I can feel it. Like it might come right out of his chest... It could be mine, but my head is far too cloudy to make sense of the harsh thrumming.

"I really want to kiss you right now."

Bellamy has kissed me plenty before this moment, but he's never told me outright like this. It's different. It feels like he needs to make it apparent, like he needs me to know that he wants me, and my touch, and my kiss. That he needs to feel my lips on his. I have no idea what my face reads, but I do know I've never felt the rush of warmth through my body that I do right now. Like a wave of fire running through my chest and my stomach. Like a rollercoaster, but... More.

"I really want you to kiss me right now, Bell," I feel like

my voice is hardly audible over the sound of rain around us.

He kisses me anyway. Part of me knows he would have either way, part of me knows he wanted to kiss me just that much, and part of me feels a need for this feeling. He kisses me, our lips slick with rain water but still clinging to each other like nothing else in the world is as important as this kiss.

Part of me wonders if that's true. That nothing could be as important... But I can't comprehend that, I can't think of this being something that is important to me... But it feels that way... It does, despite how short it feels. Despite that him pulling away is already leaving a heavy feeling in my chest. I want to tell him that. But I don't know how. I can't... So I let him open the door for me and I get in.

I realize then just how much I love the rain now.

He runs around the front of his car, and jumps in, both of us looking down at the wet clothes on our body. Our clothes cling to our bodies for dear life. I look at him, and he looks at me, and the tension shatters the minute the two of us start to laugh. Silence washes over us like the storm above us, and I feel the same heaviness return in my chest the minute the car pulls away and he starts driving home. I don't want to go, but I can't tell him I want to stay.

I pull my phone out and immediately text Sienna. I send an SOS and tell her to meet me at my apartment in thirty. I tuck my phone away, and fold my shaking hands in my lap, hoping more than anything he doesn't notice. I don't want to ruin this moment, or any of them... Honestly, I have no idea what's even gotten into me. I'm sure Sienna will talk some sense into me but for now...

"Are you alright?" Bellamy's voice is low, and I turn to look at him, forcing a smile on my lips.

"Why wouldn't I be?" The rain is hitting the top of the

Jeep harder.

"I don't know, you're just quiet... I just wanted to check..." He reaches out and takes my hand in his, and it takes everything in me to not jump at the touch, fearing he might feel the shaking in my hands.

"I'm cold," I lie, making an excuse for the shaking in my hands.

He lets go, and reaches forward, turning the heat on in the car. I feel warm air rush out, sitting well with the heat burning through my entire chest right now.

I watch out of the window, keeping my hands clasped together in my lap as I see the rain hit the window, my mind wandering back to the moments in the rain with him only a few minutes ago. My heart catches again, and I push the running images out of my head. It plays like a movie on the big screen through my mind despite how hard I try to stop it... It does feel like a movie, he feels like a movie. He feels perfect, and my brain immediately turns red at that thought, knowing it's not true. Perfection doesn't exist in people, and it doesn't exist in normal relationships.

Bellamy doesn't say anything, he doesn't touch me, he keeps one hand on the wheel, and the other on the gear shift between us, the only sound is the soft radio and rain. I partially watch him, and partially watch the road, waiting until my apartment comes into view, my eyes finally landing on comfort.

No matter what I see I feel the harsh burn that hasn't left my chest since the moment he kissed me. He turns to me as he parks on the street in front of my apartment. The rain hasn't stopped but it has settled. It's turned to a light drizzle. Not that it matters considering we're both incredibly drenched. I look over at him, and I smile as a goodbye, and he reaches forward, stopping my movements.

"I-" My words are cut short by another kiss, and I don't even think to fight it.

I welcome it, just like every other kiss he's initiated with me. Because his kiss hits like a drug that I could never recreate no matter how hard I tried. Because the violent thrashing of my heart when he kisses me is something I've never felt in my life, and I don't know if I fear it or cling to it but the skillful way he moves his lips. The way we kiss like we were meant to mesh this way... It's overwhelming. I break the kiss, and he opens his door first, running around the car to open mine despite the rain.

He helps me from his car, silence filling every space between us. Heaviness coats every part of my body as I step out of the car, and he stands in front of me, bringing his hand forward, and up to my face. He moves my wet hair to the side, and he holds me by my jaw, the tips of his fingers brushing the back of my neck. I look at him, feeling that same perfect feeling. He presses his lips together as he smiles and I do the same thing.

"Tomorrow night? My apartment?" He asks and I nod, still not saying anything. "It'll be a party. Wear something fun, and sparkly."

I furrow my brows, "Sparkly?" I ask.

"Just nod and smile."

I do, and he laughs, his chest rising and falling, and perfectly carved out under his wet shirt. I look down, and then back up, and he watches me do so. He brings his other hand up to my face, holding me the same on both sides now, his thumbs turning my jaw up so I'm looking straight at him. My vision blurs as he closes in on me again, kissing me once more. I lean into him, not wanting this feeling to ever disappear, but also searching for it, and questioning it all at once. He pushes back with his lips. My hands find his chest, the taut muscles underneath feeling warm against my chilled fingers.

I grip his shirt between my fists, pulling him closer to me, kissing him harder, and he presses his body to mine. I feel the cold metal of the Jeep behind me, digging into my back as he kisses me harder just like I want. His hand pressed to the Jeep right next to my head, his other hand still holding me. I snake my hand up the back of his neck and hold him tight to me until he feels the need to break from me. He takes a deep breath, and his eyes come into focus as I open mine. He's breathing hard, and I'm doing the same, but he has a different look on his face.

"You should probably head upstairs... "

I just stare at him. "Why?" I ask.

"Because if you don't go now, I'm not going to let you leave, ever..."

I feel warmth crash into my stomach, and throughout my entire body, and then I feel like I might throw up. I lean up and press the quickest kiss on his wet lips before I sneak around him and onto the curb. He stands on the street still, his eyes turning to me.

"See you tomorrow?" I peer up at him.

"See you tomorrow..." He speaks the words like a promise.

I turn away.

"Remember what I said!" He calls after me.

"Something sparkly!" I call back to him, and he grins at me as I walk away.

The farther I move away the more the heaviness returns, and the burning, and the confusion, and the questions. My brain feels like a puddle right now, and I can't begin to question why, not without Sienna.

CHAPTER SIXTEEN

LONELY BITCH BY BEA MILLER

I OPEN THE DOOR TO MY APARTMENT AND RUN MY hands through my wet hair, my heart rate has skyrocketed since I left Bellamy. I feel like my chest might explode, but I also don't know if that's a bad thing. It feels like there's no way this could be a good thing. Maybe I should go to the hospital because truly I think I might be having a heart attack. There's a knock on my door, and I open it without looking to see who it is. My best friend stands on the other side of the door, and I pull her inside and slam it closed, my pacing continuing.

"What is going on with you?" Sienna seems genuinely concerned for me.

I know I must look absolutely insane right now. But I can still smell him on me. The heavy smell of musk and vanilla. I smell the spice of his cologne all over me despite how subtle it is on him. I can't stop the squeezing in my chest.

"I think I'm having a heart attack," I feel warmth rushing all over my body despite the heavy wet clothes I wear.

I sigh and strip down from the dress into just a bra and underwear, and then I throw myself on the couch, reaching down to untie my shoes. I wouldn't normally completely undress myself in my living room with company in my presence but I physically cannot wear those clothes anymore. I can't have any remnants of him.

"Could you maybe explain why you think that? And also why you're butt naked now?" She follows me through my apartment.

"Because my chest hurts, and it's hot, and I'm sweating like a pig, and I feel like I might throw up too, or maybe not. I don't know," I kick my shoes off, peeling the socks off my feet. "And I'm soaking wet!"

I throw my socks on the ground and they splat on the hard floor. I lift off of the couch now, my pacing continuing.

"Calm down!" She walks forward to me. "Deep breath in, deep breath out."

We breathe together, and I stare at her, the feeling not subsiding from my chest.

"Not helping."

"Maybe explain what the hell happened and we can figure out what to do, alright?" She waves her hands in front of me, between the two of us.

She takes a seat on the couch in front of me, and my pacing starts once again in front of my coffee table.

"Okay, so we... Bellamy and I. We went on another date, and then he fake proposed to me, but he had a real ring. Not like a wedding ring but like a ring that fits me, and is for me. Well, that's the thing I don't actually know if it's for me, or if it's not for me. He didn't ask for it back though so I'm pretty sure it's for me. It's pretty though, look," I lean completely over the short coffee table, and shove my hand in her face as she sits on my couch.

"Pretty," She smiles, and I take my hand back, my feet moving before I can think of anything else.

I step over my wet clothes as I walk the same path back and forth, back and forth.

"After I got it, I was confused, right? Kind of overwhelmed and then I started to feel... I don't know... I just got all nervous, and weird, and then I really wanted to kiss him, because it was the only thing I could think about, and then he kissed me in the pouring rain, and that's on the list, but honestly, it didn't feel like he was kissing me because it was on the list. It felt like he was kissing me because I wanted him to, and he wanted to, and there was all this pressure in my chest, and I'm hot, right? Like, temperature wise, I'm so hot, and then he stops kissing me, and I hate that he stops kissing me, and then I get nervous again... and then I get quiet because I'm confused at why my chest feels so heavy and warm, and why it's burning and stuff, and then we get out of the car, and he kisses me again, and all the pressure is gone, and then I ran inside, and now I'm here, and I'm naked and confused... And the pressure is back too," I take a deep breath, finally getting air in.

"So you like Bellamy?" She asks.

"Of course I do. He's really cool and super sweet. That's not what I'm talking about. I feel like I'm going out of my mind. Or, like I said before, like I'm having a heart attack. Like I need medical attention right now. This isn't normal, it can't be normal," I start to fan myself.

"No... You like him like him. Like you want to date him and tell him you love him. You like Bellamy like a real girl-friend likes her real boyfriend," She sits up, leaning into me.

Then she gets the face that she gets when she's getting ideas.

"No. He's not my real boyfriend so that's not possible."

"Maybe he should be..."

I laugh, and then I wonder if she has lost her mind like I have.

"No..." I chuckle, shaking my head. "I told you to come over so you could talk sense into me, not so you could say things that aren't relevant or true."

"Just because you don't want something to be true doesn't mean it's not true," She shrugs her shoulders and then leans into the couch

"Sienna!" I throw my hands down, and she throws hers up in response.

"Okay fine! For argument's sake, let's say that's not true. You're just dick whipped then... And you really want him so you're frustrated or something. That's the only explanation I can think of."

I know that's not true so now my thoughts go back to the first reason she said. Do I like Bellamy really? I want him all the time, and I like spending time with him... He's hot. Extremely hot... And he's sweet, and he listens and...

And he's doing it all for the list.

So it makes sense. He's doing this to be the perfect boyfriend for the list, and only for that reason. So that must be why I feel the way I do. Because he's pretending to be exactly what I've wanted. But I'm tricking myself into liking him. All this fake bullshit is clouding my judgment. My heart is beating faster than it ever has.

"No, you're right. I do like Bellamy... But the minute I go back home to my parents it's going to be fine because none of this is real... Right? Those feelings will go away, they have to go away."

She presses her lips together and slowly nods at me.

"Um... Sure..." She isn't sure.

I know that, and I know she's agreeing with me for my

sake, not truth's sake... But I take it, and I throw myself down, my chest at rest now. I sigh, and Sienna looks at me as I sit next to her on my couch.

"Maybe you should put some clothes on..."

"That would probably be smart," I get up again and walk toward my bedroom. "Don't leave."

I go into my room. I reach for the drawers in front of my bed and pull out a t-shirt. I remove the wet bra from my body and pull the t-shirt over me. My phone starts vibrating behind me, and I look at it, and feel my heart drop. The pressure returns and my stomach feels like it's eating itself alive because of how uneasy it is.

"SIENNA!" I scream, and she runs into my room. "Bellamy is calling me, what should I do?" I ask her.

"Answer?"

I scoff at her response.

"You say it like it's easy! How do I act?" I ask.

"Normally? If that's even possible for you."

I roll my eyes at her sarcasm, and she approaches me.

"Maybe I shouldn't answer."

She reaches forward, sliding the phone open before I can react. I gasp and then shut up right away. The phone sits between both of us, answered now. She presses the speaker button, and I sit silently, wishing she would cease to exist. I reach to my side, and grab the stuffed golden retriever, hugging the plush to my chest.

"Hello?" Bell's deep voice rings out on the other end.

I don't say anything, and Sienna swats at me, pushing me to speak.

"Hi!" I manage to squeak out, genuinely sounding like a chew toy at this point.

"Are you alright?" He's got a hint of laughter in his voice.

THE LIST OF THINGS.

"Yep, fine and dandy," I sound like I'm faking it.

He's going to read me like a book.

"Everything just seemed different after we left the bar. I just wanted to make sure everything was okay..." He has charm, and care in his voice, and I bite my lip.

"Everything is fine. I feel fine... Are you fine?" I wonder what's going on in his head.

I know I'll never know, but I want to.

"More than fine. I had a really good time. I always do. I guess I'm just scared to do too much... To scare you off, and I don't want to overstep any boundaries with you... I'm just being careful," He continues to show the respectful side of him.

He never ceases to show me that which only adds to the burning in my chest.

"You don't have to be..." I tell him. "You don't have to be careful with me. Everything is fine," I promise although everything is absolutely not fine.

I am super not fine. I have every chance to let him do as he pleases. He pushes boundaries with me, and I let him, and I could stop it, but the thought makes me shake. I don't want to stop him one bit.

Sienna narrows her eyes at my lies. She just shakes her head, and puts her hands over her face, slowly dragging them down.

"As long as you say so... You'd tell me if something was wrong?"

Sienna nods her head at me, and I squeeze my eyes shut. He cannot know about any of this. The strings being left out of this was my one rule, and I'm the dumbass that is seemingly breaking that stupid fucking rule. I'm a puppeteer right now, desperately trying to attach every single string possible because I'm an idiot.

"Yep," I want to tell the truth but I know that it won't go over well.

"Good... Are you still wet?"

I choke on the air in my lungs as if it wasn't meant to be there.

"Pardon?" I ask.

"Your clothes... The rain... are you still-"

"Oh, right, the rain... Not the kiss. I get it," I nod, understanding he wasn't bringing up the feeling I had when he kissed me.

Sienna facepalms, and I shrug my shoulders, this conversation is already a shit show...

"No. I'm dry now. Fully dry."

"Good. I don't want you to get sick."

There's a small pause, and I hate the silence.

"Well, I've got some setting up to do... I'll see you tomorrow. Have a good night Ryn."

I nod even though he can't see me, "You too Bell."

He hangs up, and I groan, throwing myself face first onto my bed until I slide off, and fall to the floor, my back on the ground, my eyes trained on the ceiling. Fuck my life.

"You're down bad for him."

I can't even see her but I know she's right. She's also probably grinning from ear to ear.

"It's because you mentioned the hands. I have full faith that if I never looked at them I'd be fine," I know full and well Bellamy's hands are only a fraction of what I like about him.

"It has nothing to do with his hands, and everything to do with his dick-"

"Sienna!" I yell at her. "Stop talking about me, what about you? What about Lawson? How is he? How are you?

Are you two dating? Let's watch a movie, let's not talk about Bellamy's dick," I tell her.

"Rom com?"

I shake my head for once. I know how out of character it is for me. I know it's always a yes when it comes to romance, but right now it's the last thing I want, and probably need.

"No. Let's watch horror. Comedy. Drama. Anything that doesn't involve hot men, and feelings because I have enough to go around," I watch as she jumps onto my bed over me as I lay on the floor.

She peeks over the edge of the bed, "Alright, are you coming then?"

She holds her hand out to me and I take it. I climb into bed with my best friend, and she uses my remote to scroll through Netflix, but my mind keeps going back to the cute football player with hot hands, sloppy hair, and so much charm, and I know I'm completely fucked.

"And by the way... I have no updates on Lawson because we aren't together. We're acquaintances," She sighs.

"Why do you sound disappointed?" I ask and she shrugs.

"Because I honestly have no idea if I should be disappointed by that fact or if I should be jumping for joy over it. Lawson is bad news, football players suck," She explains.

"But what about the quarterback hands thing?" I ask, referring back to her exact words.

"Lawson isn't a quarterback. He's a... It doesn't matter. Lawson and I are... friends. I guess," She doesn't look at me.

I'm desperate to know more about what's happened between the two of them. To know if she actually wants to be his friend or if maybe she has a small crush. I have a sneaking suspicion it's the latter.

"You know just because I'm having boy troubles doesn't mean I can't listen to yours. What's going on between you and Lawson?" I finally ask the question and Sienna shakes her head.

"I would tell you if I had an answer but I don't. So I don't want to talk about it. I know you want to know but there's... There's nothing to know," She shrugs, and I know it's not true, but I've been through this with Sienna before.

When it's nothing to her it's nothing, but the minute it's truly worth talking about she'll spill it all. I know whatever is going on must be complicated. Oddly enough, I find comfort in knowing my best friend has boy problems just like I do, even if she won't admit to that out loud.

CHAPTER SEVENTEEN

I THINK HE KNOWS BY TAYLOR SWIFT

I THROW THINGS FROM MY CLOSET LIKE A MAD WOMAN, looking for a specific top that's in my mind, but for some reason, nowhere to be found in my apartment. I dig through the clothes that are scattered around and groan loudly to the point of possibly shaking the walls of the entire building. It has to be here somewhere.

"Kam, you have literally thrown around about fifty things you could wear, just pick something else!" Sienna is in the other room, but her voice carries into the closet.

"He said sparkly! The shirt I'm looking for is sparkly!" I think about Bellamy and feel the bottom of my stomach heat up.

He controls my emotions and he's not even in the same building as I am. He's not even within a mile radius of me.

"Okay, well, I promise it's not that important... Here. This will fit the theme," Sienna walks into my closet with a hot pink dress in her hands, and I turn away, almost throwing up in my mouth at the sight of it.

That isn't my color.

"No. I don't wear hot pink for a reason, it makes me look gross."

She puts the dress down, raising her eyebrows.

"So why do you own it?" She asks, her arms cross over her chest.

"Because I bought it thinking it would be cute, and then realized it makes me look gross... I know I have this shirt, it's just- AHA!"

Sienna holds her ear that's closest to me, and I hold the shirt I'd been searching for. "Found it," I smile through my words.

Sienna glares at me.

"I can see that," Her voice radiates annoyance.

I walk out of the closet, and into my bedroom, my hands greedily reaching for the black leather pants I had already set out for myself.

I strip down to just my underwear and pull on the black pants that stick to my skin. I fasten the chain metal shirt to my body, the diamonds attached to the metal, making it shimmer. The material is cold on my bare skin. I turn around, throwing my hair over my shoulder to look at the outfit on my body. It looks good. I look good. Sienna did my makeup, a dark cat eye, and I did my hair in loose curls before I got dressed. Now all I need is shoes, so I pick up my heeled black boots. We have a winner.

"Okay, I'm ready!" I stand up after putting the shoes on, and Sienna is lying across my bed, her outfit, hair, and makeup already done.

She's always more minimal than I am but always looks better than me.

Her makeup is gorgeous and perfectly done. She's in a tight fitting black dress that hugs her curvy body, and fish-nets with diamonds and rhinestones meshed into them.

She's wearing a pair of boots that complete the look. Her legs look absolutely perfect, but her body always looks good. She walks out of my room, and I follow. Both of us head to the door.

"Thank god," She turns over her shoulder as we walk out. "You look hot, he's definitely sleeping with you tonight if he hasn't already."

I shake my head as we walk down the hallway of my apartment building.

"The list says romantic first time. Though we've both already had sex, it will be our first time... Either way, he won't do it after a party, that wouldn't be romantic... Unless he has something super special planned."

I doubt he'd do it tonight. We still have plenty of time until I go home, despite how badly I want him. I have a strong feeling he's going to make me wait.

"There's nothing more romantic than being so attracted to someone you can't wait to jump their bones," Sienna isn't normally the type to speak on this, and I can't help but think of her and Lawson, wondering if she's speaking from experience...

She's not wrong, Bellamy is definitely attractive enough. I know that for a fact. Spontaneity is more my style, and not his. Either way, things that happen outside of the list only complicate things more. So maybe I'm fine with waiting too if it means we stick to the rules better. If I stick to the rules better.

"I don't know. I guess we'll see what happens. If I have to wait, then I'll wait," I smile lightly.

"God you like him more than I thought you did."

We walk from my apartment now and toward her car.

"I do not. It's like a little crush. He's just really hot."

"No, because you are always quick to have sex with

someone, and there's nothing wrong with that, not at all. You just don't seem to be rushing it with Bellamy, because it's not important to you with him. It's just different from all the other guys you've talked to."

The point she's making is prominent and poking me, and I don't like it. I do think about sex with Bellamy very often. But I also get nervous and excited about other things that have nothing to do with sex. That is a first for me.

"It is different because if I talk to other guys the intention is to get them in bed, I had no intentions with Bell at all until he made me do this list."

She shrugs, "Whatever you say."

I know she doesn't actually agree with me, but I ignore that, and we get into her car, Fashionably late of course. We drive and jam out the entire way. I call it my version of pregaming... Pumping myself up for the party. At least I'm assuming that's what's happening. He once again hasn't told me a thing. Sienna knows of course, and she hasn't denied my words when I've said party tonight. Everyone involved knows. At least I got a dress code this time, that's simply all I could have asked for.

Sienna looks somewhat nervous, her hands anxiously gripping the steering wheel. The look on her face too. I know Sienna. I know just last night she told me she had nothing to say about Lawson, but my boy senses are tingling. If she's being her normal self, she's thinking about him right now just like she was on our way to the last party we attended together. The party she suspiciously disappeared from at the same time as Lawson. She is my best friend. I never pry, I hate it and she does too, but maybe if I ask just one more time she'll give me at least an inch.

"Lawson is going to be here tonight. How is he?" I keep my voice casual.

"Hot, and available. Just like a pizza."

I laugh, still having no answer, "So you and him are just-"

"Friends," She cuts me off.

Her answer is far too quick and short. Normally I'd push this off as irritability, but she looks at me from the side, checking to see if I believe her. That's her telltale sign.

Lies. She is so lying to me right now.

"Sienna Cole. You're a lot of things, but you're not a liar," I raise my eyebrows at her, and she sighs.

"We're complicated friends," She admits. "Who might have slept together."

I swear I suck every ounce of air out of the car with how hard I gasp.

"Since when!" My voice vibrates off of the walls of the car.

"Since Leah's party last week. Don't ask. I don't want to talk about it. We're friends. That's it," Her voice is final, and I know better than to nag her anymore about it.

"At least tell me if it was good," I eye her, watching her lips turn up into a smirk.

"He has a nice penis if that's what you're asking."

I have never heard Sienna talk about her sex life, not once, and it's shocking, but I need more.

"It's not about the size of the boat, it's about the motion of the ocean, can he fuck or not?" I am practically in her lap over the center console.

"Oh my god, you are so gross. Yes, he was the best I've had, now sit down before you get us in an accident," She pushes my shoulder back, and I bounce in the car seat, practically giddy over this newfound information.

"One more question," I break the silence, and she groans.

"Kam! I can't talk about it anymore. I don't know what's happening between us, but it's not anything serious. Which is for the better. The minute I'm sure of anything will be the minute I spill it all, but until then-"

"Just tell me if you're going to sleep with him again. Word on campus is he doesn't sleep with the same girl twice," I cut her off and she sighs.

"No, never again. Not by his choice, by mine," She explains and my jaw is on the floor.

"So you're telling me, Lawson Bennet. Mr. Hot and Available asked to sleep with you again and you said no? Do you have a vagina made of pure gold? Did you hypnotize him? Sienna, you're like a sex goddess!" I'm practically shrieking, and she shakes her head.

"I don't know what he's thinking. I don't care to know. We're just friends," She sounds matter of fact. "Stop smirking, and stop asking questions about Lawson," She urges, and I cannot stop smirking even if she wants me to. I got enough information to suffice for now.

That doesn't mean I'll ever stop prying or trying to get her to have sex with Lawson again. He's hot, and she's hotter. They'd be unstoppable together.

Once Sienna pulls up to the boys' apartment complex the two of us make our way through the building, and to their front door. I can already hear music on the other side. I look at Sienna, and she smiles, opening the door. There are plenty of people crammed inside the apartment, and I scan the groups of people, my eyes inevitably finding Bellamy, who's already found me. He's moving toward me before I've fully made it through the door. Sienna is moving away, probably to find Lawson or a drink. Bellamy wraps his empty hand around me, snaking it around my lower back.

He squeezes me tight, and I hug him back, pulling away so I can look at him.

"A party?"

"Not a normal party," He turns me toward everything and everyone.

They're all wearing nicer clothes, sparkly dresses, and heels. Everyone also has tacky New Year's Eve gear, all probably from the past New Year's that happened months ago.

There are decorations and balloons, and on the TV I even spot a rerun of the ball drop from this past year, playing for everyone. I look at Bellamy, almost in shock at the effort he's put into this. I'm not sure why I'm surprised. He's gone above and beyond for every single thing we've done, but this is just... It's perfect.

"Bell..." I turn back, looking at everything again.

He threw a party for me... He sent out a dress code. He did it all for me, and my heart is turning to mush. This is not helping me and the butterflies in my chest.

"Happy New Year's Eve Ryn," He leans down, his hand holding onto my hip as he stands behind me.

He tilts his head around me, and kisses my cheek, making me laugh, "Do you want a drink?"

"Always."

We both walk to his kitchen. My stomach gets hot thinking about the last time I was in this kitchen.

Our first kiss.

I shake my head, and he reaches into his fridge, getting me a seltzer. He opens it for me and passes it over. He stands in front of me and pats the counter, the one I'd sat on before. I use one hand to push myself up on the countertop, and he stands in front of me, his eyes locked on me.

"You look really good tonight Ryn," He takes a sip of his drink.

"So do you..." I tell him, my eyes focusing on the black short sleeve button up he wears.

It's left partially open, showing off his chest as usual. He wears black pants that fit his legs well, and Converse like always. His fingers are clad with rings like they always are, and his hair is a perfect mess. I take his hand that rests by his side, and I pull him forward, closer to me. He stands between my legs now as I sit on the counter. I set my drink down, and dangle my arms over his shoulders, and around the back of his neck.

"Did I do good?" He asks and I smile with closed lips, his hazy grin showing me he already knows he did good, he just wants me to say it.

"You did amazing... You're the best fake boyfriend I could ask for."

He laughs, his eyes diverting from me as he takes a sip of his drink.

"And you're the best fake girlfriend I could ask for," He speaks casually.

My eyes catch in the corner of the room. I see Leah standing there, surrounded by her cheerleader friends. Her eyes are on me until she sees me looking at her. She looks away quickly, pretending she wasn't staring. My stomach sinks at the sight of her. Questions ripping through my brain.

"Why is she here?"

He whips his head around, looking over his shoulder quickly as if he doesn't know who I'm talking about.

"I'm not really sure. Why? Are you jealous?" He's joking so I laugh despite the anger burning in my chest.

I personally don't find anything about his ex funny

besides her fantasies and make believe she's created in her head.

"Not in the slightest. She's just got daggers in her eyes. She's staring at me."

He leans in closer to me. The uneasy feeling in my stomach isn't one I feel like sharing. He's told me before he's not using me to make her jealous. He's said it, and I should believe him, right?

"Let her," He whispers and kisses me. His lips are warm, he's warm.

Always, and I know he was trying to make me feel better but the thought of her here leaves my stomach sinking.

Bellamy has never given me a reason as to why he wanted to fake date me. Not a legitimate one anyway. Part of me wonders if maybe it was all a scheme to make her jealous despite what he said before. He seems to have no interest in her, but that one side of me never knows.

The voice in the back of my head tells me that even if he did do this to make her jealous that I have no right to be mad about that. Even though the thought of me being used without my knowledge does make me feel sick. But this is fake after all. I look at him, unhooking my arms from around him, and he starts to back away, but I lock my legs around the back of his, keeping him with me.

"Not so fast. I have a question for you."

He raises his eyebrows, "Shoot."

He nods toward me.

"This..." I hold up my hand, pointing at the ring that I still haven't taken off.

"Do you like it?"

I hesitate, "Of course I like it, but I guess I'm just confused... How did this fake proposal of yours have a real ring?" I wiggle my fingers in front of him and take a look at the ring again.

As if I haven't been staring at it for the past 24 hours like a crazy person.

"I was buying something for my sister. She graduated high school, and she's trying out for the cheer team here in a few weeks. I got her a present, and I saw that when I was there. It reminded me of your eyes, and I like giving gifts. I was going to just give it to you last night but I saw an opportunity so I took it, that's all."

It reminded him of my eyes. My heart can't handle this type of knowledge. It's not what I was built for.

"Bell, I really don't need expensive gifts."

He nods with a smirk on his lips.

"I'm aware. You don't need anything from me, and that makes me want to get you things even more because you never expect them. It's cute when you're surprised."

I shove his chest back lightly.

"You're annoying," I tell him.

It's more than annoying, it's infuriating that he wants to buy me things, and that I secretly like it.

His dimple is carved deep into his cheek as he smiles at me. That dimple makes me forget anything going through my head.

"Someone has to be," He shrugs his shoulders softly.

The unsettled feeling leaves my chest altogether. I look around us, and I look back at him. Then my ring out of the corner of my eye. It reminded him of my eyes. I shake my head and fight the urge to smile.

"I need to find Sienna really quick... But I'll be right back," I start to wiggle myself off of the counter, and he runs his hands up my thighs slowly, holding onto me.

"Don't rush babe. Have fun... Just make sure you find me before midnight," He helps me down from the counter.

I start to turn away from him, but he keeps hold of me by my hip, his fingers burning into my skin.

"Hey..." He nods his head, and my eyes land on him. "I don't get a kiss?"

I press against him, my lips brushing his. I kiss him, and he squeezes my hip once we break. He lets me go, and we separate. My eyes scan the party for Sienna, every turn I make I notice something new that he's decorated the place with. He really went all out with these decorations.

I managed to find Sienna in the dimly lit hallway that leads to the bathroom... Making out with Lawson. "Friends" my ass. I prominently vacated the area, and they yelled their apologies. I found myself elsewhere, socializing, and chatting with everyone. I talked to Griff a lot and realized just how much I liked him.

He seems to be an incredibly good friend to Bellamy. Griff is also leaving halfway through summer so he can start his training for the Raiders. He'll be living a Las Vegas lifestyle. Talking with him is easy, and it's fun. I barely realized how much time had passed. I had left him to see if Sienna had returned but I found Jade, Griff's girlfriend instead.

"Kamryn! How are you?" She wraps me in a hug.

She is a bit more under the influence than I've seen her in the past. She's wearing a tight fitting sparkly black dress that hugs her just right. I hug her back, and she looks at me.

"You look incredible... Oh my god, Bellamy, and you together too. Such a good couple," She yells over the music, and I can feel my cheeks heat up.

I don't know why I blush at her words but I do. Jade's definitely more loose with her thoughts now, and she knows we're not together. Part of me wonders if his friends are truly rooting for something more, the thought makes my stomach turn.

"Says you! You and Griff are practically perfect."

She swats her hand, "Oh stop."

She carries her drink close to her chest as we talk.

"He just talked to me about the Raiders. He seems so excited. But how does it make you feel? Him moving and stuff?" I ask her.

"It makes me feel happy. I'm going with him."

I raise my eyebrows. I don't know why the thought shocks me. Maybe it's just hard for me to think about moving for someone else... To be with someone else.

"Why? I mean I know you're dating him, but is there anything there for you?" I ask.

I know I might be projecting. I just can't wrap my head around it.

"There's always something for me anywhere I go. The school I'm going to now, Kirkland, it's just mediocre to me. I think transferring will be a breath of fresh air. It's not every day that your boyfriend gets drafted by the NFL either. I think it will only be exciting."

I can feel the excitement radiating off of her. She smiles wide too. A genuine smile, one I know is true. I smile at her, happy for her. Good. I'm glad she and Griff are as happy as they are.

Part of me feels a bit weird about the two of them not being here. I've gone to all the games. I've seen him and Bellamy play hand and hand. There's no Bellamy without Griff on the field, and vice versa. I wonder how Bellamy feels about that. I wonder why we've never really talked about it before. From the rumors I've heard there's a new Wide Receiver stepping up. One of the soon to be juniors. I've seen him step in a time or two at the games. Parker Thompson. He has promise, but he's not best friends with Bellamy. The two of them have to work together perfectly next year, and...

"Oh my god, Kamryn is that you? And Jade too?" I turn over my shoulder to look at the person speaking and to my shock, it's Leah.

Someone I never expected to be so cheery when talking to me. Maybe she's trying her best to give me a chance. Or maybe it's all fake. I tread lightly as I look down at her, her body only a bit shorter than mine.

"Wow, what a surprise. Hi Leah," I force myself to shoot her a smile.

"You clean up well, don't yah?" Her eyes are looking down at me, venom already dripping from her words.

"I could say the same for you," I tilt my head, pushing out another smile, feeling the animosity radiate from her body.

Leah has short dirty blonde hair. It's in a perfect sleek cut and she has a cute button nose. I hate that it's cute. She's cute, short, and sweet looking. The picture perfect cheer-leader, with the picture perfect body. She's wearing hot pink. I feel extremely grateful I didn't wear that pink dress Sienna suggested right now. We look nothing alike. We radiate opposite energy, and I think back once again. I wonder what Bellamy wants from me in the first place if this is his type and not me.

"So... How are you and Griff?" Leah asks Jade who stands by me.

You can read Jade's features well, as she doesn't hide anything. She looks annoyed and incredibly confused. I have no idea if it's because of the alcohol she's consumed, or if she's always straightforward like this. I'm sure Griff has told her about the drama between Leah, and Bellamy thus far. From the looks of it, Jade isn't her biggest fan.

"Perfect. How are you and... Oh, wait," Jade raises her eyebrows and tilts her head.

My lips part at the comment, creating a perfect O, signifying my shock. *I want to be Jade when I grow up.*

"And what about you?" Leah has turned her attention to me now, and I tilt my head to her, wiping the shocked look off of my face.

She ignored Jade completely, she never cared about what she had to say in the first place.

"You and Bell seem cozy. Are you just fucking. Dating?" She shrugs her shoulders, her voice sharp as a knife. The fake friendliness has left her entirely now. "I probably already know considering..." She lets her voice trail off but doesn't let her eyes leave me.

"Wouldn't you like to know?" I'm amused at her anger. "We are dating... Temporarily."

I don't lie, knowing it might get under her skin if she doesn't really know or understand this arrangement between Bellamy and me.

"What does that even mean?" Her annoyance is so vivid it's like a rainbow.

"I don't know, why do you care?" I ask.

I can see Jade beside us, her face turning back and forth as if she's watching an intense game of tennis.

"Because he and I weren't finished... You interjected yourself where you didn't belong, and I think that's incredibly below you. Or maybe it isn't considering your track record with men. You fuck them, and they use you up, then you move on. Isn't that right?"

I just look at her, wondering what that was supposed to hurt... My ego? My feelings? I open my mouth to say something, but my vision is cut off as someone steps in front of me.

I look up and see Bellamy. I step to the side, peering around him, smirking at the sight, knowing just how mad it's going to make her. There's no reason for me to care this much, but I do. I look at her, seeing her face soften only a little bit as she looks at Bellamy. She still looks incredibly angry. He's the weakness here, not just for her, but for me too. We both stare at him now.

"What was that you just said?"

She hesitates to answer Bellamy, "We were just talking."

Bellamy shakes his head to her answer, "What did you just say to her, Leah?"

I don't think I've ever heard Bellamy sound so serious.

"I said it doesn't seem to be below her to steal someone away from another girl considering her track record," She speaks confidently, and I know just how stupid that was. "And I'm not wrong either. She's slept with half of your teammates and then moved on days later. Does that not bother you?" She asks him, airing out my dirty laundry to all the people around her.

It's not uncommon to know who I've slept with. Even so, I still feel the sting of embarrassment as Bellamy hears all of it. He's known all of this, but it still feels invasive talking about it like this. It hurts knowing most of these people could be judging me. It makes it even worse thinking of Bellamy's possible judgments too. Or Jade. Or any of Bellamy's friends.

"Actually, I've only slept with three football players," I tell her, and Bellamy looks back at me. "Soon to be four hopefully."

She freezes, her eyes in a glare. I didn't think about it

before I said it. I don't even know it to be fully true after what she's doing right now. He may want nothing to do with me.

"She doesn't deserve you Bellamy, and-"

"I think it's my choice... Do you think you deserve me? Talking about someone I care about the way you are? Do you think it's going to change my mind about our breakup?" He asks, and I am frozen in place.

This is for the list... *Right?*

"Isn't it a little trashy to sleep with that many people? And to be so open about it?" She looks at Bellamy for approval, and that makes my anxiety shoot up at the thought of him giving it to her.

She's forcing me to be open about it, considering this attack.

"Don't talk about my girlfriend that way."

I fight the urge to let my jaw drop. Sienna doesn't. Her jaw is on the floor, and her eyes go wide. She smirks at me right away.

"It's trashy to-" Leah can't start before Bellamy is cutting her off again.

"Isn't it a little trashy to be acting like this in a room full of people? And to shame someone else for having sex with whoever the fuck they want? I don't know but it seems to be the only trashy person in this situation is you, Leah. This isn't you. It's below you actually. We both know that," He says, and her face changes. "You don't have to like me anymore, you don't have to like her or her friends. You don't have to like that we're together, but we are. Either get over it or get out of my apartment."

I swear all the air in the room is gone because I cannot breathe. Fuck, why am I turned on by this? It was on the list... I put it on there for a reason. Did he set this up? Is that why he's defending me right now?

"Don't come crying to me when she gives you a disease or something."

My jaw drops, and my heart does the same.

"From what I've heard she's already caught plenty," Leah looks at me.

Her insults have never hurt me. No one's have. But my heart is in my throat right now, and I don't know why that hit the way it did.

"Bitch, I know you did not just say that," I see Jade step up to the plate.

"He might not be able to hit you but I can, bitch!" Sienna stands behind Jade in my defense, and I feel a bit of warmth at the army that comes to my rescue.

All of them know that I could defend myself on my own, but the feeling inside of my chest seeing them do it anyway is unmatched.

"Maybe you should just go," Griff breaks between the two girls, and steps in front of Bell too. "Did you drink?"

She shakes her head.

"I'll walk you to your car, make sure you get out safely. But don't come back. And maybe realize that if you care about him as much as you claim to then you should let him be happy," He turns Leah around.

He's a good guy. A better person than I am by all means. Right now I'm too stunned to speak. She really just said that in front of everyone.

"We should jump her," Sienna breaks the silence, and Jade nods.

"I'm in," She agrees.

"Leave her alone. She embarrassed herself enough," My

words are drowned out by my own thoughts the minute Bellamy walks away from all of us.

I furrow my brows and look at the girls. They both shrug, not knowing what's gotten into him either.

I follow him, every feeling in my chest being pushed away. I walk right behind him, practically stepping on him to try and catch up. He makes his way into the hallway bathroom, and I put my hand on the door, stopping it.

"Are you going to pee or is there something wrong?"

He just stares at me, "Just give me a second." He speaks in the same serious tone he spoke to Leah in, his anger incredibly obvious.

"No, talk to me," I insist.

"I just need a second."

I narrow my eyes at him. He sighs heavily and pulls me into the bathroom. He closes the door and locks it behind him. I open my mouth to ask him again and he stops me in my tracks completely.

He kisses me. Hard. His lips capture mine, his hands greedy to grab my hips. My back slams to the wall as he kisses me and I lose every bit of breath in my lungs at the kiss. His hands slide down my body and under my ass. He grips the bottom of my thighs and lifts me onto the bathroom counter. *Where the hell did this come from?*

His lips press into me harder. My stomach is on fire, my face hot too, and every inch of my body feels like a forest fire as all of the heat spreads. He moves his hands up my body slowly, his lips still skillfully moving against mine. He slips his tongue into my mouth, caressing my own as he deepens the kiss, his fingers moving around the back of my neck, and his hand threading through my hair. He tugs on my hair, my head snapping back to expose my neck. I gasp at the pull, and he moves his lips down my jaw, and onto my neck, greedy with the way they move, and despite just how bad I want this to continue, I still have no answer as to where it came from.

"Bell..." I breathe out, and his breath catches as he begins to suck, and nip at the sensitive skin on my neck. "Bell... Bellamy," I force his name out of my mouth, and softly push his chest, stopping him.

He takes a second, his eyes set on me, his chest moving up and down rapidly as he tries to catch his breath.

"What's wrong? Why are you... I mean, you can kiss me anytime, but what's... What happened? Why are you..." I don't know how to make sense of what I'm trying to ask him, and he just shakes his head.

"Because it makes me so fucking mad, Kamryn," He uses my full name and I watch as he steps away from me, and out from between my legs.

I watch as he turns around, and runs his hands through his messy hair.

"You're one of the coolest people I've ever met... And you're so fucking pretty, and you can be a sarcastic asshole, but you're also really nice, and the fact that she can be so mean to you over something as stupid as who you've slept with just makes me so mad," He doesn't look at me as he rants.

"So you... Kissed me because you were mad?" I try to make sense of it but still feel confused.

"No, I kissed you because I was afraid you'd be upset and I came in here to cool off, and then you followed me. Then I was afraid you'd think I didn't want you anymore because of what she said. So that's why I kissed you. I guess I could have just told you. I just..." He rubs his hand up and down on the back of his neck. His cheeks are pink with blush.

I hold the counter between my legs, my body tilted toward him.

"So what you're saying is you want me..." I look at him with a soft smirk on my lips.

It's barely noticeable. I'm not even trying to smile, I just can't help it. He's angry over something silly. Leah is not important to me. Her words hurt. I can't lie and say they didn't. But I'm not giving them that power. Not right now. Right now I'm over it.

"Yes, I want you. I really want you Kamryn, I have fought so many urges around you so I can make it special like the list says, but god you make it so fucking hard sometimes. I do want you. I don't think I've wanted anyone more than I want you."

My stomach is plummeting and there's butterflies, fire, and everything. Excitement buzzes in my chest. Need blooms in my belly as I look at him.

"Right now?" I ask.

"Right now, tomorrow, yesterday, every day. Yes. Right now I want you, the other day I wanted you. The day I kissed you for the first time I wanted you Kamryn," He's looking at me.

His stare is intense, and I don't know what to do right now.

Normal Kamryn would fuck him in the bathroom without hesitation. But I did say I wanted something special. Something romantic. There's absolutely nothing romantic about fucking in a bathroom with a party going on right outside the door. But there is a touch of me in that. It's not completely unappealing.

"How do you want me?" I ask and watch as his eyes darken.

He looks at me carefully, his hand pressing to the bathroom counter beside me, his other hand coming up to my face. He moves my hair away and then he holds my head, tilting my chin up toward him.

"I want you in every way. I want to taste you. I want to feel you. I want to fuck you Kamryn. So bad. Is that what you want to hear? Do you want me to lay it out? Then I will. I've never wanted to fuck someone like I want to fuck you. I've never wanted... Needed something this bad."

I have never felt such a hot, searing warmth inside of my chest, and between my legs... So... Fuck it.

I kiss him first this time, wrapping my legs around his so he's pressed tight to my body. His hand is flat against my back, his skin hot just like mine. He straightens me, pushing my body upright so I can kiss him better, and I take every ounce of help, kissing him hard.

I push off of the counter, and he moves with me, my height making it hard for him. He doesn't hesitate to lean down just so he can keep his lips on mine. I move back toward the bathroom door, and his body meets me there, my back hitting the door, and his chest colliding with mine. I know the door just shook, and whoever is on the other side must know what's going on but I have never cared less.

"This is a bad idea..." He speaks between kisses, and I don't listen to him, knowing he has far more sense than I do.

Because right now my mind is telling me to do whatever the fuck I want. No matter the consequences.

Bellamy can think critically all he wants, but he can do that when his lips aren't on mine. He says it's a bad idea. His words say one thing. But the way he doesn't stop kissing me. The way his hands haven't stopped exploring. That's louder than his words.

There's a loud knock on the door, and I feel it shake behind me. Our lips part only centimeters, I can feel his breath fanning over me, and his chest rising and falling against mine. His crystalline eyes lock on me. They look at my lips, then my eyes, but settle on my lips and I feel like I'm completely helpless when it comes to Bellamy tonight.

"What?" My eyes are still on his, and our lips are still inches from mine despite my question.

He presses a finger to his smirking lips, and my lips curl up too.

"Um... It's almost midnight," I hear Sienna on the other side of the door.

I know it's her too because I have serious doubts anyone else would knock to tell us that.

"Be right out," Bellamy says and I don't say a word. My breath is caught somewhere in my chest. "We can't miss the only reason I had this insane party." He backs away from me, my body left cold without his pressed against it. "This isn't over," He says it like a warning and my stomach swirls like a whirlpool. Thank god it's not over.

"Good," I watch as he unlocks the bathroom door behind me.

He pulls me forward and opens the door, and the two of us walk out together. No one seems to notice us. That is until I turn and look at the kitchen. I see Griffin, Jade, Sienna, and Lawson pouring champagne for everyone, all of them smirking as they stare at us.

"Ignore them if they say anything," He didn't have to say anything.

They all like to fuck with Bell and me. It bothered me at the Ferris wheel date, but I don't care anymore. They know what's happening between us, and that's fine if they want to turn into something it's not. Bell and I are on the same page. Kind of.

234

"A quickie in the bathroom? Doesn't seem like you Archie," Lawson smiles wide as he talks.

Sienna is smirking right next to him, I'm pretty sure she's had a little too much to drink tonight. I'm glad she's letting loose, she's never been a very big drinker.

"We weren't fucking," I defend the two of us.

"So you were... Talking?" Griff asks, a smirk on his lips.

"Why do you two care what they were doing? Don't be weird," Jade chastises them, and I smile.

"Thank you, guys, for earlier... You didn't have to do that," I say over the chatter from the other partygoers.

Some from the cheer team, and some other football players. A mix of others too.

"Oh, but we did. I don't care if they dated for a week or four years. If she's causing problems. If she's upsetting him, or people he cares about... Aka you. Then there's a problem," Griff tells me. "And to add onto that, I don't fuck with her talking about your personal life. Whether she thinks she knows, it's bullshit. And it doesn't matter."

The fears I had are alleviated. Even though I like to pretend her words didn't hurt, I didn't want Bell's friends to look at me in a bad light. That's the last thing I want.

"What he said," Jade agrees, and I press my lips into a thin smile, my chest full at the thought of all of them caring that much. It's sweet.

"Everyone grab your champagne! The countdown is about to start!" Sienna shouts not only to us but to everyone around us.

Everyone flocks over, and Bellamy grabs two plastic champagne flutes from the counter and nods his head toward the living room. I follow him and take my champagne flute from him once we make it into the back of the living room, a perfect view of the TV, and a perfect escape route to his bedroom right behind us.

Everyone starts to filter in, and then it starts. 10, 9, 8, 7, 6....5....4.....3....2..... Bellamy looks at me, and it's not the new year. But this is new. Everything happening right now, tonight, the past week. It's all been new... And everyone around is cheering, kissing, and drinking. They're all celebrating a fake sense of new. But I'm staring at the real thing... I'm staring at Bellamy. Everyone cheers around us, and we both drink our champagne before turning to each other.

I have always dreamed of a New Year's Kiss. Because of my parents, because of the aspect of how romantic, and cheesy it might be. I know it's fake. Due to the list, and the fact that it's June, but I still feel butterflies swarming inside of me.

"Ready?" I furrow my brows.

He takes my champagne out of my hand and sets it on the table next to us. I look at him, empty handed, and he grabs me, and flips me to his other side, dipping me down so quickly that it makes my stomach drop. It's not a dramatic dip, my back isn't arched, and my leg isn't thrown in the air. But my hair is falling over my shoulders, and his lips are on mine, and I'm fully in his grasp, all the control in the palm of his hands. I laugh, a smile breaking through the kiss. He's smiling too, and I know it's not a real new year. But if it was I know I'd wish for the feeling in my chest to stay forever. It feels that good. He stands me up right and we break the kiss.

"Straight from a movie," I boost his ego more.

"Really? Was it everything you imagined?" He asks, and I smile.

"To be completely honest I didn't think this part of the

list would happen..." I'm standing close to him, my hands on his chest, his arm still wrapped around my back to hold me to him.

"I told you I would be doing everything."

I tilt my head, "What about doing something that's not on the list?" My nerves are shooting every which way.

"Like what?" His eyes are looking down on me.

"Like continuing what we started in the bathroom," I press closer to him.

"That wouldn't be very romantic, would it?" He doesn't sound like he's opposed to the idea at all.

He seems wary to mess up, I know that's what it is. He wants to make the list perfect for me, and I get it.

"It's not either of our first times anyway... We don't have to... I just..." I shrug again.

"You want to?" His face is still as he looks at me carefully.

"I do..." I look up at him and see his eyes casting down on me.

He's thinking as he stares at me, and my stomach is a big ball of nerves.

"Is that a bad thing?"

"For the sake of the list, it is," He looks at me for a second longer, and then he sighs, looking away.

He runs his hand through his thick hair, and shakes his head, "God dammit Kamryn..."

He bends down and picks me up, the party still happening around us. He throws me over his shoulder, and I squeal out, not expecting the sudden manhandling.

"Where are you going?" Sienna yells.

"To sleep!" Bellamy yells over his shoulder

"That's a weird word for se-" Lawson starts, but Sienna covers his mouth with her hand.

"Be safe!" Jade yells.

"Lawson! Don't let Sienna drive!" I yell to my friends and Sienna gasps, looking offended.

"I'm not even that-" Lawson is covering her mouth now, stopping her from lying about just how much she's had to drink

"I wasn't planning on it. Archie, don't forget a cond-"

"Bye!" I cut Lawson off, and wave to all of our friends, and Bellamy walks into his bedroom, and kicks the door closed, locking it behind him too.

"You know damn well I can't say no to you Kamryn, and on top of that... I really don't want to..."

CHAPTER EIGHTEEN

LAVENDER HAZE BY TAYLOR SWIFT

I squirm against him, and finally, he lets me go, throwing me right down on the bed, hard enough for me to bounce. My eyes focus on him, and my mind focuses on just how soft this bed is. His bed is soft. His eyes are anything but that.

"What do you want, Kamryn?" He stands in front of me, and I hold myself up on my elbows.

"I want to have sex with you."

"Are you positive this is... This is the way you want it? It wasn't supposed to be this way."

I nod quickly, "There doesn't have to be romance in everything..."

Bellamy starts unbuttoning his shirt as I talk to him, his eyes looking over me.

"I want you right now... I'd rather listen to my body than some stupid list I made," I admit.

He shakes his shirt off of his shoulders, and my mouth waters at the sight of his body. I've seen it time and time again, but it's like the first time every time. The tattoos across his chest, and his arm. His hands. His messy hair.

"No romance then. Here are the rules, if something hurts you tell me. If you feel uncomfortable you tell me. If you want to stop at any point we will stop," He crawls on the bed toward me, and I watch him as he makes his way to me, every muscle on his body contracting as he moves. He stares me down, my back flat against the bed, his body over mine.

"What are the rules?" He asks, his finger flipping my chin up so I can look directly at him.

He hooks his finger under my chin, keeping it there.

"If I'm hurt or uncomfy tell you, and if I don't want this then we stop," I say quickly, and feel my nerves start to kick in at the thought of him seeing me fully naked.

That's not me at all. I'm comfortable in my body. He's touched me before. He's seen my body practically naked. But this is real, and the longest I've waited with most guys. I don't know why it's making me feel weird but it is. I feel nervous. I feel excited.

"Lean up..." He speaks in a soft voice, and I do what he says.

His long fingers burn into my skin as they snake around my back. He unclasps the small latch of my shirt, and the sparkly metal slides away from my skin, chilling me once again as the rough material drags across my nipples. He leans down to my lips, capturing them with his, and he kisses me hard. His arm slides under my lower back, arching it, and pulling me against him, skin on skin. The friction of our bodies is heavy and hot, and his lips are harsh as they make their way down my body, and over my neck. He sucks, and nips, actually able to explore further than before. My back arches on its own as he brings his lips over my nipple. He tugs at the sensitive skin, sucking, and swirling his tongue.

"I already want you, you don't have to do all of-"

"Shut up. If I want to fuck you with class, let me," His breath fans over my entire body.

I shut up instantly. Degradation is not my thing. It never has been, but I think I'd let him say anything to me if he keeps his mouth on me like this.

He moves to the edge of the bed and pulls me with him. He's standing now, and I'm still laying here, my back to the bed, my hair fanned out everywhere, half of my body fully exposed to him.

"You have a perfect body, and I love the way you react to me. So, am I allowed to appreciate your body the way I'd like?"

I nod. He raises his eyebrows at me, waiting, and not moving.

"Yes, you can," I tell him, my breath catching as he latches his fingers underneath the waistband of my pants.

His fingers slide until they reach the button. He unbuttons them, and tugs, pulling them down my body, and throwing them behind him once they're off of me. He leans over me, kissing me again, moving down my body, but he doesn't stop at my chest this time, he continues down my stomach, his tongue working down every curve of my skin. His fingers hook around the lace underwear I wear and he pulls them down my legs. He removes my underwear, and kneels in front of me. His eyes on me now as I look at him, a pit in my stomach as I wait. He hooks my legs over each shoulder and keeps his eyes on me as he kisses up my thighs, and then he kisses me, his lips meeting my heat.

I shut my eyes out of instinct, but not only because I normally would. I shut them because it feels good, actually good. I've never had to fake it with him.

My instincts tell me to be jealous. That he learned how

to do all of this through someone that wasn't me, but I can't help but thank them because holy fuck. My back arches as his tongue flattens on the sensitive bundle of nerves, his lips latching around me too. My hands are in fists, gripping the bed sheets, and I'm incredibly thankful for the music happening outside of his bedroom right now because I let out a loud moan from the bottom of my chest. He groans against me, and I feel warmth creep into my stomach at the thought of him getting off on this... On pleasuring me. I did the same when we were reversed.

"Bell..." I moan, and he does the same, moaning once again as his tongue works me.

My body feels like there's lightning shooting through my veins. Electricity, purring in my chest, and stomach as he digs his fingers into my thighs. I open my eyes, leaning myself up on my elbows to look at him. His hair is tousled and messy.

I don't need any confirmation he's enjoying this because I can tell. I've never seen anyone look so pretty going down on me but he does. His eyes flicker open, and he takes a second to look up at me, and then he flattens his tongue again, moving it faster, more skill driven into his movements. His eyes burn through me, and my chest feels like it might collapse from how fast my heart is beating.

The muscles in my stomach and thighs tighten the faster he moves his tongue, and I pant. I can't help but cry out at the feeling. My body reacts before my mind can even process a man actually making me cum this way. He removes his lips which immediately stops the high but slides his fingers in my entrance which I know is dripping wet at this point.

I fall back onto the bed, trying to catch my breath. It's incredibly hard considering he's good at touching me like this too. My mind will never be clear when his hands are on me. He curls his fingers, and my hips jerk. Maybe at the fact that I was so close and he took that away from me.

"Not yet... Soon," He tells me, and I can't seem to catch my breath. He's looking up at me with a devilish grin.

He moves his fingers slowly, teasing me fully as he removes them from me. He slides his fingers up my heat, and stands up, his body between my legs now. I lean up on my elbows again, and stare at him, noticing just how hard he is through the black pants he wears. He brings his fingers up to his mouth and wraps his lips around them. I'm not sure why I feel my cheeks burning at the sight in front of me. He's incredibly comfortable in the bedroom, and I love that about him. I've seen this confidence before.

He fucks with the same confidence he plays with...

"You can take them off..." He tells me, and I reach forward, unbuttoning his pants, knowing he must feel relief as I pull them down.

I release him from his briefs, and stare at him once again, the sight truly not getting old.

"Condom?" I ask, and he opens the bedside table drawer.

He grabs one, and rips it open with his teeth, retrieving the rubber, and pushing it over his length.

"You're sure?" He asks me once again, and I roll my eyes. "I'm just making sure. No need to be hostile."

I reach forward, pulling him down to me as I scoot back on the bed. He moves to me, and places himself, slowly sliding in, and both of us release a heavy breath at the feeling. I feel my walls stretch around him, my body shaking at the feeling of him pushing himself deep, fully inside of me. He holds himself up over my body, both hands on each side of my head, as he stays still inside of me. His eyes screwed shut. His lips are parted as he breathes, and my body is itching to be closer to him despite how close we already are.

"You can move."

He's incredibly still right now.

"Yeah, give me a second," He hangs his head, his hair sloppy as it hangs, "You feel so fucking good."

He practically whispers the words, and I touch him, my fingers brushing over his skin. He slowly moves, almost all the way out before slamming himself back into me, his movements stay the same, over and over as he moves his hips, and I can't say a word. I won't because he's perfect.

The way he looks while he's fucking me, and especially the way he feels. He's breathing hard, his eyes open now and set on me, and I never keep eye contact like this, but it makes it feel that much better when it's Bellamy, and I don't understand it. "Ryn... Fuck," He breathes out, and I arch my back, my arms coming up and around his neck, hanging over the back of him. I run my hand up over the back of his head, my fingers laced with his hair now. My eyes squeeze shut at the feeling he brings as he rocks himself into me.

"Fuck Bell..." I moan his name and he slows, his head shaking.

"You can't call me that right now..." He tells me.

"Why?" I ask, confusion rolling through me.

"Because I'm trying to make this last, and it won't if you call me that, so don't," He warns me and then slams into me again.

I cry out, my back arching higher. I latch my legs around his lower back, keeping him where he is, and he pants, his head jerking back. "What are you doing?" He asks me, and I let his hips go, his body moving back, his dick sliding out. I pull him down, his body is easy to move in this setting. I pull him down to the bed, his back hitting it hard, and I make my move on top of him, straddling him.

"May I?" I ask, and his eyes are crystal clear, staring at me like I might have hung the moon right now.

They're glossy... No hazy is a better word for it. He looks like he's lost, and found all in one right now, and I like that he looks at me like nothing else exists in the world around us. Not his friends, not his apartment, not this campus, not football, nothing but me, straddling him.

"Please," He agrees.

I could come right now if I didn't want to make this last just like he does. Dear god, I'd pay money to hear him beg for me. I roll my hips, my core teasing him, sliding up his length. I place myself, and lower down, my body adjusting to him again in this position and both of us moan in sync at the feeling, and I get chills all over my body instantly at the knowledge of this feeling just as good to him as it does to me. I arch my back, my hands moving behind me, and holding onto his thighs as I face forward. I give myself leverage, easily able to rock my hips forward and ride him.

I do just that, slowly at first, taking my time feeling every inch of him, hitting every aching spot of mine. My body is singing at the feeling of him inside of me like this. I've never really cared which side of this I end up on because normally I have to finish myself off before the night is over. I have an incredibly strong feeling this won't be over until we've both made it across the finish line and then some.

His hands are exploring me, he moves them up my thighs, and then down my stomach. His fingers brush my pubic bones, and then his thumb finds my clit, and I'm not sure what sound I make but I know something comes out of my mouth at the feeling of him. I did tell myself I wanted this to last but I don't know if that's possible at this point.

"Bell please..." I whine out, my hips moving up and down now, my body wanting nothing more than to cross that line, but do it with him too.

I'm pleasuring myself, and the way he's moving his fingers he's aiding me, helping me. I open my eyes finally to see him with parted lips and red cheeks. He's looking at me like I've never seen him before. His chest is chiseled, his jaw tight, and hard as he clenches it. He's drawing slow circles and I'm moving slow too, the teasing pleasure feeling better than anything rough or fast right now. I'll save that for another time. I feel every inch of my stomach clench, a building pressure in my lower abdomen, and heat spreading through my thighs.

"I need to stop or I'm..." I moan as he presses harder, hitting just the perfect spot, and I stop my movements fully, knowing I need to.

"Go ahead... Use me..." His words sound sweet but are anything but. "I want you to come," He tells me, and I feel my lips part as he moves himself, aiding me more as he tries to continue the building high I felt.

My hand touches his torso, his abs flexing under my fingertips, and I ride him again, continuing the same teasing movements until every inch of my body is covered in chills. I have never come this way, but my body is shaking now, and I can't keep my eyes open. I cry out, continuing to ride him as every part of me clenches and tightens inside.

"Bell..." I moan his name and his fingers continue to circle me, and I'm not sure if he's finished yet.

I'm not sure if I'm making him wait on me, but I don't think I care at all because it feels like every part of me has melted and disappeared altogether. I slow down, and I let my hands press to his chest, finding stability. I've made a mess of him, and we both know that. I don't even need to see it to know that. I look at him, and he reaches up to me, his fingers tucking my hair behind my ear.

"Are you good?" He asks and I nod.

"Are you?" I ask.

"I'm not done with you yet..." I furrow my brows. "I've learned that nice guys finish last Ryn... So let me do that? Yeah?" He asks, and I don't even get a word in before he moves his hands up my thighs until they reach my ass.

He guides me now, his hands covering my ass in full. He's not gentle with me despite the high I just felt, and despite just how sensitive my body feels, I don't mind the intensity of his movements. I welcome them with a heavy moan, and he pauses. His breath caught in his throat.

"Fuck me, please," I tell him, and he pulls me down again, our breathing now in sync as he continues to move faster, and harder, and aimlessly.

I know this is meant to finish him off. I know that but it feels so good. The eager intensity of him filling me fully as he slams me down is enough to make me...

"Fuck... please come again... I can feel you."

The fact that he can read my body as he does makes my stomach tighten. I touch myself now, my hand snaking down my body and between my thighs. I lean up slightly, angling my hips, and I can tell by the subtle gasp, and the part of his lips that he feels exactly what I do. He slows only for a second, and then continues, now hitting the perfect spot inside of me, not just for him, but for me too.

He fucks me, but I'm still on top, one hand between my thighs, the other pressed next to his head. His eyes aren't leaving mine, and I feel like if I looked away the world might stop. My lips part as heat spreads through me again, and I can see his entire body peppered with chills, his strong arms, and his taut chest.

"Bell... I'm gonna come again..." I breathe out, my words almost caught behind my lips. "Fuck... just like that... Please."

I squeeze my eyes shut only for a second before opening them again. My body bursts, every part of me shaking, and it takes everything in me to not let myself collapse on him. He groans out, his fingers gripping my thighs, nails digging into my skin, and I whimper, feeling his cock pulse as he fills me fully once again. He stops moving his body still inside of me, every inch of my skin sensitive. He slides out, and his hands wrap around my lower back as I stay straddling him.

"You're good? You're okay?" He asks, his hands finding my face first.

He moves my hair out of my face, and his eyes are no longer dark and hazy but attentive. I hold up a thumbs up, still trying to catch my breath. My hand shakes a bit, my body still reeling from the feeling of him. He covers my hand fully and holds it tight.

"Can we move? Can I clean you up?" He asks, and my heart bursts just like my body did a few minutes ago.

I don't know if heart orgasms are a thing, but if they are he's good at those too.

"I'm okay..." I try to reassure him, and he sits up, my body still on him.

His hands haven't left my skin. He doesn't struggle one bit as he pushes himself up on the bed with me in his arms, my legs latched all the way around his naked body. There's still music playing outside of the bedroom, the chatter is not as prominent but we can both still hear it. He walks us into his bathroom and sets me on the counter, bare ass and all. I watch as he turns the water on in the shower. He turns the heat on full blast and then turns back to me.

"Um... There's some stuff in the drawer on the left that you can use if you didn't bring anything... Makeup wipe things, and shower stuff. A toothbrush too."

My stomach sinks at his words. All the good feelings slowly leave my body.

"Is it... Someone else's?" I ask the first question that pops into my head.

I'm not one to dance around the truth... At least most of the time.

"No. They've never been used before," He seems a bit nervous as he talks to me now like he doesn't want to tell me this at all.

"Bellamy, you're acting weird... Why is there stuff for me in the drawer?"

He sighs, "I wasn't sure if you'd ever stay so I had Jade get stuff you might use if you did. That's all. It's new... It's all for you. It wasn't anyone else's I promise."

His eyes are on me now. The tension in my body leaves at his confession, my heart melting again. That's thoughtful, especially considering he wasn't sure if I would stay here. Now I feel bad I never got him a sleepover kit for my apartment. I'm not as thoughtful as he is. That's incredibly blatant.

"Oh... Well, that's very sweet of you, thank you Bell..." I tell him, moving down from the counter.

"You promise you're okay after..." His voice trails off and I nod.

"I do. I'm fine... Why are you so nervous now?" I ask him.

"I'm not. I just don't want you to change your mind... and... I was wondering if you... If you were staying tonight?

You don't have to of course, I just figured I'd ask just in case... That way I could get you something to wear, or get ready so I could drive you home. If you want me to. I just figured I'd ask," He rambles, the confidence he just had completely gone now.

I smile and reach my arms forward. I hook them around his waist, pulling his body to mine. I look up at him, and he looks down at me. The comfort returns, his hands finding my face. I close my eyes, a close lipped smile spreading across my face as he holds my face, his thumbs grazing my cheeks.

"Do you want me to stay? Are you okay with that?" The question feels odd to ask.

I never stay after a hookup. I never let them stay either. I'm not really sure what this is, but I know it's not that.

"I am... I mean I do. But only if you want to stay," He tells me.

"I'll stay," I don't hesitate to agree.

I never had a morning after, or a walk of shame. But as I established before, this isn't a normal hookup.

"If you don't want to stay you don't have to. I know this is technically just a hookup... I mean we aren't... I'm not really used to the no strings attached thing is all. So I'm not really sure how this part works," He tells me, admitting why he's acting the way he is now.

He knows I'm used to this kind of thing, and that fact shouldn't bother me but it does. I always think someone is thinking something bad when in reality it's probably the opposite.

"It can work however we want it to work. This isn't really a normal hookup... It's... It's just different. I'm staying alright? It's not a big deal. I'll stay whenever you want... For the next week at least."

The truth sits in my chest as I speak it out. One more week.

"Okay... Um. You can shower. I'm going to clean up, I'll be in soon okay?" He asks and I nod.

He doesn't kiss my lips, but my forehead instead, his lips soft as he leaves the bathroom. I step into his shower, the hot water burning into my skin as I do. I don't flinch at the feeling, my skin still tingling from his touch that's gone now.

That was... It was good first sex. It was great actually. I've never hooked up with someone for the first time and had it be that good. It felt different... Bell cared about how I was feeling of course which is a giant perk. But I can't really put a finger on the exact reason. Technically we won't be sleeping together again. It was supposed to be a one time thing, but we also weren't supposed to sleep together yet.

I really don't know what's going to happen when it comes to the two of us... But if it was up to me I'd love to... Explore more with him. But he seems off now, and to be honest I feel off. I feel heavy. I feel... I feel scared. I feel scared because it feels like there are a lot of things left unsaid right now which is normally the opposite when it comes to me. Everything is usually always on the table. It could be the secret feelings I'm harboring. Though I'm 99% sure those will disappear once I get on the bus back home.

I think alone for a while and shower, cleaning myself off. The second I peek my head out of the shower to look for Bellamy, he's walking back into the bathroom. He has a towel on to cover himself now. I catch his eyes, and a soft smile hits his lips. I look around, my eyes searching for a towel, my hair dripping wet. He moves quickly, his hands reaching under the sink. He hands me not one, but two, and I take both of them. I step out, the water still running. I wrap the towel around my body, and then take the other, and wrap it around my hair.

"I'll only be a second..." He tells me, and I nod.

He drops his towel and gets in the shower.

I reach into *my* drawer once more to find face wash and a toothbrush. I wash my face quickly and then brush my teeth.

I walk from the bathroom, and into his bedroom. The sounds from outside the room have lessened. I'm assuming it's only Lawson, Griff, and Jade left now, but I don't want to leave his bedroom to look. I notice that the sheets have been changed already. What the fuck is he? Is he from a different planet? There's no way this is real life. This doesn't happen. He's just playing this up for the list, he has to be... There's a shirt folded on the bed and a pair of briefs as well for me. I drop my towel and take the clothes, putting them on my body. I throw both towels in the hamper by the door, and run a brush through my hair, letting it dry naturally. The water turns off, and I don't look behind me, I just wait and crawl back into his bed.

Bellamy walks back into his room, a towel around his waist again, his skin wet from the shower, and tempting even though I just had him... That's the problem. I don't think I've ever hooked up with someone I'm this attracted to.

Bellamy is a different kind of attractive. He's cute but sexy. He's easy to look at. He's intimidating with his strong features. Sharp jaw, and incredibly sharp cheekbones too. His nose is perfect, and the light stubble coming through might be seen as an imperfection, but I think it looks perfect on him. His lips are soft, and always pink. His face softens the minute he smiles, his dimple prominent, and his teeth pearly white. His eyes are second to the dimple... A soft pretty blue covered with thick lashes... And if his face wasn't enough his body... His hands... They are...

"You're making me feel like a science project," He's joking.

I know by the way he smiles at me, and I look away. I was really just staring so hard at him.

"Sorry. I was thinking." *Thinking about how hot you are...*

"Are you okay?" He pulls shorts over his briefs.

He throws the dirty towel into the hamper and makes his way toward me.

"Perfect," I only tell a small white lie.

I do feel perfect, and that feeling is what throws me off completely.

"Then come here," He throws himself down and doesn't hesitate to pull me with him.

We sit in silence for a few minutes, and I want to say something. Anything but I don't know how to articulate the words I'm thinking. I don't know how to sound the way I want to without sounding bad, or weird, but right now I feel so much, my body is weighed down by all of the things I'm feeling after what just happened.

"I'm sorry..." He speaks first, and I lean up, my brows furrowing as I look at him.

"Why are you apologizing to me? You didn't do anything wrong... Actually you... You did everything right... I was, well, I didn't even know what to say to you because I didn't want to sound crazy but god Bell... I just... Wow... I've never had... I mean you were... That was just... Wow... It was only supposed to be once, and I know that, and that's normally how it goes when it comes to hooking up with people... Especially for me... But even when you were walking out of the shower I was thinking about you again...

And I... I don't know... You shouldn't apologize, you were amazing."

He's smirking at me, looking like he's fighting laughter.

"What?" I ask, and he raises his eyebrows, my stomach dropping. "You weren't talking about the sex were you?"

He shakes his head. I cover my face feeling more embarrassed than I ever have. I groan, rolling onto my back.

"Oh my god that's so embarrassing," I speak out, mostly to myself, but I'm fully aware he can hear me.

"Hey, come back..." He hooks his arm around my waist, moving me back so I'm pressed to his warm chest.

"Just forget what I said."

He drops his jaw. "Absolutely not. Not now, not ever."

I cover my face again, hiding the blush of my cheeks from him.

"Stop it. That was cute... And the feeling is mutual... It wasn't... It wasn't just good for you Ryn."

I sigh at his words.

"Okay fine," I try to shake off the embarrassed feeling in my chest, and fail.

"You really think I look that good though? I can't even walk out of the shower without you wanting to-"

"Oh my god shut up," I cover his mouth with my hand and feel his smile underneath my hand.

I know my smile is just as wide.

"What are you sorry for?" I ask him, moving us back to his initial words.

"For what she said tonight," He explains and I furrow my brows.

"Leah?"

He cringes at the mention of her name.

"Yes... I was avoiding saying her name... But yes... That shouldn't have happened."

It obviously feels heavy on him for it to still bother him.

"Oh. You don't have to apologize about that, or about her. She's not your responsibility... Either way, I'm used to it."

The thought of him thinking those things about me still bothers me, even if I try to brush it off.

"What do you mean you're used to it?" His voice is serious, and his face is serious too. His defensive nature immediately returns right away, and I go silent. "What do you mean Ryn?" He asks, his hand coming to my face to hold it, just like he always does.

His features are strong, and soft all at once. I've never been defensive about the things that have been said about me. My mind flashes back to Dylan, and a few of the others. To the mean girls, I've encountered long before Leah.

"I just mean Leah isn't the first mean girl. Or guy, too. I'm not the cleanest when it comes to my history of hookups, Bell. You knew that. I'm always safe. I do everything right on the hygiene side, but when the hook up ends... And when it doesn't work out someone usually ends up hurt. Whether that's an ex-girlfriend or the guy. I've heard what she's said in a thousand different ways. I don't really care if people think that kind of stuff, it just rolls off of my shoulders... It's not your fault. If we're blaming anyone it should be me."

Only part of the truth comes out. My chest feels heavy when some of the words that have been said to me play in my head. It doesn't bother me daily, but it does sit with me. I don't just forget about it. I can't.

"That's not true," He says and I hesitate. "Kamryn... Baby..." He uses a new nickname, and warmth explodes from my stomach.

"It is partially true... I mean it hurts at the moment. I

255

won't forget about it after it happens. Sometimes when I'm down on myself I think about it but it doesn't... It's not a big deal. Most people on this campus have heard plenty. I'm a quick fuck to most, and to the girls I'm..." I shake my head, my instinct to move away from him.

He keeps me right there, pressed against his chest.

"Hey... None of what she said is true, not at all. There's nothing about you that you should be ashamed of. Especially when it comes to your sex life," He tells me. "She's jealous... I knew she would be... I figured, but I really don't want you to let anything she says get to you. Leah is not important in your life... At all."

I nod at his words. "Okay..." I agree with him. "I'm over it. I know she was just trying to get under my skin," I nestle myself into him, my head pressing to his warm skin, his heartbeat playing in my ear like a song.

"You're more than... I mean you... Your body is incredible, and you... You're amazing in bed Kamryn, but you are far more than a quick fuck... So much more than that."

I stay silent, my head against his chest, my heart in my throat.

"Thank you..." I accept the compliment that means more than he will probably ever know.

"And another thing. I know this is temporary. Everything with us is only for now, but when next year rolls around, and the year after, and every year until then... Whether you get married and have a bunch of kids or stay single forever because you chose yourself. I hope you know that it's never anyone's business or their job to make any comment on you, and what you do with your body. I know you know that. But it's your business what you do in your bed. No one has the right to change that, or alter that, or make you feel any differently. I know you know that. I just don't want you to forget it, because you're one of the most carefree people I know and you're a good person. It's just... It would be a shame to let people who don't matter take it from you..." His heart is broadcasted on his sleeve right now.

I close my eyes, not saying a word. Mostly because I have no idea what to say to him. I have no idea if I should say anything about the fact that as of right now, at this moment. Sleeping with anyone else sounds absolutely wrong to me. Not even wrong. I just don't want to. I don't know if I should tell him that the thought of what he said, me not talking to him, or not being around him next year like I was this year makes my stomach turn.

It's been a week and I've gotten used to Bellamy. Yes, in a relationship sense. But not only that. I've gotten used to him as a friend. As a person... And I don't like the thought of not having that. Despite feeling every bit of it, I keep it to myself, because I have no idea if this is a temporary feeling or if I'm starting to get too used to him being around.

CHAPTER NINETEEN

SIDELINES BY PHOEBE BRIDGERS

I WENT TO BED WITH NO INTENTION OF SNEAKING OUT in the morning, but my fight or flight got the better of me this morning when I opened my eyes in a foreign place. It was Bellamy's room. I was warm and perfectly comfortable. But I don't sleep over. I don't do that, and he and I have both talked about the lack of strings. He wanted me to stay the night but that doesn't mean he needs to cook my breakfast and bring me a cup of coffee every time I sleep over. I was afraid of how awkward it could possibly feel waking up with him.

I say that as if there will be any more. I'm not even sure if what happened last night would happen again. If it were up to me Bellamy and I wouldn't leave each other's bedrooms for the foreseeable future. I only have six days including today left before I'm on a train headed to northern Washington for the rest of summer. Bellamy and I are coming to an end sooner than not, and he needs to start focusing on summer sessions. This is an important year for him. The last thing I need is for Coach Corbin to start blaming me for anything. We've both got big plans for after college. We've both got futures in the NFL, and fake dating can't get in the way of that... No matter how real it feels.

I didn't want to sneak out, but I was afraid it would feel weird. Or he'd wake up confused. He's the nicest smelling boy I've ever woken up next to. And I can also agree to say he doesn't look completely disgusting like most do when they wake up. He's a peaceful sleeper, a heavy sleeper. He doesn't snore. Hell, he hardly even moved last night. He kept me where he wanted me the whole time we were asleep. I woke up in his arms, but he didn't budge when I got up. It'll probably work out better this way anyway.

I went straight to my apartment after I left him. I changed and freshened myself up, and then got back on the transit that runs all over campus. The bus is slowing now in front of the stadium, and I'm the only one standing up to get off. I'm in a tight pair of biker shorts, and a Seattle Pike University football shirt I got my freshman year. My black hair is in a tight ponytail on the back of my head, and my face is washed clean from the night before. I jog down the stairs of the bus and hold my small tote bag to my side, a water bottle, headphones, and a few other necessities inside. I make my way to the field, and the sun is bright as I descend the stairs.

"Hart!" I jump at the sound of my last name, not expecting anyone to be here this early.

I turn over my shoulder and see Coach Corbin walking down the steps toward me. He's got sunglasses, his typical gym shorts, and a SPU shirt on. He's taller than me, somewhat muscular, and always keeps a straight face. I know deep down he's a big softie, but he definitely doesn't look like it. I remind myself of that, knowing that's what everyone says.

"Hey, Coach Corbin!" I wave to him, and he makes his way to the same step I'm on.

We walk together now, down the large stadium steps toward the field. My nerves are at an all-time high, wondering why he's here, and why he's wanting to talk to me.

"What are you doing here this early?" He looks at his watch that rests on his arm. It's probably around 10 am now.

"I come here and run, normally I follow the football schedule and make sure that there's no one going to be here before I come. Since there's no football or cheer right now I'm in the clear," I press my lips together with a smile.

"That is until next week. I wanted to talk to you about that," He tells me, and I nod my head as we walk onto the track.

I drop my bag, and stand up straight, looking at him head on, "What's up?"

"Well, Archer told me about you earlier this year when I said I was looking to recruit some students for summer sessions. Now I don't like recruiting students, though I'm forced to most of the time. But, I've had my eye on you, all the sports you help with, all the players you help. The coaches from the other teams have nothing but good things to say about how hard you work. You seem to know what you're doing, and you also seem to really like sports too. You get into the games, and you pay attention to stats with the season. Compared to any other sports medicine student, you outshine all of them with all the extracurriculars you take part in. Your grades are stellar too, you check all the boxes," He layers on compliments which from what I know is very out of character for him.

He's normally straight to the point.

"Thank you, coach," I try not to get excited by the excessive compliments but it's hard, especially from him.

"I don't know what's going on with you and my quarter-back, but if I'm honest I don't want to know. It's none of my damn business. Now as long as you can promise me that you and that boy keep your drama off my field, and that goes for every player on my team, could I recruit you? I need someone for summer sessions, you'd learn alongside the physical therapist and athletic trainer for our team. Can we have you for the rest of the summer? That way the school can get off my ass, and I will know that my team is in capable hands."

I feel my jaw drop a bit. I was hoping to be on the field next semester. The last football season that I will be able to participate in. I wanted to be on the football team for years of course, but this is more than what I had thought I would get. Especially considering how selective Coach Corbin is, and how persistent he is on not having students on his field besides the players themselves.

"Oh... If I agree, what does this mean for the rest of the year?"

He shrugs his broad shoulders, and places his hands on his hips, "If I like you. If the boys like you, and the other coaches too then I'll onboard you for the season. But that's a big if. I'll be getting progress reports from the PT, and the Athletic trainer the whole summer. You've proved a lot from what I've seen, but I want more. And I know it's short notice, but you can think about it and get back to me alright?"

I nod, knowing how eager I look, "Thank you, coach. I'll email you with a response soon."

My emotions skyrocket the second he nods his head to

me, and turns away. He disappears through the stadium, going to the locker rooms from what I can tell.

This opportunity is one I'd be dumb to pass up, but it means I don't get to see my parents for what feels like the last time before I'm out of school. And to add to that, I was supposed to have this time to buffer before I had to see Bellamy every day at practice. I can barely look at him now without imagining him shirtless. I guess I can't really blame his ex for being the way she is. I don't know what's going to happen to my mental sanity if I see him every day for the rest of summer.

"Good morning to you too," I look over my shoulder and see Bell walking down the stairs, his shirt gone, and a duffle bag over his shoulder.

I feel my cheeks heat up, feeling more embarrassed now that I snuck out as opposed to if I hadn't. His being shirtless doesn't help either. Sometimes I feel like a teenage girl when I look at him because he's nothing short of one of those Abercrombie models from the mall.

"I figured you'd be here.. Well, actually, I figured you'd still be there when I woke up, but you weren't."

I hesitate, he drops his bag down on the ground next to mine, and approaches me, crossing his arms over his bare chest. He towers over me, and I just look up, not knowing how to explain myself.

"I just didn't want to bother you or make you feel like you had to do anything the... The morning after. I just... Yeah. I was afraid," I feel so awkward.

I wish I could sink into the field, and disappear. I don't like admitting my fear, especially not to Bellamy because it makes me feel vulnerable.

"There's nothing about you that bothers me. I've only got you for a few more days, no more sneaking out on me,"

He hooks his finger around my chin. "It's a giant disappoint-ment when I wake up thinking about you, and the night before... Then you're not there," He tells me, and I know exactly what he means by huge disappointment now.

My cheeks grow red, and he smirks, shaking his head, "I'm sorry... If I had known you wanted me to stay, I would have stayed. I felt awkward. I'm not really used to being there the morning after... To be honest I'm not even used to sleeping next to someone."

He shakes his head, "It's fine. Don't apologize for how you felt. Just know that next time, if there is one... That I don't care if you're next to me when I wake up, I'd prefer it that way actually."

I probably would have come to that conclusion if I had actually thought about what I was doing this morning but I didn't. I ran out before I could really even replay what happened last night, and now that I'm thinking about it, and looking at him, all I feel is pressure in my lower stomach, and I'm embarrassed all over again.

"Don't look so nervous... Come on... Let's just run," He nods his head and bends down to kiss my cheeks before he starts at a slow jog.

I move behind him, catching up quickly with ease. My eyes scan him as he starts to put his headphones in his ears, tuning everything else out. His face is just as perfect as it was last night and every day before... Last night... Him...

I sigh to myself. I have to torture myself for an entire summer and probably during the semester if I say yes to this opportunity. I see flashes of his body in my head, completely unprovoked images from last night and I want to rip my hair out in frustration. I told Bellamy two weeks, and then I'm gone.

If he sees me on the field he's going to think I'm just as

crazy as his ex... I can't look at him like this all summer. There's no way I can without me wanting to sleep with him again, it's inevitable. I need time to get these feelings out of my system. To detox from Bellamy Archer before the football season starts. But for now, I'd like to come as close to overdosing as I can with the few days I've got left. That is if he's okay with being my drug of choice.

"Bell..." I say his name, and he looks down at me as we run next to each other.

He pulls an earbud out, and raises his eyebrows at me, "What's up babe?"

"Do you want to come over after this? I don't know if you had any list things planned but I have to pack and clean a little bit. So I was wondering if you wanted to come. Just to hang out. You don't have to."

His lips turn up into a soft smile, "Yes, I do have a thing planned tonight, but for now, I would love nothing more than to come over Ryn," He looks like he's trying to keep laughter in, and I know it's because of how visibly sick I probably look as I make the move to ask him to hang out.

I must look insane, but I don't know how to do this, to make plans, to do things first. I'm the one people chase, not the chaser. I look at his chiseled features for only a second longer before I put my own headphone in. I'll run the tension out of my body, and then Bellamy and I can go from there.

I BURST out laughing at Bellamy as he sits on my couch, hugging the puppy dog stuffed animal. I fold my clothes and move them into a suitcase. We both showered together after our run and have been here since, exactly like this. Me doing what I've needed to do around my apartment. Him laying on the couch, keeping me company as I pack some things for the rest of summer. He turned on the movie Stuck in Love, and he's been looking past me every now and again to watch it. Most of my apartment will be left untouched for a month and a half while I'm gone... That is, if I stay gone. I haven't stopped thinking about what Coach Corbin said to me. But that's not something I can just decide on my own whenever I want. I need to think about it. I need to think a lot about it.

"Give me that," I hold my hand out for the puppy dog.

"You're taking it back with you?" He asks, and I nod, waving my hand.

He tosses the golden dog to me, and I shove it in my suitcase.

"You basically just killed the dog. I worked hard to win you that too," He shakes his head, and I roll my eyes.

"Goldie will be fine, he'll survive a few hour ride up north in the suitcase. He's not complaining, do you hear complaints?" I cup my hand around my ear, and Bellamy laughs, the room falling silent around us.

"Are you excited to be back home?" He asks me in the quiet.

I nod, smiling to myself, "I always get excited to go back, mostly because I don't plan on staying here forever. I love Washington but I want to be somewhere else, somewhere bigger, more exciting... So I spend as much time with my parents as I can for the time being," I tell him.

"What are their names?" He's propping his head up on his hand, staring at me as I sit on my living room floor in front of him.

"My dad is Dave, and my mom is Nancy," I open my

mouth again, and my words are stopped by the vibration of my phone.

I see *Mom* On the screen, I pick up my phone, sliding it open. I put it on speaker, and throw it on my coffee table.

"Baby, it's Mom," I hear her and I smirk.

"Yes Mom, I know. I have your contact saved."

"Why does it sound like I'm on speakerphone? What are you doing?" She's always full of questions.

"Because you are on speaker phone, I'm packing my suitcase for home, and I have a friend in the room so behave."

"A friend? Is it Sienna?" She asks me, and I make eye contact with Bellamy who is still laying across my couch, his face casual as he listens to our conversation.

He raises his eyebrows at me, probably wondering if I'm going to lie or not. I don't lie to my mom though, especially not now.

"No, not Sienna, someone else," My smirk forms on my lips.

I look down at the suitcase in front of me and continue to fold my clothes.

"Not Sienna? You don't have any other friends... Is it a boy kind of friend?"

I sigh, "It is exactly that type. His name is Bellamy, say hi."

"Hi, Bellamy!"

He looks at me, and then at the phone, "Hi, Mrs. Hart."

My mom gasps.

"Oh Kammi he has a nice voice, are you sure he's just your friend?" She asks and I roll my eyes.

"Mom..." I warn her with my voice, and she sighs.

"Fine. I just wanted to check in and see how you're doing. Your dad and I are excited to see you," She tells me, and I smile. "You can bring your friend too, we want to see him."

I shake my head slowly.

"No one is coming home but me, sorry... But I'm excited to see you too. I also wanted to talk to you about something. Um, the football coach, he talked to me today."

My eyes catch Bellamy who is no longer laying down but sitting up, his eyes on me, and not wavering at all. He connects his elbows to his knees, his clasped hands under his chin as he watches me. He's gone from relaxed to rigid at the mention of Coach Corbin.

"The football coach? Well, what the hell did he say?" Excitement is very present in her tone.

"He said that my friend Bellamy had told him about me earlier this year, when he was talking about recruits," I eye Bellamy, and his face doesn't change.

He's listening like a hawk, his face completely serious.

"Coach said he's been keeping up with me, and all the teams I've worked with the past year, all the games I attend, and everything. He asked me to stay for the summer and do the sessions with the football players... The ones where all the NFL recruiters are at," I hear her silence which only makes my heart sink. "But I didn't say yes yet... Because I'm supposed to be coming home, and I don't want you and Dad to think-"

"Oh please... I was just thinking about that boy you call your friend... Who seems to be going up to bat for you to the coach... Kammi, I want you to say yes. At the end of the day, it's up to you but I would tell you yes in a heartbeat. Don't say no because of us, say no for yourself, and yourself only."

I eye Bellamy, the only real reason I would say no.

"I just hadn't really thought about it, about staying. It

was set in my head, and now things have changed. I don't know... I just wanted you to know."

I think about the other things that have also changed as I look at Bellamy.

"Well, I'm glad you let me know. I'm proud of you, that's amazing that he's had his eye on you baby. And think, even if you don't go I'm sure he'll still want you for the season over all those half wits you call classmates," She insults my peers and I crack into a smile.

"Thank you, Mom... I guess I'll keep you updated," I groan out loud. "I love you Mom."

I never forget to tack that onto every phone call of ours.

"I love you. Bye, baby... Bye, Bellamy!" She calls out to him, and he smirks.

"Bye," He calls out to her, and then the line disconnects.

I stay quiet after the phone goes dead. I look around me and nod my head beside him.

"Pass me that shirt?" I ask him, and he doesn't budge.

I feel nerves skyrocket at the way he's looking at me, "Please?"

He still doesn't move.

"Fine. I'll get it myself..." I start to move, and he reaches for it, holding it in his hands.

"You weren't going to tell me?"

I shrug, "No because it doesn't really matter. I probably won't go anyway."

I hold my hand out for the shirt, watching his brows furrow.

"Why in the world would you say no? Isn't this exactly what you've been working for all these years? This is a huge deal Ryn..." He tells me and I snatch the shirt from his hands.

"It is a big deal, but so is family to me. I just had no intention of staying this summer. I never said no, I said probably no. I don't want to talk about it, Bellamy," I shake my head.

I can't talk about it. Not with him.

"I do... Were you just not going to tell me?" He asks again and I shrug and throw my hands down in front of me.

"I didn't know what I was going to do at all and to be honest if I didn't want to tell you I don't have to. Because I don't really have to tell you anything I don't want to, you're not my... You're not my boyfriend, Bell. I'm allowed to keep things to myself."

He presses his lips together and sighs.

"I'm very, very aware I'm not yours Kamryn. That doesn't mean you have to keep shit from me. We were friends first, remember?" His tone is stronger now, and there's a pang of guilt in my chest.

"You're right we were friends," I admit, feeling the weight in my words.

Were. I meant to say that too, mostly because it feels true. We were friends, and now we're confused. Because I can't be his friend now. I can't be friends with people I want to sleep with. He raises his eyebrows at my words, and I shake my head, not knowing if I meant it in the way it sounds now that I'm sitting here.

"Kamryn, you don't have to tell me everything. You don't have to give me everything. But something would be nice," His words are more true than I'd like them to be.

"I don't have to give you anything, because this is fake. It's not real, and it's just... It's not fair for you to expect anything more," I shut myself away, my walls building around me.

I say the things that might hurt him, just to get him to

go. So he'll stop asking me questions. I can't tell him I don't want to stay because of him. He'd never let that go.

"I have stuff to do..." I mumble the words, not looking at him.

"Are you asking for space Kamryn?" I nod to his words, annoyed that he can read me. "All you have to do is ask," He stands up, and walks toward me.

He crouches down in front of me, and brings me forward, his hand on the back of my head. He kisses my forehead and then stands up again, grabbing his keys from the coffee table.

"You don't have to try to hurt my feelings to get me to leave you alone. I'm trying to be your friend. Someone who can be there for you, fake dating or not. Right now, or months from now. I understand fear but you don't have to shut everyone out," He speaks softly and walks out of my apartment, leaving me alone.

I wonder how he's always doing the right thing. He's not even mad as he leaves my place. He offered to leave, and that's not normal. None of this is normal, especially not for me, and for once I feel practically helpless with all the decisions sitting in my lap. I pull my phone out and invite Sienna over, needing girl time. Truly I need anything but Bellamy time.

CHAPTER TWENTY

BAD REPUTATION BY SHAWN MENDES

Sienna and I didn't talk about Bellamy and it felt good just being with her, and not needing advice on my not relationship. She helped me pack, we did a face mask, and she did my makeup for tonight. I left my house when I decided on a party instead of talking to Bellamy. I used to be the type to go to parties alone before finals two weeks ago. I used to like being in a group of people that don't care about me. I just want to have a drink, and not feel anything for Bellamy. Just for now. That's all I care about.

I've had an incredibly hard time doing that since I walked through the doors of the frat house. I noticed how dirty, and disgusting it was, and thought of Bellamy being the exact opposite. I had to get myself a drink which hasn't happened in the past week and a half because Bellamy gets them for me. I then saw other football players lining the walls of the party and thought of him. Especially when I saw Lawson who was with some of his teammates. I have no idea if he saw me, but I saw him. I know Sienna isn't coming tonight, she told me she didn't want to go out. I wonder if that's why he's here, to let go of stress from his not relationship just like I am.

Now I'm resting against the wall, by myself for the night, debating if I should leave, and wallow in self pity, or continue to do it here instead of talking to Bellamy. My heart is useless because it's telling me to text him back. He has texted me today. Only twice. One was an apology, and the other asked if I would come over, not for a date despite him having something planned for tonight, he said he just wanted to talk. I didn't know what to say, so I said nothing. I don't want to talk because I'm scared I'll say something I don't want to say out loud.

I want to be closer to Bellamy, but I shouldn't be. I want to know everything but the knowledge would be useless a week from now because feelings are not an option once I'm on that bus home. Feelings are not an option when we are on that field together. Knowing him the way I want to is not an option. Talking to Bellamy is not an option right now. Especially because he's only perfect because of the list, outside of it, I have no idea what I'll be faced with.

I feel wrong being here. I feel bad. That's another problem. I know Bellamy isn't really mine. We aren't dating, and I said that to his face, but I feel like he should know I'm here right now. I feel like I need to reply even though I don't want to. I don't think I've ever felt more than I have in the past week. I don't like that either. I love my mom, I love Sienna. I like school, sports, and other things. I have feelings, but it's never in a romantic way. I've strayed away from that in every sense that I can.

My eyes scan the crowd, this party is way more rowdy than Leah's ever are. Frat houses are another breed when it comes to parties. There's every walk of life inside these houses. All types of athletes considering the school we're at.

I know most of them too. I catch the eyes of one of the basketball players, he's one of the more used players. I watched him a good bit on the court over the past few years. If I remember correctly his first name is Caleb. I look at him, thinking he's going to walk past but he moves forward, stumbling in my direction. I catch his shoulder, holding him off of me as I move back.

"Hi stranger, why are you so close to me?" I instantly get defensive and speak sarcastically.

Caleb settles against the wall, his hand gripping my hip, his body close to mine. He pulls me forward, but I put my hand on his chest, already smelling the alcohol on his breath.

"We're not strangers," He speaks out. "We don't have to be, I mean."

His intoxication is radiating from his body. He's too drunk for his own good, and what seems like mine too.

"We are though," I try to slightly move back, but he holds me in place.

I don't panic right away. Caleb has been known to be overly touchy, especially at parties.

"Word around is that you're doing favors now. Fucking Archer just to make his ex jealous... I was thinking-"

"I'm not... Where did you hear that?" My eyes burn instantly at the words that fall from his lips. I feel like my ears are ringing.

Maybe I just heard him wrong... But if I didn't that's everything I feared. I feared what people would say, I feared how they would react, or if they would make things up. I was right to do so.

"Everyone knows now... Hey, don't be upset. We can help each other..." He crushes me to the wall.

I can't move. Panic finally sets in. I can't think, or move, or speak.

Caleb bends down, and I try to breathe through the anxiety that's settling in my chest, The pure panic as I look into his glazed over eyes. He leans forward, and I press his chest back, but he moves forward anyway and kisses me hard. I push my mouth against him, trying to give him one kiss to move him off of me, resisting as much as I can. His teeth tug my lip between his. I taste copper and struggle against him, my body hurting from the tight feeling of his crushing mine. I groan as I try to shove him from me, but he barely budges. My muscles ache from how hard I'm pushing him away.

"Let me go..." I speak through my teeth, struggling to move from his venom grip.

"Kamryn?" I hear a voice near us, and I feel relief when Caleb is removed from me, and stumbling back.

Lawson stands there, his eyes looking between me and Caleb.

"Was he forcing himself on you?" Lawson's jaw is tense as he clenches it, his eyes set on me.

My lip is bleeding, I know it is. I can taste it. I hesitate to answer, thankful that Lawson was here at all.

"No... We were just arranging something just like her and your good friend Bellamy," Caleb steps forward, and Lawson puts his hand on Caleb's chest.

Lawson hasn't looked away from me, and at this point, my hands are shaking. I've been in uncomfortable situations in my life on many occasions. I've been scared before. But I have never been scared that someone would force themself on me. Not once until tonight. Lawson slowly turns his attention to Caleb, his eyes turn dark as he looks at the instigator.

"Excuse me?" Lawson's voice isn't timid and it doesn't falter.

"Look, Lawson. She's dressed like she-"

"That is not a fucking invitation you low life piece of shit," Lawson motions to me and what I wear.

"I need my fix just like everyone else has gotten. All I'm saying is-"

"What the fuck do you mean you need it? Need? Get the fuck away from her Caleb," Lawson steps in front of me completely now, blocking my view fully.

"You don't have to cockblock. She was into it," His words are slurring together, and they're hard for me to listen to.

I wasn't into anything with him. The last thing I need is Lawson to think I was...

"I think you should just walk away now Caleb."

Caleb tries to step around Lawson, but Lawson follows his motion, and steps in front of him again.

"Did you not hear me the first fucking time?" Lawson raises his voice, and steps away from me, and on Caleb.

Lawson's hands are on him now, pressing Caleb's chest back slowly.

"Why do you even care man? Are you fucking her too?" That was the last thing Caleb should have said in this situation.

"I should break your fucking jaw just so they wire it shut for the shit-"

I step forward, and place my hand on Lawson's arm, slightly pulling him back.

"Lawson stop... Lawson," I speak above his threats that he's still shouting at Caleb. "Lawson! It's not worth it."

I pull him back and he shoves Caleb. Lawson backs away and I let go of him, moving away as well. I knew

Bellamy's friends cared. I didn't know they cared like that. I have no idea why Lawson stepped in, maybe for Bellamy, but the strength in his defense of me seemed more personal.

"What the fuck ever. Swear to god she puts out for everyone until I step in," Caleb speaks under his breath but I heard every single word.

So did Lawson. Lawson's eyes are on me once again but his hands to himself. He's close though, and I'm not scared of him. I know Lawson would never hurt me. I know he'd protect me now more than ever.

"Are you okay?" He asks, his voice less stern, but barely audible against the abrasive music.

I press myself against the wall again, sure my body has left an imprint where Caleb cornered me. I shake my head softly, thankful Lawson stepped in when he did.

I'm not sure who specifically is making things up, and saying these things, but I'm sure it's more than one person. I'm sure Bellamy's reputation might be a bit messy when it comes to me now. Who knows, maybe I've already trashed it fully. I'm sure he wasn't thinking about that when he decided to do The List. I'm sure when he does find out, he's going to be pissed.

"I would offer to give you a ride somewhere but I don't want you to feel like I'm pushing you..."

I shake my head, "You don't have to leave because of me, it's fine I'll just... I'll figure something out, or ride the bus or something..." I shake my head again, finally peeling myself from the wall.

Lawson moves with me, not stopping me, but keeping up with me, "Hey Kam... Look at me. It's no problem, at all... I was about to leave anyway. I will take you wherever you want to go. Bellamy would never forgive me if he knew

I just let you walk out all by yourself, and find your own way home. Let me help you."

I look into his eyes. He's genuine and soft. I know Lawson is a good person. I never doubted that once. Bellamy trusts him. I nod my head and cross my arms over my chest. I know I shouldn't, but I do feel insecure about what I'm wearing now. I feel like I should have never put it on. A low-cut cropped shirt, and loose but incredibly short shorts. I want to be swallowed whole by a t-shirt at this moment. I want to feel comfort. I follow Lawson out to his car, and we get inside.

"Thank you..." My voice is hardly audible over the car turning on.

"You don't have to thank me. I swear I could fucking kill Caleb for..." He stops himself. "Just know that if it were up to me he'd be on the floor of that frat house."

"Did you do that because of Bellamy?" I ask, my eyes trying to stay focused on the street in front of us.

"Do what?" Lawson's voice is low.

I've never been incredibly close with Lawson. He and I have always been cordial, even though we weren't close. When we spoke briefly, it always felt like we were on the same page. The same wavelength in a weird way. I feel that now.

"Defend me like that... Step in at all," I explain, and he sighs.

"I'd say yes because I feel like that's what I'm supposed to say, but it's not the truth. Not all of it. At the end of the day, he's my best friend, and I care about the people he cares about. But I wasn't thinking of Bellamy at all when I stepped in, no," He admits.

I had a sneaking suspicion.

"Thank you... But why then, if not for Bell?" I ask, and Lawson laughs.

"Because you and I are the same, Kam. Truth be told I'm worse. I fuck anyone and everyone I want. I don't hook up more than once. I dress in whatever I want. I talk to who I want and I party when I want. I'm almost positive your body count is half of mine, yet I've never in my life had to deal with anyone calling me anything, or commenting on what I do. I've never been approached like you were. I've never felt scared like that. I stepped in because it's bullshit that people treat you like that and then they look at me like I'm..." He stops.

"Like you're a god for all your... conquests," I choose my words carefully and he nods.

"Because the double standard pisses me off. Because Caleb is a piece of shit for thinking like he does. I don't care if you've said yes to everyone on campus besides him, he still has no fucking right. I've never had to go through it, and I hate that you do. Even before Bellamy when someone mentioned it. When guys were fucking pigs about any girl, especially you. Bell and I both defend you. Because who you sleep with doesn't affect anyone but you," He finishes and I can't even comprehend that.

Lawson and Bellamy were my defense team even before they knew me as well as they do now.

I stay quiet as he pulls away from the crowded street. We only drive for a few seconds before Bellamy's name flashes across the car screen, a call coming in.

"I told him you were there... He was worried about you today, and I didn't expect to see you there. I'm sorry."

I shake my head. They're best friends, it makes sense. That doesn't stop me from fearing what he'll say. The last time we spoke we were fighting. And having to tell him what Caleb said, what everyone else is probably saying...

"It's okay, you can answer," My eyes drift away from the screen, my stomach heavy at just the sight of his name.

I'd love nothing more than to crawl into bed with him, with his shirt on. With his arms wrapped around me. That sounds just like the comfort I was wishing for just a second ago. I don't know if that's even a possibility right now. I don't know if Bellamy would even want to see me after what just happened.

"Do you want him to know that you're in the car..." He asks. "I won't tell him if that's what makes you feel the most comfortable. He doesn't have to know anything at all," He warns, and I shake my head, crossing my arms over my chest again.

He would keep this from his best friend because he cares. Because he's respectful. That's what makes me feel comfortable right now. Lawson being who he is, far better than I knew he was.

"I'll end up telling him if you don't. It's fine, say what you want," I can hear my voice shaking.

I don't know if I'm cold or if I'm scared, or if I'm anxious. It could be all three. I really don't know how I'm feeling at all right now besides hurt. Lawson answers the call and waits for Bellamy to speak.

"You don't sound like you're at a party," His voice is over the loudspeaker of the car.

My chest burns at the sound of his voice. I shake and Lawson reaches forward, turning on a light stream of heat in his car.

"I left... Something happened, um...Kam...Kamryn is in the car with me, I told her I would take her somewhere else," He tells his best friend.

"What do you mean something happened?" Bellamy's voice changes from normal to serious in a matter of a second.

"Caleb, the point guard of the basketball team. He happened. I stopped him before he got what he was looking for. She stopped me before I killed him for trying something like that," Lawson won't look at me.

He's angry, he has been since he left. Lawson has always been somewhat hot headed, I've seen it on the field and I'm seeing it now.

"Ryn, are you there?"

My heart beats faster the second he says my name.

"I'm here," I hardly recognize my own voice.

"Are you okay? Did he hurt you?" When it was happening it didn't feel good. It did hurt as he pressed against me, but I'm not hurt now.

"I'm fine."

"Baby, you don't sound okay. Are you okay to go home? Do you feel safe?"

I let out a shaky breath and I don't think about it before I even speak.

"Can I come over?" My question surprises me.

Mostly because it's unlike me. Mostly because I thought that I would be tolerating him throughout this entire endeavor, not relying on him to comfort me. It's shocking because I'm afraid of rejection, and I know that he could tell me no right now, but all I keep thinking about is being in his presence so I have to try.

"Always," He says and I feel heat flow through my stomach, and tears burn my eyes. Relief is prominent in me. "Hey, Lawsy..."

"Yep," Both of Lawson's hands are on the wheel, and his eyes are on the road.

His knuckles are white from how hard he grips the steering wheel.

"Thank you," Bellamy's voice is sincere.

"Of course. I'm going to be there in a few minutes to drop her off. The apartment is yours tonight," He tells his best friend, and I let out a short sigh, trying to not cry right now.

I didn't hesitate to ask to go to his place, but I know it's the place that will make me feel the most comfortable right now. Bellamy makes me feel simple. He makes me feel like things aren't the end of the world. He makes me feel like stuff isn't as bad as it feels, and I want to feel like this wasn't that bad. I want to feel okay right now.

I want to work through what happened, but I don't want to do that alone. We drive in silence, no music, no nothing. I notice the normal apartment building that I've been to a few times now, and Lawson pulls up to the front. Bellamy is already standing out front. He's not wearing a shirt, only sweatpants. It looks like he ran from the apartment the minute Lawson said he was dropping me off.

"Tell Sienna that I'm okay... And tell her that I'll call her and tell her everything tomorrow."

Lawson nods, "Um... I... I will. Are you okay though? Really?"

I have no idea what's really going on with Sienna, but I'm sure he'll talk to her tonight before I do.

"I will be. Thank you. I was afraid you thought... I was afraid you thought I was trying to hook up with him, or that it was my choice because-"

"I could see how scared you were, Kam. I didn't think that for a second. I'm sorry I didn't step in sooner," He speaks out to me. "Be safe."

I open the door, and start to get out of the car, "You too."

Bellamy steps forward, he doesn't touch me, he just looks at me, and leans down. I walk forward, not hearing what he says to his friend as I step inside the apartment building. I cross my arms over my chest, feeling exposed right now. Bellamy walks in, his hands in his pockets.

"You're staying the night?" He asks and I hesitate. "You're more than welcome to. I want you to. Only if you feel comfortable," He puts me first without hesitation.

My heart melts.

"I want to stay with you," I admit.

"I already have clothes set out for you."

The butterflies reign free in my stomach, just like they have every single day since I went out with Bellamy. We get in the elevator, and Bellamy is looking at me. I can feel it, but I don't know what to say other than I don't want to be looked at.

I don't know what to tell him. I don't know how to talk to someone I feel like I barely know, but know so well all at once. The elevator opens, and he leads the way to his apartment, and once he opens the door, I step in first, and we walk into his bedroom together. Just like he had said, there are clothes ready for me.

"Go change, or shower, or do whatever you need to do. I'll wait. I can sleep on the couch if you're not comfortable being next to me... or you can stay here with me," He motions to his bed.

I just look at him, not sure how to respond to his kindness, especially not after how I ignored him today. I know we need to talk about that, but I can't... I don't think I can even think about what happened today... All I feel like doing right now is pretending. All I'd like to do is to be with Bellamy Archer and pretend with him. Just for one night.

CHAPTER TWENTY-ONE

I DON'T KNOW YOU AT ALL BY LIZZY MCALPINE

I CHANGE INTO THE LARGE SHIRT THAT SWALLOWS ME whole, just like I wanted. After I'm dressed I dive into my drawer in Bellamy's bathroom. I brush my hair and my teeth. I remove my makeup, and I get as comfortable as I can.

The second I finish, I open his bathroom door slowly, looking into the bedroom. I look around carefully as I step in, and Bellamy isn't there at all. I didn't put any pants on because of the size of the shirt on my body. I move to his bedroom door, and open it, looking outside to see the living room. Bellamy is laying across the couch on his phone, music playing in the background. I step out of the bedroom, and his eyes catch me. He sits up right away.

"Hey. Are you... Are you okay?" He asks me, and I nod and shrug.

"I'm okay. I'm just shaken up. I'm embarrassed I guess," I hate that I have to tell him this happened because it never should have happened.

"Do you want to tell me what happened?" My eyes roam on his body, and back to his eyes.

I contemplate it. I look at him, wondering how exactly I will get it out, scared about how he will react. What if he's upset by what's being said about me, and possibly him? What if it bothers him? I feel my lip shake, and I see Bellamy's face completely change to full concern.

"Baby..." He stands up, and comes straight to me, not hesitating. "Can I touch you right now? Is that okay?"

I move my arms around his torso, not looking at him, but pressing my cheek to his chest, hugging him. He holds me too. He slides one hand up my back, and into my hair, the other hand pressed flat against my back as he hugs me.

"What did he do?" He's quiet as he speaks to me.

"He cornered me," I'm crying now. "I'm sorry Bellamy."

I hate this more than I can explain. I don't want him to be upset. Not about what happened or about his reputation. He has to know how bad this will look to others. How people might see him if they think...

"What do you mean he cornered you Ryn?"

I shake as I think about it again, "He walked up to me, and he stumbled up, and I tried to push him back, but he grabbed onto me. My back was pressed to the wall and I couldn't move. He said he was... Someone told him about our arrangement. Not the truth of it. He said that I'm..." I can't talk.

My voice is shaking at the thought of this ever happening again, other people knowing about this, or about Bellamy. About me.

"It's okay..." His thumb moves back and forth on my head, his hands warm against my skin.

"Someone told him I agreed to have sex with you to make... To make your ex jealous... He... He-" I hesitate again. "He kissed me, and he might have done more if Lawson didn't say something and I didn't want him to. I kept trying to push him off. I told him we weren't. That it wasn't what he had thought it was and I tried so hard. I'm sorry."

Sobs wrack my body, my face is so wet with tears at this point I know they've transferred onto him now.

"I'm not really sure why you're apologizing to me baby," His chest moves as he speaks.

I find comfort in the way it rises and falls. His arms are strong around me.

"Because people are going to think... People are going to associate you with me. Your reputation-"

"Means absolutely nothing to me," He finishes my sentence. "And if you're going to apologize to me for kissing him, you have no reason to."

That's another thing I was already apologizing for. He took my words out of my mouth.

"If you wanted to kiss him, you would still be there kissing him, not here with me," His understanding is over-whelming to me.

"And I'm sorry about earlier today, and-"

"I don't want to talk about earlier today or anything else right now. I want to talk to you, and make sure you're okay... Lawson told me you were there alone at that party. That he was keeping an eye on you to make sure you were okay and I'm glad that he did. I'm glad you're all in one piece. You're okay. That's all that matters," He pulls me back to look at my face.

His hand comes up, slowly moving my hair out of the way. He slowly wipes the tears from under my eyes, his thumbs resting on my cheekbones.

"I wanted to see you... And to feel comfortable so I came here... I... I felt so wrong, I was just scared..." My words are shaky and uneven.

My voice doesn't belong to me right now.

"I was scared for you and if I wasn't here, and I wasn't with you I promise I would be driving to the frat house right now, and ending Caleb's entire basketball career as we speak. I still plan on doing that at some point for putting his fucking hands on you. Let me see..." He keeps holding my face with his left hand but brings his right down.

His fingers brush the bottom of my chin, and his thumb grazes my lip, looking at where Caleb drew blood.

"Does it look bad?"

Bellamy shakes his head, "He did this? Does it hurt?" He asks and I nod my head to both questions.

"He bit my lip when he... Um. It stings, but it's fine. I'm fine."

"As for what he said to you... Baby, no one that matters believes that bullshit. If they do, they don't deserve to know you, or me," He speaks quickly, his eyes drifting between both of mine.

He slowly brings himself to me and kisses my bottom lip as softly as he can. Not in a sexual way, no ulterior motive to the kiss than to comfort me. My heart throbs at the gesture. My heart aches knowing how badly I feel for him. How this right now shouldn't be happening but it is, and I feel every ounce of it. He brings his lips to my forehead now, and I close my eyes tight.

"I wish this was all real sometimes," I speak before I think.

"What do you mean?" Bellamy asks slowly, if it wasn't a crazy thought I'd have sworn I could hear hope in his voice.

"I mean all of this is fake. For the list. This comfort and all of this isn't real, and sometimes I wish I knew this wasn't just for some list... That someone was as kind as you are in real life," It's not like me to be honest like this.

But I guess my normal is out the door for the night.

"Do you not think you deserve that? The kindness..." He asks and I shake my head.

"I don't know. I deserve a lot of things. I want to feel like I deserve kindness from everyone but I don't. I just don't think it's fully obtainable. Comfort from humans can happen, it's just... too hard to find, and I found it, but this is just for the list, I know that. I just... I want to keep it right now and pretend," I speak quickly, not wanting him to interrupt me.

"Ryn..." His features soften.

I know I still have tears in my eyes. He's looking directly at me, that electrifying gaze locked in on every inch of me.

"Pretend," I speak before he can say anything else.

He looks at me with the same soft face. The same bright blue eyes.

"Tonight I want to know you and I want it to mean something. So pretend with me."

He slowly tilts my chin even more. He moves his hands, putting us in a dancing stance.

"What do you mean you want to know me?"

"I want to know things that most people don't know," I admit.

"I want to know you, too," Bellamy sways me, both of us dancing to the music that he's playing.

I tilt my chin back down, and Bellamy brings his hand to caress my cheek, his fingertips brushing behind my ear.

"What makes you feel the most comfortable?" I ask him softly, his heartbeat playing in my ear louder than the music that makes us sway.

"Hugs and warm blankets. I like ice cream but not anything chocolate or caramel... I like the raspberry or strawberry kind, it was my mom's favorite, and all we had in the house when I was growing up. So I ate it all the time with her. The smell of laundry makes me comfortable. Lawson and Griffin. Um... You. You make me feel more comfortable than any of those things."

My heart leaps up to my throat.

"What about you?" He asks me as if he didn't just send me into cardiac arrest with his words.

"Big t-shirts. Sienna because she never judges me. Football games. Rom coms. Your friends make me feel comfortable. Um, hot coffee, and you... You make me feel more comfortable than I have ever felt," I tell him.

His hand slides up my back and through my hair, somehow we're closer now. If it was possible I'd mesh with him at this moment. I'd be as close as I could ever get if there was a way.

"Who's your favorite artist?" He asks me.

"Music?" I ask back, and he nods. "I love Kings Of Leon and boy bands. And I love Taylor Swift too."

"I love the same things, but I've told you the music I listen to before," He answers, and he's right, I do already know the music he loves. "How do you take your coffee?"

It's not something he'd ever need to know. It's not something he'd probably remember in a week or two, but he asks like it's the most important thing in the world to him right now.

"I like it with sugar and vanilla soy milk. And I like caramel flavoring. What about you?" I ask him.

"I'll take it, however, it's given to me. I'm indifferent about coffee," He tells me.

I want to gasp, but it seems just like Bellamy to not care. It seems just like him to drink the first thing he sees on the menu at some small cafe. Or he'd order whatever I got every time we got coffee together, I smile at the thought.

"I talk in my sleep sometimes... and I sleep in the fetal position most of the time... But I like something under me, under my face when I sleep whether that's a person, or a pillow, or a blanket," I tell him.

"I normally sleep on my stomach, TV off always, no noise, no light."

"My favorite holiday is New Year's," I continue to rattle off facts.

Like if I don't get it out tonight, he's never going to know. Which is probably true. This over sharing isn't a usual occurrence for me. I don't have much longer with Bellamy anyways... I don't tell anyone about my favorite holiday. Mostly because people never truly get it. Sienna knows. She likes that my favorite is something different, but now Bellamy knows. Mostly because I know he'd never judge me, just like my best friend.

"Really?" I feel that childish excitement when he asks.

The kind that you get when you feel like someone cares, like someone is excited to be around you, and you are realizing it for the first time. I'm realizing that now.

"Yes, really... It has been since I was younger," My mind wanders to the fondest memories of my parents.

"Why?" I feel like Bellamy asks questions because he really wants to know.

Because he really cares about what I'm going to say, and that's something I love about him.

"Because my mom and dad always used to throw neighborhood parties. All their work friends and our neighbors would come over, and I was always young. I stuck with my parents, and when I got old enough I could invite my friends. It was always so eccentric. Our house was... It was transformed, and I would cook with my mom always, all day long. My dad always made it a point to kiss my mom at midnight. I remember one time, my mom was in the kitchen with a friend and didn't realize it was close to midnight. My dad was going crazy, he couldn't find her, and he couldn't miss the kiss. I just... I love the excitement. The hope. The gathering without the promise of presents. Anyone who is there actually wants to be there with you. I like the outfits."

The memories flashing through my head are the most fond memories I have. My favorite memories.

"And you always dreamed of someone looking through a house of people for you. Just so they could make sure they kissed you into the new year... You dreamed of something real like that didn't you?" He asks and I almost feel sick to my stomach at just how easy it is for him to read me.

"Yes, actually."

"So you didn't put New Year's Kiss on the list from some movie, you put it on there because of your parents?" Bellamy asks and I nod.

"My parents are the only example of real, and true love. I've never had any other family members stay together. Not my aunts, uncles, and grandparents. All of my friends have dealt with shitty relationships. Sienna went through one for years, but my parents... What they have is magic. He... My dad and how he loves my mom is magic," I speak softly.

"I'd search for you at midnight..." No one in my entire life has said something to me that's made me want to cry happy tears.

This sentiment makes me want to cry overwhelmed, happy, and emotional tears. It takes everything in me not to cry them right now. I don't speak at the confession. Mostly because I don't know where it comes from. I don't know if it comes from him feeling like he should say that to make this more real. I don't know if he means it. I don't know anything when it comes to Bellamy except how hard it is not to fall head over heels for the man. Especially when he says things like that.

"You don't mean that," I keep my eyes shut and he doesn't stop us from moving or swaying.

"I do mean it because I did do it... I didn't actually have to search for you because I couldn't stay away from you long enough to lose you before the clock hit... You don't get it Kamryn..." His breath is light, his lips brush against my hair and I fight the urge to cry again.

I fight the urge to let every single emotion crash through me right now.

"Bell..." I whisper his name, not knowing what else to say to him.

This night is all so much. So much for me, and so much for us. I... I feel so deeply for him right now, and I don't understand it at all.

"I think you have the purest heart Kamryn..." He says and I feel my so-called pure heart melt. "I know that no one knows about your romance obsession besides Sienna. And I know that it's not common knowledge, and I get that, but I know that it makes you feel. And I think the way you love, and the way you hope, and the way you talk. It's just perfect. You're so much sweeter than you show to the world, and I like that about you because you keep it for the people that matter. You keep that for yourself."

He's genuine, he's sweet and he's perfect. He's too good for someone that has such a vindictive outlook on relationships the way that I do. He needs someone with the same ideals and the same outlook on life. He needs someone who would be able to trust and love him the way I can't. He's the optimist, and I'm the pessimist, and I want to tell myself that sometimes that works. But I don't think either of us deserves the disappointment when it doesn't work.

"You're too kind for me," My voice sounds like a warning and maybe it should be.

"No one is too kind for anyone... Kamryn baby..." He pulls me back and looks at me. "You're the kind of person people write romance books about. Don't accept less than that."

My words are caught in my throat. He looks at me, directly in my eyes, and I swear if I didn't know better I think I'm falling in love with him right now, just from looking at his eyes like this. His eyes lose their focus. They shift to my lips first, and then to my eyes. He's fighting himself to look back down again.

"Can I kiss you?" He asks and I kiss him instead of answering.

My lips are hesitant to kiss him, but they do. My lips are tender, and I kiss soft, sure not to hurt myself.

He doesn't overpower me. He doesn't take any ounce of control but he does kiss me back. The weight this kiss has on my chest, it feels like a thousand pounds are laying on me, suffocating me. He holds my face with both of his hands, and I push myself against him now. He gasps at the sudden movement, and the sound from his lips is so sweet. So addictive. I wonder if anyone has ever made him gasp like that. I wonder if, well, I wonder if he wants me now, if he wants me after what just happened. Or considering the list and the fact that we've already checked it off...

He crushes his lips to mine. It's not gentle, but I've never felt so much passion from one person. The gap is lost between us now as his tongue slips past my lips and into my mouth, colliding with my own. His lips are sweet, and his tongue is a drug because all I want is more. More of him. More of his kiss. More of his kindness. His hands, his body, his entire being right now.

I slide my hands around his hips, I let them slowly make their way up every single muscle, every inch of his carved body until they are flat against his chest. I think about the list. I think about the rules, all of them, and I let my lips break off of his despite the almost painful feeling of them leaving mine.

"The list said once. We were only supposed to-"

"If you want me to be honest right now Kamryn I couldn't give less of a fuck what the list says, I want you. I want to be sweet to you, and I want to worship your body, and I want to make you come tonight, and as many times as you'll let me until you walk out that door to go home tomorrow morning," He confesses and I think my soul has completely left my body. "Tonight you said you wanted to pretend, but this is not pretend. There was no romance last time, and that's all I want with you right now. I want to be gentle with you, and I want to savor this... If you want it, it's yours."

I just look at him with so much confusion, wondering how he exists, fake or not. It doesn't feel possible even though he's standing right in front of me.

"Okay..." I almost whisper, mostly because he captures my words with his lips the minute I agree with him. He consumes me with this kiss.

I forget how strong Bellamy is until moments like this happen. Until Bellamy lifts me with such ease, not breaking our kiss, or letting any of the heat between us disappear. My legs are wrapped around his hips, and my lips are kissing his, slow, but eager as they move. My arms are lazily slung around his neck, holding on to him. Bellamy doesn't throw me down. He brings me to the bed carefully, as if I could break at any second.

My back is against the soft bed, and that's when he

moves his hands under the shirt I wear, and he exposes my body, slowly bunching up the shirt and then pushing it off, and over my head altogether. His eyes scour my body, no shame in the way they take me in, and I want to blush. At first, I tell myself to feel anxious, nervous, or shy but there's none of that with him at all. It doesn't exist in this space. The way he looks at me makes me feel like I'm insane, and I don't think I've ever been so happy to feel so crazy.

Bellamy kisses me everywhere, his lips finding new places to explore, and new ways to pleasure me. I let him do whatever he wants, and I don't fight any of it because it does feel good. He does exactly what he said he wanted to. He's gentle with me, and kind to my body. He uses me and cares for me all at once. And I see now, I feel that he can't get enough of me, and I feel the same way. He brings me to shower, and he fucks me there too. We barely get out of the shower before he lifts me up on the counter, and starts over again. I'm happy to let him do so.

CHAPTER TWENTY-TWO

ORDINARY PEOPLE BY BLAKE ROSE

THE NEXT MORNING BELLAMY DROPPED ME OFF AT MY apartment after we ran together bright and early. We didn't sleep much, only bits and pieces of the night. He picked me up and he didn't even warn me, he just showed up at my door again and didn't give me a single second to finish getting ready. He said he needed it to be casual.

He really meant casual because I am in sweatpants, and his shirt once again, that I still haven't given back. My hair is down and natural from my shower after our run, my face is bare. He's in a pair of running shorts, and a plain white shirt. His casualness still looks just as good as his normal, and it's completely unfair.

"Are you ever going to give me my shirt back?" He asks and I can see the smirk on his lips.

He obviously doesn't want it back by the way he's smiling. Knowing him it probably boosts his ego when he sees me wear it.

"I can give it back to you right now if you want it. You say the word."

He shakes his head. We never exchanged a single word

about last night, or about yesterday after the phone call with my mom.

"I'm alright. I can do without a shirt. Or two, or three. You can have all my shirts if you want them," His hand is around mine as he drives, a comfort not only for him, but for me too, and my head is reeling over what's going on with me.

When I said what I had said yesterday. About how we used to be friends. I've been thinking about it since he dropped me back off this morning. I feel bad for saying it, but I don't think I want to take it back because it's true.

I like Bellamy far too much in and out of bed to be his friend, and that's why this can't be more than what it is. As much as I know these feelings will fade, the urge to want to sleep with him every chance I get won't. It's funny just how little time can make so much change. Bellamy Archer is decorating the walls in the corner of my mind that he's taking up. He's making a cute cozy little home there, and I'm not cool with it.

"I was thinking, and I wanted to ask you before I did anything. I don't think Caleb should be able to get away with what he did. I know you're not happy with the thought of me causing him any physical harm which is what I want to do. So I thought maybe you could talk to the basketball coach. Or the head of sports admin... Only if you're comfortable, that way he doesn't get away with anything like this again."

Bellamy's intentions are sweet and come from a good place. I know him and I know that, but he's thinking like a boy right now.

"Even if I wanted to say something, do you actually think any action would be taken? We're a top ranking athletic school, meaning our teams are highly ranked across the country... He's the best player on the team, they won't care if he committed murder... They'd cover it," I explain and Bellamy's knuckles are white as he grips the steering wheel.

"I know that. I know how much they let people get away with, not just people but men. That doesn't make it right. I'm sure if they tried to cover it, and anyone got word of it that it'd cause an uproar. Ryn, he should know what he did isn't going to be tolerated. The school should at least be warned so that if there's ever another report, or if there was one in the past, maybe it'll get taken seriously because of yours. It makes a difference. If you don't want to tell for other reasons, so be it. It's your choice, but I think that maybe it would be a good thing... Just trying," He shrugs, gently nudging me in the right direction.

"I don't want the basketball coach, or any other coach looking at me in a bad light. Thinking I'm causing problems or taking the side of Caleb instead of me. This kind of thing could dig me into a hole I can never get myself out of... If I'm running to the coach to tell on his best player," I explain.

It's not that I don't want to. I would love for someone besides Bellamy and Lawson to know that the star basketball player is a scumbag. I just don't know if the repercussions on me would be something I can handle.

"Then don't say anything... Lawson can say something. He already offered. He said he would when I was at home. Let him talk to the coach, let him tell the coach what he saw, and he can say you have no idea that he's saying anything. As shitty as it may be, he might believe it more if Lawson tells him," Bellamy explains, and there's anger burning in my stomach at the last sentence he spoke.

Not at Bellamy, but at how truthful it is. That anger is enough to make me nod my head in agreement.

"Yes, I'd be okay with that. If Lawson wants to, you can't make him do it," I explain, and he shakes his head.

"This was Lawson's idea. He wanted me to talk to you about it. I told him I didn't want to push you, he just told me to ask so I did. I'm glad I did too. I'll let him know," He holds my hand, and squeezes.

I smile at him. Bellamy's friends are almost as caring as he is, which is incredibly hard to do.

"Where are we going?" I change the subject.

We've been in the car for a while, and I don't recognize where we are at all.

"Somewhere that I added to the list. A date of choice if you will."

My stomach flips, "That's against the rules."

He looks completely unphased, "So was having sex in an unromantic way but we did, and having sex more than once, but we did that too. I've also been adding things to your undetailed list since we started. Rules are for losers."

The mention of sex makes my cheeks heat up. Why am I embarrassed to talk about sex with Bellamy? Maybe because he's so good at it? Maybe because he knows he's good too. Maybe it's because the people I have sex with never speak to me after, and I have never in my life had to face someone who gave me an orgasm. Maybe that's it.

"Fine, carry on," I motion, and he turns off the road, and my eyes scan the area around us.

It's dark outside now, and there's not much happening around us, we're practically in the middle of nowhere.

"Are you going to kill me?" I ask and he laughs. "This was your plan, a cute date, and then homicide?"

He doesn't stop laughing.

"There were easier ways to kill me, you didn't have to romance me first. An ax to the head would have sufficed."

He shakes his head, parking the rusty old Jeep in the middle of an empty field.

"I'm not killing you, and I have no plans to," He speaks through his spouts of laughter.

"Yet," I say and he nods with a smile.

"Sure."

It hasn't felt weird since he picked me up, and I was afraid it would after the past day. He's good at making me feel comfortable though, and that's a huge part of why I haven't run away screaming.

"A date to nowhere?"

He turns his car off, getting out. I don't move, waiting for him to open the door for me. He does, and helps me out, keeping my hand in his as he goes to his trunk. He takes out not one but multiple large quilts and blankets. He nods his head to the pillows, and I grab them, following him to the front of the Jeep. He starts spreading things out and makes a giant palette for the two of us. I'm still confused until I hear it. The engine of a plane, loud over us. It looks like a star as it passes over, and I realize just where we are. The airport is near... It has to be.

"See now?" He asks as I sit down on the plush blankets.

"Where did you find this place?" I look up at the sky as Bellamy sits next to me.

"Freshman year on the team, all the seniors used to come out here and get drunk... They'd get all of us drunk actually. Which isn't very romantic but that's how I found it. Then I kept coming back every now and again because there was a good view of the planes coming in and out. I just thought it was nice."

I feel a tinge of jealousy in my chest knowing there's

probably been other girls here before me. I see why, and I don't fault him for bringing me either. It just annoys me when it shouldn't at all. I push the jealousy down.

"This isn't from a romance movie," I remind him.

"Do you know how many romance movies have a romantic airport scene? Do I need to list a few? Sleepless in Seattle, Love Actually, Garden State. There are probably a million more. We'll just use one of those," His knowledge of the movies only makes me more jealous.

I knew he had it but that mixed with the thought of him being romantic and bringing other girls here, I can't help it. The taste is bitter in my mouth.

"Why do you look mad?"

"I'm not mad."

His eyes are locked on me.

"Why are you mad, baby? Don't lie to me," He tilts his head to the side, waiting for an answer.

"Have you ever brought anyone else here?" I blurt out and wish it didn't sound as crazy as it feels coming out of my mouth.

I don't want to intrude. I honestly have no right to but my mouth works quicker than my mind in too many situations. He has a life outside of me, and he's going to continue that. Especially with the rules I've set in place.

"I have never brought another girl here, Kamryn. If that's what you were wondering," He lays himself down, his eyes looking up, and I do the same thing, copying his movements.

I was wondering about that but I won't tell him. I don't want him to know, he can be left to wonder. We lay side by side, with no contact at all, just our eyes looking up to the sky, waiting for a plane to pass by. I feel the anxiety I felt earlier creeping back up my throat. The words I had said to him yesterday, and the silence sitting between us. I press my lips shut, trying my hardest to stop myself, but I can't.

"Bellamy, about what I said yesterday before you left. After I talked to my mom on the phone..." I start.

"You don't have to say anything, I get it."

I furrow my brows, "What do you mean you get it?"

"I mean that I get there's really no chance of a friendship after this. It makes sense, at least for me it does. It would be really hard to go from... From sex to just friends."

I'm shocked he only referred to the sex, but I nod, my chest tight. That's what this was. Fake dating. Fake sex. Fake. It hurts to admit that to myself more than it should. It hurts to hear him say it like that too. It shouldn't, and I want to tell myself to not feel that but I do. I can't help feeling what's right in front of me.

"I'm sorry."

"I am too," Bellamy agrees, and I don't know why my heart is in my throat but it is. "Why were you so against doing this list? Or dating, or doing anything romantic at all?"

I'm shocked at how blunt he is. I was never keen on answering this question, only because Bellamy seems like the type to convince me of why I should give it all a chance. He wants to change my mind... But I don't want my mind changed, and I think he's realized that by now.

"Um... There are a lot of reasons why," There's no sense in hiding any of this anymore from him.

Sadly, we did grow closer. Close enough I feel like I could share anything with him.

"Care to share?"

I sigh and clasp my hands together, resting them on my stomach.

"Have you ever heard the phrase 'Never meet your

heroes' before?" My clasped hands rise and fall as I breathe, my back flat against the ground just like Bellamy.

"I have."

"Romance was like my hero, and I know that sounds dumb but it's the easiest way I can explain it. I loved the romance movies, Bell. I did and I loved books, romance plots, and my parents. I love my parents, and I looked up to them so much growing up. How much they loved each other. I still have yet to meet two people as in love as my parents are."

Images of them through the years flash through my mind.

"My parents were the same..." He speaks in a tone that shows me just how fond he is of them, and my heart aches for him as he sits next to me.

I can't imagine losing people I love that much.

"Keep going," He urges, despite the weight in my chest.

He has no idea it's there, but I feel the pressure.

"I did meet my hero, romance... or I tried to, and I realized that nothing will ever compare to it. No one will be a romance movie, and no one will be a stupid book trope. I will never find what I see on the screen, or read on pages, or imagine in my head, it's never going to work that way. My parents, what they have is unattainable. I swear I don't know how they did it," I feel like I sound crazy.

There's no sensible way to explain this.

"And how did you come to that conclusion?"

"I started to realize it before I got to college. It was a dumb relationship. I know high school romances are silly and superficial, and whatever, but it still hurts my feelings. I know I said I never dated anyone before Dylan, but that's because I don't count high school. It's not a real relationship, it doesn't matter."

"Stop downplaying the way you feel to make everyone else feel comfortable around you."

My mouth opens but nothing comes out. He really just called me out.

"You did it the other day after Leah was mean to you. You pretended it wasn't a big deal when it was. If it hurts then it hurts, that's just it. It's okay if something makes you feel something else."

His words sound so simple but they're anything but.

"Okay, fine. It hurt my feelings a lot and it didn't feel superficial to me at all. My boyfriend at the time cheated on me with who I thought was my best friend, and it made me feel like complete shit. So I said no more boyfriends until after college, and then that's when I started hooking up with people occasionally," Talking about this is easy with him.

It feels like second nature.

"I hated how helpless I felt and how sad I felt, and I hated more than anything that someone else had done something to make me feel that way and there was nothing I could tell myself to make it better. There are a lot of worse things in the world, but having your heartbroken still really hurts... Far more than it should."

I vividly remember how hard I took that breakup. How devastated I was.

"So if you swore off dating from then on out, why Dylan?"

I almost gag at the name.

"Stupidity? Lapse of judgment?" I joke and he laughs softly. "He was one of the only people I've hooked up with that almost made me come... Which is a horrible excuse to date him, but the sex wasn't that bad, and he was really good at talking, back then at least. Now when he talks it sounds like nails on a chalkboard. He's such a dick too... Before you and I started all of this when we were at Leah's party... He called me out for sleeping with people. He said I'd let anyone in my pants, and I agreed with him because I let him in there. But he cheated on me too. So why would he expect me to stay?" I finally get it off my chest and feel relief as I do. I never talk about these things.

"Because he lacks every bit of common sense he could ever possess," He tells me. "I'm sorry... That he cheated, that anyone did."

I groan, "And it's such a disappointment that men that exist in books and TV shows don't exist in the real world. We grow up hearing and reading about Prince Charming, but where the fuck are all the Prince Charmings? I'm getting all the Gastons you know? The assholes and the shitty ones. I know the real ones, the good ones are there, but is it really worth it to look when you're going to get hurt a million times?" I ask.

I don't stop though, my mind is on a roll.

"It's just so stupid. All of this, relationships, feelings, emotions... Love is like... It's like a con job and men? Such a fucking letdown."

He continues to laugh next to me.

"You're not wrong," He agrees with me, which is a shock.

"Bellamy you are the only man I've ever in my life been with who made sure I came first which should be the bare minimum, but here we are... And you did that twice the first time, two whole times. Then last night? That was like a miracle... And it's not reality. None of this is, these stupid feelings, and all these dates, and everything that's happening is awesome Bellamy, but it's not real, it's all for a list, and it's just... So frustrating. That's why I'm against dating and romance because it's not worth the fallout. It never has been."

We sit in silence as I catch my breath after spilling my heart.

"I had no idea. I thought it was just because you were scared of commitment or something. You actually have plenty of reasons. I get it," He tells me. "So that leads me to my next question. Does that mean it's forever? Your hatred for all of this? Don't you want kids and a family one day?"

I shrug, "I mean if I'm honest the idea of it sounds great. Married to someone, with kids, a dog, and a grumpy cat. A big house somewhere nice, a vacation home, and college funds set up for all of the kids. I have a perfect image of it in my head but the only problem is getting there. That's what I can't handle. I can't deal with all the dating, the breakups, and the constant letdowns... Because that's what relationships are, they're constant letdowns. You of all people know that. You've been in far more than me."

"I have and I'm always going to be open to more."

I can't comprehend it. I feel like that should be considered a form of masochism.

"But why?"

"Because being hurt by relationships is kind of meant to happen, I guess? It's not meant to hurt unless you really force it to. That's something I've noticed... Like when Leah and I broke up. It didn't start really hurting me until she started doing what she does. It's like when you try to force a puzzle piece together or something. It was never meant to fit, it's never going to no matter how hard you try. But you've got to keep trying other pieces till one finally fits," He tries to make it make sense in my mind and I do get it. Somewhat...

"I guess I see where you're coming from," I agree. "Are

you not going to try and convince me that relationships are worth it? Or that not all men are complete shit?" He sighs next to me.

"No. I don't see a reason to."

Once again. Bellamy's words take me by surprise.

"Okay, but why?"

"Because you have reasons to feel the way you do. And all of those feelings come from experience, and that's valid... So why would I, a man, try to convince you that men don't suck? Why would I try to convince you of anything? There's no power in words in this type of situation. I can only hope that one day someone will show you. That's all."

This is another moment where I feel like he's not real. He always knows what to say. And he's always respectful about it. His words also sting because the hopeless romantic in me is telling me that he has shown me. That he's right here, doing just that. Showing me, but I know that's not the truth. He's showing me a fake version of himself. This List version.

"I appreciate you..." I don't think before I speak, but it's true.

Bellamy is far better than most, even as a friend. He's just a good person. He's quiet now, probably not knowing how to respond to me. I watch as another plane shoots across the sky, the lights looking just like more stars.

"My parents were the same as yours. When me and my sister were younger they were around a lot more. They would do family dinner every night and we all cooked together. My mom loved cake and desserts. My dad loved baking them. I want what they had, that's what I want with my future. I want my kids to love each other the way I love my sister. I want to love my wife the way my dad loved my mom. That and football of course. The NFL."

"Football is important to me too. The NFL. Just like it is for you. I want to be on the field, always," I smile at the thought.

It's all I've wanted for years.

"Wouldn't that be something?" He asks and I look over at him, seeing him stare up at the sky, a plane passing just as he does.

"What?" I ask.

"Us, years down the road. We both graduated, and we both moved on with our lives. What if I'm working and just see you on the sidelines one day, wouldn't that be something? Even better if you were working for my team."

I smile, imagining how good it would feel to see his face after years of not. He'd probably be married, with kids. The picture perfect romance he deserves. If I've ever said anything true it's that. Bellamy deserves to be loved so hard by someone.

"That would be something," I smile to myself, despite the small tinge of hurt I feel thinking of it.

Thinking of me feeling the same thing in my chest for him that I do now all those years down the road. Thinking I might love him, but never actually knowing if I do. You can't fall in love with someone this soon, can you? You can't truly build a real relationship off of someone you're fake dating for a fake list, can you? No. You can't.

"I want you to stay for the summer. Not for me, but for you. I won't make it weird. I won't even talk to you if you don't want to if that means you'll stay. I just want you to get the future you want, just like me," He tells me and I shake my head.

"It's not you. It's more than that," I admit, knowing I won't be telling him the full reason.

"Good, because if you turn this down because of me I'm

going to be pissed," He has no idea that he just called me out.

I won't tell him either.

"Tell me about your sister..." I offer up something I know he won't be able to shut up about, changing the subject away from me.

Bellamy starts talking about her, and not only her but his family. His grandparents, and his parents too. He doesn't stop and it's obvious he's proud of who he was raised by. It's obvious he misses his parents more than anything, and that he's his sister Brianne's biggest fan. It's blatantly obvious that Bellamy Archer has the biggest heart of anyone I've ever met in the entire world, and that thought alone makes me feel like a big ball of messy unresolved feelings. Things with Bellamy are so much more than they were supposed to be. This feels cluttered, and it feels confusing, but more importantly, it feels so, so good...

CHAPTER TWENTY-THREE

CRAZIER BY TAYLOR SWIFT

WE LOOKED AT THE PLANES, AND THE STARS FOR A while, but decided to leave before it was too late. The second we got in the car the music was turned up loud, and I realized that Bellamy really does have a thing for boy bands. I didn't know how serious his obsession was until now but it turns out we both share a huge love for the '90s bubblegum pop, and even the new age stuff too. He might have a bigger crush on Harry Styles than I do.

I sing along with him as we drive home, the air light as it whips through the open Jeep. He smiles brightly when he doesn't care, and I think it makes me feel the best knowing he feels comfortable around me like this. Part of me wonders if he ever felt like this with Leah, or anyone else. If he ever felt like he could be the way he is with me. The thought loses itself as he slows the car down, turning off the main road. I look around and see the pretty street we've stopped at.

"What are you doing?" He stops the car haphazardly on the street.

His parallel parking is anything but good.

"Doing what I signed up for. Come on," He motions and he gets out of the car.

I don't wait for him to open my door, I just get out. He keeps the engine running. I look at the small quaint street, during the day I'm sure it would be just as pretty, but right now it has bistro lights strung around, and over. Some people are milling around, but most of the street is empty and quiet.

Bellamy leans into the car through the open window and grabs his phone. I watch him as he fiddles with it, moving quickly. He cranks the volume in his Jeep, playing something slightly different from what we were listening to before. Crazier by Taylor Swift blasts from the car, and he jogs up to me, not hesitating to grab my hand and pull me into the middle of the street.

"Was this planned?"

He starts to sway me, our chests pressed together tight. His large hand is spread on my lower back, pulling me close to him. He keeps my hand in his, and my other hand rests on his shoulder as I look up at him.

"Not in the slightest. I saw the street and knew if I pulled over it would feel just like this," He says and I feel it too.

It's just like a movie. Like *La La Land*. I imagine myself in a pretty dress, my heels clicking on the ground as he starts to dance with me. Outside looking in we look absolutely insane and I'm very aware of that. Me in sweatpants and a t-shirt, him in his lounge clothes just the same.

Two random strangers dancing in the middle of the street we don't seem to belong on. Or maybe people aren't looking at us like we're crazy but like we're something else. Like we're something out of a movie or a book. Like we're two people so in love that nothing exists around us. Like we're something that doesn't exist in the real world, but we're here, and we're doing this, and we do exist. The thought settles in my chest, and it fills it to the brim with feelings. My heart throbs so hard it almost hurts. The song choice too. It's him. It's just so Bellamy.

"Don't you have to buy the entire Hannah Montana movie soundtrack to be able to listen to this song?" I ask him, my voice soft, but I know he can hear me because I feel him laughing under me.

"Yes, you do. Once again, I have a little sister," He hesitates for a second.

I look up at him, narrowing my eyes, knowing it was more than just his sister that influenced this choice.

"It's a good movie, okay?" He defends himself, and I can't help but smile.

We go quiet again, and I watch his eyes. Normally I wouldn't be fond of eye contact like this, but Bellamy's eyes are so pretty. Especially when they reflect the twinkling lights the way they are right now.

"How does it feel?" I talk first, playing off of his words from before.

He hesitates. He thinks, and I watch as he starts to smile, "Like it should last for a long time."

His eyes drift elsewhere. I lean my head forward, resting it on his chest, my eyes closing as we sway back and forth, dancing in the street. As if this couldn't feel more like a dream. Like some crazy fantasy I've thought up in my head, Bellamy physically lifts me off the ground. He twirls the two of us, causing laughter to break from my chest. He's strong in the way he holds me, but that doesn't stop me from feeling like I'm falling. We move together, and I feel like I need to pinch myself to wake up.

"You're so perfect," I whisper the words, not wanting to

say them but feeling like I have to. "And you deserve to be loved. You deserve the world."

I shouldn't say it. I know it's insane that I'm letting myself but I can't help it. Not with him.

"You don't know what you're talking about," He's talking softly too, just like I am.

"I do, and I mean every word. You deserve everything good. You deserve everything you want," I tell him, continuing the honest streak.

"And I'm going to pretend this is real for a second, and let you know that you've given me a taste of what I deserve in a little under two weeks. Perfect doesn't exist, but you're pretty good at showing me what it feels like Ryn..."

I don't know what to say to him. His kindness is welcomed in my chest. My chest is tight at the thought of this possibly being real. No pretending, no lying. I think I want that. I think I want this feeling, but the thought of it going south makes my stomach turn.

Bellamy spins me, my hair whipping around me, and when I stop he stares. His eyes are heavy as they look at me. They read so many things, so many things left unsaid, and I don't know what's sitting between us at all right now, but I do know I've never been looked at the way that Bellamy Archer is looking at me right now.

We're not dancing anymore. He's moving my hair from my face, then he's stepping close to me, and then he's in my space altogether. I take a step back, and Bellamy takes a step forward. He closes the space between us, rushing to kiss me like he could die if he didn't do this right now. If he didn't completely take me over with just one kiss that's causing a million things in my chest. It feels like a car crash, like something sudden and instant hits me so hard it almost knocks the wind right out of me. This is the kind of feeling I want to bottle so I can go back to it, and feel it again one day.

My heart is thrumming, loud, and heavy inside of me, the feeling immense as it takes me over. I really like Bellamy Archer. Far more than I should. So much more than I ever thought I would. If I didn't know any better I'd be convinced this feeling in my chest was the feeling of falling in love. But I do know better. I break from his lips, catching my breath, knowing our night doesn't end here.

"We can't stay here all night," I break the dream in my head.

"Where do you want to go, Ryn?" His voice is quiet.

"Back to my apartment," I look up, my eyes meeting him.

He brings his hand to my face, cupping my cheek.

"Come with me?" I suggest.

"I don't know if I can stand another night on your incredibly uncomfortable couch, but I'll stay for a little bit."

My cheeks heat up.

"I expect you in my bed, not on my couch," I feel my stomach drop as the slight smirk returns to his lips, his eyes burning bright.

I kiss him hard as I push him into my bedroom, the journey up the stairs, and into my apartment is agonizing, but finally over. My hands are under his shirt, and feeling every muscle I can as we back into the room, not needing to close the door, but still doing it anyway. He takes me by the shoulders and turns me around, my body coming in contact with the door of my bedroom. I gasp, but without a second to think or breathe he crashes into me again. His lips are harsh and hungry on my own as he kisses me.

There's no hesitation now. There's no gentle energy like there was last night. He wants me, and I want him, and we both fully understand that. A few nights ago I questioned if this would ever happen again, and now I know if I had even spoken that out loud to him he probably would have laughed. Looking back on it I want to laugh.

Bellamy brings his hands to my throat, the warm skin wrapping around it before moving up the side to hold my face. His hands explore, always thorough. His tongue slips into my mouth, and I moan as he kisses me, a gentle smile appearing on his lips. He pulls on the shirt I wear, his shirt on my body.

"Can I have this back momentarily?" His voice is low.

"Momentarily," I warn him, and he tugs on the material pulling it over my head, and my hands are greedy as they take his off just the same, revealing his taut muscles I might never get used to looking at.

Well, I have to. I have to get used to this, to him.

He grabs my jaw, turning my head up to the ceiling as he attacks my neck with his lips. He kisses me harshly, and his hands move around my body, taking their time to find the waistband of the sweatpants I wear. He pushes them down greedily and brings his hands back to my ass as I kick off the pants. He lifts me, his hands firm on my backside, my legs latching around him, not an ounce of fear that I'm too heavy for the football player.

I arch my back against the door the minute he bites, and sucks on my neck, my breath hitching in my throat. It drives me insane to feel his smile on my body, my neck, my lips, wherever it may be. I know he's grinning out of cockiness. Because he feels good knowing it's him who makes me moan, and react, and I'm far too invested in these moments to be annoyed by it. The way he kisses me wherever his lips are found I know the feeling will be a hard one to forget. The way our tongues tangle, and our body heat transfers.

He pushes himself hard into me, and I feel him, I feel how hard he is, and I look down between us, and then at him, his eyes hungry, wild. His hair is disheveled, and his lips are swollen from the harsh kisses. He's pretty when he's breathless. He's pretty when he doesn't try to be. I take my legs from around him and slid my way down so my feet were touching the floor again. My hands leave from around his neck and go to his chest, and then the waistband of the shorts he wears. I tug on them and push him back, our bodies continuing to touch. I palm him, his hard length pressing against his briefs, and he grabs my wrist, moving my hands from him.

"If you don't stop doing that-"

"I know the repercussions, and I want all of them," I take my hands from his grip.

He sits himself down on the bed, and I climb on top of him not bothering to take anything else off.

"Condom?" He asks, and I lean over without removing myself from him.

I pull one out of the package in my bedside drawer. He doesn't question it once as he rips it open. We both pull his briefs, and he puts the condom on. His eyes find mine, and before he can even ask, I speak.

"Yes I want you, I'm positive..." My breath is ragged and completely uncontrolled.

I push my underwear to the side, and he places himself. I revel in the feeling of him once again. This time feeling different as I sit on him, filling myself fully this time. He holds me tight, his hands spread across my lower back, his breath rattling his chest as I lay him back, and come down with him.

"This is okay? Me on top again?" My breath is heavy.

"There's not enough time in the day to have you in every way I would like Kamryn, but you like this is one of those ways."

I feel my stomach tighten. I move myself not talking but feeling everything as I ride him, his hands moving up my thighs, and around to my ass. He watches me silently, his eyes tight on my body, my face, every inch of me. His stare is like a wrecking ball, it crashes through you and turns everything inside to ruin, that's what he's doing right now. I lean down, bringing my lips to his, wanting to feel him everywhere, not just in one place.

So much feeling crashes into me as he wraps his arms around me, similar to a hug, pulling me into him as he moves his hips instead of me moving mine. His body rubs against mine, a sweet spot, and perfect friction. I kiss him slowly, my lips writing poetry on his. He indulges in every slow, savory kiss, his hands holding me like our lives depended on it, and I don't care if he can feel my rapid heart but it's beside the point. It doesn't matter if the entire apartment hears it, or the entire world. He feels good. He feels heavenly pushing in and out of me slowly just like our kisses, filling me fully every time.

I whimper into his mouth, feelings crashing into my chest, and pleasure hitting my core deeply. I squeeze my eyes tight and turn my head down as white hot euphoria ripples through me. I feel it coming, and I whimper again, the feeling of him inside me almost too much for my chest to handle. It's more than sexual pleasure, it's far more than that, and I'm panting now.

He kisses my forehead, his hand lacing through my hair

as he moves inside of me, his hips perfectly slow. I moan out, waves of pleasure hitting me faster until they break down every wall, my body fully giving in to my orgasm. I moan, and he leans up, turning me over so my back meets the sheets.

His hips are faster, and I feel everything more intense now. He holds himself up, each hand on each side of my face. He speeds his movements, and I watch as his brows furrow, pinching together. I reach forward, my hand holding his face. My lips parted, my breath still rapid as he moves, and I can't help but pull him down. Our lips crash together, and he pulls my bottom lips between his teeth, a moan leaving his lips, our foreheads resting against each other as he reaches the peak of his high.

"Fuck Kamryn," His words are sloppy, and I smile as he slows his pace, my chest still feeling that heavy unyielding feeling as before.

He kisses my cheek, my neck, and my face all over. He pulls out of me and then pulls me up with him.

"Where are you taking me?" I ask as he throws me over his shoulder like I weigh nothing.

My laughter is hardly stoppable at this point. He reaches into the open bedside table drawer, grabbing a handful of condoms.

"I told you there wasn't enough time in a day... And the day isn't over yet," He tells me and heads to my bathroom. He doesn't let my feet touch the ground before he kisses me again, his mouth just as hungry as before, but playful, just like his movements. The comfort between us has returned because Bellamy now knows my body, and my mind too. There's simply one thing he hasn't figured out yet, and that's my heart, but I'm not sure if I'll ever let him at this point.

CHAPTER TWENTY-FOUR

MEDICINE BY LEVI RANSOM

I WAKE UP WITH WHAT FEELS LIKE A WARM HUG wrapped all the way around me, and my first instinct is to panic. But then I remember last night, Bellamy. I asked him to stay, and he did, and he's mentally stable unlike me, and won't run away in the morning. So he's here, and we're cuddling, which is a weird word to me. Not only that but it feels weird that I like it so much. It's almost like a weighted blanket.

I settle into him, my lips brushing against his ear as I move into his warmth. We woke up together yesterday too, but like I said before, we barely slept. Last night I had what felt like one of the best nights of sleep in my life. Bellamy is the perfect person to sleep next to. It's like he's dead for a few hours, honestly.

"Are you trying to kiss me? This early, Kamryn?" His voice is husky with sleep. "Good," He speaks before I can, and turns his face to me, planting a kiss on my lips, and my cheeks, and he takes hold of my face to kiss me all over, making me laugh as I try to brace myself.

"I've never met someone who's an all day kind of

318

person, but you are that person," I tell him, shoving him away from me. He leans up, coming into my space again to lean halfway over me. His finger curls around a strand of my hair as he looks at me, twirling it around his finger.

"What do you mean?"

"You're not a morning person, and you're not a night person. You're both... and it's honestly annoying."

He raises his eyebrows at me, a shocked smirk on his lips.

"Annoying? Don't be mad because you can't compete Ryn," He moves off of me, and my stomach turns but settles at the sight of his body. My mind is finally starting to get used to him, and the way he looks.

"Get ready. We're watching clouds today, just like *Up*."

I smile. I get out of bed, and he takes my hand pulling me into him.

"I'll be back in an hour," He kisses me quickly and starts to move toward the door. It almost feels like an instinct to tell him. To tell him I love him, and my chest bursts at the thought. I don't love him, there's no way.

"Text me when you get back. And then when you're on your way here again."

He nods and leaves quickly.

Now I'm alone in my own thoughts and instantly my mind is reeling wondering if that's even possible. I've known Bellamy through friends and others for a long time. I've known of him, but I didn't actually speak to him until this year, not until I started tutoring him this past semester. I was aware of him, but not like now. I've only truly known him for almost two weeks now, and I don't think it's possible to fall in love in less than two weeks. In a normal circumstance, this would be insane. I would be admitted. So I think it's infatuation, not love, that's final.

BELLAMY PICKED ME UP, and he hasn't taken his eyes off of me since. It's been hard for him to even focus on the road. He's got his normal sunglasses perched on his nose, and his hair done, but still perfectly messy. He wears a normal white shirt with khaki colored slacks. He paired it with a white pair of tennis shoes, and he looks just as good as normal. I wear a black dress, one that hugs my chest, and billows out at my waist. It has a cut out in the back exposing my skin there. I paired it with a pair of Dr. Martens, and it seems like he's got some sort of problem with it. I look at him with a question in my eyes.

"Is there something wrong with the way I look? Do I have something in my teeth?" I show my teeth and then look in the mirror, and he takes my hand finally.

"No. There's absolutely nothing wrong with the way you look, baby."

I slump back in the car, and look at him, "So why are you staring at me like I'm from another planet?"

"Because sometimes you look so pretty I think that might be the only way you exist here," He refers to the other planet I mentioned. I pause, knowing I'm blushing like an idiot in front of him, but I don't think I've ever in my life been complimented so blatantly. I look at him, and he's smiling as he looks at the road. "Black is your color."

I smile to myself. I thought I looked really good today too, and I didn't need him to seal that thought, but it does feel good hearing it.

"Thank you, Bell."

He squeezes my hand three times, an odd number, but I squeeze it back, watching as the houses roll by us. He's taking us pretty far away for just cloud watching. I don't speak my thoughts, and let him drive, knowing he wouldn't tell me if I asked.

The area is pretty, but somewhere I've never been despite having lived in the state my entire life. This is a wealthy area, near Seattle. I know that just by looking at some of the neighborhoods, and houses that pass us as we drive. I hear a familiar song on the radio and gasp.

"Bellamy Archer. Is this Sparks Fly by Taylor Swift?" He's played a few of Taylor's older songs, but he normally sticks to the newer stuff.

"Listen, I grew up with a sister who loves Taylor, and this was her favorite album. Either way, it's a good-"

"I LOVE this song," I take his phone from the cup holder, and use it as a makeshift microphone.

I whip my hair and sing, really channeling my inner Taylor Swift as I belt out the lyrics, probably hurting Bellamy's ears at this point. I look over at him, and I don't think I've ever seen him smile wider. The chorus hits, and I don't hesitate to lean into him, and his smile that is quite literally making sparks fly in my chest. He rolls to a stop light, and then he cuts my singing off altogether. He has a hand on each side of my cheeks, his lips are so sure on mine, and the world disappears around the two of us.

A car honks behind us, and I jump. Everything comes back into focus, and Bellamy pulls away. He still has a million dollar smile on his lips. I have a million and one butterflies scrambling inside of my stomach at the thought of him, the song, and the moment. Every moment with him. I smile to myself, still humming the rest of the song. Slowly he pulls into a parking lot off the main road, and I notice a widespread area of green. A park, so vibrant. There are a few trees scattered, but there's a huge tree in the middle of the park, with so much shade underneath it.

"This place is beautiful," I tell him.

There's a nice breeze today, probably because it's going to rain later. I'm happy we can both enjoy the sun together while it lasts. He parks the car, and as soon as he's out, he runs to my side to open the door for me. I thank him, and he helps me down even though I don't need any help. He's incredibly aware all the time, and that's something I've noticed since all of this started. He's not the type to let anything go undone or unnoticed. Even when I don't need help he wants me to know he can and will if I do end up needing it. He's thoughtful. More than most.

Bellamy retrieves the blankets and a cooler from the back of the Jeep, and I feel like it's routine between the two of us. These kinds of dates don't feel repeated though, they feel just as fresh every time he takes a blanket from the back of his car to take us anywhere.

He walks ahead of me, not letting me carry anything, and he brings us to the tree. It's shaded, and nice, but he doesn't bring us right under it. He sets everything down and spreads the quilt along the ground right on the edge where the tree won't block our view. He brought pillows too, and I don't know what's in the cooler, but Bellamy is always ready to eat something, so I'm not surprised he brought it.

"There are only three more things on the list," Bellamy's voice is soft.

I think of the list in my head. I never memorized it, I was only reminded of the things I wrote during each date. But It doesn't feel like we've done as much as we have. It also feels like I could do this for months and months with him. Like I don't want it to end.

"What's left?" I ask him.

"Beach trip at midnight, playlist, and carving our initials in a tree, but I plan to do that one today before we leave,"

He nods his head to the tree behind him. He brings himself down to the blanket and I do the same thing, turning over on my back, and inching myself closer to him. I rest my head on the pillow partially, and partially on his shoulder as well.

"Are you excited to get rid of me?" My tone is light as I joke.

"I've actually had a lot of fun the past week and a half. I didn't really think we'd finish this early, you've got a few days left before you leave."

To be honest I didn't think he'd finish at all.

"I hate to admit it, but I also had fun," The words are bittersweet in my mouth as I speak them.

"Hate to admit it?" His eyes settle on me as he turns his head.

"I told you I didn't want to do it, and I told myself it would be dumb, and I'd hate every second. I hate being proven wrong, and I was. So, yes, I do hate to admit it, but it's true. I had fun dating you."

He lets out a triumphant "Hmmm" and I don't say anything about it, I just let him sit with that fact for a little bit. My eyes focus on the clouds, something I never normally watch, but am enjoying staring at right now.

"I see a giraffe with a cowboy hat," I point to the shape in the sky.

"Exactly where do you see that?" There's laughter behind every single word he speaks, signaling he doesn't see a thing.

"Right there," I point, bringing my finger in his line of sight, he lifts his hand, pointing to the same spot.

"There? That's not a giraffe, that's a dinosaur."

I scoff, he must have vision issues.

"You're insane, that looks nothing like a dinosaur," I laugh, and my hand falls, the sun hitting us perfectly now.

The breeze is constant, and soft on my skin as I lay next to Bellamy. I sit myself up partially and look around at the quiet park.

"How did you know about this place?" I ask. It's beautiful, and close to the city but still quiet. It's perfect.

"Well, I grew up right down the road. My parent's home, my home now. It's down the street."

I furrow my brows, "What do you mean your home now?"

"When my parents passed away they left me everything. They left my sister money of course too, but most everything was in my name the second I turned 18. The house, money. The Jeep. It was all theirs, and they gave it all to me. So... so the house is mine, but I don't live in it obviously. My grandparents and sister live there now."

I don't understand that kind of pain, and I don't ever want to, but as always I feel sad for Bell and his sister at the thought of their loss.

"Do you ever want to live there again?" I feel him shrug against me.

"I'm not sure... I guess it depends on the future. Whoever I end up with might not want to stay here, or if I play for the NFL I may not live here so there's no point in letting a house go unlived in. So maybe I'll sell it, or sign it over to my sister if she decides to stay here. I have no idea what could happen."

My heart beats faster at the thought of who he ends up with. My heart aches over it.

"When did your parents pass away again?" I ask and he takes a second before answering me.

"When I was in high school."

My hand moves over the blanket until it finds his. I lock my fingers with his.

"Did they call you when they were gone on work trips?"

"Me and my sister every night," He nods while he speaks. "I know it seems like something to be sad about or feel bad for me for, but it's not. I miss them, but I've grown up, and I've learned how to handle that pressure. And I had them for a long time. It wasn't enough time but it was longer than a lot of other people have had their parents. I think that's one of the things about you that makes me the most happy, Kamryn. Your relationship with your parents."

I didn't expect him to turn the conversation around. Now I'm confused.

"What do you mean?" I need elaboration.

"A lot of people our age don't really appreciate what their parents do or have done. I know there are some circumstances that make everyone's situation different. I know I don't know everyone's story, but it makes me happy to see that you call your mom like you do. That you're as close with her as you are, and that you're close with your dad too. It makes me happy to see how much you appreciate them."

I feel my chest heat up.

"My parents are a handful but they love people, and that's what makes it easy to love them."

"I've never met them, but they made you... So I can imagine how wonderful they are."

My chest keeps its warmth, and I feel it spread to my cheeks. Bellamy was always open with flirting, but for the past two weeks the compliments are new, and they make me nervous, but in a good way. They don't feel like casual flirting, they feel intentional.

"I think both of us turned out pretty okay," I tell him.

He squeezes my hand again, one two, and three times. I squeeze back, and we sit, pointing at clouds for what feels like hours. Bellamy pulled me along with him after the clouds started to turn dark, and we found our way under the tree. He pulled out a pocket knife I never knew he carried, and he began carving, K first and then a B. He even drew the cheesy heart around it, and it makes me happy and sad all at once. We ran from under the tree to his car, the soft rain starting to pour down on us. There's one date left. Only one. I want to say it went by far too fast, but isn't that what I wanted? Didn't I wish for these two weeks to be a breeze?

CHAPTER TWENTY-FIVE

THE ARCHER BY TAYLOR SWIFT

"Do you mind if I stop by my house? Since I'm already here I figured I could see B and my grandparents," Bellamy asks as we sit down, finally out of the rain, and inside the cover of his Jeep.

"That's perfectly fine."

He probably doesn't see them as much as he wants to considering it's a long drive from our campus, "You don't have to come in."

I tilt my head in his direction.

"Do you not want me to meet them?" I ask.

I don't even know if I want to meet them. Isn't that something only couples do? Usually, but I've heard so much about his sister, I feel like I should meet her. I don't know if it's what he would want though.

"No, I do. I would love for you to meet them, you can meet them. I just didn't want you to feel like I was forcing you because I wanted to stop in. I was just giving you the option to stay in the car if you wanted it."

The thoughtful side of him shows once again. He turns down the road, exactly where he had pointed, and I look at everything around us as we drive. I'm sure it won't rain for long, maybe an hour or two. It's not as hard as it normally is when it rains.

Bellamy pulls into a neighborhood, and it takes everything in me not to gawk at the size of the houses we drive past. Each one is big enough to house a family and probably all their friends if they ever had a party. I know the inside must be far prettier than the outside which is truly saying a lot.

I didn't grow up without money. My family was well off, but not like this. Not like Bellamy. I watch as he pulls into a driveway, three cars parked in it, all of them fairly new looking compared to the old beat up Jeep that he told me belonged to his dad. The sentiment of it still makes my heart swell.

"Your house is beautiful," I look up at the white brick house, black shutters, and matching details all around.

"Thank you," Bellamy gets out, and comes around to my side.

Once we're both out, he keeps his hand on my lower back as we walk in through the front door. My eyes are scanning everything as we walk, looking at every beautiful detail of the home. This place is where a family is raised. It makes sense here, it's perfect here.

"Ma, Pa! I'm home!" Bellamy calls out, one hand cupped around his mouth.

"Belly?" I hear a girl's voice and look around.

Around the corner of the walkway, a beautiful girl steps into view. She's wearing gym shorts and a tight athletic shirt. Her hair is long and brown, with beautiful natural curls that hang down to her lower back. This is his sister. Brianne. I can see the resemblance between the two of them.

"Hey, B," He smiles, and she runs down the long entryway until she's jumping to hug her big brother.

He hugs her tight, and I smile at the reunion, the two of them making me wish I had a sibling. He lets her go, and her eyes go to me, and back to Bellamy.

"Oh. Bri, this is Kamryn, and Kamryn this is my sister."

I smile, and wave, and his sister goes past that, wrapping me in a hug. It's nothing like the hug she just shared with Bellamy, but it's still warm.

"It's so nice to meet you. Bellamy doesn't bring girls here, he only brings those meathead football players he calls friends over," She rolls her eyes, and I laugh, watching Bellamy shove his sister to the side.

"I'm letting Lawson know you said that, he's going to have a mouthful to say to you when-"

"Oh I'd like to see Lawsy even try to get a word in when I'm in the room, he has no chance," She argues back, and I love seeing Bellamy in his element.

This is his element just like football is. Being with his family is comfortable.

"Belly is that you?" I hear from upstairs.

"It's me!" He calls back.

"Come up here for a minute, we need your help with something," The older voice of a woman speaks.

"Coming!" He yells up. "Do you want to come with me?" I open my mouth to agree with him, but I don't get a chance.

"No she can stay with me," Bri takes my hand, and pulls me from the entryway, and to the other room before I can even say anything else, so I shrug my shoulders toward Bellamy, and turn toward his sister instead.

"I'll be down soon. Don't be annoying B!"

She rolls her eyes as she pushes the door open to a very

clean, and simple bedroom. It's clean but lived in. There's a desk with books and schoolwork. She's far more put together than I am. At least Bellamy and his sister have one thing in common. She jumps on her bed, and she pats it too, signaling for me to sit down.

"You're really pretty. Bellamy was right."

I smile at the compliment.

"I wasn't aware Bellamy had been talking about me at all," I raise my eyebrows, and she smiles, just like I am right now.

"Obviously. He's been telling me about you since February. I don't remember, but he said you were his tutor right? And I thought it was a little bit silly that he needed a tutor, especially in math because he's super smart. He tutors me in math every time he comes home."

My stomach drops a bit at the confession. Her math must not be too complicated if Bellamy is the one helping her. He's smart, but... He's been with me once a week every single week since February.

"Oh, he does? Well, he seemed completely clueless when I was tutoring him," Realization strikes me hard.

Has he been lying this entire time? He was so believable. He couldn't have been. His sister shrugs her shoulders, completely unaware of what I'm thinking.

"But either way, I've been hearing about this crush he had, and now I finally get to meet you because you and Bellamy are dating right?" She doesn't understand that she's ratting him out right now.

And I can't tell if I'm happy or mad.

"Oh... It's complicated... Not dating... But-"

"I totally get it. Complicated is better than nothing. Sorry, I just never really get to meet any cool people through Bellamy, they're all gross, and like throwing balls for fun."

I laugh, despite the uneasy feeling in my stomach. At least she has a similar sense of humor to me.

"You don't have to apologize. You seem close to Bellamy, I think it's sweet you're excited to meet his... Friends," I fumble the words, and she smirks as she notices.

"We are close. Bellamy is my best friend. Boy problems? Bellamy. Math problems? Bellamy. If I just want to talk? Bellamy. He's always here. And I wanna be just like him too. I'll be going to SPU next semester. I just graduated and I got accepted to the university early admission last year," She tells me, and I raise my eyebrows.

"What for?" I lean myself into her, wanting to know her well. I don't know why. I have no idea why but she's sweet. And she's funny.

"Oh, I cheer. My parents had us on the field together despite the age difference. I was always on the older teams anyway because I can do all the tumbling, and I'm small so they can throw me in the air. I'm going to get a BFA in dance. I want to be an NFL Cheerleader one day,"

I laugh at her energy. She's far more talkative than her brother, but I like that about her.

"Okay, enough talking her ear off B," Bellamy pushes the door open, and my stomach sinks at the realization of what his talkative sister had said.

Bellamy lied. But she must not know what she's talking about. At the same time she talks about how close they are, how would she not know? My mind is fighting itself as I look at him, but I manage a smile.

"She's sweet. Don't be mean," I defend her, and his sister smiles next to me.

"Yeah, listen to your girlfriend."

Bellamy sighs, "I didn't tell her that."

I nod, believing him, "I assumed that much."

I smile awkwardly and he nods his head.

"We were just stopping in, but I'll come back next week, and stay for a few days alright?"

I get up and walk with him. He guides me out of her bedroom, and his sister follows, jumping behind us.

"Bring Kamryn! Please! Kamryn, please come, I'm inviting you firsthand, right now."

Bellamy hesitates. He looks at me. He's not used to dancing around the truth with her from what I can tell. He probably hasn't explained our arrangement to her.

"I'm going home to my parents in the next few days actually or else I would... I would love to... To meet everyone."

I feel bad for not fully telling the truth. I probably wouldn't come even if I was staying on campus. Because after our last date, there's nothing left between us.

"Another time," She nods her head, and I don't say anything, I just nod.

Bellamy hugs his sister, and we both say our goodbyes before he ushers me out of the door, and back in the car. I stay quiet, my mind dancing with theories, and answers to the questions I continue to ask myself.

I don't want to think that all of this was some giant ploy. Something that he's been plotting this entire time? Since I started tutoring him. I never once gave in to his advances, but he never once made any in the sense of asking me on a date, or inviting me anywhere with him. He never tried. I wouldn't have said yes, but he never made his attraction apparent. I just thought he flirted with me because it was his personality. I thought he flirted with me because he's a stupid boy.

"Are you okay?" I have no idea how much time has passed since I zoned out, but we aren't anywhere I recognize anymore.

"Fine," I force another smile, and he furrows his brows, a question on his face. "I'm fine, really," I try again.

"Did it bother you that she called you my girlfriend? Bri is a lot sometimes, but she was joking."

I shake my head.

"No. That wasn't what bothered me," My words leave a question hanging between us. He can sense it right away.

"Did she say something else?" His hand hangs loose on the steering wheel as he drives.

"She said a lot of things. She said you were incredibly smart and very good at math which was a shock to me. She also knew about me, and not from the past few weeks, but for months, and months. Apparently, she's heard a lot about me."

His grip tightens on the steering wheel as he continues to drive.

"So I guess my first question is did you even need tutoring?" I ask.

He shrugs, and I'm not usually blunt like this asking Bellamy questions, but there's a bit of anger I feel in my chest. Confusion, and anger, and now as I watch him shrug his shoulders. I feel anxiety spreading.

"I did at first," He admits.

"At first?" I ask, and he sighs.

"Look Ryn-" I stop him right away, not wanting to hear him admit to anything at all right now.

"Bellamy. You lied to me. You never needed me, you... You what? You wanted sex? Is that what it was? You thought this would be the way to get it? Faking stupidity?" My voice doesn't raise once.

My words are more harsh than I had intended.

"I never faked stupidity, I just am stupid. God Kamryn, do you think there was a way I could casually speak to you outside of class without-"

"Yes! There were plenty of ways! There are thousands of other ways besides wasting my time. You... Ugh! Bellamy, why did you do the list? Don't make up some bullshit lie either. Tell me the truth."

He sits in silence.

"You're not going to like my answer Kamryn."

My stomach drops, a thousand reasons crossing my mind.

"But I want to finish it with you..." He says.

I let out a small laugh, "Bellamy..."

I shake my head, my eyes locking outside of the car, not on him. I can't look at him.

"Kamryn... One more date, that's all I'm asking."

I sigh, wondering how he's even going to ask me that right now.

"You lied," I speak the words again.

"I did, but... Kamryn, give me the last date, give me the beach just to hear me out. Let me mend some things. Please. I'll tell you everything."

"I just want to go home," I admit.

What was his reasoning? Why did he do the list? Why was he so persistent? Why did he go so far as to add his own date? My heart sinks at the possibilities, and the fact that he knows I won't like the answer. There are only a few good reasons, but most of them sound horrible rolling through my head.

"I'll take you home then. I've never once wanted to do anything to upset you Kamryn. And I only lied once. Only once," He tells me.

"What's that supposed to mean? You shouldn't have lied at all."

He nods, "I know that, and you do too, and I'm sorry. Once doesn't make it better but I'm telling the truth," His voice is timid.

He's not being aggressive as he tries to explain himself. That doesn't make me want to hear him out, though.

"I'm sure you are sorry, and I want to think about all of this, and I'll text you tomorrow about the date, but for now I just want to go home."

My head is already full of muck, and tarnished thoughts of him, and what we've done the past two weeks.

"Kamryn, I never used you for sex," He says and I feel relief but not fully. "I wouldn't do that to you. I wouldn't. So please don't think that's what all of this was."

I look at him, and he looks worried, his face showing distress I've never seen on him before, "I believe you."

His words from before are replaying in my mind. His words about the insecurities I've shared, about the insults that have been thrown at me. Bellamy might be dumb sometimes, but he's not cruel. He's not heartless. I have to believe him.

"Kamryn, is that the only reason you're upset?"

I shrug. I feel hurt. Not just upset but hurt. I shouldn't because none of this matters. Fake dating, then done. No strings, but it feels like I'm a puppet being pulled by about a thousand strings right now. There are so many strings I've tangled myself in it feels like I might never find a way out, and that's not his fault. It's mine. I let feelings get in the way, and if this was between me and anyone else, his lies wouldn't bother me. They wouldn't surprise me, but with Bellamy, it just feels different. So I'm lying now. I shake my head no, and shrug.

"No, I'm not even upset. I guess it just took me by surprise is all. You just...You took me by surprise," The lie burns in my mouth.

I don't want to lie to him, but he lied to me. For months he lied, and I hate the thought of all of it. I hate that I wasn't something that happened, I was something that he planned.

"I could say the same for you Ryn," He speaks softly, and I stay quiet after that.

I want my time to be without him, and then I want my date. I want my date. I want one last night with Bellamy before I cut it all off. That's all I want. Bellamy drives us the rest of the way back to my apartment and he looks at me the minute he parks the car. I open my door without waiting for him to open it for me, and he doesn't fight it.

"I'll see you tomorrow night," I tell him even though I don't know if it's the truth or not.

He starts to say something but doesn't get it out before I get myself out of the Jeep, and head to my apartment, silence filling the air, but not my mind.

BELLAMY HASN'T TRIED ONCE to text me in the hours it's been since he dropped me off. I made myself a sandwich and didn't eat it. I tried to take a nap, and couldn't sleep. I tried to watch New Girl, but couldn't focus. My mind is spinning with thoughts of Bellamy the past semester, wondering if every word was something calculated, and planned. I think back to every tutoring session trying to pull everything from the depths of my head, trying to see if there's something I missed at the moment. He had good intentions. But it shouldn't matter. He still lied about everything.

I send Sienna a text, an SOS. I wait for her response. When she replies, I'm relieved. She started training for fall ball, and spring season with her teammates. She's serious, and I know the rest of the teams are too. She tells me she's on her way, and I sigh to myself, not even knowing what I'll be able to talk about. Not knowing how I'm supposed to feel now with everything between Bellamy and I. Sienna is walking through my door not even twenty minutes since I sent the text. My knees are pulled up to my chest, and my apartment feels empty right now. I hug myself and she looks worried.

"I feel sick to my stomach," My words sound hollow.

"Are you pregnant, or did Bellamy do something?" She moves quickly toward me.

"I'm not pregnant," I tell her, not even questioning why she would suspect that.

"So what did he do?"

I tell her everything that happened today, what his sister said, and how he responded. Sienna presses her lips together tight.

"The worst part of all of this is the fact that I feel like I can't be mad. I feel like it would be... I don't know. I just feel like it's wrong. I feel like I'm not allowed to have feelings at all."

"You're more than allowed to have feelings, and you're allowed to be mad at him for lying. But I don't think he did it to have sex with you," She tells me. "I think maybe he was just trying to get to know you. Maybe he just thought you were cool, and didn't know what else to do."

Sienna is always the best at playing devil's advocate. I swear it's her favorite thing to do. But I've been through this kind of thing before. I've been through the lies, and the hurt, and this is exactly why I steer clear of feelings.

"Even if that was the case, it's still not fair. It's not fair because Bellamy and I swore on it all along that this was meant to be nothing. No strings. No ties. Nothing. So if he went into this with different intentions. If he went into this already having feelings, big or small then that's just. I don't know," I say.

It's unfair.

"It's romantic. Just like all the movies he was trying so hard to replicate with you," She argues.

I don't know if I feel warmth because I'm angry, or if that just sparked something inside but they feel one in the same right now.

"It's crazy because I feel like I know him. I feel like I've really known Bell for months... Even for years, but I haven't. Bellamy confuses the hell out of me, and I just don't know, Sienna. I've never been so lost for words and for a plan on what to do next."

There's no way I can stay on campus for summer sessions. There's no way. I'm not hurt by his lies, I'm confused. I'm a little angry too. I feel like I was blindsided a bit.

"I know it's really messy, and it feels unusual but maybe you should for once just do what your heart is telling you to do, and then maybe you can deal with the repercussions of that later. I think you should hear him out tomorrow. Just understand his reasoning for lying about the tutoring, and going into this whole thing with you. Maybe it's not what you think."

I contemplate it.

I was going on our last date tomorrow night already, it was set in my head before Sienna had even come, but I still feel sick. Every time I think of going home while feeling this way, tears threaten my eyes. I'm not the sensitive type, but that's all I've felt since I got out of Bellamy's car. My phone buzzes and I look, seeing Dylan's name on my phone. I groan. Sienna's eyes catch his name on my screen.

"What does he want? Why didn't you block him?"

I slide open the text. My stomach sinks, a picture, and a message.

"I thought this was your new boyfriend?" It reads.

The picture is incredibly incriminating and it was taken today. Bellamy is in the same clothes he was wearing with me earlier. He's at a coffee shop, and he's smiling, but he's with Leah. She's smiling too, and his hand is threaded through her hair. It looks like the two of them are backing away from a hug. Maybe even a kiss. Maybe I'm looking too far into it. But that sick feeling returns in a wave as everything clicks in my mind.

"That son of a bitch."

I don't look away from the picture, the tears pooling in my eyes again, but staying this time. He used me for tutoring. I'm assuming Leah hated that too. He did The List for what? To make her jealous. I feel manipulated now. Like I was used. I had thought about the possibility of this. Of Bellamy doing this to get her back, to make her jealous. He never told me why he invited her to my New Year's party. He never explained that to me, and now I know it was to make her jealous.

To see him defend me, and stand up for me. He wanted her to see that he cared about someone else, and it worked. I already felt betrayal sitting low in my chest at the confession from his sister, but seeing this. Having my original fear set true in my brain. It's not a good feeling. Anger and hurt in my chest, and so many questions in my mind.

"He lied because he wanted his ex back..." I don't want to speak the words out, but I need to hear them.

They settle between Sienna and me. I think of every-thing... Everything I trusted Bellamy with. I think of going to him after the frat party. Getting a fucking tattoo. Every-thing was all for nothing. And even before that, it was all based on a lie. I have no idea what's true, and what's not.

"I'm sorry Kam..." Her hand comes to my leg to show me she's here for me.

I laugh, tears slipping out of my eyes.

"I just don't get why he went as far as to sleep with me. He knew she was jealous that night before he slept with me, so why do that? Why let me tell him about my life, and why beg to complete the list? Did he feel guilty? Because he real-ized I'm a fucking person, not some object he can just use? God I feel like a fucking idiot," I wipe tears from under my eyes, and probably makeup too.

I've used people for sex, but they know they're being used before it happens. I would never do this. I would never go to such lengths to just get sex. If it wasn't for sex, if it was to make Leah jealous he could have told me from the start. I would have gone along with it. I wouldn't have caught feel-ings for him.

"You're not an idiot at all, maybe he was really good at faking a relationship. Or maybe he wasn't faking it at all, and this is a picture from your shitty ex who you don't trust at all..." She tells me and anger boils deeper in my chest.

"I don't trust Dylan, but I don't really trust Bellamy right now either. He's been lying this entire time Si. About more things than one from the looks of this picture. Even if it's not what it looks like, he never even told me he was going to see Leah, going to talk to her..." I writhe in my anger and Sienna sighs.

"Lawson told me you got mad at him the other day for wanting you to tell him about summer sessions. He said you snapped at Bellamy and told him you're not dating and you don't have to tell him anything. Why should he tell you where he's going when he's not with you if that's how you were treating him?" She asks, calling me out completely.

I stare at my friend blankly, hating that she's right. It doesn't ease my anger.

"I have every right to be mad at him," I argue and she nods.

"I agree. You should be mad at him for lying about the list. But not for a picture sent by Dylan. Kam, sometimes you jump to conclusions, and normally I jump with you because we do everything together, but this... I don't think you should. As for the tutoring thing, leave. Don't finish the list, stop caring, and just leave and go home. If he's willing to lie about something like that and it makes you not trust him, then don't give him any more. I support you, you know that," She ensures, and I know she does support me, but she's also my voice of reason.

If she thinks I have reason to be mad, then I must actually have a reason.

"I do care about him. And I care about the picture too, more than I should, and I feel stupid because despite the rules I do have feelings for Bellamy, and I knew this was a bad idea, and I was dumb enough to think it might have been real. Just a little bit, he made it feel real. The sex, the talks, the dates. Everything felt real, he felt real, and I shouldn't be mad because I made the rule, and he followed it and I didn't. I thought he had feelings though. I really did. So I will leave, and I won't let this stupid list burden him anymore. I'll just take the rest of summer, and I'll move on."

My mom is going to be surprised. She's also going to hear an earful about him too.

"What about summer sessions?" She asks and my heart sinks all over again.

"I can't... Not when she'll be on the field practicing too. They'll just be rubbing it in my face. I just need to take the summer. I'll get over him, and then I can... I can be on the field, and I'll pretend, just like he has been. I can pretend too. Besides, I don't need summer sessions to make it to the NFL. I have to get my master's first anyway, I don't need them," I try my best to give a convincing smile.

"Can I come visit you? At least once..." That's the best part of Sienna, she's not the kind of person that will try to get me to do something I don't want to do.

She trusts my instincts and I'm thankful for that.

"I don't think I'd be able to last all summer without seeing you," I laugh through the tears and accept the hug she throws around my shoulders.

CHAPTER TWENTY-SIX

ANYTHING BY DODIE

Sienna helped me finish packing up what I would need for the next few months that I'll be gone. I felt wrong leaving which is a feeling I've never had when leaving campus to go home to my parents. I think it's because I've never in my life left feeling unresolved. That's what I feel right now. I feel like I was lied to. I don't know if I should be mad at Bellamy for the picture. I never gave him a chance to explain, but whatever that was mixed with his lie... It's enough to lose my trust. Especially after I told him everything I did about barely having trust in the first place.

My mom picked me up from the bus station, and it's been silent since she picked me up. I feel like I haven't opened my mouth to talk in ages, and I'm glad because I don't feel like talking at all right now.

My mom seems like she can't sit still. More than normal as she drives us back to my childhood home. She looks pretty right now. Her dark hair pulling back into a tight bun, her glasses resting on the bridge of her nose. She's got on her normal red lipstick, and pretty makeup. I swear she looks like she hasn't aged in years.

I don't know what's gotten into her, but I know she knows there's something wrong with me. Her hands have been tapping the wheel, and she keeps looking at her phone that's propped up on her dashboard. She keeps looking at me too, like she's waiting for something. She knows me better than anyone else, and she can read me as easily as a children's book. She knew there was something wrong the minute I wanted to come home early, she just hasn't asked yet, and I know she will.

"Why are you so fidgety?" I finally speak.

My voice sounds like a phantom, like it isn't me talking at all.

"I'm not fidgety... Why are you so quiet?" She asks and I shrug. "Does it have anything to do with the fact that you decided to come home a few days early?"

I shrug again.

"And does coming home early have anything to do with your so-called friend Bellamy?" She pushes.

I keep my eyes out of the window, not looking at her once as I watch everything pass by us. There's really not much out here. It's barren compared to the city. I hate how my mom always has an intuition about what's going on in my life. I hate that she knows even when I've never told her anything. The minute I mentioned a boy to her without her forcing it out of me she knew he was more than a friend. I thought he was at least.

"That's all he is," It's the truth despite the feelings I have inside.

All he is now and ever will be is a friend. Lesser than a friend at this point.

"That sounds like a lie," Her voice trails off.

I know when my mom doesn't want to push me for

answers. She doesn't want to right now, but in normal mom fashion, she's going to do it anyway.

"Bellamy and I had a silly little fling, and it didn't mean anything, and that's it. It was a mistake, and it was stupid."

It was a mistake, but it wasn't stupid, and it wasn't silly, or little in my head. It was special to me. Bellamy's words ring in my head, telling me not to diminish my own feelings to make everyone else feel comfortable. I push it away, he lied to me, I shouldn't be thinking of any of the things he said, good or bad.

"Why do you think that?" She asks and I don't respond, relief crashing through me when I see the familiar home.

My mom pulls into the driveway, and I still keep my mouth shut.

"Kamryn..." My mom tries once more and I shake my head.

"I don't want to talk about it, Mom. I don't want to think about Bellamy, that's why I left. He wasn't who I thought he was, and he just... He's just not what I need."

I watch as she presses her lips together. The words taste bitter in my mouth, but I force them out because they're more than true.

She shuts off the car, looking disappointed as she looks around us. I look around too, trying to understand what she's looking for and disregard it when I see nothing. I grab my things from the back of the car, and my mom helps, both of us approaching the side entrance of the house, and walking up the brick stairs. I hear a car behind me, tires screeching to a halt, and both my mom and I turn at the loud sound.

"Oh, he made it," My mom sounds relieved, but I feel everything but relief.

My eyes rest on the beat up Jeep, and Bellamy getting out at the bottom of the driveway. He slams his door, and he looks disheveled as if he just raced three hours to get here. I have no idea how the hell he got ahold of this address but I have a feeling it has to do with my mom which only leads to more questions. I feel anger, I feel nauseous. I turn away from him and don't wait for him to make it to the top of the driveway despite his jogging. I walk through the doors, drop my bags, and slam the door behind me, leaving my mom outside too.

"Kamryn..." My mom opens the door.

"What is he doing here?" I ask as she steps inside, closing the door behind her softly.

"Why don't you stop acting like a little girl, and come out here, and find out?" She calls me out and I hate that she's doing it.

"Because he hurt me, and I want nothing to do with him anymore," I feel odd arguing with her. I don't fight with my mom.

Not now, not ever because she would... *Because she would never do something if it wasn't for my benefit.* Never. I stop. I think, and I squeeze my eyes shut. Dammit.

"How did he even figure out where I live? What did you do?" I ask, and she raises her eyebrows, probably at my tone, but I'll get the lecture on that later.

"Sienna gave him my number, and I gave him our address because I think you jumped over too many important details and left without explanation. From him, or to him," She argues, her hands on her hips.

I keep my arms crossed over my chest as I look at my mom.

"He drove all the way here, just to talk to me?" I ask, and she nods.

"Just give him a chance to explain himself," She looks at

me with warm eyes, and I don't say anything as I open the door.

My mom would never tell me to do something unless she thought it was right.

"Don't snoop," I warn her, knowing she'd press her ear to the door, waiting to hear everything.

Though she really doesn't need to. I'll probably cry to her tonight after I force him to leave. I walk outside, Bellamy already standing at the door, waiting.

"Cross my heart," My mom gives Bellamy a thumbs up.

I take a second before I look at him, and when I do I still feel like the breath in my lungs might get knocked out of me. I deserve an explanation. That's all this will be, and then I can get over it.

"You skipped out on me..." His voice is so soft.

Looking at him, it looks like he's got a million things going through his mind like he doesn't know which one to say first. I'm nervous to see what he chooses.

"You lied to me, and you used me," I watch his eyes shut, and his head shakes slowly.

"I didn't use you Kamryn. Sienna told me about the picture, and I'm sorry. I'm sorry you saw that, and I'm sorry for everything. I am not with Leah, I never wanted to be. This wasn't some ploy to get her back or make her jealous, and it never was. It was always about you, always."

My brain is now a jumbled mess of mixed emotions. That makes no sense in any capacity unless...

"What are you talking about? I saw the picture of you two, you holding her like you had... Like you were kissing her, and-"

"No. I didn't kiss her. I don't want Leah. I was at the coffee shop on my own, she happened to be there, and she wanted to talk to me. I let her talk, I forgave her for acting the way she has the past few months to me. She asked to apologize to you and I said it was up to you. I hugged her, she held on, and I backed away, I told her she needed to stop acting the way she has to me. I told her she needed to leave you alone while you and I are together. That picture just makes it look far worse than what it was. Because it was nothing. She's my past Kamryn; I didn't use you. And I said a few words to your ex too for fucking all of this up."

I cross my arms over my chest. Half of me wishes I could have seen the confrontation between Bellamy and Dylan, and the other half of me is yelling to stay on track right now, and not think of anything else but the problem standing right in front of me.

"You drove all this way to make sure I knew you didn't use me?" My heart betrays me as I feel it warm my entire chest, a burst of energy spreading throughout me.

Just as Sienna said, it's something right out of a movie scene.

"I drove all this way to tell you what I was going to tell you if you had stayed and come to the beach. I came all this way because in every stupid cheesy romance movie, there's always a big confession, and a big scene at the end where everything is laid out on the table. It wasn't on the list, but the list doesn't matter anymore. I couldn't just go the rest of the summer thinking what if. What if I did it, what if I didn't. You might hate me, or be mad at me, or never want to speak to me again after and that's fine, but I came all this way to tell you it was never about a list to me," Bellamy pauses, and my heart stops.

I have no words, my mouth is dry.

"It was never about sleeping with you, and it was never about anything but getting the opportunity to be near you, and spend time with you Kamryn. That's all this ever was.

It was me being an idiot and hoping for something more with you. I knew the rules. I was still dumb enough to hope."

I'm shocked. I don't hate him, but I still feel a subtle hint of betrayal.

"So the tutoring?" I ask him.

His sister said he didn't need it. She said he's had a crush on me all semester.

"At first, I did need help. Only for a few weeks, that's it. But I thought you were funny, and the prettiest person I had ever met. I knew that you would never give me a chance. You are so far out of my league Kamryn, there's no way you'd even let me ask, I was positive. So I never tried, and I was going to let it go as just that. I was going to keep it in, flirt when I could, and see you for tutoring, hoping maybe I'd build up the courage to ask you to go out with me just once, and then I saw the list, and that was the day I was going to ask you out since it was our last tutoring session. But again, I saw the list, and I took a chance, and I didn't... I shouldn't have. It was dumb, and I lied, and I'm sorry, but there were always strings attached for me because I've had a crush on you since February Kamryn. I'm... I'm sorry."

I stand speechless in front of him. Half of me is screaming to just agree, and forgive him. The other half, the sensible half is saying everything but.

"You knew that I had been lied to before. Cheated on, lied to, hurt, all of the above. You knew my trust was limited, and you let me trust you while you openly lied about your intentions Bellamy. If you can start all of this by hiding the truth, then what else would you lie to me about?" I ask, knowing part of me could be projecting, but the other part of me is trying to preserve what I have left of my heart.

"Probably little things," He answers honestly, and now I truly am speechless.

Did he just admit that out loud?

"Little things like when I tell you I'm at the gym but I'm really at the store buying you flowers. Or if you ask me if your breath smells bad in the morning, and it does, but I'll lie and say it doesn't just so you'll kiss me anyway. I'll lie and say I won't buy you a million things for your birthday or Christmas, and then I will. I'll lie when I tell you I don't have to go, even when I do, just so I can spend more time with you. I'll lie when I have to just so I can make our time together more special. I'll never do anything behind your back, decisions are made together, and I didn't let you decide, and I'm sorry Kamryn," He pleads with his voice.

"Bellamy..." I stare at him, ocean blue eyes looking back at me.

He's got his heart on his sleeve, and my heart is practically beating out of my chest. I can't believe he said all of that. I can't believe I'm believing all of it either. My brain tells me no, but the way my chest feels is telling me to give in.

"The list... You went into it thinking what? That I was going to fall for you?" I ask, not wanting it to sound mean, but knowing it does.

I don't want to hurt Bellamy, but I need to understand all of this. All of him.

"No. Half of me figured you'd never speak to me again after it. I went through the dates, and I was hoping that maybe I would be let down. I didn't want you to be perfect, and I didn't want you to be what I wanted, I was hoping that maybe you'd be some awful person, or you did something that just made me not want you because I knew wanting you wouldn't end well but I couldn't find a single thing. You are everything I want. You love what I love, and you get along with my friends, and you're funny, and so fucking smart. You treat me like I matter Kamryn, and you're careful with me. You know me, and you'd be happy to get to know me more. You're just. God, you're better than I ever thought you would be. So I did everything I could to make sure it didn't end as badly as I thought it would."

I look at him blankly, my heart racing faster than it ever has in my life. He's laying everything on the table, not one thing left out. I want to turn him away. I want to hate him for lying to me, for convincing me to do this list with ulterior motives. But I don't. I'm not sure if hating him is possible.

"I know this is a lot to take in, and I know you probably think I'm crazy, but you're about to think I'm crazier because I've wanted you for months, and now that I've had you I know that you are literally the best I've ever had in every single sense, and I'm in love with you Kamryn. I love you. That's why I came here. I couldn't let you think I didn't care when in reality, I care more than I probably should," He finally takes a second to breathe, and I think my heart might have stopped altogether at the confession.

He truly is breathless. He spoke quickly like he was trying to make sure he got every word out before I got a single one in.

"You... Love me?" Outsiders probably think it's insane, but to me, it doesn't sound crazy.

Not at all because I think I feel the exact same way he does.

"I do."

I can see the small ounce of fear in his eyes, and I get it. I feel it too. But part of me isn't surprised. Bellamy is the nesting type, just like I told myself from the start.

"I knew this would happen. That's why I didn't want

this, that's why I never should have agreed to this dumb list," I turn away from him, not wanting him to see my face.

Emotions pour through my chest like a heatwave. It was just a list, that's what this was. It wasn't real. The feelings are only real until everything gets ugly. We made it perfect, but perfect doesn't exist.

"Look at me and tell me you don't have feelings for me. Kamryn why would... Why were you upset about Leah if you didn't care? If you didn't want this?"

I laugh to myself because if I don't I might cry.

"It's not about feelings Bellamy, I developed feelings for you before the first week was finished. I honestly thought you knew, I thought you could feel it. Every kiss, every night, everything was real. It felt real, and I wanted it to be real, but that's just it. None of this is real. This was all stupid dates and a made up list. This isn't what we would be, this is fake. This isn't the fights, and the hard times, and the crying, and screaming, and this isn't what it would feel like if we had to break up. If you got an NFL contract, and I stayed here, or you cheated, or found someone better. This isn't that, this isn't real."

He shakes his head and steps up the last stair, now on the same level I am.

"It can be real. All of this can be real Kamryn. I wouldn't treat you any less than I have the past two weeks. I would care about you, and I would defend you, and I would love you every second of every day like I already do. You... You are a dream Kamryn, and I have no idea what the world will look like in a year when we graduate, and I have no idea if the NFL is anywhere in our future, but I do know that no matter what I'm doing I'd like you in my life. I want you, good times and bad times, and I want this to be real. I feel like I only just got to know parts of you and I want to know everything. Kamryn I'll do everything I can."

I press my lips together.

"How do I know that?" I challenge him again.

"You don't, you just have to trust me. And I know how hard that can be, and I know that you might have to work on it and figure it out, especially after I broke your trust. I'll do everything in my power to gain it back... But I'll wait. I'm fine with waiting, and I'm fine with figuring it out. I'm fine with going at your pace, but what I'm not fine with is just shutting this down because of fear. You are fearless Kamryn. The last two weeks were not enough time to show you how loved you deserve to feel," He steps forward, and I feel my chest squeeze.

I feel tears threaten my eyes, but I know the closer he gets the easier it will be to give in to him.

"I have never seen you back away from a challenge," He inches closer, and I feel his warmth on my skin now, his hands moving down my arms. "Don't back away from this now, please..."

I stare up at him, his hands interlocking with mine. I feel heat and panic settling in my chest. I feel nervous, happy, and confused, and I know that feeling because it's something I've never felt before. I do love him, even if it's based on fabricated things.

"I'm scared," My voice is fragile as it comes out.

"I know, and that's fine. It's fine, and I'm positive I completely overwhelmed you. I know your head is probably spinning because mine is too so take your time. You don't have to tell me. You don't have to talk to me at all, but you do have to come back to campus in a week for summer sessions. We can talk when you're ready."

"What if I'm never ready?" I ask and he shrugs his shoulders.

"Then that's fine too but I'll be waiting if you change your mind."

Pressure builds in my chest and claws up my throat.

"Okay," I'm overwhelmed right now.

I just got home. Then I found out that everything I'd been sitting on for the past day wasn't true. Bellamy is in love with me, and I think I love him, but that feels so wrong to think. It doesn't feel true. Like it's impossible for any of this to be true at all.

"Okay, you'll think about it?" He asks, and I nod.

"I'll think about it."

He smiles, pulling me forward. He wraps me in a hug, and my body responds, naturally hugging him back, his body tight against mine. His heavy scent fills my nose, and I breathe him in. The sweet smell of the spicy vanilla cologne he wears. Soaking in his stronghold.

"I'm sorry... I never wanted to hurt you Ryn," His lips brush my hair as he speaks.

I just hug him tighter, feeling his arms around me, not knowing if I'll ever feel this again.

"I'm going to go now. But I'll see you at summer sessions," He pulls away, and I let him despite my not wanting to let go.

He just drove all that way to turn back around. A simple phone call would have sufficed. He knew I wouldn't answer, and he's far more romantic than the normal guy. He completed the cheesy romantic love confession that's in every rom com, and it wasn't even on my list. He drove here with one intention, and now that he's completed it, he's turning around, and going right back to campus.

I watch as he walks down the driveway, and makes it to

his car. He turns around and waves to me before he climbs inside. I watch as he sits on his phone for only a few minutes, and then he looks up at me. I feel my phone vibrate in my pocket, and I look at him. He points to his phone, and I reach for mine, pulling it out of my pocket. I look at the notification and see a link from him. It leads straight to Spotify. The playlist he made me. He texts again.

"I started making this after our first date, and added songs anytime something felt right."

I look up again, tears welling in my eyes. For once my heart feels incredibly fragile as I watch Bellamy pull away, the same million dollar smile on his face. I wish he didn't have to leave.

CHAPTER TWENTY-SEVEN

WHILE I HAVE YOU HERE BY JOHNNY KNOX

I WALK THROUGH THE DOORS OF MY CHILDHOOD HOME feeling a rush of every emotion all at once. I don't know if I want to cry, or scream, or break something. I don't know if maybe I just want to shut down completely. I have to go back. I have to go back to campus in a week because the opportunity is far too big to pass up, especially now that I know the truth of what the picture was. I was stupid to leave campus because of Bellamy in the first place. That's not who I am, but all of this. It's all so much.

"Kamryn?" My mom calls and I squeeze my eyes shut as I stand in the entryway. "What happened? Where is he?"

I leave my things, walking into the kitchen first. I see her in the living room, and I walk in, hugging her instantly.

"Thank you..." I squeeze her, and she hugs me back.

"What happened?"

"I just never would have known if you didn't let him come here."

She still looks confused as I let her go.

"Can you tell me what happened?" She asks me again and I nod, moving toward the couch.

I don't want to have to explain everything, but I know if anyone can help ease my mind my mom will be the one. She's always been that person for me.

So I start at the beginning and I tell her everything. Every detail from the ferry boat to the last night before I left to come back here. I tell her about when he made me feel better after the frat party. I tell her how his friends care about me and defend me. She listens to everything, not interrupting once as I explain where feelings came into play, and when I felt butterflies. When he took me to the most special places and how we talked about the most personal things. I show her my tattoo in person, and my mom seems happy as she listens to the story. She seems so calm.

"And when he came here, he told me. Well, he told me he loved me. That he was in love with me, and that he's been looking for an opportunity to ask me out since February. He's just..." I stop finally, shaking my head and covering my eyes.

Every emotion crashes to the surface, and I finally let it out, tears coming to my eyes.

"He lied though. As sweet as he is, and as good as he could be, he started all of this with a lie. I just don't know how I'm supposed to feel," I admit through my tears.

"You feel whatever is in your heart, and you let it figure itself out. You don't ignore that, and you don't push those feelings away. He lied. It was wrong that he lied. He's acknowledging how wrong that was though. It's the bare minimum, yes... But everything else he's done is far above that bare minimum, don't you think?" The question she asks is fair.

It's truthful too. Everything Bellamy does is above the bare minimum.

"How do I know any of this is real, Mom? This was all for a list, every single feeling is. It's fabricated, it's based on something superficial and fake, and what if it's not the same?"

"It probably won't be the same. There will be really bad days, and there are going to be times where it feels off, and not perfect. But I'm going to tell you something Kamryn. You have dreamed your whole life to live in one of those silly movies, and I know the way you look at your dad and me. I know you've always wanted that, and you'd be a fool to run away now because that's exactly what you have. Bellamy jumped through hoops. He spent money. He even got his best friends involved to make sure every task was completed and then some. He made you feel welcomed, and comfortable, and he never once did anything that was even somewhat alarming, Kammi. That boy drove three hours to make sure you knew he cared about you, and that he was set up to look like the bad guy. He drove three hours just to make sure you knew he was sorry for lying. He's always going to go up to bat for you. If he hasn't proved himself yet, I don't know what else he could do. I don't know what anyone could do. He's not perfect, but he's about as close as you're ever going to get," She defends.

I take a shaky breath. He already put it into perspective, but she is drilling it in.

Every word she said made my chest light up. Just the thought of Bellamy makes my heart swell, and the recollection of everything these past few weeks too. He really did take me, and turn me around with how I feel about all these things. About relationships, love, and feelings, and he wasn't intentional in that. He was just hoping for the best, and the best happened, and my stupid impulsive self ruined that for him. I know he's not perfect but he's real, and he tries his best, and he doesn't skip past anything. He's thoughtful and intentional.

"So how do I fix it? What should I do?"

"You spend time with your dad and me this week, then you take my car, and you go back to that school for summer sessions, and you finish that damn list. You have one date left."

I laugh at my mom.

"And after that?" I ask.

I feel better already. Because my mom always makes me feel better no matter what happens.

"After that, you tell that boy you love him just the same, and then years down the road you marry him and have his babies," She says and I cringe. "Okay no babies, not if you don't want them, but you better marry that man. He's a cute one, and he's tall too. Kammi, you found a real man, not like that scrawny little thing you dated-"

"Ew! Mom, stop talking," I try to cover her mouth and the two of us start laughing together.

"I missed you, Kammi," She hugs me tight and I hug her back.

"I missed you, Mom," My tears dry up.

"And just in the past few months, you've grown up so much. I can't wait to see you after this year. You know your dad and I bought tickets to every home game."

I back away from her, my eyes wide.

"Mom! What if I didn't get asked to be on the field? What if they never-"

"Then I would have sold 'em! But I knew you would be. You're too hard working. You're too good not to. I knew they would see that."

I hug her again. That's one thing about her that I know is true. No matter what. No matter how big or how small my mom will always believe in me. She will always root for me, and she will always push me, and so will my dad.

My mom is my best friend, and right now all she's got to do this week is give me every ounce of courage to go back to that school and talk to Bell. I know the minute my dad is home from work, and he hears about a potential boyfriend he might die on the spot. He's never cared if I date or not. He's always just as supportive as my mom, but I never really brought anyone home after I went to college. This will be news to him.

"Go get some rest. I'm cooking your favorite tonight."

I've never once told my mom that chicken Alfredo isn't my favorite. I'd prefer spaghetti. She seems to love cooking the Alfredo for me though so I don't ruin that for her, and let her think it's my favorite.

I think of the playlist I now have on my phone that I still haven't even looked at and now I rush. I grab my things where I left them, and rush up the stairs of the house, straight to my bedroom that's completely untouched since the last time I stayed in it. It's the same light pink it was throughout high school, with white bedding, and light green accents.

I drop my things and jump on the bed. I land straight on my stomach and kick my legs back like a teenager. I pull my phone out, and click the playlist, instantly playing it. He titled it *"The List of Songs."* My heart melts at the play on words.

I don't know why this feels different. Especially considering I've most likely heard these songs before. But even if I have, they mean something different now that they remind someone else of me. I look at the songs on the playlist and recognize plenty of them.

Hot for Teacher by Van Halen. I laugh out loud. Of course he would.

Tattoos Together by Lauv. My fingers draw over the ink on my arm.

Cliche by Cece Coakley. The most perfect song to describe me.

Ahead of Myself by James TW. The honesty of these songs starts hitting me hard. The vulnerability only makes me wish I followed him back to campus.

Talking Body by ToveLo. I could say the same for him. That's when I feel tears prick my eyes. Mostly because I see everything else that lies ahead. Never once have I cried to Talking Body by Tovelo. I guess there's a first time for everything.

Wannabe by The Spice Girls. Our Karaoke date. I twist the ring on my finger that he gave me, still having not taken it off.

Ordinary People by Blake Rose, my heart stops at this one.

Magic by John K. I feel like an asshole for not seeing him. Seeing his heart before right now.

Satellite by Harry Styles, I can't stop myself from falling in love with him all over again. The thought of him feeling this way is almost too much for me to process.

Mastermind by Taylor Swift. I laugh. I shouldn't but I do. The effort and care he put into this. The time. Bellamy Archer waited and went into this fully aware he could end up hurt but he did it anyway, just to have a chance.

Certain Things by James Arthur. I adore him. Bellamy is so loyal it's not good for him at this point. He's persistent, but he's caring. He's a good person. The best person I've probably ever met.

New Year's Day by Taylor Swift. I am filled with memories of the party, it was days ago and it feels like forever. But I feel just how wet my cheeks are as I listen to the lyrics.

Crazier by Taylor Swift. Dancing with him was one of the best nights I've ever had. I fell so hard for Bellamy that day. Even if I knew it before this, I remember feeling like I was falling then.

Sparks Fly by Taylor Swift. The other day. I sang it to him in the car, and he couldn't stop himself from kissing me. My heart melts.

Use Somebody by Kings Of Leon. This is the kind of song I've always wished made someone think of me...

Anything by Dodie... I've never heard this song. I've never cried to a song the way I do right now. Guilt settles deep into my chest.

While I Have You Here by Johnny Knox. I contemplate going straight back to campus right now after hearing this song. I wish I knew he felt like this before I ran away from him.

It takes me a while to get through every song, but the minute I reach the last one. I can't help but cry. I repeat the song over and over again. I listen to the lyrics every time, hearing them through Bellamy, and my heart breaks.

I don't like that he lied to me. I don't like how that made me feel. But I'm not dumb enough to think he's anything like Dylan. I'm not silly enough to let my past get in the way of Bellamy, and what he could offer. I just don't know how I'm going to translate that to him. Words and feelings have never been my strong suit.

CHAPTER TWENTY-EIGHT

SATELLITE BY HARRY STYLES

IT'S BEEN A WEEK. I GOT BACK ON CAMPUS A FEW hours ago. I drove three hours back, Bellamy's playlist for me on shuffle, just like it has been the past week. I spent every second I could with my mom and dad. They always clear my head, and I'm glad I have a place I can always go back to no matter what I need.

I haven't talked to Bellamy. I haven't talked to anyone except Sienna all week. To get my mind off of things I've begged her for any ounce of juicy details between her and Lawson, but she swears there isn't any. She says she hasn't seen him since the New Year's party which she claims she didn't sleep with him at. I don't know if she's telling the truth but she says I need to worry about fixing Bellamy and me before I worry about her and Lawson. Fair enough.

I was surprised that Sienna wasn't waiting inside my apartment, bouncing off of the walls with excitement the minute I got back. We never go too long without seeing each other. Summer is the worst because we have to go at least a month before she cracks and comes up to see me for a week or so. Lucky for us, I called Sienna and invited her over to come and sleep over tonight. I'm sure she'll have a million questions about Bellamy.

I'm at the stadium field right now. Summer sessions don't start until tomorrow. Meaning the field will be empty today, and it's afternoon so I know Bellamy won't be here. I want to run, clear my mind more, and get myself in the right headspace for not only talking to Bellamy but summer sessions. I park my mom's car, and get out, bringing my bag with me. I'm still wearing Bellamy's shirt. It's my favorite now.

I make it inside the stadium and start down the stairs, my eyes focusing on a group of cheerleaders, making their way off of the field, and up the stadium stairs. My heart sinks straight down to my ass, panic setting in. I don't see her right away, and then I do, her short blonde hair flashing from within the group. She has it half up half down, a sparkly cheer bow tied into it. I'm not sure how she still looks good after what I assume was a practice but she does.

I make eye contact and then divert my eyes. She hates me, and I kind of hate her. I don't need any more drama or trouble. I'm not one to back down, but for my sake, and Bellamy's, I think confrontation needs to be avoided. Even if that is against my normal judgment. I pass by the group, no words exchanged, and let out a quiet sigh of relief. Thank god.

"Hey girls, I'll be up in a second, okay?" I hear her voice, and I cringe, knowing what's about to come.

I keep walking though, pretending like I didn't just hear that.

"Kamryn, wait up!"

I want to pretend like I didn't just hear her, but insanity would be the only explanation since she was loud and clear.

So I stop, right at the entrance of the field, and I turn to see her jogging back down the steps.

I'm short. At least compared to most, but Leah is a different level of short if she's smaller than I am. I angle my head down to look at her. I take her in, her nervous look. I don't think I've ever seen her with anything but a scowl on her face. *Be nice, be nice, be nice.* I repeat it in my head, knowing it will do me no good to be a bitch to her. Even if she does somewhat deserve it.

"What's up, Leah?" I ask, staying neutral.

"I wanted to talk to you..." She starts strong, and I just stare at her. "I wanted to apologize to you, and I know you like to talk, so just don't do that right now so I can say what I need to say," She speaks quickly.

"The floor is yours," I wave my hand between the two of us, letting her have what she wants.

"I shouldn't have said the things that I said. I was mad, and I was jealous, and I thought I was making him see something he couldn't see before. But that was dumb because Bellamy is... Well, he's a good person and he doesn't care about all the stupid stuff... The stuff I shouldn't care about either. It's not my business who you, or anyone sleeps with. Even if it is my ex-boyfriend," She clarifies. "To be honest, I said it without thinking which doesn't make it better. I just always saw you as someone who didn't care. I was saying what I did so it would hurt him, not you... and when I saw the look on your face, and all of his friends react the way they did. I realized that I did more than what I intended so I'm sorry," She finishes.

I raise my eyebrows. "Can I talk now?" I ask, and she nods, resting her weight on her left side. "I'm assuming you were the one telling people I was fucking Bellamy to make you jealous... That we had some deal going on?" I ask and she sighs.

"No actually, it was one of the girls on the cheer team. She thought it would get her brownie points from me, that I would buddy up with her, but it just made me feel worse. I never wanted people to hate him or you. I just wanted my ex back, and I realized after your party that wasn't going to happen. He was always a good guy but he wasn't good for me. Bellamy never looked at me the way he looked at you. He never cared the way he does with you. Or maybe I never let him, I don't know, but it doesn't matter. I shut the rumor down. I told her if she ever said anything like that again that I'd have her suspended from the team."

Leah's words are shocking. I never expected her to admit to any of this. To own up to it.

"I appreciate your apology. I'm assuming you said the same thing to him?" I ask and she nods.

"Something similar. I also apologized for just being a bitch to him in general. About you, about our break up. For breaking up with him. I don't always have the best judgment at times," She explains.

"So, what does this mean then?" I ask.

"It means we go through senior year civilly. We still go to each other's parties and we stay neutral. Even if you are sleeping with my ex," She shoots me a look, and I wait for a beat.

Both of us stare at each other and it's slow, but both of us break into a smile. I laugh softly, my eyes trailing to the ground. Leah and I have never been close. We've never been best friends. We've never truly gotten along and this newfound civility isn't going to change that.

"Alright, that's fine with me," I nod.

"I'm not going to hug you, though. I still kind of hate you," She explains and I smile, nodding.

"I still kind of hate you too," I agree, and she takes a step up and nods.

"Good. I'm going to go now," She starts to leave awkwardly.

I watch her go and sigh.

"For the record, Leah... I'm not just sleeping with him. I don't know if that makes this better or worse, but I actually have feelings for him," I tell her, and she stops and looks at me.

"It doesn't matter how I feel because it's not my relationship... But it does kind of make it better," She nods and looks down.

Then she turns around and leaves.

I feel good knowing that I've made amends with Leah. I feel like even if I'm not someone's biggest fan that girls have to stick together. That we have to be on each other's side, and as much as Leah and I don't get along, I know it would've picked at me if I didn't at least hear her out.

I GET out of the shower, my body fresh after my run. I went harder and longer today than normal. Usually, I only do a mile, and call it, but today I ran almost three. I needed to relieve the stress I feel over tomorrow. It's not all gone either. Running helped though. I drop my towel and throw on a hoodie, and a pair of underwear. I brush through my wet hair and walk from my bedroom to my living room.

"Ahh! What the fuck, Sienna!" I shout, noticing her rummaging through my fridge.

She opens the freezer door now.

"What? I told you I was coming over," She shrugs, turning back to the freezer. "When did you go to the grocery store?"

She pulls out the brand new tub of strawberry fudge ice cream and opens it before I can protest.

"This morning when I got home. Can you start buying your own groceries for my apartment?" I ask her, walking over to the kitchen.

I open the utensil drawer and get a spoon. I push myself up on the counter, and Sienna stands in front of me, both of us, eating the ice cream straight from the carton.

"Have you talked to Bellamy yet?" She asks and I shake my head.

"No, I don't want to say anything before summer sessions start. Just in case shit goes wrong," I explain.

"Nothing is going to go wrong. What could go wrong?" She waves her hands, the ice cream carton waving in them.

I follow them with my spoon, trying to dig out more ice cream from the moving carton.

"Everything. It's me, I'm me, I don't do this. Everything could go wrong in this situation. With my luck I'll get struck by lightning or something the minute I tell him I love him," I shove my mouth full of strawberries and chocolate fudge.

"Fid wou just saw the L wod!" Sienna's words are a muffled shout and even though I can't understand her I still cringe at her volume.

"Ow," I bite back with my words.

"Hello, answer? Love? Kamryn Hart is in love?" She asks and I narrow my eyes.

"Did I forget to tell you that part?" I ask and Sienna waves her hands manically.

"Um yes! That's like the biggest part of all of this! You

don't just forget to tell me you fell in love with a big stupid jock! Hello?" She asks and I laugh.

"You can't say anything about me and my big stupid jock considering you're fucking a big stupid jock," I correct.

"Ah! Incorrect. I fucked a big stupid jock. Past tense. It only happened two times," She clarifies and I choke on my ice cream.

"TWO TIMES?" I scream, and her eyes widen.

"Did I forget to tell you that part?" She asks and I scoff.

"Oh, you are such a hypocrite," I roll my eyes but keep the smirk on my lips. "Tell me, was his dick bigger the second time?" I ask and Sienna rolls her eyes now.

"For someone who has had sex at least a million times, you should know the anatomy of a male better than I do. No, it was just as big as it was the first time," She shakes her head and I smile.

"It's at least a billion times at this point and I don't know if it gets bigger the second time. I normally only see them once and chase them away," I clarify.

"Well, you didn't chase one of them away," She raises her eyebrows and I shrug my shoulders, and shake my head.

"I don't know about that," I watch and she sighs.

"I guess we'll see tomorrow at summer sessions," She gives me a smile and I smile back. I'm happy to be reunited with my best friend. However, I'm not so happy about the sinking feeling in my stomach. I'm nervous about summer sessions. I'm more nervous to see Bellamy. Especially because I never told him I was coming back.

CHAPTER TWENTY-NINE

GENTLE BY LEXI JAYDE

Sienna drives me to the football field, inevitably making me feel like I'm being dropped off for the first day of school. I am fully capable of driving myself. But the thought of being behind the wheel right now with my nerves seems like it would be not only a danger to me, but to everyone else on the road, and innocent pedestrians as well. I look at the stadium in front of me, my stomach turning. I would have turned myself around and gone home had I driven myself here.

"I think I'm going to throw up," My thoughts are on Bellamy, and the thought of proving myself to coach and the rest of the boys. I barely slept last night thinking about it.

"As long as you don't do it in my car, and don't puke in front of the team, I think that's a normal thing to feel," She slightly chuckles.

"I didn't tell him I was coming back. I didn't text him once while I was home, I didn't even know what to say. I just feel so much when it comes to Bellamy. I can't put it into words," I tell her.

"I know, but it's not about Bellamy right now. It's about

summer sessions and wrapping the players, and learning from professionals. And doing it before the scouts show up, and before the coach has your head for being late, so go. Worry about your stupid jock later," Sienna physically shoves my shoulder and I groan.

"What if I-"

"I swear to god if you say you're not going to go I will physically drag you to the field by your hair. Get. Out," She raises her eyebrows and I know just how serious she is.

Memories replay in my head from when I was going to tell Bellamy I would do the list. How we had a similar conversation before that. I sigh.

"Fine," I grab my things, a giant duffle bag of supplies, and my phone as well.

"Tell me how things go when you're home. I'll be over asap if you need me, alright?" She asks and I nod as I climb out of the car.

Sienna drives away and I take a deep breath, heading to the steps and down them toward the players who are already on the field warming up.

"There you are, Hart. I thought you were going to be late," Coach Corbin says when he sees me.

I saw in the football forum on social media that they made the coach pull younger sports medicine students. They get to take notes and observe all summer. I wish that was a thing when I was their age. I see the bright eyed upcoming sophomores and juniors. Then I see Bellamy's head turn at the mention of my name. I keep my eyes on the coach, not looking over to Bell right away. My stomach is in knots.

"On my first day? I wouldn't even think of it," There's a wide smile on my face.

It's forced, but the coach doesn't know that. He doesn't

need to know that. I'm only forcing it because of how nervous I am. I'm forcing it because if I don't smile I might puke on the field in front of everyone. I can't fuck this up.

"Set up on the side near the benches. I see you brought your things, but there are more over there. This is Tamara and Danica. They'll be teaching you for the entire season," He motions to the two beautiful women standing on the sidelines.

They wave to me.

"Boys! Get wrapped now!" The coach calls and they listen instantly, a few boys heading toward where I'm walking to.

"I'm Danica. Coach Corbin told me that you have a very good eye, and you've worked hard. I'll do the first few, and then you can jump in after if you feel comfortable," She instructs.

I nod, letting her start. Parker Thompson smiles at me, and I give him a thumbs up as she wraps him. Parker has light facial hair and it's perfectly managed. His hair is a dusty brown color, and a curled mess, but it fits well with his light green eyes. He looks so excited, and I can only imagine the anxiety he's feeling. Danica is perfect, and precise in the way she moves. I want to be just like that. I watch for a few more players, and then she steps to the side.

"I'll be just over here if you need me. I think you've got it from here, but if you have any questions just shout," She tells me.

"Thank you, Danica," I smile at the pretty woman, and she goes to the other woman, Tamara, and both of them get set up.

Lawson is first in line now, and he smiles at me, his blonde hair flat on his head for once because it's going to go under a helmet.

"Glad to see you here," He sits himself down on the bench.

"I'm glad to be here," My words are truthful.

I'm glad I'm not missing this opportunity. I'll be more glad when my nerves subside.

"He didn't know you were coming back," He says and I know he's talking about Bellamy.

"I didn't tell him. I wasn't sure if I should, especially before summer sessions," I start wrapping his ankle, crouching down in front of him, doing what I know how to do best.

Lawson is good at reading people. I can tell by the way he's reading me right now.

"You have nothing to worry about. Bellamy cares. I promise you he does. I've never seen him like he was this past week. He barely left his room."

I instantly feel guilty. I know that wasn't Lawson's intention. He never has bad intentions especially when it comes to Bellamy. But I still feel bad. I hate knowing Bellamy was hurting.

"I'm sorry," I don't know why that's my first response, but it is and Lawson is shaking his head.

"You don't have to be. You came back. He was going to blame himself if you turned this opportunity down. We're all just glad you're here."

I stretch his ankle, looking up at him.

"Does that feel fine?"

"Feels perfect," He says and I stand fully. "Thanks, Hart," He gives me another big smile, and I smile back, turning around toward the other players, and right away I'm faced with Bellamy who stands further back.

He's wearing a SPU tank top, his arms beautifully displayed to me. I look at him as he walks toward me, the other players staying back, and waiting their turn. He approaches without a word, my stomach tight and warm, full of swarming butterflies. He passes me and brushes against me as he does, every nerve in my body shooting every way at the simple touch. Bell sits down, and I hold out my hands to him, knowing he'll need his right wrist wrapped first, his throwing hand.

"Hi..." He calls and I feel my stomach sink at the sound of his voice.

"Hi," I peer up at him, my eyes catching him.

He watches me intently as I touch his hands, my chest feeling so constricted I feel like my next breath might hurt. My heart is in my throat, and my hands are starting to sweat. I wrap his hand, my eyes focusing on it hard, not daring to look up at him. I think this is the only time since getting close to Bellamy I've chosen to stare at his hands over his face.

"I didn't think you were coming," He breaks the silence again and I shake my head.

"I wouldn't miss this for the world... I couldn't just leave," I look at him, and I speak more about him than football, and I think he knows that.

He smiles slightly, my stomach dropping again at the sight of his dimple carving into his cheek.

"I'm glad you're here," He squeezes my hand tight.

I smile back at him, the tension in my body tighter than it's ever been. He's not giving me any insight into how he's feeling or what he's thinking. He wanted me back. I know that. But I don't know what to expect off of the field.

I hesitate before crouching down to wrap his ankles. He watches me carefully as I do it, my fingers brushing his legs as I begin to do my job. I wrap each ankle of his, feeling more nervous than I ever have to wrap a player. I finish, and he flexes his muscles. He stands, stretching himself out.

I keep my spot in front of him, and I take his hand once more, wrapping each finger, protecting every single one from injury. I can feel his eyes burning into me as I touch him, and I feel myself burning up at the thought of him looking at me the way he does. I move to his other side and look at the intricate birds tattooed on his hand, my heart beating faster at the sight. It looks good. He looks so fucking good, and touching him, even if it's small. It feels just as good.

"Thank you."

Our chests touch, and my eyes swiftly look into his. He's smiling, and incredibly confident as he takes my shoulders and moves around me. I feel relief, tension leaving my body the second he's no longer in my bubble. The next player moves forward, and I get to work. I notice Tamara, and Danica, my mentors and teachers both getting to work on other players. I should be focusing, and I am. I notice their techniques as they work closely next to me, and I take them into my work. I do a good job, but my mind is on Bellamy Archer the entire time.

The boys start their warmups, and they're all completely in it. I'm always excited to watch from the sidelines, but I'm practically giddy watching this team. I'm excited to finally be on the sidelines for football. I watch each player carefully as they run their drills.

It's odd seeing all of them without Griff. He leaves soon for the NFL which I know must be one of the most exciting things. Parker Thompson is the wide receiver that's moved into Griff's spotlight position, and he's good. Really good. He's a year younger than Bell and I. He's been on the team since his freshman year. He got some playing time but not much because of Griff. Parker is meshing with Bell, really well. Bellamy moves, and so does Parker. They're going to be a good team on the field next year.

I keep my eyes on Bellamy without even meaning to. Every play, or snap I just drift to him when I have nothing else to look at. He's captivating on the field. The boys look to him for answers and authority. They don't have a team captain here, but he's the unspoken one, it's obvious.

I knew all of this about him before right now. I knew all this from just seeing him last season, but it's elevated now. I'm far more into it as I watch him. The boys practice their plays, Bellamy snapping the ball, keeping his stance as he throws the football down the field. He's incredibly skilled. He's swift. His skin is glistening now, the sweat coating his tattooed arms. The fake play ends in a touchdown thanks to the throw from Bellamy. Parker is dancing in the endzone.

I watch as Bellamy celebrates with the new running back, a few of his teammates hyping him up as he does so. I see his smile as he pulls the helmet off of his head. He pulls Lawson into him, both the boys smiling as they walk from the endzone. Coach Corbin blows his whistle and the boys break, and I stand, moving my notes to the side. Danica motions for me to follow, and I do. The three of us pas out the named water bottles to the boys. Once they've got what they need I walk away from them, back to my binder with all my notes.

"What are you working on?" A voice asks and I turn to see Bellamy and I smile, showing the binder.

"Oh um... Player tendencies. What sides do they tend to use more, or their dominant hands, it's like... Like a profile for each player. It just helps me."

He looks at everything, his eyes scanning what I've written when the coach blows his whistle again.

"Run 'em again!" Coach Corbin yells, and I look at Bellamy.

He looks back at me, wanting to say something but not letting himself. There's something unspoken in the look he gives me, something that tells me we're going to talk soon, something tells me that he couldn't wait because he's waited long enough. We both have.

I sit on the sidelines of the field. All the players have vacated as well as the coach, the scouts, and the onlookers in the stands. I talked through things I need to work on and practice with my two mentors. I really like them and I have a really good feeling about this summer. All of my nerves about the sessions and football, in general, are gone now that I know the two women I work for are kind and helpful. The giant stadium lights are beating down on me now, the sun having escaped the sky, and hidden itself away.

Today is supposed to be the longest day of summer sessions because it's the first day. It's the day all the new players meet the seasoned ones. It's the day everyone gets used to something completely new but somehow not at the same time. Every ounce of field time felt like a rush. It felt like a dream and only confirmed that I had picked the right sport. That this was the place I wanted to be for the rest of my life, the sidelines just like this. Whether it's pro or not, I don't care.

I look out to the turf field. I smile to myself, proud, and happy. I made the right choice coming back. I'm deciding right now, no matter what happens between Bell and me.

This is where I'm meant to be. I hear shuffling to my side, and I peer toward it seeing a wet haired Bellamy. He walks up slowly, his duffle bag on his shoulder. Parker and Lawson walk by his side. They're all smiling, obviously coming down from the high they just felt.

"We'll catch you later," Lawson nudges Bellamy's shoulder. "It was good seeing you Kam."

Lawson's smile is bright and I can't help but think of Sienna when I look at him now. I avoid smiling, and showing that on my face.

"Bye Lawson, bye Parker. You guys did good today," I smile at them.

Parker and Lawson walk toward the stadium stairs and Bellamy keeps moving forward toward me.

"I hoped you'd still be out here."

I look at the field again, "I was just taking it all in..."

He's used to this. He's done it the past four years, I haven't.

"It's a lot to take in. I get it," He must have felt it when he first got to school.

When he first got to play on a field this size, in this capacity.

"I'm really happy I came back," My stomach is nervous, and uneasy for a different reason now. Feelings crash through my chest, and my stomach, and I feel nauseous as thoughts of what to say next hit me.

"I was relieved to hear the coach say your name today. I was... I was happy to see you on the sidelines every time I turned around today," His words are careful and subtle which is unlike him.

"So..." I say and he raises his eyebrows.

"So..." He repeats. "I wasn't going to push. I left the ball in your court, and I was keeping it there until you...

Until you wanted to make a move. If you wanted to at all."

I can understand why. He's being careful for his own sake.

"I didn't... I don't know how... I don't want to ruin anything or mess anything up. I don't want to scare you or hurt you, and I wasn't sure if you even wanted me to bring it up so I didn't," I'm rambling like an idiot.

He shakes his head in response.

"I've been waiting for something since the day I left you with everything Ryn," He says and I nod to myself. "So you can start with whatever you want. Whatever you're most comfortable with."

I stand up, a distance between us. His eyes follow me wherever I move.

"Well, there's one date left... One place left on the list."

His face melts into a soft smile, "You want to go to the beach?"

I nod, "If you want to, I'd like to."

I extend an invitation and feel sick again.

"Are you asking me on a date, Kamryn Hart?"

I roll my eyes at him, "If you don't agree I might die of embarrassment, and nerves, so just give me an honest answer. You can say no."

He walks forward to me, snatching my duffle bag from the ground. He hangs his arm over my shoulder and walks with me toward the stairs.

"The day I say no to you is the day pigs fly, Ryn. Let's go," He starts walking us to the stairs, my body tucked into his.

We walk together in silence, the same comfortable stillness creeping back in between us. I climb into his car and send Sienna a quick text updating her.

Bellamy has changed into a pair of jogging shorts, and a simple black hoodie. His hair is drying in soft waves, and his eyes are pretty blue against the dark sky around him. He drives, and I sit quietly, the music he plays familiar because it's the same songs I've listened to since the day I came home. He plays the playlist he made for me, and my heart starts to beat faster as I see the sign for the public beach.

"We're breaking the rules again... It's not midnight," I tell him.

"I think we've both come to the conclusion that when it comes to The List of Things, we don't follow the rules," He smiles and puts the car in park.

I smile to myself, happy there's no uncomfortable tension between us.

He gets out, and like a routine he comes to my side, and opens my door for me, helping me from the Jeep, and then to the back of his car, retrieving what I've now decided to call the date blanket because it's one that's been everywhere with us. We walk together, both of us taking our shoes off, and leaving them at the edge of the sand, feeling the cold gritty texture under our feet, and hearing the sound of the crashing waves in front of us.

There's a breeze, and it's far colder than it would be during the day. It's not midnight, but it is later. Closer to 10 pm. Bellamy spreads the blanket, and I sit just as he does. We're quiet at first. The stars look pretty as they reflect the ocean. The moon looks split right now, with only half of it showing its face right now. I sigh, my courage built up as much as it could be in this moment.

"I've thought a lot about everything the past week..." I start while Bellamy stares at the ocean in front of us. "I've thought about every date, every time we went out from start to finish. I thought about every kiss. I thought about the sex.

I thought about every word and every simple morning. The little things that you did that weren't a part of the list. The things we did that weren't there. I listened to every song on that playlist front and back, and I felt so fucking stupid Bellamy," I admit.

He looks at me carefully now as I say the words, and I see a small amount of confusion spread across his features. I know he wasn't expecting that.

"Why?" He doesn't look hopeful.

I hate that, especially because now I recognize that's what he had every day two weeks ago. Hope on his features every single date we went on.

"I felt stupid because I should have seen from the moment that I went on that first date with you that this was more than what it was. I should have known the minute you kissed me, and I felt like I couldn't breathe, and I should have known when you went above and beyond what was intended. I should have known, and I should have never left. I shouldn't have run away."

His knees are pulled up and his hands are clasped together, his arms hanging over his legs. He looks down.

"But I understand why you did. I get it. And I'd get it if you did now, if you turned this... Me down," He speaks to me like he doesn't want to say what he does.

Like it's hard for him to get it out, but I appreciate him.

"I'm still mad at you for lying to me. And for going into the list with different intentions. But I can move past that. I can trust you when you say you won't do something like that again. I'm also giving you a chance now to tell me anything else that you've lied about, or that you've kept from me," I give Bellamy the floor, but he shakes his head.

"Nothing else. It doesn't make it okay, but that was the only lie I told. When I said I didn't and wouldn't catch feelings," He explains and I nod, swallowing the lump in my throat.

I can't believe this is happening. I don't know how to say these things. I've never had to before now. The movies make it seem so much easier.

"I love you," I practically blurt the words out.

I don't look at him. I look at the waves, hearing nothing else. His silence is deafening. I'm glad too, because I need to keep going before I let him talk.

"I know because every single time you did something that no one has ever done for me before, I felt something I've never felt before. I felt so much build up in my chest. Kind of like that feeling you get when you're anxious. Where your chest is tight, and you feel like your heart might stop. And you feel like if you try to speak it might not come out. You cared for me without me even knowing, and it made me feel loved without me even knowing that's what it was. And I know it's absolutely insane to feel the way I do, especially because I feel like I barely know parts of you, but never in my life have I wanted to know someone more than I want to know you. And I know I love you because when I look at you, and I see the way you smile at me it makes me feel absolutely insane. I love you, and I want... I want to try," I think my heart is going to come right out of my chest.

It feels like it's begging to be let out with how hard it's beating.

"Fuck..." He shakes his head, and I watch as his smile breaks out on his face, like he couldn't contain it.

He throws himself back, his back hitting the blanket. He brings his hands up to his face, covering it, and then he runs them through his hair, and I watch him carefully. I twist the ring he got me around my finger, fiddling with it nervously as I watch him, and he closes his eyes.

"You have no idea how badly I've wished for you to say that," His voice just above a whisper.

Bellamy sits himself up, shaking his head, and I feel the small tinge of insecurity running through me, the small feeling that I could still be rejected.

"If you think we shouldn't. I mean if you think we shouldn't rush anything, or you want to wait. Or if you think maybe all of this isn't-" Bellamy catches my lips with his, shutting me up instantly.

Every emotion in my head rushes to my chest and explodes like fireworks on New Year's Eve.

His hands hold my face, his thumbs on my cheeks, and his fingers are spread to keep me exactly where he wants me. He pushes into me, kissing me hard, every emotion he feels pouring into me. He breaks from me, and I catch my breath, every insecurity having vacated my head. My heart somehow feels louder, like it's beating harder, and faster than before. I don't open my eyes reveling in the feeling he left on my lips.

"I think that you'd be absolutely insane if you thought that I wouldn't jump at the opportunity to be yours Kamryn. And I think fake dating should become real dating because I love you just the same."

I feel him back away, so I do the same, my eyes opening and finding his.

"I don't know. Having a real boyfriend would do horrible things to my reputation..." I say and he raises his eyebrows.

A slow spreading smile etches itself on his face.

"Oh really?" He asks, and I nod.

"Really," I hum, and inch closer to him.

"It was all real to you?" His voice is soft and serious.

"It was all real to me. It's all real now. It's been real

since you kissed me and I want it to be real for a long, long time Bell..."

He kisses me again, and the sound of my heartbeat drowns out everything else. Nothing has felt more real than this right now.

EPILOGUE

ALL THE TIME IN THE WORLD BY
STEPHEN DAY

BELLAMY ARCHER:

I pack everything I still have. All the other things have been sold, mostly because I'll just buy new stuff when I get there. College felt like it ended abruptly this past summer. It had been a long time coming. I had waited for it and wanted it for so long until it finally came. We graduated only a month ago, and it feels like it's been a lifetime already.

No one really ever tells you just how scary it's going to be when you graduate. It's worse than you'd expect. No one else thinks you're meant to go out and make a name for yourself right away, but I felt like I needed to. I felt like I didn't get to rest, wait, or sit still. Especially since I was a first round draft pick for the Giants. The New York fucking Giants. That's why I'm packing. Training starts in two weeks.

"Bellamy."

I look to the door of my apartment to see her, her long black hair trailing down to her stomach. She's got half of it pulled up into a messy bun on the back of her head, the rest of it naturally curly. She's got a clean face mostly because she's been packing all day, just like me.

After she came back for summer sessions and told me how she felt, I barely let her leave my side. She did practically perfect on the field during the summer sessions, and even better during the season. Her mentors let her ride solo a lot, and I could tell it boosted her confidence higher than it already was.

Our friend group got closer, and everything felt so much more natural. So much easier senior year compared to the other three here at SPU. After Lawson went to the basketball coach about what happened to Kamryn, she was called in to give a statement. Coach Corbin went with her after everything, and stood by her side in all of it, just like me and the guys did. Just like Sienna did too. Caleb was suspended for half of the season because of what he did, another girl had come forward against him after Kamryn did, and it solidified everything. He deserved worse, if it were up to me, he'd get it.

That brought all of us even closer. Being here, being with Kam, and Lawson. Going to see Griffin for home games, and him coming back to see us. It's like a second family.

Ryn and I didn't really leave each other's side all semester unless she was leaving me to go to see her friends, or I had workouts with Lawson and Parker. We figured after having so many sleepovers at each other's apartments that it was dumb to keep going back and forth with sleepover bags. It was tiring, so Kamryn ended up moving into my apartment right before SPU's holiday break started.

She invited me up to her parent's house for the holidays. I came to meet her dad, and officially meet her mom as well, then we came back to campus together before the break was over. She met my grandparents too. They showed enough embarrassing baby pictures for a lifetime, but seeing the way Ryn smiled at them... I'd let her see every single one if it meant she'd do it again.

"What do you need?" I ask and stop what I'm doing to watch her.

"For you to pinch me because I still don't believe it," Her voice is somewhat somber.

I get it. I feel it.

"It is real..." I barely believe it myself.

Since the moment the two of us started officially dating, all of this has felt like a dream. The thought of leaving it all behind. It's bittersweet to see things change this way. To see things change for both of us in such drastic ways.

"I'm going to miss-"

"Don't say it," I pull her down to my bed with me, my back hitting the bed first, her hitting my body next.

"I am though."

Neither of us has really known anything different than right here... I understand it completely.

"At least I won't be missing you..." She speaks, and my heart warms at the thought of her moving with me.

I wasn't sure if she would want to. But she mentioned it before I even had the chance to ask her. She's been saving her money, and she's going to get her masters in New York. She's continuing her education on a full ride scholarship. I'm not surprised considering the glowing recommendation from Coach Corbin who has another national championship under his belt after this past season.

"But this is what I've always wanted, Ryn. This is it. Well, not the New York Giants... But you, and an NFL contract. That's what I've always dreamed of," I joke with her, knowing good and well that she was over the moon when I was drafted by her favorite team and not mine.

Her lips are warm as they greet me. She's happy, and I've seen her the opposite this past year. I've seen her stress, and struggle, and I know this is the perfect place for the two of us. The perfect place to be a family. To be together. To discover, and to find ourselves even more. This is the perfect place for a legacy to begin. This is our start, and despite the past year, we have a long road ahead of us.

"The Giants are great, they have you," She boasts about me, and I roll my eyes. "They were great before you even if you can't see that... But they're even better now."

I kiss her quickly one more time before pushing us up.

"Come on, we've got to pack, no being lazy."

She groans and I pull her from the bed. She whines some more but laughs as I smirk at her. My chest warms up seeing her laugh.

She's going to be a part of the same team as me one day. And I can't wait to look on the sidelines and to see her there just like I did this entire past season. That is if I get any playing time. No matter what happens, I know Kamryn will be there. I know that we've got each other. Kamryn is loyal. She is hard headed, but she loves harder than anyone I've ever met in my life.

Once her shell was discarded she turned into the most romantic person I'd ever met. She loves cooking with me. She enjoys coordinating our date outfits, and she thinks it's fun to have skincare nights where she goes at my face, in her words "making it more perfect than it already is."

We've learned the ins and outs of each other, and it was hard to mold our lives together, but she was willing, and so was I. Before Kamryn, I wasn't really sure if I believed in soul mates. I know she hadn't either, not in real life anyways. The small part of me that did believe in them wasn't sure if I'd ever even meet mine. Then I met her, and I got to know her. Kamryn Hart is easy to love. She's without a doubt in my mind, my soulmate.

I think about what it took to get us here. I think about the torturous tutoring sessions and the aspect of playing dumb around her just to spend time with her. She never knew, but I stole every glance I could. I tried as best as I could to get anywhere... The list was the perfect in for me, it was the perfect way for me to get her to just go out with me, even if it was only once. It was also one of the dumbest ideas I've ever had. It almost cost me her altogether. I'm still lucky for that list even if it was stupid for me to use it.

She doesn't know it but I still keep that silly list folded up and shoved in my wallet. It's some of the happiest moments I've experienced. Since I started seeing Kamryn she has felt like family, like a safe space, and when she looks at me she confirms it. Everything is set into place when she looks at me, no matter where we go, or what we do. No matter what happens I have a partner for life with her, just like one of those movies, or those silly books. Kamryn is my happy ending. She has been since the very first date.

ACKNOWLEDGMENTS

Author's Notes are weird to me. Mostly because I'm used to writing something short and sweet, asking for opinions at the end of every chapter because I'm used to writing books on Wattpad. If you know me already then you know that but if you don't it's nice to officially meet you. Thank you for reading my first officially published book.

I don't know if it's a common thing to talk about how someone got into writing. How someone realized this is what they wanted to do with the rest of their life. I'm going to tell you though, even if it's not normal because it feels right. I mean hell. You just read my first book. I think we're on this level of trust, to say the least.

A lot of you will relate to me when I tell you fanfiction was my entire life when I was far too young to be reading such... Descriptive things. But reading them made me feel like I could take a crack at making one of my own. I'd like to pretend that's the end of it, and I wrote something wonderful, and that was that. But I have to tell you the first book I wrote was shit. I'm pretty sure it wasn't even a hundred pages at all, but it was something. And it was so fun to write and share among my friends. I enjoyed playing make believe.

Fast forward a few months. My freshman year of high school. In class with my favorite teacher. His name was Charlie. I'm not going to tell you his last name. What I actually referred to him as, mostly because I don't think he remembers me or even realizes that eight years later what he did still impacts me to this day.

Charlie was a teacher who pushed me. And he made me excited to read boring school assigned books and write boring nonfiction papers that I never enjoyed writing. He gave us a short story assignment in my freshman literature class. He asked us to write something that was five pages long, and completely fictional. I remember writing something, and not being able to stop. I was enthralled in a fictional world I had created. I couldn't send it at five pages. So I did ten. Double what was assigned, and normally any teacher would accept more than what was assigned.

Charlie meant what he said when he told us to only write five pages. When it was time for our rough drafts to be turned in, I skipped the class. I didn't go, and I didn't turn in my short story because I feared others' eyes reading something that I created. I didn't want to be let down. I didn't want a teacher I looked up to to hate something I put a lot of work into.

My teacher reached out to me, and he knew my story was finished. He knew there was no way I worked as diligently in class as I did if I really didn't complete the assignment. So he asked me what was wrong. I told him how long my story was. He told me to shorten it, and I made it clear that I made it as short as I could. Nothing could come out of my story. He said to me, "Then it better be damn good." And I was scared but confident at this point. If I fail I fail, I liked my story.

I turned it in, the final draft only. I remember scouring through, editing until my eyes crossed sometimes. I treated this ten page story like it was the end and beginning of my own life. I awaited my grade, and a week later I remember watching Charlie walk around the class, handing back short stories. I never thought much about writing before that day. I never thought about it being more than a hobby. When my paper was returned I looked for bad notes. I look for a scratch of a red pen that marks anything but minor grammatical errors. The only sentence I saw was written on the last page at the very bottom. The note he wrote.

"I want more."

And I'd never felt as much relief as I did at that moment. Charlie told me after class that I should keep writing. Always keep doing it, even if it was for fun. So I did just that. Just for fun. Just for me, never released on any account, or any web page. Only through class, and to my friends.

When 2019 came around I released my first fanfiction. A lot of you already know that. But after that, the rest truly wrote itself. The readers I gained. Millions of them. They made it very clear that my writing wasn't something I should use for fun. But for my future. So I did just that. Thank you, Charlie. Thank you, readers.

I've written a book. It's weird to say it. A book. A whole book. I want to thank some people. First off being the people that made this book possible. My wonderful editor Sabrina Grimaldi. She made the process of writing and fixing my book so easy. I would also like to thank the designer of my book cover Kassandra Camponi. She worked so well with me and made it easy for my vision to come to life. Without these two wonderful women, my work would have been so much harder, and my vision, and story never would have come to life. Self publishing is a crazy hard journey, and it has challenges all throughout it. These two made navigating it easier.

I want to thank my friends that gave me time, and space to bounce ideas off of them, and the friends who read my story as I wrote it. Ashley, Autumn, Alesia, Callie, and Becca. The friends that were there through this whole process, and not only those friends but the friends who have supported me in my writing in the past few years. Heather, Emma, and Sofia. You have all changed my life. You have made me a better writer, and I know you will continue to do so.

I'd like to thank my parents Christine, and Jeff, grand-parents Julie, and George, and my sisters Alaina, and Lea because they might not have specifically pushed me to be an author or to write, but they always pushed me to be creative, and artistic. They let me keep my head in the clouds, and imagine different worlds. They bought me books when I was young, and were the reason that I even found a love for reading in the first place. And they still support me to this day, even though I'm writing sex scenes now. Sorry, Mom and Dad.

I want to thank my husband Levi. He's one of the biggest supports I have and he doesn't fully understand it. He doesn't understand all of the romance in these books, and my infatuation with it, but he is my real life book boyfriend. He tries every single day to make me feel like I'm living in a fairytale, and he pushes me further and further to always keep writing. He asks questions about what I'm doing, and what process I'm in even though I'm positive he doesn't understand what any of it means. I think he's the perfect example of "If he wanted to he would." I'm thankful every day for that.

I will never hesitate to thank you, my readers. Especially my readers that have been here from the start. As weird as some may think it is, I will never be embarrassed by my past in writing. I started with fanfictions, and I am incredibly proud of them. I am proud of what they taught me, and I'm proud of what I have become because of them.

I am forever grateful for the people who read those books and pushed me to write this one. I am thankful for the continued support you have all shown me online, and I will never in my life be able to repay you for the love and kindness you have shown me through my words.

It baffles me that words that spill from my head can change someone, or make someone feel something. This story is just the start, but I thought it was a perfect one for me, and for all of you. A perfect step away from what I used to write to what I want to write for a long long time now.

I've had the story of Bellamy, and Kamryn in my head for what feels like years now. I have imagined their story in a million different ways, with a million different settings. None of it was perfect, but then I told myself it was never meant to be that. I am fully aware that there is work to be done for myself, but I am proud of the story you have read.

Bellamy and Kamryn first started off as Jaxon and Lucy, thankfully, I found a better set of names that fit them more. I have a million different versions of The List of Things that Kamryn created, and I think the final copy might be perfect in my eyes. This writing process was messy, and it was stressful. The hardest part was starting, and the easiest part of that was falling in love with my characters to the point that I couldn't wait to tell their story.

Though I went through many drafts, and ideas and thoughts I will say the one constant was the excitement from all of you to finally get your hands on my book. And I am happy I have a space to allow myself to share this with all of you.

This is the first of many books from me. I cannot wait to take you all to different worlds, through different relationships, and through different emotions. I am most excited to push myself and learn along the way. There are not enough ways to thank you, but my words are the start. Once again, thank you.

-With great love, Emma.

Milton Keynes UK
Ingram Content Group UK Ltd.
UKHW042312020823
426203UK00004B/220